D0435456

# SECRETS *so* DEEP

ALSO BY GINNY MYERS SAIN

*Dark and Shallow Lies*

# SECRETS *so* DEEP

GINNY MYERS SAIN

RAZORBILL

An imprint of Penguin Random House LLC, New York

First published in the United States of America by Razorbill,
an imprint of Penguin Random House LLC, 2022



Visit us online at penguinrandomhouse.com.

LIBRARY OF CONGRESS CATALOGING-IN-PUBLICATION DATA
Names: Sain, Ginny Myers, author.
Title: Secrets so deep / Ginny Myers Sain.
Description: New York : Razorbill, 2022. | Audience: Ages 14 and up. |
Summary: Seventeen-year-old Avril Vincent returns to an exclusive theater camp to uncover the truth of what happened when her mother drowned there twelve years ago.
Identifiers: LCCN 2022019107 | ISBN 9780593403990 (hardcover) |
ISBN 9780593528860 (trade paperback) | ISBN 9780593404003 (ebook)
Subjects: CYAC: Theater—Fiction. | Secrets—Fiction. | Drowning—Fiction. |
LCGFT: Thrillers (Fiction) | Novels.
Classification: LCC PZ7.1.S2456 Se 2022 | DDC [Fic]—dc23
LC record available at https://lccn.loc.gov/2022019107

Printed in the United States of America

ISBN 9780593403990 (HARDCOVER)

ISBN 9780593528860 (INTERNATIONAL EDITION)

1st Printing

LSCH

Design by Rebecca Aidlin
Text set in Arno Pro Regular

*To my twin flame, Wes . . . the one I will always find my way back to.*
*Keep pushing me to sing louder, love braver, and live more honestly.*
*This is for all the times we crossed the world while it was asleep.*

# SECRETS *so* DEEP

Lord, we know what we are, but not what we may be.

—**Ophelia**

*HAMLET* BY WILLIAM SHAKESPEARE

# ACT I: SCENE 1

I was five years old the night stars fell from the sky. They tore loose somehow and came down like rain. I remember the heavy, dull sound of them hitting the water.

*Plop.*

*Plop. Plop.*

*Plop.*

I'm watching—waiting for them to do that act again—but tonight they stay pinned to the vast blackness above us. Where they're supposed to be. Which is more than I can say for us, because we're supposed to be in our cabins. Curfew was like an hour ago.

But here we are on the beach.

The salt hangs heavy in the air. It prickles my skin.

Burns my lips.

Tickles my memory.

I think the girl's name is Viv. The one with her arm around me. We're cabinmates. She has the bunk across from mine, and we are perfect opposites. My hair is the color of ice. More white than blonde. It falls just below my shoulders, hanging straight and limp in the dampness, but Viv's inky curls tumble all the way down her back. Like laughter. Our eyes are almost the same shade of green, but hers are lined in that sexy cat-eye style I can never seem to master. She's swaying back and forth, and she pauses to whisper in my ear. Then she laughs, throaty and low. And I laugh, too. Because Viv is the kind of girl you want to laugh with. The truth is, I didn't catch what she said. Her words were lost to the crash of the waves. The cresting swell of voices all around us.

"Avril!" she shouts. "I'll be right back! I gotta pee!" And that I hear, so I nod and take a deep breath. I'm grateful for a few seconds alone in the crowd. A little time to just stand here and take it all in. This is why I came down to the beach tonight. I thought about skipping the party, but I had to be here. In this place. Something inside me wouldn't wait—couldn't wait—for morning.

I've always been drawn to the water. Even from landlocked North Texas, I've felt the pull of the tides. Craved the brokenness of the coastline. And now, finally, here I am.

Again.

Here I am again.

There are so many people, though. And I'm not really great with big groups.

Or small groups.

Or people in general.

I haven't met the tall girl writing her initials in the sand by the fire. Or the shaggy-haired guy who's sitting beside her, picking out chords on the guitar. Fragments of melody that Viv and I were trying—failing—to sing along to.

I do know the redhead who's walking toward me with a couple of beers. His name is Lex. I met him at dinner, and evidently that makes us besties now.

"Holy shit," he says, and he hands me one of the sweating bottles. "Can you believe we're actually here?" He raises his own half-empty beer in my direction, and his blue eyes come alive with reflected flames. "To the first night of the best summer ever!"

Each year, high school juniors from all over the country apply for a chance to attend the four-week theatre intensive at Whisper Cove. They all want the opportunity to study with Willa Culver. And we made it in—me, my new pal Lex, and everyone else milling around us. This secret after-hours welcoming party makes it official.

Lex is playing with the fringe on a light scarf that's expertly draped around his neck. He's all freckles and gorgeous red-gold hair in the firelight. Barefoot with his jeans rolled up, he looks like a stylish Tom Sawyer, and I suddenly feel plain in my cutoff shorts and concert T-shirt. "You ever been to Connecticut before?" he asks me.

"Once," I tell him. "A long time ago. You?"

"Nope," Lex says. "I've never even seen the ocean before."

I detect a southern drawl, elongated vowels that clink together like ice cubes in a glass of sweet tea, and I remember he told me at dinner that he's from somewhere just outside Nashville, Tennessee. Franklin, I think he said. Or something like that.

"It's not really the ocean," I correct him, even though it makes me an asshole. "It's Long Island Sound."

"Whatever." He rolls his eyes, totally unbothered. "It's basically the ocean. And it's pretty, right?"

He's not wrong about that.

Tonight a full moon hangs huge and low just above a horizon that looks like it's been stitched with golden thread, and below that, waves rise and fall in a shimmer of silvery brilliance. In the distance, silhouetted against the black, a lighthouse is the tent pole holding up an expanse of dark sky.

The view doesn't look real. It reminds me of a storybook I had when I was a kid. Something Dad used to read to me at bedtime. About mermaids.

Or maybe they were pirates.

Lex and I stand there. Staring. Toes buried in the sand.

"Avril! Hey! You decided to come!" I turn to look over my shoulder at the sound of my name, and Jude is making his way toward us with a big grin on his face. He's the program assistant who picked me up at the train station earlier this evening. My flight from Dallas to New York City was delayed, so I had to take a later train out to Connecticut, which meant I was the very last one to arrive. I got here just in time to drop my bags in cabin number one before dinner. "And Alexander," he adds when he sees Lex. "Shit." He snaps his fingers. "Sorry. You said you go by Alex, right?"

Jude is cute. Dark brown skin and big, warm eyes. His hair is shaved short except for a cascade of perfect charcoal-colored ringlets in the front. I see Lex run a hand through his own red hair before he throws a grin back in Jude's direction. "It's just Lex. I go by Lex." He's playing with the fringe on his scarf again.

"Lex." Jude nods. "Got it." And I notice the way his eyes linger on Lex for a second, even though he's talking to me. "I told you the bonfire would be awesome. It's kind of a first-night tradition. You get settled in okay?"

"Yep," I tell him. "Like you said. Hilton by the sea."

The temperature has dropped, and I wrap my arms around my

chest. I wish I'd grabbed a sweater. I keep forgetting I'm not in Texas anymore. By mid-June, Dallas is already sweltering. Even at night. But here, with the breeze sweeping in off the water, it's chilly.

"Yeah." Jude laughs. "The cabins aren't exactly luxurious." That seems like an understatement. I think of the paper-thin bunk bed mattress and the leaning dressers with their crooked drawers. "But you'll really just be there to sleep anyway. Willa keeps everyone busy." He laughs again. It's an easy sound, and it makes me a little jealous. I wish I could be easy like that. "Oh man, you guys are gonna love Willa. She's a trip. In the best way. You'll meet her before breakfast tomorrow."

"Whoa," Lex mutters under his breath, like he can't quite comprehend it. "Willa fucking Culver."

I knew she'd be here, of course. We all knew she'd be here. But Lex's reaction is still understandable, because Willa Culver is a theatre legend.

"The one and only," Jude tells us. "Y'all get ready, because for the next four weeks, Willa's gonna be your director, your teacher, your boss, your mom, and your best friend all rolled into one."

"You sound like you know the whole drill." Lex gives Jude a flirty little wink. I'm impressed, and I can't help wondering if he's always that brave, or if the beer and the moonlight are making him bold.

"I actually did the intensive last summer," Jude tells him. "But Willa picks someone from each group to come back the next year and help out. Manage rehearsals. Make van runs into town. That kind of thing."

"Did you have fun?" I ask. "Last year."

"Best four weeks of my whole damn life." The way he says it, it's clear he's telling the truth. "And God, I learned so much. That's why I jumped at the chance to come back as a program assistant." Jude looks a little sad all of a sudden. "Man, this month will fly by. So make the most of it." That grin is back. Friendly brown eyes. He pops the top off a beer he's been holding, and I watch him slip the cap into his pocket like a quarter. "That's just a little free advice from someone who's been where you're standing."

"Noted," Lex says, and I'm glad he doesn't wink again. Because that would be overkill.

Viv the dark-haired beauty comes back to the fire. "Avril!" She grabs me by the arm. "Come swim with me!"

"Hey, hey!" Jude raises his bottle to greet her like an old friend. "Val, right? From the City of Angels."

Shit. He's right. It's Val. Not Viv.

Valeria from Los Angeles. I remember that now.

And how the hell does Jude know everybody's name? There are like two dozen of us, and he just met us all today.

Val tosses her hair over her shoulder. "Good memory," she says, and I hope like hell I never called her Viv to her face. "Come on, Avril." She's tugging me toward the water. I turn back to Lex and Jude.

"You guys wanna swim?"

"Swim?" Jude laughs and shakes his head. "Oh, hell no." He swallows a long swig of the beer he's been holding.

"You scared?" Val teases.

"Me?" Jude lifts his chin and brushes those charcoal-colored curls back off his forehead. "Nah. But listen, California girl, these are not the warm waters of your misspent LA youth." He shivers and jerks his head toward the waves. "The sound is cold. Especially at night."

Val rolls her eyes. She's staring at Lex now. He swallows the last of his beer and shrugs. "I don't have a swimsuit."

Val throws her head back and laughs, but Lex just stands there. Waiting.

"Oh," she says. "You're serious." And she raises one eyebrow. "Who cares? No swimsuit? No problem." She's already stripping off her sweater.

"I'm in," I say, not because Val convinced me, but because that dark water has been tugging on me since I first laid eyes on it. I bend down to plant my half-empty beer bottle in the sand, and I'm rewarded with a huge smile from Val. She grabs my hand and pulls me toward the shoreline.

"Jesus Christ!" I can't help but squeal when the waves lap over my feet. Jude was telling the truth. We don't have water this cold in Texas. Not even in the middle of winter.

"It's fucking freezing," Val hisses under her breath, and she tightens her grip on my hand. She turns to yell back in Lex and Jude's direction. "Come on! It's not that bad!" Then she looks at me, and we both crack up, because it's cold enough to stop your heart.

The guys exchange a skeptical look, but they stick their bottles in the sand, side by side, and follow us down to the water.

"Holy shit!" Lex does a little dance as the sound licks at his toes. "I thought the ocean was supposed to be warm, y'all!"

"Easy, Nashville," Jude tells him with a smirk. "You're thinking of Florida. You see any palm trees here?"

Val lets go of my hand and slips out of her jeans like she's shedding her skin, splashing into the water in just her tank top and underwear. I blink, and she dives beneath the black surface and comes up gasping. "Oh my God! So cold!" Her dark hair stretches even farther down her back. Heavy and wet now.

Lex hesitates, but then he strips off his scarf and his T-shirt and tosses them onto the sand like he's throwing down the gauntlet. His skin is baby-smooth and china-pale. Dotted with freckles.

He grabs Jude by the arm and tries to tug him into the waves, and I see so clearly the moment Jude decides to let him get away with it. And the two of them laugh.

Val reaches for me again. A cold hand tight around my wrist.

And just for a second, I'm frozen.

Five years old.

Afraid.

Then Val and I both shriek as a big wave nearly takes us down, and that flash of almost memory is swept back out to sea. Gone. Washed away. Like maybe it never existed.

We're all playing and splashing now. Shouting. Darting up and down the beach, in and out of each other's grasp. Sandy fingers reaching and wet hands slipping. The sound of our laughter mixes with the pounding of the surf.

The water is like ice, but after a few minutes I don't mind the bite of it anymore. It almost feels good. Wispy bits of seaweed brush the backs of my knees like floating spiderwebs, and soft, deep sand squishes between my toes.

My T-shirt and shorts are already soaked, so I wade in deeper until I can lift my feet off the bottom and float. And then I can't feel the cold anymore. I can't feel anything anymore. So I let the current pull me out even farther, past a floating swim dock and beyond the clanging safety buoys.

I can still hear the others carrying on and having a good time. But it's like an echo. I'm separate from all that chaos now. I stretch out on my back and let the water hold me up. Carry me away. I'm far enough from shore that there are only gentle swells. I rise and fall with them. Like breathing.

It makes me feel safe. That painless, floating feeling. The numbness of it. And the dark. Like being rocked to sleep. Suspended. Inside a cocoon, maybe.

Or a womb.

I stare up into the emptiness and think about that night. Twelve years ago. When I was five.

This beach.

These waves.

That sky.

I'm trying to remember something real. A tight hand on my wrist, maybe? But that moment has slipped away, and I can't get it back. There's just the same impossible memory as always.

Stars falling into the sea. Like rain on fire.

The heavy, wet plop of them.

And, always, a voice that seems to come from nowhere. From no one.

*Look at the stars!*

Water is sloshing around my ears, but somehow I hear shouting. Not memory voices. Real ones. Muffled words tinged with panic.

"Avril!" It's Jude. "Too far out!" Then something I don't catch. Dangerous. Undertow something. "Come on back!" I open my eyes and let my feet drop so that I'm treading water. It's so much deeper here than it was along the edge.

Darker.

Colder.

Val and Lex are waving at me like they're signaling an aircraft. Motioning for me to swim toward them. Lex yells something about sharks.

I spin in a slow circle. In one direction, I see my new friends. Jude and Lex and Val. The fire burning on the beach. The lights of Whisper Cove Theatre shining in the distance, at the top of the hill behind them.

But in the other direction, there's open water. The lighthouse, and then just black. A slick, wet nothingness that seems to go on forever and ever.

And for a second, I don't know which way I want to swim.

I hesitate. I'm looking for someone. Waiting for her.

Hoping she'll find me.

I've been searching for my mother for years. In creeks and rivers. In muddy Texas lakes. Our neighbor's bottomless swimming pool. The bathtub. And I've never found her.

Or she's never found me.

But surely here. In this place, of all places.

This ocean, dark and deep.

I wait. Tread water. Count my heartbeats. Bleed an invitation out into the depths.

*I'm here. I came back.*

There's nothing, though. There never is. So I start swimming. Toward the light. I'm slicing through the waves. Pushing against a current that's trying to pull me even farther into the emptiness. I spit out water and keep going.

The others are waiting on shore. I haul myself out of the sound, panting and dripping. Sand clings to our feet. And legs. The sea runs down our back in little rivers, and we shiver together.

My mother is still lost to me. Still dead. But I'm alive. The ragged breath in my throat and the burn of my muscles is enough to make me know it. At least in this moment.

I'm alive.

The beach is almost empty now. Everyone else is gone. Or leaving. They're shaking off their towels and heading back up to the cabins, but someone's left an abandoned blanket near the fire. Jude grabs us a couple of new beers from the cooler—one for him and Lex to share and one for me and Val—then the four of us pile in close, greedy for warmth, as the water evaporates and the salt tightens on our skin.

Jude and Lex and Valeria are fishing for information about each other. They're sharing carefully curated pieces of themselves, passing little bits of their lives around like shiny gold coins.

Val has a boyfriend back in LA. He keeps texting her. Chester. She makes a face when she says his name. "I know, I know. It's a horrible name," she tells us. "It sounds like somebody's weird uncle. But he's hot . . . so . . ." She shrugs and shows us a pic on her phone, and he's all brooding eyes and bad boy energy. But she's not sure she loves him.

At least not that much.

She wants to be an actress. Movies, though. Not the stage. "There's no money in live theatre," she warns us.

Jude's from Macon, Georgia. He's a year older than the rest of us, so he's heading off to college in the fall. University of North Carolina. Chapel Hill. He wants to study dance. Ballet, to be specific. "My mom thinks it's stupid, though." He runs a hand over his chest, and I see the glint of dried salt crystals against dark skin. "She's pissed because my sister's studying eighteenth-century British poetry or some shit like that, so we're both gonna be broke as fuck. And who's gonna take care of her in her old age?" He shrugs. "She wants me to major in accounting. And she's paying, so it's whatever."

Lex tells us he has two goals for the next four weeks. "Learn everything I can from Willa Culver and have a hot summer romance." I see him blush and sneak a hopeful glance at Jude. "Like Sandy in *Grease*." He's grinning when he says it, but there's something almost sad underneath that mischievous sparkle in his blue eyes, and I wonder what his story is.

Then they're all looking at me. Waiting. So I take my turn handing out the scraps of myself that I've deliberately chosen. I live with my dad. It's just the two of us. My mom died when I was little. Acting is so deep a part of me that I can't even imagine my life without the theatre. I don't have a boyfriend right now. Or a girlfriend. I miss my cat. And I'm glad to be out of Texas for a few weeks. Because of the heat.

I hold up those pieces of me like it's show-and-tell. But there are other pieces I keep hidden. Truths I stuff down into my pockets. Secrets I choke on like seawater. At least for now.

I don't admit that I came here searching for something.

For someone.

Or that I've been here before. I don't mean to Connecticut. I mean right here. To this exact spot.

And I definitely don't tell them that this is where I died.

# ACT I: SCENE 2

"To new friends," Lex says, and he lifts his beer in a toast before handing it to Jude. Fingers touch. Flirty smiles. The wordless exchange of the slick bottle. Lip to lip.

"To summer," Val chimes in, and we all drink to that.

"To George," Jude adds, and everyone looks confused. "He's the one who bought the beer."

"Who's George?" Lex demands.

"The Whisper Cove caretaker," Jude explains. "He gets paid extra to keep an eye on things at night. But if you slip him a little weed, he's happy to look the other way."

"To George, then," Val says.

A chorus of gratitude and bottles clinking. "To George!" More laughter.

Then it's my turn. I feel the space they've left open for me.

"To the stage," I offer. And they all applaud. Drink again.

"You ready for auditions tomorrow, Avril?" Val's face is relaxed. She's sifting sand through her fingers, but there's an edge under her words that I recognize. Sure, we can be friends, it says, but don't forget that we're also competitors. Because auditions tomorrow night will determine what role each of us gets in the play we'll be working on together.

Willa Culver's play. The one that made her famous.

"Yeah," I say. "I think I'm ready." But suddenly I don't feel so confident.

"Good." Val laughs, and that edge disappears. "Then you can help me with my monologue. It's a mess. I just finished memorizing it on the plane this afternoon."

Lex pulls a crumpled cigarette out of his bag, and we pass that around between the four of us. The fire is getting low, so Jude and Lex go off to gather more driftwood. I watch them down the beach, doing more flirting and laughing than wood-gathering.

Val gets a call from Chester. She rolls her eyes and steps away for some privacy. I can't hear what she's saying, but that hand planted on her hip tells me she's annoyed, and I almost feel sorry for the poor guy.

It's finally quiet for a few minutes then. Just the sound of the fire dying. And the hypnotic repetition of the waves. I lean back on my elbows and breathe in smoke and salt. The fire and the sea. It's almost more intoxicating than the beer, that smell. If somebody could invent a candle that really smelled like this, they'd be so rich.

Then, from somewhere behind me, I hear voices. Hushed and secretive and carried on the wind. I can't make out the words, but there's something familiar about the barely there sound. It brushes against my memory the way the seaweed brushed the backs of my knees.

More whispering.

I think it must be Lex and Jude. But when I sit up and look

toward the water, I see the two of them standing close together, arms full of sun-bleached driftwood. The moonlight makes it look like they've been gathering bones.

I glance over my shoulder and there's no one there, but I still hear the sound of muffled whispers. Leftover partiers, probably. A half-drunk couple hooking up in the tall grass.

I get to my feet and take a few steps away from the fire. Toward the dunes. And that whispering sound.

"Who's there?" I ask. My voice is soft, almost a whisper itself. But no answer comes back to me on the damp night air, so I try again. Louder this time. "Is somebody out there?"

There's nothing now. No sound at all. So maybe I never heard anything to begin with.

I turn back toward the water to find Lex and Jude and Val again. Just to make sure they're not messing with me. I count heads. One. Two. Three.

"Hey."

A voice from the darkness. Not a whisper this time. A solid word.

I spin around to look behind me, and a figure is walking out of the blackness. A guy about my age. Someone I haven't seen before.

"Looks like I missed the party," he says.

My muscles tense. There's something about the way he moves. Too slow. Too easy. Too sure of himself. Like he owns the place or something.

He stops a few feet away, still mostly in the shadows. All I can really see are his eyes. "I'm Cole." There's a pause. Like maybe that should mean something to me. "Willa Culver's son."

"Oh," I say, and I relax a little because at least that means he's not a weird drifter with a necklace made of human teeth. But I'm also surprised, because I didn't know Willa Culver had a son. Or any kids at all.

Cole is just staring at me. Like he's waiting for me to say something else.

"So, do you have a name?" he finally asks with a little smirk. "Or . . ."

Shit. Now I look like an idiot.

"Avril," I tell him, and we stare at each for a few seconds. "Avril Vincent."

He takes a step closer, and now he's lit by what's left of the fire. I make note of the tattered jeans paired with an expensive sweater. The dark, wavy hair above wild, dark brows. The hard angles of him. Features carved out of rock. I feel him run his eyes over my wet T-shirt and shorts. My sandy bare feet.

My face.

There's something strange about the way he's staring at me now. The change in his breathing. I feel it. And I wonder if maybe I was wrong about that necklace of human teeth. But then he smiles.

And damn. My stomach drops.

I pull my eyes away from Cole's to peer around him. Into the blackness. "Who were you talking to?" I ask, and he gives me a funny look. I'm still searching the dunes behind him, waiting for another shape to emerge from the night. "Just now. Who was out there with you?"

He shakes his head. Slips his hands into his pockets. "Nobody." I still feel his eyes on me. "Why?"

I don't think I believe him, but I also haven't heard that whispering again.

I shrug. "I thought I heard something." My damp hair is clinging to my face. It's in my mouth. My eyes. I reach up to tuck a strand behind my ear. "I just—" I stop and listen, because maybe it's almost there again. That whispering sound.

Or maybe not. I can't tell anymore. The waves are so loud.

The way Cole is studying me makes me uncomfortable. "Forget it," I tell him. "It doesn't matter." I shiver and wish again that I'd gone back to the cabin for a sweatshirt or something. I turn and walk back toward the dying fire. Cole follows me.

"You're cold," he says.

"A little," I lie. My teeth are starting to chatter.

"Here. Take this." He pulls his sweater over his head and tosses it to me. The T-shirt he's wearing underneath hugs his chest and his arms, but I don't let myself stare, because he's just standing there watching me with this slightly amused look on his face. "I mean, unless you enjoy freezing."

The sweater is soft in my hands. Thick and warm. And it smells like sandalwood and summer.

But that cocky grin pisses me off.

"Thanks," I tell him. And I toss the sweater back. "But I'm fine. Really." I force my muscles to relax. Refuse to shiver.

He shrugs and pulls the sweater back on. "Suit yourself."

"Cole!" Jude shouts. He and Lex are heading back in our direction. "Good to see you again, my man!" They pile on the driftwood and get the fire going.

Val comes back, too. Drawn by the flames. She sits close to the fire and tucks her long legs under the blanket, jeans spread out to warm in the heat beside her.

Jude handles the formal introductions.

Lex.

Val.

Avril.

Cole.

"Willa's son," Jude tells us, and Lex and Val seem appropriately impressed. Which is probably the reaction Cole is used to. "We hung out last summer." Jude fishes the last floating beer out of the cooler and wipes the wet bottle on his damp shorts before he hands it to Cole. "He's gonna be a senior this year. Same as you guys."

"Are you doing the intensive, too?" Lex asks. I figure he's sizing up the competition—like Val was with me—but Cole shakes his head.

"I'm not much of an actor. Music's my thing." He pops the top off his beer. "I'll be around, though."

Jude keeps Cole busy answering questions about the past year. Everything that's happened since they last saw each other. But I notice how Cole's eyes drift in my direction. The way he keeps looking at me through the fire. Between the flames.

I try not to stare back, but there's something about Cole Culver that makes it hard for me to look away.

"So you grew up here?" Val asks him.

"Lived here my whole life," Cole answers. "Right next door to the theatre."

"I was just telling Lex some of the stories about this place," Jude says, "but he didn't believe me."

Lex rolls his eyes. "I didn't believe you when you said it was haunted."

"Every theatre has a ghost," Val tells us. She's drawing lazy circles in the sand with one finger. "It's like a requirement or something."

Jude laughs, but I'm thinking about our high school back home. It's only a couple of years old. All chrome fixtures and big windows. Bright lights and fresh paint. The fine arts building sits on the site of a former JCPenney.

No ghosts there, except for maybe the ghosts of sales gone by.

That's one of the reasons I love it so much. I actually feel less haunted on that stage than I do most places.

Cole shakes his head, like Val got it wrong. "Every theatre has a ghost *story*," he corrects her. He drains the last of his beer and tosses the bottle into the fire. "But that's not the same thing." He looks at me then, and there's something about his eyes. "Whisper Cove is different."

"Well, fuck," Lex says, and he giggles. But it's a nervous giggle. "I did not sign up for ghosts. That was not in the brochure, y'all."

Cole looks around our little circle. Faces lit by firelight. "You guys know how this place got its name?"

We shake our heads. Say that we don't.

"Oh shit," Jude says. "Here we go." He raises an eyebrow at Lex, passes the bottle in his direction. "Better have another drink."

"There used to be a little whaling village," Cole tells us. "Right here, on this property. Back in the 1800s. A dozen or so little houses up on the hill, where the theatre is now. A general store and a tavern." He looks around to make sure we're all paying attention. "The story goes that, one summer, the men went off to sea, like usual. But when they came home six months later, the village was deserted. Totally empty. All the houses abandoned. Plates still laid out on the tables. Vegetables rotting in the gardens. Laundry flapping on the lines." He shrugs. "But not a soul to be found."

Cole may not be much of an actor, but he's a born storyteller. He's got us eating out of his hand. Everyone looks around, as if we could see the laundry now. Those silent houses standing sentry at the edge of the sea.

But all we can see is the dark at the edges of our circle where the firelight doesn't reach. And the strange glow of the lighthouse off in the distance.

"So they start asking around," Cole goes on. "Where are their wives? Their sweethearts? But nobody will say. And finally this one old guy tells them what happened. They're all drowned, he says. The womenfolk are all dead. They walked into the sea."

"Jesus." Lex shudders.

"Told you," Jude says, and he reaches for their shared bottle. "Haunted as fuck."

"That's not even the worst of it," Cole tells us. "They took their kids with 'em. Grabbed their toddlers by the hand. Carried their babies in their arms."

"You're full of shit," Val accuses, and Cole shrugs.

"I'm just telling you how the story goes." He pauses to lick dried salt from his lips, then looks around our circle again. His hair is damp from the night air, and it shines like obsidian in the firelight. "People around here believe the sea was calling to those women. Luring them to their deaths." Cole turns to look in my direction. He brushes the hair out of his eyes. "Whispering to them."

And now I get it.

He's messing with me. Trying to freak me out.

That's the point of any good ghost story, after all.

"Seriously?" Lex says, and Cole nods. He picks up a stick to poke at the fire. Sparks explode like a fountain.

"Swear to God, that's how the story goes."

Jude leans in close to Lex's ear and makes a whispering sound, and Lex gives him a shove. "Asshole," he mutters. But one corner of his mouth twitches up.

"Anyway," Cole says, and he wipes his sandy palms on his jeans, "that's why they call this Whisper Cove. And they say if you start to hear that whispering, it gets inside your head. The sea, it'll start calling to you. Whispering right in your ear at night. And if you're not careful, you'll end up just like those women more than two hundred years ago. Drowned." He pauses to look around our little group again. "Because what the sea wants, the sea will have."

The words hang there for a second. Suspended over the fire.

Then Val laughs and Cole's spell is broken. She rolls her eyes. "Oh my God," she says, and she reaches for the bottle I'm holding. "So dramatic." Her dark eyeliner is all smudged now, but somehow it only makes her more beautiful. "What the sea wants, the sea will have. That's a great line."

Cole shrugs. "It's not a line." He looks in my direction. Our eyes meet again, and I don't let myself look away, because I want Cole Culver to know that I'm not afraid of his campfire tale. I've been living with ghosts my whole life.

"Look," Jude tells us, and he rubs at his arms. "I know it's corny. But I get fucking goose bumps every damn time I hear it."

"It's just a story," Lex says, almost more to himself than to us. He's finger-combing that gorgeous red hair of his, but he stops to look around the circle. "Isn't it?"

"Maybe," Jude adds. He shifts closer to the fire. "But every story has some truth to it."

"It's a bunch of bullshit," I say, and they all turn to look at me. "People die. The sea is dangerous." My mouth suddenly feels like it's full of sand, and the words come out rougher than I intend them to. They're gritty on my tongue. "You don't need a reason to drown."

"That's true most places." Cole gives me a look, almost like the two of us are sharing some kind of secret. An inside joke I don't quite get. "But Whisper Cove is different."

"He's right about that." Jude glances around at the rest of us. There's something I can't read in his big brown eyes. "You'll see for yourselves."

The fire pops and crackles.

The waves moan.

The beach is alive with night sounds. Singing frogs. The buzz of insects.

And the clanging of safety buoys. They ring like alarm bells.

But nobody speaks for a long minute, and then Jude mentions that it's getting late. And we have to be at breakfast early. So we all get to our feet. Start to gather up our stuff. Val pulls on her jeans, and most everyone wanders down to the water's edge to collect the things they discarded there. Shirts. Socks. A sweater or two. Val is shaking the sand out of her hair, and I see Jude say something to Lex as he goes to pick up his scarf. The quiet way Lex laughs lets me know it was a joke meant just for him.

I don't have any clothes to collect, so Cole and I stay behind with the heat of the fire between us. A smothering fog has started to roll in off the water. I feel it clinging to my skin.

He reaches up to run a hand through that dark, wavy hair, and I notice a little tattoo. Some kind of four-point star on the inside of his wrist. He catches me staring.

"It's a compass rose," he says, and he moves around the fire to show me. "I got it last year when I was sixteen. Used a fake ID. One point for each direction. See? North, south, east, and west."

"Cool," I say, and I glance toward the water. I can hear Lex giggling now, but I can't see him anymore. I can't see any of the others. The fog has settled like a curtain between us.

Cole is studying me again. His eyes are gray. The color of smoke. Or ash. "Sailors thought a compass rose tatt was good luck," he says. His voice comes from deep in his throat, and there's an almost-hypnotizing ebb and flow to it. The words move against my ear with the rhythm of the waves. "They thought it would protect them. Keep them safe at sea."

"Are you a sailor?" I ask, and he laughs.

"No. My mom is deathly afraid of the ocean." He rolls his eyes. "We live right here on the water. And we don't even have a boat."

"Then what do you need protection from?"

He gives me that little smirk from earlier. But there's honesty in his eyes this time.

"Myself, mostly." He moves in closer, and he's really staring at me now. My face flushes, and I feel his breath on the top of my head. "What do you need protection from, Avril?"

"Nothing," I tell him. But he's still staring at me. I'm relieved when the others emerge out of the fog then, sandy and stringy-haired and yawning. I see Lex take note of the way Cole and I are standing close together. The way his eyes are locked on mine.

And then I feel that warm breath on the top of my head again. Heat. And proximity. “What do you need protection from, Avril?”

Cole is staring down at me. Waiting for an answer. I look around. We’re alone. Where is everyone?

“I . . .”

I blink. And the others are stepping toward us out of the fog. Again. Lex cuts his eyes toward Cole. Then me. Just like before.

The sand shifts under my feet, and I lose my balance. Cole shoots out a hand to steady me. “Easy,” he says, but I take a stumbling step back. Away from him.

The beer is making me woozy. Everything feels strange.

Off-kilter.

Jude smothers the fire with sand. Val gathers up the empty beer bottles. Someone rolls up the blanket.

Everyone is quiet as we start back toward the theatre together. The fog follows us up the boardwalk and over the dunes, across a salt marsh where the sickly sweet smell of mud and rot fills up my nose. The overwhelming scent of decay.

And then we’re deposited on thick grass. The boardwalk spits us out and we bunch up, tripping over each other as we struggle to get our shoes on.

We make our way up the great sloping lawn toward the cluster of buildings gathered at the top of the hill. The big yellow farmhouse where we all ate dinner earlier this evening. The red barn theatre. And the twin blue cabins on the other side of the field.

In the thick fog, I can just barely make out a green-striped awning extending off the back of the farmhouse.

The sea porch.

I know that somehow. I hadn't remembered it earlier when I saw it at dinner. But I know it now.

I remember it.

Cole says good night when we reach the gravel driveway, and Jude starts off toward the cabins. Lex and Val follow him, but when I turn to go with them, Cole grabs my hand to stop me. His touch is hot against my skin. I feel that shifting sand beneath my feet, even though I'm standing on solid ground now.

He reaches into his pocket and pulls out something small, then presses whatever it is into my palm. He closes my fingers tight around it, and I feel the smooth coolness of his gift.

"Sea glass," he tells me, and I open my fist to stare at the little blue chunk. It's beautiful. Frosty and polished. Round like a pebble. "You find it all over the beach here. The waves and the sand wear it down."

"What do I do with it?"

Cole laughs low in his throat. "Just keep it. It's a good luck charm. I have a ton of it. All different colors." It's my turn to stare at him now. "It's for protection."

"I don't believe in lucky charms," I say. For a couple of years, I carried around a rabbit's foot. It was dyed hot pink, and I won it at the Texas state fair. I threw it out, though, once I realized it obviously hadn't been lucky for the rabbit. "And I don't believe in ghosts."

Even if I've spent my whole life looking for one.

"I don't believe in ghosts, either." Cole shrugs. "But there are lots of ways to be haunted." He gives me a little smile. "Just take it."

I never asked for a party favor from him, but I give up and slip his treasure into my pocket.

"Welcome to Whisper Cove," he tells me, and something flickers behind those smoke-gray eyes again. I'm almost surprised when he doesn't correct himself with *Welcome back, I mean.* But he doesn't. Instead he just vanishes into the dark, and I stare after him for a second before I hurry to catch up with the others.

I'm grateful Jude knows where he's going. The fog has me all confused. Turned around. And disoriented. I would have sworn we were headed the wrong direction.

# ACT I: SCENE 3

We follow Jude through the fog to the first of the blue cabins that sit huddled together on the other side of a muddy field. One for the girls and one for the boys. He reminds us about the breakfast meeting with Willa Culver before he and Lex disappear into the mist, headed for the other cabin just a few yards away.

Val and I trudge up the front steps to our temporary home. She pushes open the door, and I close it tight behind us. I'm not really afraid of serial killers, but I don't want that fog to follow us inside and fill up the room.

Swallow us whole.

The walls of the long, narrow cabin are lined with a dozen or so bunk beds, and a threadbare green rug fills up the floor between them. Most of the other girls are already asleep, so Val and I tiptoe by cell phone light, try to keep things quiet. No sense in pissing off our new roommates on the very first night.

Her phone vibrates. It's Chester. Again. CALL ME BABE. She shows it to me and rolls her eyes. Then she deletes his text without a reply.

I pull Cole's sea glass out of my pocket and tuck it into my over-crowded dresser drawer, between my socks. I still need to finish unpacking, but it'll have to wait until tomorrow. I'm too tired to think about it tonight. "Where's the bathroom?" I whisper. "I need a shower."

"There's a building out back," Val mumbles. She's flopped down on her bunk with all her sandy clothes on, and it makes me itch just thinking about it. "Like an outhouse, only with electricity and plumbing and stuff. Just follow the path." I'm digging in my suitcase for some clean shorts. "Want me to come with you?" Her voice sounds so sleepy.

When I turn back to answer, her eyes are already closed, so I grab my things and head toward the door. But as soon as I step into the fog, I'm suffocated. Disoriented again. I wish I'd packed a real flashlight. Dad told me to, but I ignored him. Because I'm seventeen, and I don't need to be told what to fucking pack.

Clearly.

I feel my way down the steps—one, two, three—until I hear the crunch of a gravel path under my feet, then work my way around the little cabin until my eyes find the flicker of a fluorescent light not too far away. I head in that direction, but it seems to take longer than it should to get there. Like someone keeps moving it just out of my reach. I'm relieved when I finally feel an old-fashioned doorknob under my fingers. The grit of crusted salt on smooth, worn metal.

It's chilly in the bathroom, but at least the light is bright and the water is hot. I'm exhausted and my muscles ache. I lean against the shower stall and let the steam soak into my bones. Was it really just this morning that Dad dropped me off at the airport in Dallas? It seems like so long ago.

I think about the big fight we had back in February when I first told him I planned to apply for the summer intensive at Whisper Cove.

*Pour l'amour de Dieu. Pourquoi?*

For God's sake. Why?

He'd shouted the words at me in our little kitchen, his hands white-knuckled, gripping the back of a chair.

My father is French, and it pisses him off to no end that I'm less than fluent in his native language. He was a university professor in Paris, until he met my mother and fell in love. She was a graduate student on a study abroad trip, but he decided he couldn't live without her. So he followed her home to Texas, only to wind up living without her anyway. Now he teaches beginning French to uninterested freshmen at a private high school he could never afford to send me to.

And when he's irritated—which is most of the time—the French comes out.

*Why would you want to go there?* he'd asked. *To that place. Why drag all that up?* We fought about it for days until he finally threw up his hands and declared, *Do what you want. Je m'en fiche.*

I don't care.

He didn't tell me not to apply, but he obviously didn't understand. Maybe he would have if I'd told him why I wanted to come so bad. If I'd explained how disconnected I've always felt. That I just need to find some link to a mother who's never been anything more than a ghost to me. Some hint of who she was. Some anchor.

So maybe I'll know who I am.

But I couldn't tell him any of that, because Dad and I stopped talking—I mean really talking—in English or French—years ago.

I can still see the look on his face when he found out I'd actually been accepted into the program. All pale and thin-lipped. Afraid. The last words he said to me at the airport this morning were *Whatever you're looking for, Avril, it won't change anything. Elle sera toujours morte.*

She'll still be dead.

So maybe he understands more than I think he does.

The water starts to go cold. I dry off and put on clean clothes, then brush the fuzz of cheap beer from my teeth before I head back to our cabin. The wet, worn wood of the front steps is slick as glass under my flip-flops, and my feet almost go out from under me. I suck in my breath from the surprise. "Shit." A sharp sound in the dull fog. I grab the handrail to steady myself. I can't seem to find my footing tonight.

"Avril?"

I turn to look over my shoulder, and I'm instantly blind. Squinting against the glare. Bright light bouncing off the moisture in the air. Hitting me square in the face.

One second, I'm seventeen. Standing on the steps.

The next, I'm five.

Standing in thick, wet grass.

Blinking.

Against that sudden blinding light.

Paralyzed.

I can't see.

My chest tightens and I can't breathe. Can't move. Can't call out for my mother.

"Avril?"

The redhead—Lex—lowers his flashlight. And I can see again. He's standing at the bottom of the steps.

I'm standing on the porch.

We are seventeen.

The return feels like being sucked backward up a vacuum cleaner hose.

"You okay?" Lex asks.

"Yeah," I say, "I just . . ." But I don't know what the next words are. Because I don't know where that thought came from. That memory. Or whatever.

The bright light in my eyes.

It's like having amnesia and déjà vu at the same time.

"I was on my way to the bathroom," Lex says, "but I heard something." He hesitates. Stares at me. I'm still half-frozen. "I wanted to make sure everything was okay over here." He waits. "Av?"

Nobody's ever called me that. A nickname. I guess we really are besties now.

"Yeah," I say again. "I'm fine."

Lex looks around. But there's nothing to see. We're walled in by fog.

"Can I hang for a minute?" he asks. I start to say no, because all I want is to go to bed, but Lex turns off his flashlight and settles on the top step without waiting for an answer. "I don't think I can sleep yet. I'm nervous, I guess. About auditions tomorrow and everything."

I take the towel that's draped around my shoulders and spread it on the boards to protect myself from the slick wet, then settle down to sit beside him. I pull the sleeves of my sweatshirt down over my hands.

"So what do you think of Whisper Cove?" Lex asks me.

"It's good," I say. "Like summer camp without the stupid canoeing."

"I never went to summer camp. My mom never had the money," he admits. "So I'll have to take your word for it." He nudges me with his shoulder. "I saw the way Cole was looking at you tonight." Lex raises one eyebrow and gives me a sideways smile. "Not bad. Willa Culver's son."

"Did you know she had a son?" I ask him. "Before you came here?"

Lex shakes his head. "I didn't know anything about her personally. I just knew the play."

I know the play he means, of course. Everyone knows *Midnight Music* by Willa Culver. Our Intro to Theatre class read it in ninth grade, and I remember being so swept away by the heartbreaking beauty of it. It was the first play that ever moved me like that. I carried the script in my backpack all the rest of that year, just so I could take it out and reread my favorite parts whenever I had a free moment.

"Yeah," I tell him. "I didn't know much about her, either." And that's certainly not a lie, but I'm thinking of a photograph that I have tucked away inside a notebook back in Dallas. My mother with long hair—icy blonde like mine—in a black cap and gown. College graduation. She's laughing, and her arm is around another young woman, this one with hair as dark as my mother's is blonde.

Willa Culver. The famous playwright. Only she wasn't famous back then, of course. And her last name wasn't Culver.

They were college friends. That's all the info I was ever able to get out of Dad. That's how we ended up at Whisper Cove that summer, my mother and me. When I was five years old.

"He's fucking hot," Lex says. And it takes me a minute to bring my mind back around to what he's talking about.

Who he's talking about.

Cole Culver.

And Lex is undeniably right about that, but there's something about Cole that puts me on edge. So I change the subject.

"What about the way you and Jude were flirting?"

Lex blushes. "He's cute, right?"

"He is," I say. "For sure." It's my turn to nudge him. "You're a fast mover."

"No," he says. "I'm not. But I've only got four weeks." He shrugs. "So no time to waste." Lex sighs, and his grin slips a little. "I just don't want to drag my feet. If there's something there, I wanna find out. You know? Before it's too late." His face has clouded over, and I know that cloud must have a name. But he doesn't tell me who it is that made him sigh like that, so I guess I was wrong about us being besties. We aren't quite there yet.

Lex digs around in his bag and comes up with a cigarette. He offers it to me, but I shake my head, so he shrugs and lights it up for himself.

"You ever wish that you could erase certain memories?" he asks me. "Like how you can turn off a light switch. Or like . . . fuck . . . I don't know." He sucks in smoke and holds it for a minute before he breathes it out again. "The way you can pull a weed up out of a garden or something."

It's a weird thought to me. Wanting to forget. I've spent my whole life trying so desperately to remember. "What memories would you erase?" I ask him. "If you could."

Lex laughs, but it's not that same playful giggle from the beach. This laugh has a hint of bitterness to it. Like coffee grounds left at the bottom of a cup.

"Oh, I don't know," he says. "The shitty ones?" But then he stops. Puts the cigarette to his lips again. Takes another long drag. "Actually, the happy ones, maybe. The really good ones. Like the best fuckin' ones. Those are the memories that hurt the worst sometimes. Right?"

It's quiet for a long minute, and I stare out into the fog. It plays tricks with my depth perception. The light on the front porch of the big farmhouse, just across the little field, looks like it could be the light on a cargo ship far out at sea.

"Do you ever wonder," I ask, "if maybe you're dead?"

I feel like we're drifting. Untethered. The only two people in the world. And that's probably why I say it. Because it's not something I've ever asked anyone else before. Not something I ever would have asked. Not in a million years.

But even though I've only known him a few hours, there's just something about Lex that feels right. Something about him makes me feel seen.

Recognized.

Safe, maybe. As weird as that sounds.

He's watching me. His cigarette smoke mingles with the fog.

It floats lazy and thick around our heads. "I know this is crazy," I tell him, "but something happened to me. A long time ago. And sometimes I have this thought that maybe I'm living out a scene from one of those movies where the main character doesn't know she's dead. You know? That she hasn't survived the accident. Or whatever."

Lex thinks about that for a few seconds, like it's a totally normal question to ask an almost stranger.

"Sometimes I wonder if I've ever really been alive," he finally says. "Is that the same thing?" He offers me the last of his cigarette, and I take it from his fingers and suck in hard before I hand it back to him so he can put it out on the porch steps. It makes me cough something awful, but I like the way it starts my head spinning.

"Yeah," I choke out. Words wrapped in smoke. "I think maybe it is."

A long, low sound reverberates through the still air—a sort of soothing, sustained baritone—and at first I can't figure out what it could be. But then it comes again, and I realize it must be a foghorn.

I like the lonesomeness of it.

"I better get to bed," Lex says, as if the foghorn had been some kind of reverse alarm clock. He stands up and stretches. "Night, Av."

"Good night," I say. I'm already falling in love with that Tennessee drawl of his. It makes me think I could get used to having a nickname. "See you in the morning."

I lose sight of Lex as soon as he steps off the porch, but I hear the crunch of his feet on the gravel path, heading toward the bathroom. I listen to his footsteps until they fade away.

And then I'm all alone.

But I don't go inside. I'm too tired to get up, and I keep thinking about those new almost memories. Those flashes. Or whatever they are.

The one on the beach with Val. A cold hand tight around my wrist.

And the sea porch. How I knew what it was called. That green-striped awning.

Then the moment on the steps with Lex. Blinding light in my eyes.

I've never been able to remember the night my mother died. Or anything before that, either. It's like the sea washed everything away. It stole all my memories and spit me out clean. Oxygen deprivation, the doctors said.

I drowned, after all.

But what if being here is opening up some kind of locked drawer inside my head?

I know that's what Dad was worried about. And I swore to him that I could handle it. Because if I could find just one real memory of her—of my mother—it would make all the difference in the world.

Suddenly I'm overwhelmed by a familiar ache. It's such a deep, constant part of me, that longing for my mother, but it still takes me by surprise when it strikes fast and hard like this. It feels like being hit in the stomach with a baseball bat.

It sucks the air out of my lungs and leaves me gasping.

I reach for the cigarette lighter Lex left on the steps. I flick it with my thumb, and the flame comes to life in my hands. It's a familiar feeling, and just holding it makes me feel more in control.

I touch the lighter to a string hanging from the edge of my towel, and the flame eats it alive. Gobbles it up in a rush of light. A bright flash. And then it's gone. I burn another string. And then another. And another. Until there are none left. Then I take my other hand and hold my palm just above the lighter's flame. I like the heat it gives off. And the brightness. The pain of it. Like the catch in my lungs and the ache of my muscles after that long swim back to the beach.

The burn proves that I'm alive.

I slip Lex's lighter into my pocket, and I sit there listening to the low moan of the foghorn.

And then maybe there's another sound—a barely there sound that drifts into my ears like cigarette smoke—and at first I think Lex has come back from the bathroom. I stand up. Say his name into the darkness.

And that's when the whispering starts.

# ACT I: SCENE 4

"Avril, wake up. We're gonna be late."

Someone is shaking me. I open my eyes and blink a few times before Val's green eyes and dark hair come into focus.

I push myself up and look around.

"What time is it?" I mumble. All the other bunks are already empty.

"Seven thirty," Val says. "Meeting starts in fifteen minutes."

Shit. I wonder why my alarm didn't go off. Val heads out to the bathroom to brush her teeth, and I tell myself I need to get up and get dressed. A quick glance toward the window lets me know the fog is already gone. All I see is blue sky and sunshine.

I throw back the sheet and swing my feet to the floor. And that's when I notice the dried mud. And the grass. On the bottom of my feet and in my bed. There's not a lot of it, but for a few seconds I just stare, trying to make sense of it. I remember being out on the porch last night. I remember Lex. And the foghorn. But after my shower, I never left the gravel path and front steps. So where did the mud and grass come from?

And then I remember the whispering.

But that part doesn't seem real now. It's like a dream, maybe. Something I imagined.

I feel a little dizzy—slightly hungover, probably—but I shake it off and stumble into some clean shorts and a T-shirt. I brush off my sheets before I run a comb through my hair and shove my feet into my flip-flops, then grab my toothbrush and hurry to the bathroom. Val's already on her way back, but she promises to wait for me. I get ready in record time, and we start across the field toward the farmhouse.

"Hey! Av! Wait up!"

I look over my shoulder to see Lex waving at me. He and Jude are jogging toward us, and we pause to let them catch up.

"Mornin', boys," Val says, and she bats her mascaraed eyelashes. "Ready to set the world on fire?"

"Ready for breakfast," Jude says. "That's for damn sure."

"You sleep okay?" Lex asks me.

"Yeah," I tell him. But that starts me thinking again about the grass in my bed. The mud on my feet. I brush it out of my mind, though, the way I brushed it out of my sheets. I must have picked it up on the path somehow.

The day is perfect. The sun is warm, but the breeze is crisp and it carries the kiss of salt. I stop for a second to take in the crumbling rock wall that surrounds the garden. The sloping green lawn and the brilliant sparkle of the sea beyond. It's like something out of an impressionist painting.

"Jesus." Val throws her arm around my shoulders. "The beach in LA never looks like that," she whispers, like she's letting me in on some kind of secret. "We have fucking amazing sunsets, but we don't get that kind of blue."

"It's incredible," I say. You'd think I'd remember a view like this.

But then, you'd think I'd remember a lot of things.

We've almost made it to the front porch when a man steps out from a cluster of trees next to the farmhouse. He's older, with sandy-blond hair and a weathered face, and he's carrying a giant pair of hedge clippers. Jude raises his arm in a friendly wave. "Hey! George!" he shouts. "Good to see you, man!"

So this is the infamous Whisper Cove caretaker. The one with a fondness for weed and a reputation for looking the other way.

George gives Jude a dismissive scowl, then lifts his clippers to lop off a low-hanging branch. "Still can't believe they let you back in here," he mumbles. He shakes his head and bends to pick up the clippings at his feet. When he straightens back up, his eyes lock on mine, just for a second. There's something about the way he looks at me that makes my arms break out in goose bumps. Maybe it's the way I feel his eyes moving over my body—or maybe it's the giant clippers in his hand—but I'm instantly uneasy, and I'm relieved when he disappears into the trees again.

"He loves me," Jude assures us with a grin. "I promise." And I tell myself that I just imagined that weird feeling. That being here has my mind playing tricks on me. I shake it off and tell myself to focus on more important things. Like how I'm about to be face-to-face with Willa Culver.

The farmhouse is painted bright yellow, and it seems to spread out forever with no clear plan, the way houses do when they've been added on to and then added on to again. We all gather up on the big front porch, since that's where the welcome meeting is supposed to be.

A bunch of the others are already there. It's crowded, so I perch on the railing between Lex and Val. I run my hand over the worn wood and think about how my mother probably touched it. I already feel closer to her here than I ever have in our apartment back home. Dad erased all trace of her there years ago, but here it's easy to picture her strolling across the lawn. Or sitting in the shade of one of those big trees, reading a script.

"Y'all ready to meet Willa?" Jude asks us. His smile is so wide. It's clear how much he adores her. "She's the one who really put this place on the map, ya know. A decade or so ago, Whisper Cove was just another struggling summer theatre. It was about to go under for good. But Willa's play changed all that. She—"

We don't get a chance to talk any more, because the most striking woman I've ever seen suddenly bursts through the screen door and onto the porch. She's tall and elegant, with long legs and long, dark hair streaked with steely silver. She has on jeans and heeled boots. Dangly earrings and jangling bracelets. A flowing yellow scarf trails behind her like the tail of a kite.

But it's those eyes that really demand my attention. They're gray. Unflinching. So much like Cole's that, even if I hadn't spent the past couple of years staring at that photo of her younger self, I'd know without a doubt exactly who she was.

There's a flurry of activity and excited murmuring, because this is Willa Culver. Right here in front of us. In the flesh. She's the reason theatre kids from all over the country compete for a chance to come here. They all want an opportunity to study with Willa.

I can't stop staring at her for another reason, though. Because standing right here in front of me is someone who knew my mother. Someone who called her a friend.

"Hello, my lovelies!" Willa is beaming at us. "Welcome to Whisper Cove!"

I was such a little girl the last time she saw me, and my name is totally different. And I know there's just enough of my father in my face to keep Willa Culver from recognizing me. But I have this sudden urge to stand up and shout out my truth to her.

*My mother was Nicole Kendrick!*

Instead, I bite my lip and stick to my plan. I'll tell her after auditions. After the play is cast. That's what I decided on the plane.

"Okay, okay," she tells us. "Let's get down to business. First, I want to say congratulations, and I want you all to take a moment to consider that you are among greatness. Right here on this humble farmhouse porch." Willa looks around our group, and we wait with a hushed anticipation that's settled on us thicker than last night's fog. "The two dozen of you here this summer were chosen by me personally, handpicked from among hundreds of applicants. I was looking for something special. Something that stood out. And each and every one of you had that." She gives us a dazzling smile. "So please know that each one of you is already extraordinary."

Val leans over to whisper in my ear. "Holy shit." She's twisting a long strand of dark hair around one finger. "Can you believe this is real life?"

I glance around and everyone is staring, rapt, at Willa. Lex. Jude. All the others. They're hanging on her every word. I know she's talking about us, but there's obviously something special about her, too.

"You may be aware," Willa starts, "that a while back I wrote a little play." Everyone giggles, of course, and Willa laughs with us. "But seriously," she says, "*Midnight Music* is the greatest achievement of my life. It's the reason this theatre is still here. It's the reason I'm still here." She pauses for a deep breath. "And now it's the reason you're all here." A cheer and a round of applause go up from our group, and Willa pauses another moment before she continues, one hand over her heart. "And for that, I am eternally grateful."

She goes on to explain that our mornings will be filled with classes on everything from stage combat to dialects. "We've arranged for some of the industry's top theatre professionals to work with you this month." Naturally, she teaches playwriting herself.

In the afternoons, we'll have our work assignments. Because there's no cost to attend the intensive, the work assignments are how we give back to Whisper Cove. Willa tells us all to check the call-board on the front porch to find out where we'll be working. But I've already done that, so I know I'll be at the reception desk.

"Classes start tomorrow," Willa lets us know, and she tucks a strand of long, dark hair behind one ear. Silver bracelets jingle. "That gives you a little more time to settle in. But work assignments start this afternoon." She pauses, and her eyes sparkle. "Which brings us to this evening's auditions."

A hush falls over the group. We all lean forward like we're scraps of metal, powerless against Willa's magnetic pull. It reminds me of the way we listened to Cole's story last night on the beach.

Those deserted houses with their rotting gardens.

"As you're probably aware," Willa says, "each year the students present a workshop performance of *Midnight Music* on the final day of the intensive."

Lex has stopped breathing beside me. He's gripping the porch railing, and the freckles on the backs of his hands stand out like tiny drops of blood.

"But you don't need to look so worried," Willa says. "Everyone gets a part. All worthy roles, I assure you. I happen to know the playwright." She winks at Lex, and he giggles. It comes out super high-pitched. Nervous. And he clamps a hand over his mouth, embarrassed. But then Jude tosses him a grin, and he starts to breathe again.

"And, of course, Jude here will be our trusty stage manager." Willa waves a hand in Jude's direction, and he lights up under her attention. "So no worries about tonight," she says. "You'll all be stars, I promise."

We wrap up the meeting by going over the rules, and there aren't many. Be on time. Work hard. Love each other. And one last thing. Nobody outside the cabins after eleven o'clock. It's a rule we've already broken, but nobody volunteers that information.

"Here's a thought for the day," Willa adds before she dismisses us. "In act four of *Hamlet,* the beautiful but doomed Ophelia says, 'We know who we are, but not who we may be.' I want you all to remember that. Think about it every single day while you're here. Every moment, even. You came to Whisper Cove as one person, but if you're lucky, you'll leave here as someone else. Someone you can't even begin to imagine yet." She looks around our group again. “Let this summer set your soul on fire. Let it bring you to life, my lovelies. That is the real magic of the theatre.” She claps her hands. “Meeting adjourned. Now, someone please get Jude some breakfast!”

There’s another round of applause, and we all float in the screen door on a wave of chatter and excitement. A small woman stands up from a reception desk to greet us. Her curly brown hair is just barely held under control by an overworked headband. She doesn’t look very old. Late twenties, maybe. It’s hard to tell because of her huge glasses.

“This,” Jude announces, “is Glory.” He swoops in to give her a big hug. “Think of her like your big sister. She knows this place inside and out. You have any questions, or you need anything, you talk to Glory. She’s the real boss around here.”

Glory blushes. “Don’t listen to this one,” she warns us, and I notice her Boston accent. Or maybe it’s New York. Either way, it’s definitely not the Texas twang I’m used to. “Jude’s too charming for his own good.” She’s running her hands over her wrinkled skirt. Picking cat hair off her cardigan sweater. “Everyone knows who’s in charge around here.” She gives us all a nervous little smile. “Whisper Cove is Willa’s baby. I’m just lucky to be a part of it. But do let me know if you need anything.” She offers us each a peppermint from the bowl on her desk. “We want you to feel at home here.”

She seems kind, and I’m glad, since I’ve been assigned as her assistant. I start to introduce myself, but just then the phone rings, and Glory turns to answer it. “Whisper Cove Theatre. This is Glory. How can I help you?”

She gives us all an apologetic wave, and Jude blows her a kiss as he ushers us on down the hallway, around a corner, and through a set of swinging doors into the little cafeteria.

A hot-food line with buffet-style serving tables sits along the far wall, and there's a drink station in one corner. A salad bar fills up the middle of the floor. Last night, at dinner, it was overflowing. But it's empty now. The rest of the room is taken up with round tables.

We all grab trays and make our way through the line, filling our plates with scrambled eggs and sausage. There are biscuits, too. Big fluffy ones. And fresh strawberries.

All around the cafeteria, kids are splitting up into groups. We've only been here one night, but everyone seems to have found their people already. It reminds me of the school cafeteria back home. I guess some things are universal.

I fill my glass with orange juice from the dispenser and head toward a spot in the middle of the room where Jude, Lex, and Val are waiting for me.

"What'd you guys think of Willa?" Jude asks as we slide our trays onto the table. His plate is piled high with biscuits. "I told you she was a trip, right?"

"She's fucking amazing," Lex says as he reaches for the pepper. "Exactly like I thought she'd be."

"I keep thinking about what she said," Val tells us. She's dressed all in black this morning. Ripped jeans and another tank top. Cat eyes and red lipstick. She looks like a rock star. "About how we know who we are, but not who we may be." She pops a strawberry into her mouth. "That's deep shit."

"So, who are we going to be four weeks from now?" Lex asks,

pepper shaker frozen in midair over his eggs. He sneaks a look at Jude. "I don't wanna leave here the same person I was when I showed up."

And I don't, either. But I don't know yet who it is I want to become.

Maybe none of the others do, either. Maybe that's what this summer is about. For all of us.

We fill in some more gaps about ourselves between bites.

Val has done some modeling in LA. Just stuff for a local mall, she tells us like she's halfway embarrassed. But the rest of us are impressed.

Lex got suspended last year for skipping classes. But he still had straight As. So fuck 'em.

And Jude plays sax in the marching band. "Played," he corrects himself. He probably won't have time to keep it up next year. In college. The look on his face tells us he already misses it.

I dig around inside my brain for something that feels safe to share. Something easy and comfortable. The kind of thing you can lay out on the breakfast table next to the biscuits and the butter. But I've never been good at this kind of thing. I settle on a funny story about playing the part of an apple tree in *The Wizard of Oz,* even though I'm allergic to apples.

And that seems to satisfy them.

At least for now.

The rest of the talk over breakfast is about auditions. The monologues we've prepared. What we're wearing. We harass Jude with questions about what to expect, but he just grins and says his lips are sealed.

We're almost finished eating when a man in khakis and a wrinkled blue dress shirt comes into the cafeteria. He's going bald, but he has a handsome face. I watch him stop at the hot-food bar and load his plate up with eggs and biscuits. Jude waves, and he comes over to our table.

"Morning, Jude!" His voice is louder than I expect it to be. "These must be some of our new recruits."

"Lex, Avril, and Val," Jude says, "this is Brody Culver. He's the artistic director here at Whisper Cove."

And just like that, I'm face-to-face with someone else who would have known my mother that last summer of her life. I want to ask if he remembers her. But I don't. Not yet. I just stare at him and wonder.

"He's also Willa's husband," Jude clarifies. But we all knew that already.

"Most important part of my title," Brody says with a chuckle. "Mr. Willa Culver."

And he's Cole's father, of course. But there's no sign of Cole in this man. Cole is all dark hair and intensity. Like his mother. This guy is almost too relaxed and casual. Too laid back to be genuine.

"Sorry to fill my plate and run," Brody is saying. "But I need to get back to my office. You won't see a lot of me. My focus is on the professional shows we have going up the second half of the summer. But you're in good hands with Willa." He slaps Jude on the back. "And with my buddy Jude here, of course."

When he's gone, we finish our breakfast and dump our trays, then everyone splits off to work on their audition monologues. Lex and I make plans to rehearse together, but Jude catches us on the way out of the cafeteria. "Hey, Avril," he says, "do you mind if I steal Lex for a little bit?" He's talking to me, but those big brown eyes are trained on Lex. Just like last night on the beach. "I promised I'd show him around this morning."

"Oh," I say. "Yeah. Sure." I almost add that I'll come, too, but the way Lex is blushing clues me in that this is meant to be a private tour.

"You don't mind, do you, Av?" Lex looks worried. Like he feels bad leaving me alone. But I'm used to being alone, so I shake my head and tell Lex that he should go with Jude. Because Jude is leaning against the door frame, grinning, all gorgeous curls and long eyelashes and flirty smiles. So, yeah. Of course Lex should go with him.

We promise to meet back up for lunch, and I decide to head out to the sea porch. I've been thinking about that green-striped awning since I saw it in the fog last night.

I try finding my way through the house, but the rooms and hallways are like a maze. After I get lost the third time, I give up and backtrack to the cafeteria so I can head out the side door and follow the stone path around to the back.

When I come around the corner of the farmhouse, I stop dead in my tracks. I wonder if I'll ever get used to it all. That stunning view. Or the coolness of an ocean breeze in the middle of June. And the way the air smells here. Fresh, but with a little bit of a bite. Like salt and flowers and seaweed. And something that reminds me of the way clean, crisp sheets feel against your skin in the summertime.

I listen to the faraway song of the waves. Watch them breaking down at the beach in a line of white foam. Seagulls cry overhead, and colorful sailboats dark back and forth against the horizon. It's perfect.

Magical.

So much more beautiful than anything I've ever seen in Texas. It seems more like another planet than another state.

It's more than just pretty, though. There's also something about it that just feels right. In almost the same way that Lex feels right. Like this is where I belong. On these wide back steps with the lighthouse standing guard.

I let my eyes travel the distance to the water.

Green lawn.

Brown sand.

White foam.

Blue sea.

Then I look up. There's something so familiar about that striped awning covering the huge porch.

I wait. Just in case. But no new memories come to me, so I take out my phone and return a few texts from Dad. I promise him I'm fine. Really. That everything is going great. Then I pull the script for *Midnight Music* out of my bag. It's a dog-eared edition from when I first read it in ninth grade. I need to go over it again and make some notes before tonight.

But something stops me.

Down on the beach, a figure is climbing out of the surf. It's too far away for me to see his face, but that shock of dark hair tells me who it is.

Cole Culver.

I watch him bend down and pick up a T-shirt. Shake out the

sand. Pull it over his head. Then I lose sight of him. He disappears into the dunes, and I can't see him anymore. Not until he emerges onto the green lawn a few minutes later.

He's running now. Not jogging. Full-out running up the big hill toward the farmhouse. Like some kind of monster is hot on his heels in pursuit. And I can't seem to tear my eyes away from him. There's something beautiful about the way he moves across the bright green grass. Like he's pure energy. His feet don't touch the ground.

I manage to force my eyes down toward my script when he gets close, but he keeps on coming. He doesn't stop until he reaches the sea porch, and then he leans down, hands on his knees. Breathing hard. And dripping. Salt water sliding down his cheeks and arms. His neck.

Not that I'm looking at his neck.

"Hey, skeptic girl," he pants. "You busy?"

I look up, like I only just noticed him, and Cole is standing at the bottom of the steps, grinning at me. It's weird seeing him in the daylight, almost like I'd imagined he was a ghost himself. But here he is with his annoyingly good hair and his smoky eyes.

"Reading," I say. And I hold up my copy of the script.

Cole smirks and takes the steps in one long stride. He settles down beside me, just like I'd invited him. "Is it any good? I've never read it."

I can't tell if he's being a smart-ass.

"It's not bad," I say with a straight face. "I think it could be a big hit." Cole laughs then. It's a real, genuine laugh, and it kind of makes me forget how cocky he was last night.

"Hey," he starts, almost like he can read my mind. "About that story I told at the bonfire. I wasn't trying to freak you out. I just—"

"You didn't freak me out," I say. "I don't believe in that kind of stuff. I told you that."

"Yeah. You did. Right."

Cole reaches into his pocket and pulls out another little piece of sea glass. This one is a pinkish color. It reminds me of a shell. He rubs it between his finger and his thumb as he stares at the water, and I wonder what he's really doing here.

He has on dark blue swim shorts and a faded gray T-shirt that matches his eyes. It sticks to his back and his shoulders, where he's still wet, and I can see the angles and edges of his body. He's all lean muscle and bone. The only thing soft about him is that dark, wavy hair.

Cole's hot, like Lex said, but there are things I can see in the daylight. Things I didn't notice last night on the beach.

Those black circles around his eyes.

The chewed skin at the edges of his fingernails.

That tension in his jaw.

He catches me looking at him, and I turn back to my script.

"For whatever it's worth," he says, "most people say it's just the wind in the dune grass. That whispering sound you heard last night."

I have this sudden twinge of fear. Just the smallest shiver. And I want to tell him I didn't hear anything—on the beach, or later, on the cabin porch.

Cole tosses that pink sliver of glass into the air and catches it in his hand like a game of heads or tails.

"But that story about the mass drowning is true," he tells me. "There's a little graveyard not far from here." He jerks his head toward the tree line. "Where the women are buried. And the kids."

The idea of a cemetery, rows of little graves, makes me uncomfortable. So I change the subject.

"Were you swimming?" I ask him, and he nods. Runs his fingers through his still-wet hair.

"I swim every morning. A couple of miles. Up the coast to the state park and back."

That explains the leanness of him. Those taut muscles and that agile grace.

"You swim for exercise?" I say, and he shakes his head.

"I swim because the ocean scares me."

We look at each other for a few seconds.

He told me last night his mother was afraid of the water. He didn't say he was. My eyes find the soft skin of his wrist. That compass rose tattoo.

"But you're safe," I tease. "You've got that magical tattoo, right?"

He laughs out loud again, and I realize it wouldn't take me long to become a fan of Cole's laugh. If I let myself.

"Yeah," he says. "Totally safe." He's watching me. But I'm staring at my toes now. "You should come with me some morning."

"Maybe I will," I say. And then I'm not sure what to say next.

He looks down at the script in my lap. "Have you read it before?"

"Yeah," I tell him, "I've read it lots of times. I just wanna make sure I'm ready for auditions."

"Don't bother." Cole reaches down to swat away a horsefly that's buzzing around his ankles. "You can't prepare for Willa Culver, trust me."

"What does that mean?" I ask him, and he shrugs.

"She'll surprise you every time." He smiles. "Did you know she wrote that in one single weekend? Just went into our study and typed it up." He shakes his head. "Nobody even knew she was working on a play."

"That's incredible," I tell him, even though I'd heard that before. It's part of the fabric of theatre lore. The stuff of myths and legends. "Does that talent run in the family?" I'm teasing him now. Flirting, maybe. Or at least trying to.

"The talent for keeping secrets?" he asks. "Yeah. As a matter of fact, it does." He pushes himself up off the steps. Looks down at my script again. "Let me know how it ends."

"Sure," I say. But I still can't tell if he's messing with me.

"And break a leg tonight." He tilts his head to one side and grins. "Or do you not believe in luck, either?"

"I've never needed luck before." I figure two can play that cocky game of his.

"Yeah, well," he tells me, and he steps out from under the green-striped awning and into the bright sunshine, "you've never been to Whisper Cove before, Avril Vincent."

And only one of us knows that isn't true.

# ACT I: SCENE 5

My second encounter with Cole Culver leaves me almost as off-balance as the first one. And there's no fog to blame it on this time. So I chalk it up to his dark hair. The beads of water on his eyelashes.

That laugh of his.

And I warn myself to be careful.

I gather back up with Lex, Jude, and Val at lunch. We're all talking about our favorite shows. The best roles we ever played.

Val was the witch in *Into the Woods* this past spring, and Jude was Sky in *Guys and Dolls*. "It was incredible," he says. "Man, there's nothing like that feeling when you know the audience is just right there with you. In the palm of your hand." He shakes his head. Sticks a few french fries in his mouth. "Pure fuckin' magic."

Goose bumps break out across my arms, because that magic Jude's talking about has always run so deep for me.

I tell them about playing Madge in *Picnic,* and Lex says his favorite role ever was Tom in *The Glass Menagerie*. "God," he says. "I just felt it so much, you know?" And I do know, because it's like emotions get amplified onstage. There's so much feeling in everything.

Lex turns those bright blue eyes in my direction. "What is it you love about theatre, Av?"

"Freedom," I tell them without hesitation. "I can be furious. Or heartbroken. Or head over heels in love. Whatever. I can take it all to the extreme. And there's no danger in it. Because it's not me."

"Yeah," Val says, like she gets it. She swallows a bite of her ham and cheese. "It's like you can play with the flames and not get burned."

And that's it, exactly. Really being in the moment onstage feels like being lit on fire. Only you know, when it's all over, you won't have any scars to show.

No blisters. Or scorched places.

We finish our lunch, and when we're dumping our trays, I ask Lex about his tour with Jude. "Did he show you what you wanted to see?"

"Not yet," Lex says with a sly little grin. "But he will. What'd you do this morning?"

"Not much." I shrug and push Cole's face out of my mind, because I'm still not sure what to make of him. Or the way he makes me feel. "Just studied the script."

After lunch we head to the first day of our work assignments, and Glory offers me another peppermint when I show up at her desk. "I hope you're a hard worker," she says, and she pats down her frizzy curls with one hand. "This is the only month of the year I have an assistant, so I have to make the most of it."

The first thing she teaches me is how to make the coffee. "Job number one," she calls it. Then she hands me a thick stack of folders and shows me how to sort them into her overstuffed filing cabinet. After that, we go over the copy machine and the phone system. "Brody gets a lot of calls," she warns me from behind those huge glasses of hers. "Especially as we get closer to the big professional shows coming in next month." She gives me a little smile. "That's one of the reasons I'm so thrilled to have an assistant."

We're almost finished for the afternoon when Glory sends me upstairs to drop some files off for Brody. He isn't in his office, so I leave them on his desk. But as I'm walking out, I notice rows of framed photographs neatly hung on one wall. Each one is almost identical to the others. A big group of people arranged on the wide back steps of the sea porch. That green-striped awning overhead. A year is scrawled at the bottom of every photo, and they're all in chronological order.

Something catches my eye, and I take a quick glance around before I go over to sneak a closer look, because I know I shouldn't be messing around in Brody Culver's office.

There she is, though. Third row. Second photograph from the left. My mother. Green eyes and white-blonde hair, like mine. Except hers is longer.

We could almost be twins. If I didn't have my dad's nose.

There must be thirty or forty people in the picture. Actors and techs, probably, from the professional shows that summer. I know that's why we came up here. Dad did tell me that much. He said Willa begged my mom to take a role in one of Brody's productions. This was back when Whisper Cove was a tiny summer theatre with a shoestring budget. Before Willa's play changed all that. Put this place on the map. Isn't that how Jude said it?

I lean in closer to study my mother's image. Her sunglasses are balanced on top of her head like a tiara, and her face is turned to the side. She's looking at the person next to her. Her hand is on his arm, and she's laughing. At something he said, maybe. That's how it looks, anyway.

It takes me a minute to recognize the guy, because he has a full head of curly brown hair. His face is the same, though. It's Brody Culver. Willa sits on his other side, smiling and laughing too. They all look so young. And so happy.

My mother is wearing a yellow top and denim shorts. Gold strappy sandals. Hot pink polish on her toes. And she's beautiful. Radiant. But as soon as I see those toes, I feel sick.

Not just sick. Scared.

Terrified.

And then I'm not standing in Brody's office anymore. I'm hiding underneath one of the big picnic tables out on the sea porch. Rough boards scrape my knees. My hands are over my ears, but I can still hear the low hiss of angry words. All I can see are my mother's shoes.

Strappy golden sandals.

Pink polished toes.

Someone gasps behind me. That brings me back to reality, and I spin around to find Brody Culver standing in his office doorway staring at me. His mouth is open and he's gone all pale. He recovers fast, though.

"Did you need something?" he asks. His face is relaxed now. That easygoing smile I saw at breakfast is back. The change is so fast it unnerves me a little.

"Just dropping off some files," I say. "From Glory." And I dart around him and out the door before he can say anything else.

There's a bathroom down the hall, and I duck inside and lock the door. My legs are shaking. I stand there for a minute, leaning on the sink. I'm trying to get myself together. But that terrified feeling is lingering. And I keep thinking about that gasp. The look on Brody Culver's face.

Almost like he'd seen a ghost.

When I do finally lift my eyes to look into the mirror, it takes me a second to realize what I'm seeing, because the mirror is old and cloudy, and the distortion throws me.

But then it becomes clear. I'm looking at me. But it's my mother's eyes that are staring back at me. I know them from my hidden photograph, even if I can't remember them from real life.

Her eyes.

Bigger and wilder and a slightly darker shade of green than my own. Flecked with bits of gold.

I stare at those eyes for a few seconds before my reflection begins to change. The subtle differences ripple across the mirror like someone running their hand across the surface of a still pond.

First the nose.

Then the chin.

And the lips.

It only takes a few seconds for me to disappear. And then my mother is looking back at me from inside the rectangle-shaped prison of the bathroom mirror.

I reach for the faucet with shaking hands and turn on the cold water. I lean down and splash my face, then feel for a paper towel to dry it with. And when I look up again, my mother is gone. Of course.

Because she was never there to begin with.

It's only me.

It's always only been me.

I head back downstairs, and Glory looks up from her desk. "There you are," she says with a smile. "I was starting to worry you'd gotten lost." Then her expression changes. "Avril? Are you okay?" Her eyes are worried, and she lowers her voice to a whisper. "Did Brody—"

The screen door bangs open, and Lex and Val tumble in, laughing together. They're both sweaty and grimy from working with the grounds crew all afternoon.

"Oh my God," Val says. "I have never been so ready for dinner in my life."

Lex gives me a big grin. "We've been planting flowers. In the dirt!" He laughs and holds up his earth-streaked hands. "George showed us how to do it."

Val rolls her eyes. "Don't lie," she teases. Then she turns to Glory and me. "I did all the digging. Mr. Useless here just handed me the flowers." She grabs Lex by the arm and pulls him down the hallway. "Come on," she says. "I'm starving."

He cranes his neck to look back at me. "Coming, Av?"

"Yeah," I say. "I'll be right there."

"I guess I lost track of time," Glory tells me. "I didn't realize it was five o'clock already."

"Me, either," I say.

The fear I felt when I saw that photo in Brody's office is finally sliding off my back, the way water does after a swim. And that memory of hiding under the picnic table on the sea porch doesn't seem any more real now than what I saw in the bathroom mirror. Or the whispering I heard last night.

I'm embarrassed for letting my imagination get the best of me. I've been looking so hard for my mother that I'm seeing her ghost around every corner.

"We'll pick back up tomorrow, then." Glory smiles. "You were great today. My best assistant so far." She hands me another peppermint as payment, and the wrapper crinkles as I slip it into my pocket.

I start down the hallway, but Glory calls my name and I turn back to look at her. "Let me know," she says, "if there's anything you need. Okay?"

"Yeah," I say. "Thanks." Glory looks like there's something else she wants to tell me, so I wait for a second, but then the phone rings. She turns to answer it, and I head on down the hallway.

Val and Lex may have been laughing when they came through the door, but the tension mounts during dinner. Everyone is thinking about auditions. Jude cracks jokes and tries to keep things light, but we're all nervous.

Val says she's too freaked out to eat. She keeps going over her monologue again and again. I watch her mouth the words to herself as she rearranges chicken fingers on her plate.

Lex is fidgety. He's playing with his scarf. His silverware. His napkin.

We're all counting the minutes. It's that weird combination of being excited and terrified. The one we all crave, but somehow never get used to.

By the time we get cleaned up and head down to the big red barn, we're all just ready to get the whole thing over with.

We gather up out front. Waiting. Jude tries to keep us entertained. Distracted. He tells us the buildings that make up Whisper Cover were part of a working farm, back in the day, and this really was a barn. The outside doesn't look like it's changed much since then. "There's a joke Willa loves to tell," he says with a laugh. "She says that some poor farmer probably spent his whole life shoveling horse shit out of this barn, and now theatre people spend every summer shoveling it back in."

We all giggle, and I'm grateful. Because it helps break the mood a little bit.

Willa shows up just then. She's wearing high-heeled boots and a long, sweeping skirt. Those jangling bracelets. And she has a huge silver key ring in one hand.

"All right, my lovelies!" she announces with a grand flourish. "It's showtime."

My stomach is in knots, at least until she opens the theatre door.

It's funny how there are places I could walk into completely blindfolded and still recognize, just by smell alone. My favorite pizza place back home. My kindergarten classroom. As soon as Willa pushes open the door to the barn theatre, the scent of something so familiar hits me. It's sawdust. And paint. Old wood. Musty curtains.

It's home.

I breathe it in, and I start to relax. Because this is where I belong.

It's more than just the smell, though. I feel my mother here. There's still some part of her lingering in this space. Like her soul has soaked into the wood and the walls, and when I breathe in that theatre smell, I'm breathing her in, too.

I run my palm along a wooden railing at the edge of the stage. It's worn smooth from years of being touched, and I think about how my mother's fingers probably rested where mine do now. It's the same thought I had about the porch railing this morning, and it hits me that this is the closest thing I can remember to the feeling of holding her hand.

There's no lobby in the barn. The big double doors open directly into the performance space. And it's dark, at least until Jude moves to a small booth at the back to turn on the lights.

We all blink at the sudden brightness, and I'm mesmerized by the bits of dust floating through the air like snow.

A rectangular stage stands in the middle of the huge room, surrounded by bleacher seating on three sides. A big black curtain hangs across the back. Above our heads, a loft holds even more seating below the original beams of the barn.

"Find a chair, everyone," Willa says. "We need to go over a few things." The way she's smiling at us, it makes it hard to stay nervous. That energy of hers is so contagious. "I'm sure you know all this," she begins, "but *Midnight Music* is a love story." She raises one eyebrow. "With a little bit of a twist."

It strikes me again how wild it is that we're all sitting here with Willa Culver. *The* Willa Culver. *Midnight Music* is a beautiful play, and it was a huge success on Broadway, but that's only one part of the mythos and mystique surrounding Willa. She could have gone on to have this extraordinary career as a brilliant New York City playwright, but she didn't. She took all that newfound fame and those connections, and she brought it right back here to Whisper Cove and invested it into making this little theatre something extraordinary instead.

I read an interview with her once where she said she'd come back here because this is where her heart was. She'd never written another thing, before or since. But she hadn't needed to. *Midnight Music* was an instant classic, and she was an overnight celebrity. The mysterious and reclusive darling of the theatre world.

"In this story," Willa is reminding us, "a musician named Orion falls in love with a girl named Eden, and when Eden dies, Orion refuses to let her go. He decides to call her back to him the only way he knows how. With a song. And the crazy thing is, it works." Willa stops and grins at us. "But of course, there's no 'happily ever after' for the two of them, because true love is never simple, is it?"

Her eyes are bright and her cheeks are flushed. Even after all these years, it's clear she still loves talking about this play.

Her play.

Back when I was in ninth grade, Dad saw my *Midnight Music* script lying on the table. "You know, your mother knew her," he told me, and then he went back to grading his French quizzes. Like it was nothing, that bombshell he'd just dropped.

It took weeks of constant badgering to get any more information out of him. I finally found out Willa and my mom had been college friends, both of them undergrads studying theatre at the University of Texas. This was back before my mom and dad even met.

I also found out that we'd been here, at Whisper Cove, when my mother died. Up until then, I'd only known that she drowned—we drowned—at a seaside theatre where she was acting that summer.

He'd refused to tell me anything else, though. *Je ne sais pas!* he'd shouted when I pressed him about Willa for the millionth time. *I don't know. I only met the woman once!*

I didn't ask again, but one night not long after that while he was out, I dug through the shoebox on the top shelf of his closet, the only lingering hint of my mother that remained in our apartment. Tucked in between some insurance papers and her death certificate, I found the graduation photo with NICOLE AND WILLA written on the back. I took it and kept it hidden in my room. Proof that my mother had existed.

And that she'd known Willa Culver.

We go over a few more details, and then Willa tells us that Jude will call us up one by one to audition in front of the whole group. I cringe, because I hadn't realized we'd be auditioning in front of everyone. Judging by the looks on their faces, nobody else had, either. "It's a learning experience, my lovelies," Willa assures us with a smile. "Break legs! And remember to breathe."

I'm sitting between Val and Lex. Lex won't quit bouncing his knee, and it's driving me nuts. I finally reach over and put my hand on his leg to stop him. *Sorry,* he mouths.

Val leans over to whisper in my ear. "I can't remember a word of my monologue." But when her name is called, she knocks it out of the park.

And so does Lex.

It's a long process, but we work our way through the whole group. Until, finally, there's only me left. The very last one. Of course.

"Avril Vincent," Jude says in an official-sounding voice. "You're up."

Lex reaches over to give my hand a quick squeeze. "Blow her away, Av," he whispers.

Willa's sitting in the front row, and it shocks me a little how close she is. Just a couple of feet from where I'm standing. I could reach out and touch her if I wanted to. My high school theatre in Dallas is huge. It seats like two thousand people. So there's a lot more distance.

This feels much more personal.

A lot less safe.

"Okay, Avril," Willa says. "So what part of the script did you work on for your audition?"

"Eden's monologue toward the end of act one, after the dance with Orion. The scene where she realizes she's in love with him." I swallow my nerves. "It's one of my favorite parts of the whole play."

"Good choice!" Willa says. "It's one of my favorites, too. I'd love to hear that. Just start whenever you're ready." She leans back in her seat and waits.

I take a step upstage, toward the center, lifting my face to find the light that's shining down on me from the loft. Because a good actress always finds her light.

And suddenly I feel my mother so strongly, almost like she's standing right behind me. Like maybe if I turned my head really fast, I could catch a glimpse of her.

Dark green eyes flecked with gold.

The sense of connection to her here—on this stage—is like nothing I've ever felt before. It almost brings me to my knees, because this is what I've been searching for my whole life. It's the part of me that's always been missing. The something I could never find back in Texas.

This is why I came to Whisper Cove.

My hands are shaking, so I take a deep breath to center myself. I let go of Avril and open myself up wide to Eden. I feel her wash over me like a wave crashing over rocks on a beach. She fills up all the empty corners and the quiet places inside me.

I start the monologue, and when I speak, it's with her voice, not mine. By the time I reach the last line—"I'm flying in love!"—I'm standing with my arms spread wide, and everything inside me feels like it's cracked open.

And it's so good, that feeling. It makes me hungry for more. I hadn't fully realized—or maybe just hadn't admitted—until this moment how much I want the lead role in this play.

How much I need to be Eden.

"Wow," I hear Willa breathe. "That was great, Avril." She's leaning forward in her chair.

"Thank you," I say, and I start to head back to my seat. But Willa stops me with one raised finger.

"Stay right there," she commands, and she calls all the other girls back to the stage to join me.

"I'm going to ask you all to do something kind of unorthodox," she tells us. "Are you feeling brave, my lovelies?"

We all nod, and Willa beams at us. "Good. I've got a piece of music from the show here. Something I want you all to hear. It's the melody that Orion plays for Eden, the song he calls her home with. In the show, Orion will play it live on the guitar. But for now, I'm afraid a recording will have to do." She gestures to a big boom box sitting at her feet. The old-fashioned kind with a tape player.

One of the guys sticks up his hand. The shaggy-haired boy from the bonfire. Guitar dude. "Um," he says, "I could play it if you want. If you have sheet music for it." He's grinning, one hand on the guitar that's leaning against his knee. He must keep that thing with him twenty-four seven.

Willa turns her dazzling smile on him, and it's like he almost melts. "That would be lovely!" she exclaims. "What a treat!" And she pulls a single sheet of music from a folder tucked into her notebook. "There's no replacement for live music, is there?" She studies the rest of the boys seated in the audience. "Do we have any other musicians among us?" The rest of them all shake their heads, and Shaggy-Hair lights up like somebody plugged him in. He gets up to take the music from Willa's hand like he's accepting a Grammy. "The important thing," Willa continues, "is that this bit of music really breathes Eden into life. It's like she lives inside these few measures. Do you know what I mean?" I nod along with the other girls, even though I'm not sure I understand.

"So, we're just going to listen to this piece of music, and I want you all to move. That's all. It can be whatever you want. Whatever you feel like. It doesn't have to be dance. I mean, it can be, if that's what you feel led toward, but I just want movement." She's studying me again. "You've all shown me that you can bring Eden to life through her words, but so much of this story is visual. I need to see if you can make Eden live without the words. Does that make sense?"

I'm starting to panic, because this isn't really my kind of thing.

I'm not a ballerina. Not by a long shot. I find Lex's blue eyes, and he flashes me a little thumbs-up.

Willa nods at the boy with the guitar, and he nods back. Looks at the paper in front of him. Squints a little. Stretches his long fingers. And then the music starts. It's beautiful. Happy and sad at the same time. Like nothing I remember hearing before, and still somehow hauntingly familiar.

A few of the girls start to dance right away, showing off their skills with graceful moves I don't even know the names for. But I just stand there for a few seconds, absorbing the music more through my skin than through my ears, kind of swaying back and forth and letting Eden fill me up again. And when I finally start to move, it feels so awkward at first, especially with everyone watching. But I just keep reaching inside to find Eden. Because I know she's in there.

She's flying, I think.

No. That thought separates me from her.

*I'm flying.*

Twisting. Turning. Reaching. Arms outstretched. Then bending low to sweep the ground.

Every time I blink, I see her, Eden, on the insides of my eyelids, flickering like an old movie. She's twirling in time with me, her dress flying out as we spin in slow circles. She moves when I move and laughs when I laugh, and I know that's because we're the same person.

My eyes are open, but all I see now is Eden. I reach for her, and she breaks apart into a hundred thousand girls, like the images in a fun-house mirror maze. And I laugh out loud. Because she's so beautiful. The Edens are all around me. They go on forever. They are infinite. And they are all me. And we are all dancing, holding hands and flying free together. When we move, our connected bodies make kaleidoscope patterns—shifting and changing. In and out. Around and around.

Then we throw our heads back and lift our eyes to the night sky. Our hair falls away, and for the very first time I can see our faces.

I can see our eyes.

And I realize I was wrong. We aren't us at all.

We are not Avril.

And we are not Eden.

We are my mother.

The scent of lavender fills my nose. So strong that I'm choking on it.

We're Nicole.

All of us.

Every one of our faces is her face.

Our eyes are her eyes.

We blink against the blinding light.

And then the stars are coming down like rain. I gasp because they're so beautiful.

*Look at the stars!*

The words echo loud inside my head.

Someone grabs me by the wrist. Tight. Cold fingers. It hurts and I try to pull free. But I can't.

And then I'm falling. Just like the stars.

Falling

and falling

and falling

and falling.

I fall for so long that it starts to feel like flying. I fall for what feels like a hundred years before I finally hit the ground. Hard.

And all of that vanishes.

I'm grateful for the suddenness of the stage floor.

For the pain in my twisted knee. And the throbbing in my elbow, where I banged it when I landed.

For the real.

"I'm okay," I say, more to myself than anyone else, and I push myself up with every bit of strength I have. I'm smoothing down the yellow sundress I chose to wear tonight. Brushing my hair back out of my face.

Val is instantly beside me, a hand on my arm.

"Do you need a minute, Avril?" Willa has gone all pale. The boy with the guitar isn't playing anymore, and it's suddenly quiet enough to hear a pin drop. Willa is searching my face. Looking right through my skin to somewhere deep in the middle part of me. The way Cole did last night. "The bathroom's over that way."

I glance toward the corner, where Willa is pointing, and I catch sight of George, the Whisper Cove caretaker, staring at me from the shadows. He's leaning on a push broom, but he isn't sweeping. He's just watching me. Not moving.

Nobody is moving. They're all frozen in place.

Tears sting the corners of my eyes. I'm humiliated. Bruised. I've totally botched the audition. Obviously. But it's more than that. I don't have any explanation for what just happened.

"I'm fine. I . . ." But I lose my train of thought then. Because everyone is staring at me. "I'm so sorry," I say. "I don't know what happened. I just got dizzy, I guess. I—"

"Your name is April, isn't it?" All of the air leaves my lungs in a whoosh. My knees go weak, and I'm grateful for Val. She doesn't let me hit the floor again. Willa has me pinned down with those steel-wool eyes of hers. So I know there's no escape. "April Kendrick."

There's a confused murmur from everyone else. They all know something big is happening, but they don't understand what.

"It was." I pull away from Val to stand on my own. Because I refuse to be weak when I say this. "A long time ago."

Dad had my name changed when he took me back to Texas with him. When he came to get me.

After.

I guess with my mom gone—dead—he wanted a fresh start for me. For both of us, maybe. So April Kendrick became Avril Vincent. Avril because it's French for April. Vincent because that's his last name, even though my mother had never legally claimed it for herself. Or for me.

I couldn't remember anything from before anyway, so it was almost like I'd just been born.

A brand-new name for a brand-new person.

"Oh my God," Willa whispers. She's forgotten how to blink. "Oh my God." She's still repeating that phrase over and over as she gets unsteadily to her feet and crosses to me. She grabs me and pulls me into her arms, and I feel her trembling. Something inside me breaks, and I start to sob, even though I couldn't say exactly why.

"You look so much like her," Willa says when she finally pulls back to look at me again. Her hands are on my wet cheeks. She runs her palms over my hair. "Of course. I should have known when I first saw you. When I saw that audition tape last winter. Your headshot. But I didn't." She's still staring at me like she can't quite believe it. "Not until I saw you onstage just now. Alive. In that moment. And then I knew." She smiles. "I knew." She hugs me tight again. "I've only known one other actress who had that kind of power to just wholly transform herself." She chokes back a little sob, and it starts me crying again. "And it just hit me. *Bam!* I knew it had to be you. You had to be Nicole's daughter."

"But I fell," I say, and I'm embarrassed all over again thinking of how I hit the floor. What that must have looked like to Willa. "I messed it all up."

"No." She shakes her head. "Oh my God. No. Sweetheart. You were beautiful. Transcendent." She smiles at me. Lays her hands on each side of my face. "You were Eden." Willa takes a shaky breath. "Holy shit," she says, and that makes us both laugh a little bit. "This is just unbelievable." She touches my face again. "But absolutely expected, too. Inevitable. Because of course you had to find your way home."

We look at each other for a few seconds, not sure what to say. And then Willa seems to remember that there are two dozen or so other people in the theatre. I glance around, and nobody else has moved. They've all become statues with identical chiseled faces.

Wide eyes.

Open mouths.

Willa tells us all that we can go. The audition is over. She reminds us of the rule. Nobody outside the cabins after eleven o'clock. "You need your rest," she warns us. "The next few weeks will be busy."

I move back to my seat and gather up my things. Everyone is still staring at me, but I manage to get my backpack and start toward the door.

"Avril," Willa says, and I turn back to look at her as the others file out, whispering to each other. "Nicole was special. She loved this place, and it loved her back. What happened that summer was an unbearable tragedy, but it doesn't change that." She pauses for a moment. "Whisper Cove will love you, too, if you give it the chance. I promise."

"Thank you," I tell her, and I run my hand along the rough wall of the barn. Feel the wood floor under my feet. *My mother was here,* I think. She was alive here in this place. And for the first time in my life, I feel like I have a home.

I know everyone is gathered in front of the barn. I can hear the murmur of voices, but they all fall silent when I push open the big double doors.

Lex slips a protective arm around my shoulders. "Jesus Christ," he mutters as he guides me over to the edge of the crowd where Jude and Val are waiting for us. "Everyone back the fuck off."

"What the hell just happened?" Val asks. She looks worried. Like she thinks I might pass out again.

"Wait. Wait. Hold up." Jude is staring at me like he's trying to make sense of something. Big brown eyes blinking in disbelief. "Your mom was Nicole Kendrick?"

"Yeah," I say. "She was."

"Who?" Val asks.

"My mom was a friend of Willa's," I explain. "She drowned here. One summer a long time ago."

"Oh my God," Val gasps.

"I almost died, too," I tell them. "They found me washed up on the beach."

"Holy shit." Jude breathes out the words in a long, low whisper. "Wow."

"Someone please tell me what's going on." Lex looks so confused.

"It's like an urban legend around here, what happened to Nicole Kendrick." Jude stops and shakes his head like he can't quite believe it. "Or a rural legend. Whatever. Everybody knows the story." He pauses a moment. "She was called into the sea. Just like the women Cole told us about back in whaling times."

"Jesus, Jude," Val says. And she reaches for my hand.

"That's the story." Jude's apologizing to me with his eyes. "That's all I meant."

"It's not this big, mysterious thing," I tell them. "What happened to my mother was an awful accident. That's all."

"God," Val says. "This must be such a mindfuck for you. Being back here." Her long, dark hair is spilling over her shoulders. She squeezes my fingers. "I can't even imagine."

And it's weird how it all makes sense when she says it like that. Suddenly I have a way to explain all the strangeness of the past two days. The weird bits of memory. The things I've seen and felt.

A total mindfuck.

"Why would you wanna come back here?" Lex asks.

"To do the intensive," I say. "Like the rest of you." I almost leave it at that, but there's this part of me that wants to tell them the whole truth. And that's a weird feeling for me. "But also because I never got to know my mother. And I really want to."

"You don't remember your mom at all?" Val asks.

I shake my head. "I don't remember anything that happened before I woke up in the hospital."

No memory of my mother lighting birthday candles when I turned five.

No memory of her walking me to school on my first day of kindergarten.

No Christmases.

No Halloweens.

And no memories of that last summer we spent together. At Whisper Cove.

No memories of her at all.

Val's fingers are intertwined with mine. "I never knew my dad," she tells me. "He was long gone before I was born." Her green eyes are brimming with pain, and I remind myself that everyone has holes. "It sucks—I know—walking around with that piece of yourself missing."

"So, what do we call you?" Jude asks. "April? Or Avril?"

"Avril. My name is Avril."

April was a totally different person. She was a girl who had a mom. And I can't remember her any better than I remember my mother.

Lex and Val and Jude are all looking at me. I'm holding my breath. Wondering if this changes everything between the four of us.

"Well, you were incredible, Av," Lex tells me. His arm is still around my shoulders, and he gives me a little squeeze. "Like Willa said. You took my breath away."

"You were great, too," I tell him. "Everyone was."

"All right, then," Jude says, and he flashes that trademark warm grin. "Give yourselves a round of applause, people. You all survived auditions." He waggles his eyebrows at us. "Willa always announces the cast at the first rehearsal, so you'll know your fates by tomorrow night."

And I know then that it's okay. They know. And it's okay.

"There's always something else to be nervous about, isn't there?" Lex says with a sigh.

Val laughs. "That's life in the theatre, baby."

"That's life, period," I say, and everyone agrees.

The four of us head back toward the cabins together. It's dark, but there's no fog tonight. At least not yet. And the dark doesn't bother us. Theatre people have a special ability to peer into the blackness and walk through it to the other side. I guess that's a talent that comes from finding our way offstage during the scene changes.

Before we say good night, Lex hugs me hard. I stiffen up, because I'm not really a hugger. But I don't pull away, because I know he'd be hurt. And also because I need that closeness tonight. Now that everything is out in the open, he says, maybe it'll help me remember. I tell him that I hope he's right, and I can't help noticing the way Jude hangs back to wait for him. How they smile at each other. The way their shoulders touch as they walk into the dark together.

At least one of us is already on his way to becoming the person he wants to be. So maybe there's hope for me, too.

Val and I climb the cabin steps, and I glance over my shoulder toward the farmhouse. I catch sight of Cole. He's sitting on the railing, bathed in the dirty yellow glow of the porch light. The expression on his face is unreadable. And I'm too far away to see his eyes. But I raise my hand in a little wave, and he waves back. I watch him toss a shining piece of sea glass into the air. Catch it in his palm.

Heads or tails.

I wonder what he'll think when he finds out who I really am.

I follow Val inside and ignore the other girls' stares while I get ready for bed. I'm exhausted, and I fall asleep even before someone switches off the overhead light.

But sometime after midnight, an old nightmare finds me. I'm crouched in the dark, and the stars are falling into the sea.

*Plop. Plop. Plop.*

*Look at the stars,* a voice tells me. And I want to look, but I can't. Because I'm suddenly blind. The burning brightness hurts my eyes, so I squeeze them closed. And I'm cold. So, so, so cold. My wrist aches, and my feet have turned to blocks of ice. My teeth chatter so hard they hurt.

The lonesome moan of the foghorn wakes me up, and I'm still freezing. Shivering in my bed. Those words echo in my ears.

*Look at the stars.*

My mother's voice, I guess. It seemed so familiar in my dream, but now that I'm awake I can't remember the sound of it. And that makes me feel like crying. It's an ache that's always hiding somewhere down inside me, that feeling of wanting her.

Needing her.

I can shove it down in the daytime. But sometimes in the dark—

I roll over and close my eyes. Try to go back to sleep. But the sheets are soaked. Everything feels wet. My skin. My hair. My pillow. Even the air in my lungs.

The curtains flutter in the night breeze. That explains the cold. And the damp.

I slip out of bed and tiptoe to the window. Bare feet on the icy floor. The fog is rolling in now, but it's not so thick yet. Not like last night.

So I can see her clearly.

A woman is walking across the muddy field between the farmhouse and the cabins. Moving in and out of the fog and the shadows. She's made of moonlight. And the heavy scent of lavender. And she dances with a grace that makes my heart ache.

Reaching. Twirling. Bending low to sweep the ground.

She turns in my direction, and we lock eyes across the darkness. Arms outstretched. She's reaching for me. Long fingers. Bone white.

I stop breathing. Take a step back. Away from the window.

The woman's mouth opens. Then closes. Her voice is the sound of the foghorn. I blink and she's closer now. I could reach outside and touch her.

A woman with ice-blonde hair.

A woman who looks exactly like me.

Or my mother.

# ACT I: SCENE 6

My heart is pounding in my chest. I blink and she's not there. Of course. She was just a trick of shadow and fog. A product of sleeplessness and the strangeness of the day. Of being in this place.

Like Val said. A mindfuck.

My imagination dressed in moonlight.

How can I believe in ghosts with like twelve other girls snoring just a few feet away?

Except the smell of lavender lingers in the cabin.

I close the window. Then I head back to bed and pull the covers up to my neck, and somehow I fall asleep again.

When my alarm goes off the next morning, the cabin is almost empty. I grab my stuff and head to the bathroom to get ready. Val is standing at the sink brushing her teeth. "You okay this morning?" she asks.

"Yeah," I say. "I'm fine."

She takes my arm and runs her fingers over the bruise on my elbow. Her touch is so gentle, but I still flinch, and she looks concerned.

"Just a little sore," I say. "No big deal."

All through breakfast, there's chatter about the first rehearsal coming up tonight. Everyone is so excited. It's contagious, that buzz. It fills up the whole cafeteria.

"You guys don't know what you're in for," Jude tells us with a grin and a shake of his head. Those charcoal-colored curls. "Working with Willa will blow your minds." And that makes me think of what Cole said yesterday afternoon on the sea porch steps, about how you can't prepare for Willa Culver.

Only when Jude says it, it sounds like a good thing. The way Cole said it, I wasn't sure.

After breakfast, we all cram into a cozy little library right off the cafeteria for the first of our morning class sessions. Today's workshop is on script analysis, and Willa's gotten a big-name director friend from New York City to come teach. It's normally the kind of thing I would love, but I keep getting distracted by the room itself. There's something familiar about the dark paneling and overstuffed couches, the shelves lined with books and scripts. I breathe in the smell of polished wood and leather.

"I think I used to play in here," I tell Lex and Val when we take a short break, and I wander over to the window to feel the thick floor-length curtains. "Hide-and-seek, maybe."

"Who with?" Lex asks, but I shrug.

"My mother, I guess." It's just a feeling I have. Not a real memory.

Willa sticks her head into the library then. "Morning, lovelies!" she says, and I watch her search the room until her eyes land on me. "Avril, meet me in the cafeteria when class ends." She smiles. "I'd like the two of us to have lunch together. If you're up for that."

"Sure," I say. "That'd be good." I feel everyone staring at me, and I hope I sound less nervous than I feel.

"Wonderful!" she tells me. She waves a hand, and I hear the jangling of silver bracelets. "Now, back to work, everybody! No rest for the wicked!"

"You're her Eden," Lex whispers when Willa's gone. "I'd bet you a million dollars."

"You might as well start learning those lines," Val adds.

My stomach drops. I want that to be true, but then there's so much I want from Willa. And the lead in her play is only part of it.

Our instructor comes back from the restroom, and we jump back into script analysis. But now I can't even pretend to pay attention. I'm still thinking about this room. Those long curtains tied back with gold cords. But I'm also freaking out about eating with Willa. Just the two of us.

And about how much I want to be Eden.

As soon as we break for lunch, I grab a few slices of pizza off the buffet and hurry over to where Willa is waiting in the doorway with her own tray. She leads me down the hall, through what looks like a conference room, and toward another door. I figure maybe she's taking me to her office, so I'm surprised when the door opens directly out onto the sea porch.

"I thought we could eat out here," she says. "The afternoon breeze is always nice after being cooped up inside all morning."

"Sure," I say, and I slide onto the picnic table bench across from her.

For just an instant, I have another flash of five-year-old me hiding under the table. Hands over my ears.

I see my mother's gold strappy sandals. Her pink toes.

And I freeze.

But then Willa reaches across the table and takes my hand, and there is so much warmth in her touch that it pulls me back to the present. My eyes fill up with tears, and I don't even know why. I've never been a crier. Ever. At least not before I came to Whisper Cove.

"Oh, Avril," Willa says. "I don't even know where to start."

"Me, either," I say, and that makes us both smile a little.

"You probably know this, but Nicole and I weren't much older than you when we met as college freshmen. Very first day of classes." Something so sad crosses Willa's face. It's almost like looking into an open wound. She lets go of my hand and picks up her fork, but she doesn't touch her salad. "We were inseparable for the next four years," she says. "Just the two of us against the world."

"I wish I could remember her," I admit, and that is the hugest understatement ever. But anything more than that feels precarious. Dangerous, even. I might slip and fall. And I learned a long time ago that hurt is like quicksand. It'll suck me under if I let it. Best to tiptoe around the edges. Not say too much. Hold on to the rope.

"Why didn't you tell us who you were when you sent in your application?" Willa is staring at me like she's looking for clues. Or resemblances, maybe. I wonder if she sees that I have my mother's eyes.

"I didn't want that to be the reason I got accepted. I wanted to earn it on my own, you know?"

"That's exactly what your mother would have said." Willa forks a little tomato and pops it into her mouth, and I force myself to take a nibble of pizza. I have to choke it down. It's like I've forgotten how to chew. "It would mean so much to Nicole to know that you're an actress. Like she was."

"The funny thing is, I didn't even know that about her when I started. Dad didn't tell me until later."

Willa frowns at the mention of my father, but it doesn't last long. Just a brief slip. So small I might have made it up.

Except I didn't.

"Well," she says. "The stage is clearly in your blood." She tilts her head to one side and gives me a long look. "You have an awful lot of your mother in you, I think."

My heart swells and I can't talk. My throat has closed up, and I'm blinking back stupid tears again. Because nobody's ever told me that before. I mean, I know I look like her. I can see that in the few photos I've found. But being like her is different.

Deeper.

It means more.

Willa's eyes are sympathetic. She nods like she understands. "I'd like to get to know you, Avril. Really know you. The way I knew your mother." She stops. "If that's all right with you, of course." There's a slight quiver in her voice, and now I'm worried maybe she's going to cry. But she doesn't. She just takes a deep breath, and when she speaks again, that quiver is gone. "Nicole was the best friend I ever had."

"Okay," I tell her. "I'd like to get to know you, too."

And I'd like to get to know my mother.

Willa beams at me. She reaches up to tuck a strand of long, dark hair behind her ear. Those steely silver streaks catch the afternoon light, and I hear the jangle of bracelets. "It'll be a summer of discovery, then." She nods. "For both of us."

We eat the rest of our lunch punctuated with little bits of sharing.

She asks about school. What classes I enjoy. What subjects I'm good at. My friends. My likes and dislikes.

But she never asks about my dad.

"Nicole was fierce," Willa tells me. "That's what drew me to her in the beginning. She was tough as nails. And I admired that so much." She looks over my shoulder, out toward the sound in the distance. "I knew she was destined for something truly extraordinary. And, God, whatever it was, I wanted to be part of it."

Even though Willa doesn't really tell me much—she loved black-and-white movies—she always had cinnamon gum in her purse—she cried when she was angry—it's more than I've ever known about my mother. In the two days I've been at Whisper Cove, she's already becoming real for me in a way she never has been before.

I've always felt like the child of a ghost. Two ghosts, really.

And now I know my mother was fierce.

She loved gum.

She was destined for something extraordinary.

When we finish eating, Willa heads down to the theatre so she and Jude can get the rehearsal space ready for this evening, and I report to my afternoon work assignment. Glory smiles and offers me the usual peppermint, but she seems even more nervous and awkward than usual.

Over the next few hours, she teaches me how to update the contract databases on her computer. She shows me where all the office supplies are and how to change the toner in the copy machine. The trick to replacing the ink in the ancient printer that sits on her desk. I learn how to handle Brody's calls and what to do with his emails.

Jude wasn't kidding when he said Glory knew this place inside and out. It's wild, seeing how much of Whisper Cove's day-to-day operations depend on her. There's plenty to keep us both busy, but almost every time I look up, I find Glory staring at me. And I figure that's because she's heard the news.

Nicole Kendrick's daughter is back from the dead.

She never brings it up, though, and I'm grateful. Talking to Willa was so good, but it left me feeling a little overwhelmed. I'm not used to talking that much.

Or feeling that much.

So I'm happy just to sit in silence with Glory and stuff envelopes. We work together all afternoon. Side by side. And there's a kind of comfort in being with Glory. There's something about her peppermints and her frizzy hair and her nervous smile that makes me feel at home.

My breathing is easier.

My heart rate is slower.

And my palms are less sweaty.

And it takes me a long time to realize what that feeling is. It takes all afternoon. But by five o'clock, I've figured it out.

It's familiarity.

I remember Glory.

# ACT I: SCENE 7

At dinner, everyone is gearing up for the announcement of the cast list and our first rehearsal. They're telling themselves not to get their hopes up because they probably won't get the part they want. But secretly, their hopes are all so high. They always are. They have to be. Otherwise there's no reason to audition.

I'm especially counting the minutes, because I know that becoming someone else will give me some room to step outside myself and breathe. No matter which role I end up with.

That's a big part of what's always drawn me to theatre in the first place. To leave myself behind, even if it's just for a few hours, always feels like such freedom.

I walk down to the theatre with Jude, Lex, and Val. And even before Jude pulls open the door, I feel the tingle of shared energy. All those dreams and all that nervousness, all crammed into the old barn. It fills up the whole space, from the scuffed floor to the big wooden beams of the ceiling. It's palpable. Thick as the fog that creeps up the lawn at night.

Willa is waiting for us onstage, and she directs us all to sit in the front row. She stands there with her clipboard and looks us all over, and it hits me again how striking she is. That long, dark hair streaked with gray. Those intense eyes. So much like her son's.

A hush falls over the group, and Willa cocks her head to one side. She waits. And we wait. The air is humming. It snaps and crackles with excitement. "There's always such beautiful possibility at a first rehearsal. Isn't there?" Everyone nods and agrees. We're on pins and needles, and she knows it. "Before I announce the cast for our show, I want to remind you that each one of you is on a personal journey. Don't compare paths, and don't compare roles. There's plenty of room for everyone to shine."

Willa starts calling off names and characters, starting with all the smaller parts. All the kids in the dance scene. The waitress. A police officer. One by one, people get up and move to Jude's stage manager table to pick up their scripts. Lex is playing Orion's best friend, and Val is Eden's older sister. Not the leads, but they're both great parts with really good scenes.

I'm waiting. Holding my breath. Every time Willa announces a female role and it's not me, Lex looks at me with this *I told you so* look on his face. I'm starting to feel a little dizzy with the excitement of it all. The anticipation.

The hope.

"I told you. It's you," Lex whispers in my ear. "Holy shit. You're Eden." But I refuse to let myself think it. Not until Willa says the words.

We're running out of parts. Almost everyone is holding a script in their hands, and my heart is really starting to beat in my throat. Then the door creaks on its hinges.

"Nice of you to join us," Willa says without looking up from her clipboard. "You know you're late."

"Shit," Val whispers. "Somebody fucked up already." I can't see the door from where I'm sitting, but I know Val's right. Somebody's in big trouble. Because Willa's rule number one was *be on time.*

"Sorry," a familiar voice says. "I got a little lost." Cole Culver slips into a seat at the end of the front row, and I feel my stomach flip-flop. "First night of rehearsal and all."

Willa sighs and rolls her eyes. "I've got some bad news to share, lovelies. One of your fellow students had to leave the program this morning due to a family emergency. That leaves us one actor short." I look around to try and figure out who's missing, and I know right off. The shaggy-haired guy with the guitar. Jude gets up to hand Cole a script, and Lex elbows me hard in the ribs. "And," Willa goes on, "since we don't have any other musicians in the group, Cole has agreed to step in. He'll be playing the part of Orion, opposite Avril."

For a second, I think I must have misheard her, but then Willa turns to look at me, and there is so much in her eyes. She smiles, and my heart almost explodes.

"Yes!" Lex shouts. "I fucking knew it!"

I reach for my script with a shaking hand, and Jude leans down to whisper in my ear as he hands it to me. "Nobody else was even close," he says. "It had to be you."

"And now that we're all here"—Willa gives Cole a pointed look—"we might as well jump right in. We have less than four weeks to get this show up and on its feet, so screw your courage to the sticking place, my lovelies. Everyone on your toes!"

We start with some warm-up exercises. Stretches and vocalizations led by Jude. I try to breathe deep. Relax my spine. Find my center. But I keep accidentally finding Cole's eyes instead.

Then Willa claps her hands together. "Okay. Let's take it from the top. I need Eden and Orion onstage for scene one, please."

Cole grabs an old acoustic guitar that's leaning against the stage manager's table, and Willa gestures to a small wooden bench, the only real piece of scenery we have so far. "This first scene takes place in the park. Eden, when the lights come up, you're sitting on the bench there, eating lunch and reading your book. Orion enters, walks up, and sits down next to you. Got that?" Cole and I both nod. "Good." Willa gives me a reassuring wink. "And so it begins."

I sit on the bench, and Cole walks up and looks around before sitting down beside me. He leans the guitar against his knee, and we read from our scripts.

**ORION**: I've read that book. The one you're reading. It's good. The ending isn't very nice, though. It made me sad.

**EDEN**: I like it. So far, anyway. I haven't read very much.

**ORION**: Do you mind if I sit here? I'm Orion.

**EDEN**: I know.

**ORION**: You do?

**EDEN**: I saw your band play at the club last week. I thought you were really . . .

**ORION**: Awesome?

**EDEN**: Loud. Actually, I was going to say loud.

Cole laughs, and I have to remind myself to focus. I'm looking at my script, but I can feel his eyes on me. So I glance up, and he grins.

**ORION**: I like that.
**EDEN**: You like what?
**ORION**: That you told the truth. Most girls don't.
**EDEN**: Most people don't.

Cole looks at me for a few seconds.

**ORION**: Do you want to hear a song? I just wrote it.
**EDEN**: You mean before you got here?
**ORION**: No. I mean just now. When I saw you sitting here. I wrote it in my head for you.

Cole picks up the guitar and strums a few notes. The opening of Eden's melody floats across the barn. It's the same song we heard at auditions, but it's different hearing Cole play it. I get so lost in watching his fingers moving across the strings. Then I remember I have a line.

**EDEN**: No one's ever written a song about me.
**ORION**: It's not about you. It's for you.
**EDEN**: Like a gift?
**ORION**: Like a gift.
**EDEN**: No one's ever written a song for me, then.
**ORION**: I have.
**EDEN**: I'm Eden.

Cole puts down the guitar.

**ORION**: Do you eat lunch here every day, Eden?
**EDEN**: Almost every day. I like to sit and look at the river. Do you come out here often? To write songs.
**ORION**: I haven't. But maybe I will now.
**EDEN**: I suppose I'll be seeing you again, then, won't I?
**ORION**: It sounds that way.

Cole stands up. He picks up the guitar and takes a few steps away from the bench before turning back and going on with the next line.

**ORION**: Do you want to know how the book ends?
**EDEN**: That would ruin the surprise.

Cole pins me down with those smoke-gray eyes.

**ORION**: But what if it makes you sad?
**EDEN**: I'd rather take my time to find out all the lovely things that happen along the way, without worrying about the ending. Wouldn't you?

I smile at Cole, and he smiles back.

**ORION**: Yes, I think I would, too, now that you mention it.

"Blackout," Jude calls from the stage manager's table, and I realize I've been holding my breath. I let it out and tell myself to relax. I'm acting like I've never been onstage before. "Do you want to go back over that?" Jude asks Willa. "Before we go on?"

"I think so," Willa says. "It's so short, but there's a lot happening." She puts her hands on her hips and I hear the jangle of bracelets again. "So, what is this scene all about, lovelies?"

Rehearsals are supposed to be a learning opportunity for everyone, so she addresses the question to all of us, not just Cole and me.

"It's a plot necessity," Val says. "They can't fall in love if they don't meet each other."

"That's technically right," answers Willa. "That's its structural purpose. But what's it really *about*?"

"Lust!" one of the guys shouts. "He just wants to get with her." Everyone giggles, and Cole smirks. I feel my face flush.

"Well, yes," Willa says, and she laughs. "Ultimately everything is about lust of one kind or another. But what else is this scene about?"

"Potential," I say.

"Yes!" Willa whirls around to face me. "Yes! That's it, Avril." She crosses toward the bench where Cole and I are sitting. "Potential for what?"

"For love?" Lex offers from the front row. He grins at me, proud of himself.

"Yes! Absolutely!" says Willa, but she doesn't turn around to look at Lex. She's still staring at Cole and me. "But what else?"

"Potential for a story," Cole offers. "Eden wants to know if they have a story to tell. It's about letting that story play out to its end. Whatever that ends up being."

"That's it!" Willa practically shouts. "Yes!" She raises one eyebrow at Cole. "Not bad for somebody who couldn't find the theatre." She crouches down in front of the bench where Cole and I are sitting. Her eyes are so full of fire that it's almost hard to look at her. "And we have the potential—perfect word, Avril—for all of that laid out in less than a dozen lines here in scene one. You two are off to a great start with this."

Cole gives me a little grin. He runs one hand through his dark hair. And just for a second, I can't move.

Alarm bells are sounding in my head. Because I have a feeling this boy could be dangerous.

At least for me.

And then I realize that Eden is feeling the exact same thing. So I tell myself to lean into it. Because that's what we do in the theatre.

We run that section a few more times, and each time I feel myself becoming more and more Eden. I let myself feel her hope, that little spark of curiosity about this boy. That tiny flicker of *maybe* in the back of her mind.

But also her fear.

By just the third time through, Cole and I are able to put down our scripts and run the whole thing off-book, and Willa says that's earned us a break.

"Company, take five," Jude announces in his best stage manager voice, and he notes the time on his rehearsal report.

Most everyone drifts away to wait in line for the bathroom or step outside for some air. But I stay put. And so does Cole. Val starts in my direction, but I see Lex grab her by the hand and drag her outside with him.

"Not bad for a first rehearsal," Cole says.

"I thought you said you weren't much of an actor," I tease him, and he shrugs.

"You can't grow up being Willa Culver's son and not learn a thing or two about playing a part." He's staring at me now. "Besides, I couldn't pass up an opportunity to share the stage with an old friend."

"She told you," I say. "About my mother."

Cole nods. "I don't remember much about that summer," he admits. "I don't even remember you. But there's a framed photo of your mom that sits on the piano in our living room. I've grown up looking at it." He's studying me, and I see his mind working behind those gray eyes. "You look like her." Something crosses his face then. Something I can't decode. "I should've known it was you all along."

It's weird to think about Cole growing up looking at that photo of my mother. My own father has always kept her memory locked in a tiny shoebox, tucked away on the top shelf of his closet. In the dark.

But Willa keeps her in the sunshine. On the piano in the living room.

"I should have told you," I say. "On the beach. That first night. But—"

He cuts me off. "You didn't owe me your truth. Everyone has secrets."

"Even you?" I ask him. I'm staring at that little tattoo on the inside of his wrist. The compass rose. A protective mark for a sailor who's never been to sea.

Cole shrugs. "I've got a few." He drops his eyes back to the script in his lap. "You hear any more whispering?" he asks, and there's a funny sound in his voice. Something that's almost teasing, but almost not.

"You said it was the wind in the dune grass," I remind him, and he looks back up at me.

"I said that's what most people believe." He reaches over to run his fingers across the inside of my wrist—the spot where the little tattoo marks his own skin—and I shiver. It's just the lightest touch, and he pulls his hand away almost before I have a chance to feel it. But it makes it hard for me to think straight. "You might wanna think about getting your own compass rose," he tells me. "We all get lost sometimes."

I don't get a chance to say anything else, because people begin drifting back into the theatre then, and Jude calls the end of the break.

"Back at it, my lovelies!" Willa tells us. "Let's take it from the top."

We work that first scene a few more times before we go on to a scene with Orion and his bandmates. The one where they're all teasing him about this girl he met at the park. It's fun watching Lex attack the scene as Orion's best friend. I thought that gorgeous red-gold hair was my favorite thing about him. Or maybe that Tennessee drawl. But I'm starting to think it's his fearlessness. There's this ferocity about Lex, onstage and off. He just puts it all out there, and that's exactly the kind of energy I need in my life.

We're starting to wind down for the evening, but I don't want this to end. The barn is warm and cozy and bright. And Willa is so open and intuitive as a director. I feel like I'm learning so much from her already, even when she's working with someone else. We're all hanging on her every word, eager to answer her questions about the script. Feeding off each other's understanding of these characters as we put the puzzle pieces of this play together. There's so much shared energy. This is exactly what a good rehearsal is supposed to feel like.

When we're finished, Willa asks us to circle up onstage and hold hands. A Whisper Cove tradition, she says. "This is how we leave things." It feels almost like a prayer circle, and I guess it is a kind of prayer. In a way.

"This," she tells us. "This is why we come to the theatre. This connection—with the words on the page—with an audience—with our fellow actors—with ourselves, even." She looks around the circle. "This is why we come to Whisper Cove." She pauses. "There's something so intimate about it, isn't there? Even in a theatre full of people."

Suddenly I'm thinking of my mother again. I'm wondering if she felt that. The magic Willa talks about. Because I've only been here a few days, and I feel it so strongly already.

"You have a chance to become someone remarkable here," Willa finishes. "To step into a life of true greatness. Don't let that opportunity pass you by." Her thrumming presence fills up the whole barn. It's like standing a few feet from the sun. "Don't be satisfied with anything less than amazing. Be anything but ordinary, my lovelies."

Everyone is busy gathering up their things, but I'm suddenly feeling a little overwhelmed again. It's all so much. I feel tears threatening to fall, so I slip away to the little bathroom in the corner of the barn. It's dark inside. I feel around for a light switch, and the bathroom fills with a flickering, buzzing light as the single fluorescent bulb comes to life overhead.

I stand at the sink and stare into the cracked mirror. The reflection looking back at me stays mine. There's no hint of my mother hiding inside my eyes, and that makes me a little sad. I'm almost wishing for a glimpse of her tonight. I've felt so close to her all evening, here in this theatre where I know she lived and breathed.

I use the bathroom, then cross back to the sink to wash my hands. Only, when I'm finished, I can't turn the faucet off. It's stuck. And the water keeps running. The drain must be clogged, because the little porcelain bowl is filling up fast. I panic. But the knob won't budge.

The sink is full, but more water keeps flowing from the faucet, so now it's spilling over the edges and splattering onto the tile of the bathroom floor. It makes a sound like rain hitting the pavement. And then, as I stand there watching, the flow from the faucet becomes a torrent, and the splashing sound becomes a deafening roar. Like Niagara Falls.

I feel it splash over the tops of my feet. Ice cold. Like stepping into the sound.

Soon the water is up to my ankles. And it's rising fast. Panic claws at me with sharp fingers.

It's up to my calves.

My knees.

My thighs.

Water.

Up to my hips.

My waist.

My chest.

Bubbling and swirling all around me.

Up to my shoulders.

My neck.

My chin.

I clamp my mouth closed, and my panic stiffens into slicing terror as the water creeps up past my nose and over my eyes. It washes over the top of my head, and I am fully engulfed.

Embraced.

The water fills every inch of the tiny bathroom. I swim up and touch the ceiling. The fluorescent bulb flickers underwater, like a swimming pool light on a summer evening.

No air.

No way out.

I swim back down and try again to turn off the faucet, but it's no use.

My lungs are burning.

And there she finally is in the bathroom mirror. My mother, reaching toward me with graceful hands. Stretching through the glass like it's an open window.

Skin slipping from bone.

I open my mouth to scream for help, but I'm not sure if I'm screaming for my mother to save me, or for someone to save me from my mother. It doesn't matter, though, because screaming underwater just sounds like silence and bubbles. Liquid rushes in to fill up my lungs.

And that's when I remember that I've done this all before. Because this is what it is to drown.

I swim to the door and grab on to the handle. Turn the knob. Jiggle it hard. Try to push it open. But it's no good. I'm floating away. Drifting backward. Out to sea. Everything starts to go black.

Then, suddenly, the door is being pulled open from the outside, and I'm swept out with the surging water, tumbling into the stillness of the barn.

George is staring at me. He's leaning on a mop, and I'm sprawled on the floor. Everything is dry.

"Whoa there," he says. "Take it easy."

I run a hand over my clothes. My hair.

I'm dry.

Bone dry.

George offers me a hand up. But I don't take it. I push myself to my feet. I'm shaking all over. Teeth chattering. Knees wobbling. I feel unsteady. George is staring at me again. In that odd way he has. "The door was stuck. I panicked, I guess." I try to smile. Like it's no big deal, drowning on dry land. But it's not my best acting work, and George doesn't look convinced.

"It's an old building." He shrugs. "Things stick sometimes. Around here." He hasn't taken his eyes off me. "It can be dangerous. If you're not careful."

"Yeah," I say. But he's still staring, and I wonder if he was waiting for me. Hanging around after the barn cleared out because he knew I was in the bathroom. That thought gives me the creeps, so I push past him.

"Watch yourself," he growls.

But I'm already gone.

I grab my stuff and hurry outside. When I push open the door, I hear Jude call out from the little booth in the back of the theatre. "Going dark!" A stage manager's warning before he shuts off the lights and plunges the stage into blackness.

Lex is waiting for me out in front of the theatre. It doesn't surprise me to see him there. It's weird how fast the two of us have settled into a kind of routine. Waiting for each other. Checking in. Saving a seat.

The best friend I never knew I needed. Or wanted.

He takes one look at me and slips an arm around my shoulders. "Come on," he says, and I'm grateful when he leads me around the corner of the barn. Away from the bright glow of the outdoor lights.

I knew there was an amphitheater at Whisper Cove, but I hadn't seen it until this moment. It's bigger than I expected, with rows and rows of concrete risers stretching out below us and a wooden stage at the very bottom. It reminds me of something out of a theatre history textbook. A thing the Greeks might have built.

"Wow," I say as Lex and I settle on the very top row, high above the stage where we'll perform *Midnight Music* at the end of the month.

"Cool, huh?"

"Yeah," I tell him. "Very cool." The thought of acting out here gives me goose bumps.

Lex is watching me. Red eyebrows drawn together. Nibbling on his lower lip. I've already come to recognize it as his worried face. "Did something happen?" he asks.

"No," I say, but I'm still shaking. "I just . . ." I stop and take a deep breath. Try to come up with something that will make sense to Lex. And to me. "It was just a lot, you know? Becoming Eden. Being on the stage where my mom used to act." And it sounds so rational when I say it like that. Because of course it's been a lot.

It's a mindfuck. Right?

A huge fucking mindfuck.

Lex nods. "After everything that happened last night, I thought today might be hard."

"It's just been weird," I say. "I talked to Willa, and that was great. But so strange, you know?"

"I can't even imagine what this must be like for you." Lex smiles. His eyes are so bright. "But how cool that Willa wants to get to know you. I can't believe you ate lunch with her!" He collapses against me, and I can't help but smile, too. "Tell me everything."

"She told me all kinds of stuff I never knew about my mom. Just little details, but it all felt so important, you know? Because I never get that from my dad."

"That's intense." Lex is looking at me. "No wonder you're a little freaked out."

"Yeah," I say.

A little freaked out.

It's quiet for a minute, except for the always-present sound of the waves down at the beach.

"It'll be weird when we get to that scene, huh?" Lex's worried look is back.

"What scene?"

He's staring at me. "The end of act one." Lex blinks. "The scene where Eden drowns."

Shit.

It's not like I didn't know that happened. But I hadn't really thought about it until the words came out of Lex's mouth.

How many times will I have to drown in my life?

Once when I was five.

Over and over in my dreams.

Again tonight in the bathroom.

And how many times onstage? During these weeks of rehearsal as Eden.

Then the performance, of course.

The idea scares me, but I file it away. Tuck it into a drawer and slam it closed.

The concrete is hard and cold underneath me, and I shift positions. There's no way to get comfortable, though.

"They put out cushions all along the risers," Lex tells me. "When they have a show out here. That's what Jude says."

"How are things going with Jude?" Lex's face turns red, and his freckles glow like hot coals. "He's adorable," I say.

"He is." Lex grins. "I know." Then that darkness drifts across his face, and I wonder again what his story is.

"You should go find him," I say. "It's a nice night. You could take a walk." Lex raises one eyebrow at me, and I laugh. "Or something."

He shakes his head. "I don't wanna leave you alone."

But he's not responsible for me. I don't need a babysitter.

And I refuse to be afraid of things that aren't real.

"I'm a big girl," I tell him. "I can find my way back to the cabin. I promise."

"You sure?" he asks, and he's already getting up. I fight the instinct to grab him by the hand. Swallow the urge to tell him how I almost drowned in the bathroom.

Because if I tell him that, I'll have to tell him about all the other weird things that have happened to me over the past few days. I won't be able to stop myself, and it will all come spilling out of me. Like that water flowing out of the bathroom faucet.

My muddy feet the first night here. The bathroom mirror in the farmhouse.

I'll have to tell him about the whispering.

And the woman outside my window.

Then there's no way he'll leave me alone. I already know that about him. He'll spend the next four weeks glued to my side. And I want him to have this. Whatever this thing is with Jude. Because something tells me he really needs it.

So I just say, "Be good." And he blows me a kiss.

"Oh, believe me," he says with a wink, "I always am."

I laugh and watch him walk away until he gets swallowed by the dark. And it feels strange to be alone. My phone says it's 10:45. Just a few minutes to curfew. I glance around the amphitheater, but there's no trace of fog. The air is cool and dry, and I tilt my face up to find the stars. They twinkle and shine, but none of them fall out of the sky. They're all firmly anchored tonight.

I think about that voice. The one from my dreams. The one I can never remember the sound of.

*Look at the stars!*

I try to conjure up it up. But there's only the waves breaking down at the beach. The call of the foghorn. And the constant, empty ache deep down inside me somewhere.

The hole where my mother should be.

It's bigger than usual tonight. I feel it spreading like water poured on a tile floor. It bleeds out into my whole body until I'm made of so much nothing.

And that's when the cold sets in. Like always.

I dig around in my bag until I find Lex's little purple lighter. The one he left on the front steps of the cabin our first night here. Because I know what I need. I flick it with my thumb, and it springs to life. I like the heat of its tiny flame. The brightness of its small light.

It doesn't feel like enough, but that's okay. Because I know an old trick.

I reach over and rip a handful of pages from my notebook. I crumple them up and arrange them in a little pile on the concrete at my feet.

I touch them with the lighter, and the glow from the flames is immediate. Brighter. Warmer. And I'm grateful. But it's only a few seconds before the tiny fire eats through the paper and starts to die. So I rip another page from my notebook and add it to the pile. The flames devour it with a silent hunger, and something deep down inside me feels hungry, too.

I hold my hands low over the fire until I feel the burn. I don't let myself pull away. Even when it starts to hurt. Because at least I know I'm alive.

Real.

Not a fucking ghost.

"Hey."

I whirl around to look over my shoulder, and Cole Culver is

standing right there. I'm panicking and I start to step on the little inferno I've created.

"Don't," he says. "Don't put it out." And he comes to sit beside me.

I feel trapped. Naked and exposed. I have to fight the urge to run.

"It'll die in a minute anyway," I tell him. "It's just a little one."

I see him glance toward my open notebook. He picks it up and rips out a page, then crumples it up and adds it to the fire. But it's too late. The flames are already fading, so the paper doesn't catch.

I pull the lighter from my pocket and hand it to Cole. When he takes it, his fingers linger on mine longer than they should. I shiver, and Cole studies me for a second, then takes the lighter and flicks it without a word. I'm hardly breathing as the flame kisses the little pile of paper and it comes roaring back to life.

He leans down low and holds his hands just above the fire. I wait for him to pull away from the burn, but he doesn't.

"Be careful," I warn him, and when he turns those gray eyes on me, I feel myself get twisted inside out.

"Careful really isn't my thing."

Another piece of crumpled paper.

Another flick of the lighter.

*Snick. Sizzle. Whoosh.*

A long, low horn cuts through the night, and I look around. Somehow the whole amphitheater has filled with fog. It must have been creeping in on us, and I didn't even notice. Because right here, where Cole and I are, there's a little pocket of light.

And heat.

So much heat.

I remember what Willa told us yesterday morning, on the front porch of the farmhouse. *We know what we are, but not what we may be.*

I've only been here a few days, but I already feel myself *becoming*. Like Willa said.

I hand Cole another page. He flicks the lighter under his thumb. Then he holds the paper in his hand while we watch it burn.

And I'm not afraid anymore.

When we run out of things to light, we blow away the ashes together. They float up toward the sky. Get lost in the dark. Then Cole walks me back to my cabin.

We stop on the steps and look at each other. Neither of us seems sure where this goes now.

"Is that something you've done before?" he asks me. He's leaning against the railing. Gray eyes lit up by the porch light. "Starting fires?"

"A couple of times," I admit. But that's not really the truth. Because I do it pretty often.

"Why?" There's no judgment in the question, or in the way he's looking at me. Just curiosity.

"To make sure I'm not dead."

Cole nods. "I walk along the edge of the cliff," he tells me. "Sometimes I close my eyes and take ten steps. Or twelve. Fifteen, if it's really bad. Right along the very edge. Just to feel that rush." I'm staring at him, and he shrugs. "It's better than some of the other things I used to do."

"It never helps for very long," I tell him. "The cold always comes back."

Cole reaches over and takes my hand. He laces his fingers through mine. I wasn't expecting that, and it makes my stomach flip-flop again. He squeezes hard.

"Do you feel that?" he asks. And I nod. "You're not dead, Avril. And neither am I." He gives me a half smile. "Not yet, anyway."

The heat of him travels all the way up my arm. That's the effect Cole Culver has on me. Just that little touch can spark a fire. No lighter required. And the truth is that I'm more afraid of that than I could ever be of ghosts.

But I don't pull away.

And he doesn't let go. Not until he gives my hand one more squeeze.

Then he leaves me standing on the front porch, and even after he disappears into the night, I feel warm.

Later, though, my old nightmare sneaks in on the fog. It finds me in my bunk and tangles its wet fingers in my hair.

A thousand shimmering stars are falling into the sea. *Plop. Plop. Plop.*

*Look at the stars.*

A long blast jolts me awake. The low vibration of the foghorn rattles my bones. It comes again a second time, and I feel the echo of it deep in my chest.

I open my eyes and the world turns upside down. Nothing makes sense.

I'm standing in the ocean. The tickling kiss of wispy seaweed against my skin. The burn of salt in my nose.

On my tongue.

Waves sweep over the tops of my knees. And I shiver. Fight against the clawing panic.

Because this isn't a dream.

And it isn't something I'm imagining inside my head.

I'm wide awake now, standing mid-calf in the ice-cold surf of Long Island Sound. The fog presses in from all sides. I can't even tell which way is the shore and which way is open water.

And I have no idea at all how I got here.

# ACT II: SCENE 1

My muscles seize and I'm frozen in place. Wave after wave crashes into me, but I'm too afraid to move. My feet and legs are numb from the cold. Finally, I make myself take a shuffling step. But the water gets deeper. It's up to my thighs now, so I retreat in the opposite direction. One tiny step at a time. Until the waves are just barely washing over the tops of my feet. A few more backward steps and my legs give out. I sink to my knees in the sand.

This is real.

This is real.

This is real.

What the fuck?

What the fuck?

What the fuck?

This is not like what happened at auditions. Or the water in the bathroom. There's no cold, hard floor to bring me back to reality.

I'm shaking so hard that my bones knock against each other. A choked sob tears its way out of my throat and immediately gets swallowed up by the thick fog and the noise of the waves, like I never made a sound at all. I lift my head to look around, but I might as well close my eyes again, because even with them open I can't see anything. Not even my own hand in front of my face.

I get to my feet somehow. I'm barefoot. Wearing the tank top and shorts that I sleep in. No phone. No flashlight.

No lighter.

No idea how to get back to my cabin. I'm already disoriented again.

Which way was the sea?

I turn in a slow circle, and I have no idea.

Then the hair on my neck stands up, because I know that I'm not alone out here. I sense something coming toward me. Moving slow and silent through the fog. My heart stops, and I go rigid with fear. Something is there. Breathing. Just a few feet away. I feel its presence, even if I can't see it or hear it.

Sudden bright light. So blinding that I have to shield my eyes.

Just like on the cabin steps with Lex.

Like the night my mother died.

The night I died.

I scream and stumble backward into nothing. But I trip. There's something buried in the sand. Something wide and flat just under the surface. I land hard, and it knocks the wind out of me.

"Avril?" There's a voice behind the light. "It's okay. It's me."

"Lex?" It doesn't sound like him, but I don't know who else would be out here in the night, looking for me. An outstretched hand emerges from the fog. Disembodied and strange. I still can't see a face.

"It's Cole." He squats down low beside me. Our faces are inches apart, but all I see is the glow of his eyes. "Nice night, huh?" I'm so confused. And so cold. He slips off his jacket and drapes it around my shoulders, then takes my hand and pulls me to my feet. "Are you hurt?" he asks. But I can't answer. Because I don't know. "Come on."

Cole leads me through the fog. The beam of his flashlight barely makes any difference at all. It can't cut through the gray that walls us in. But his grip is strong, and I almost cry out in relief when I feel the wooden planks of the boardwalk under my bare feet.

We feel our way through the emptiness together. Board by board. Step by step. Inch by inch. Over the dunes and across the marsh. I know it by that sickly sweet smell. The scent of rot. And eventually we come to the thick, soft grass of the great lawn.

"You okay?" Cole asks me again. But my teeth are chattering too hard to speak.

He stops to pull his jacket tighter around me. Then he leads me on up the hill toward the farmhouse. When we get close, I see lights burning in some of the windows, and I've never been so grateful to see anything in my life.

"Come on," he says. "Let's get you warm." He leads me on through the fog, and I think he's taking me back to my cabin. But then I hear the jingle of keys and the squeaky hinge of the old barn door. "I thought you might want to clean up," he tells me. "Maybe dry out a little. Before I walk you back to your place."

As soon as Cole opens the door, an overpowering odor floods my nose. But it's different than before. This isn't paint. Or sawdust.

"Smell that?" he asks me, and I nod.

It's musky. Sweet and earthy. Like fresh sweat and hay and manure. It smells like—

"Horses," I whisper. My voice creaks like the barn door. And Cole nods.

"There haven't been horses in this barn for more than thirty years."

He ushers me inside and closes the door gently behind us. A single light bulb glows at the edge of the stage, and I stand, transfixed, and stare at it.

"The ghost light," Cole tells me. "It's tradition to leave it burning at night." I want to tell him that I know that. Of course I know that. But I have trouble getting the words out.

I let him lead me over to the little bathroom. The one I stood in just hours ago. When I drowned on dry land. I don't look at myself in the mirror as Cole runs warm water in the sink and dampens stiff paper towels to wipe the crusted salt from my face. The sand from my arms and legs. His touch is so gentle that it makes me cry. Because I'm exhausted and scared and frozen. And I don't know what any of this means.

He reaches out to tuck a strand of damp hair behind my ear. "Avril? Look at me." I can't make my voice work, but I manage to find his face with my eyes. "You're safe," he tells me. And I nod.

Cole leads me over to the stage, and we sit together on the edge. Bathed in the ghost light's glow. It's warm in the barn. And I feel myself start to thaw.

"What were you doing?" I finally ask him. "Out there?"

He laughs. It's a low, gravely sound that comes from somewhere deep in his throat. "I could ask you the same thing." I flinch at that, and the hard angles of his face soften. "I walk sometimes." He shrugs. "At night when I can't sleep. Which is always."

I run my tongue over my lips, and they feel raw. Chapped by the night wind and the salt spray. How long was I standing out there? In the surf. Before the foghorn woke me up?

"I saw you," Cole tells me. "I was sitting on the back steps of the farmhouse, and I saw you walk by. You passed near the porch light. And I saw your face."

"I don't remember," I tell him. "I don't—" The words get hung up in my mouth.

"You were sleepwalking," he says. "Is that something you've done before?"

"Never," I say, and my voice cracks. Because I remember the bits of mud and grass clinging to my feet. "Not anywhere else. Not before I came here." I turn to look at Cole, and his eyes are so intense. But there's a softness in them I haven't noticed before. He reaches out to brush sand off my cheek with his thumb.

"Yeah. Well. I tried to tell you. Here isn't like anywhere else."

"You followed me," I say. And he nods.

"I lost you in the fog. And it took me a while to find you. I was afraid—" He stops.

"Afraid of what?"

He hesitates, but his steel-gray eyes never leave mine.

"I was afraid I'd be too late."

Fear settles in my stomach again. I feel the lead weight of it. Solid and heavy. The metallic taste of it in my mouth.

*What the sea wants, the sea will have.*

Cole runs a hand over his face, and I realize how exhausted he looks. Not just tired. The kind of bone-deep weary that comes from years of never resting easy.

"I told my mother not to cast you as Eden," he says. "I begged her to give you some other part. Any other part. But you can't argue with Willa Culver."

"Why?" I ask him. "Why would you do that?"

"You've already drowned once," he tells me. "It's enough. You shouldn't have to do it again."

"I can handle it," I say, even though I'm sitting here sandy and wet and terrified. "I—"

But Cole cuts me off.

"You need to go home," he tells me. "Tomorrow. Call your dad and tell him you made a mistake coming back here. Get Jude to drive you to the train station."

"I don't want—"

"It's not safe for you here," Cole says, and there's this desperate sound in his voice. "It's not safe for—" He starts to say something else, but then he clearly changes his mind. "It's not safe."

"I'm not going home," I tell him, and I hear the undercurrent of anger bubbling beneath my words. I don't like to be told what to do. Not by Cole Culver.

Not by anybody.

"Jesus, Avril. I need you to listen to what I'm saying." Cole reaches for my hand. He turns it palm up and traces a compass rose onto my wrist. Like he's marking me. "We're alike, the two of us. And I knew it the moment I saw you. That first night. I felt it. Before I knew who you were, even." His eyes have turned dark around the edges, and he tightens his grip on my hand. "I didn't remember you. But I knew you. In that instant on the beach." He lets go of me, and I can breathe again. "I fucking knew you."

I know what he means. Because I felt it, too. With him. That instant shock of recognition. Some kind of deep pull that threw me off-balance. Powerful enough to scare me, right from the beginning.

Cole looks at me for a few seconds, like he expects me to get it. But I don't. Nothing makes sense tonight. It's like the fog has found a way inside my brain. So he spells it out. "I hear that whispering, Avril. Same as you. I've heard it my whole life."

The stage is spinning. "I feel sick," I manage to say. I can't talk about this. Not now. Not with him. Not with my clothes still damp from the waves. I'm not ready. And I don't even know if I believe any of it. "I need to go to bed." Cole nods.

"Yeah. Of course." He stands up and leads me back into the night. Across the gravel and over the grass. Right to the porch of my cabin. It isn't until we stop on the front steps that I notice my hand in his. His grip is strong. Sure. There's heat in it. And my whole body goes warm when I remember that fire we lit in the amphitheater.

When he lets go, I miss his touch immediately. I hand him back his jacket, and I feel his eyes on me as I lean down to brush the last of the dried sand from my legs.

When I stand back up, he's holding out his hand. Two more little chunks of sea glass rest in his palm. A pretty red one and a pale yellow one. "Take them," he says. But I don't reach for his sailor's charms. "Red and yellow are the rarest colors."

"Are they really good luck?" I ask, and as tired as I am, I can hear the skepticism in my voice.

Cole holds up the bits of polished glass so they catch the porch light. And I like the way they shine. The soft glow of them. He gives me a little smile. “I found you, didn’t I?”

“Yeah.” I breathe my answer into the night. Because he did. And so I let him press the smooth pieces into my curled fingers.

There’s a moment when either one of us could pull away.

But neither of us does.

“It’s almost five o’clock,” he says. “Sun will be coming up. The fog should be lifting soon.” I’m so confused. None of this makes sense. “Try to get some sleep. While you can.”

“You, too,” I say. And he laughs under his breath.

“Yeah. Maybe.”

And then he’s gone. I’m alone in the fog again.

I search the field between the farmhouse and the cabin. I’m looking for my ice-blonde hair. Gold-flecked eyes. The figure of a woman.

I’m looking for my mother.

Like always.

But I can’t see her tonight. Maybe because she isn’t there and never was. Or maybe because the fog’s too thick. Either way, my mother is hidden from me. Lost to years and memory. The same as she’s always been.

Even if she doesn’t roam the grounds of Whisper Cove at night, I figure that makes her a ghost. So I guess I believe, after all.

# ACT II: SCENE 2

I push open the cabin door as quietly as I can and tiptoe inside. I change into a clean T-shirt and shorts, and when I pull my damp tank top off over my head, the smell of horses floods my nose again.

Nobody stirs when I slip into my bed. Just like I imagine nobody stirred when I slipped out of it.

My head feels fuzzy. Like it's full of cotton. My arms and legs are heavy, and my body aches from the cold. I'm so empty. All I want in the world is to sleep, but it seems like the minute I close my eyes, my alarm is going off.

The first things I see when I wake up are Cole's little treasures, those bits of red and yellow sea glass, resting on my pillow.

So I know it all really happened, even if my mind is trying to make it into a dream now.

The cabin is empty, and I figure the others must already be in the bathroom. I force myself out of bed and dig around in the bottom drawer for something to wear, then slip on my flip-flops and grab a towel. Hopefully I have time for a quick shower.

The sky is a beautiful, clear blue, and the air feels so perfect. But none of that does much to ease my mind. Not when there's still sand clinging to my body from last night. All I can think about is washing away that proof. Because if I can rinse off the sand, maybe I can rinse off the memory of waking up knee-deep in ice-cold water.

It doesn't work, though. I watch the sand swirl down the drain. But the terror still sticks to me.

I hurry back to the cabin after my shower. I'm running late now. Everyone else must already be at breakfast. But I still pause to stare at that sea glass on my pillow for a few seconds. Then I reach for the two shiny charms and slip them into my pocket.

I'm still not sure they're magic. But I like the way they feel between my fingers. The cool smoothness of them calms me a little.

I start across the field toward the farmhouse. Cole is waiting for me on the front porch. He's leaning against one of the support posts, and his posture is so casual. But there's a fire burning in his eyes.

"Hey," he says. "Sleep okay?" Like we're an old married couple meeting at the breakfast table over French toast and the morning paper.

"Not really," I tell him.

"We need to talk," he says. My head hurts. The sun is so bright. And I don't think I'm ready to have another conversation with Cole Culver. Not yet. "I need to show you something. I promise it won't take long." He looks at me for a few seconds. "It's important."

I think about how he found me last night. How he saved my life, probably. I remember the strength of his grip on my hand. The comfort in that. And the heat.

"Yeah," I say. "Okay." I leave my backpack on the porch, and Cole leads me across the grass and down a little hill toward a long, low building. It's painted bright white, and the words **SCENE SHOP** have been burned into a board nailed over the door.

George is sitting on an overturned five-gallon bucket out front, smoking a cigarette. "Ya need somethin'?" he asks, and I can feel him looking at me, but I avoid his eyes. I'm relieved when Cole just shakes his head, and we keep moving. I've had enough weird moments with George to last me the rest of summer.

We don't go inside the scene shop. Instead, Coles takes me around toward the back. A few pieces of scenery sit drying in the sun, and a couple of dusty sawhorses rest in the shade of a tree. The plywood silhouette of a skyscraper leans against a light pole. We pick our way between stacks of old lumber and discarded paint cans. "Back here," he says. "Watch out for nails."

And that's when I see the name on the back of the building.

**NICOLE KENDRICK**

It's painted in red. Capital letters. Big and bold. There's a familiar date there, too. The day my mother died.

And beneath that, in cursive brush-stroke script—

*What the sea wants, the sea will have.*

The words look so jarring against the white boards—like the bloody title credits of a horror movie—that at first I don't believe I'm really seeing them. I'm frozen for a second. Staring.

I reach out to touch the N in my mother's name, and the damp grass slips under my feet. My whole world tilts sideways. Suddenly, I'm drowning. Eyes open. Water rushing in over my head. The burn of it in my throat. The weight of it in my stomach. Pulling me down like a stone.

Cole stays close—watching me—but he doesn't say anything. "What is this?" I manage to ask.

Cole leans against the building. He runs his fingers through his hair. Touches the tattoo on his wrist like a talisman. "It's a sort of graffiti memorial," he explains. "It gets painted over every few years. But theatre people are superstitious. So somebody always puts it back. It's supposed to be protection. To keep us all safe."

"That's ridiculous," I tell him. "We were night swimming. And we got caught in a riptide. Somehow, I survived. My mother didn't. That's all there is to the story."

Dad told me that years ago. *It happens all the time,* he said. *People forget how dangerous the ocean is. Mais la mer est mortelle.*

But the sea is deadly.

"Avril—"

I tear my eyes away from my mother's name so I can focus on Cole's face. "You don't really believe that old story, do you?" It's one thing for him to say it at night. Around a campfire. Or in the barn, huddled under the ghost light. But here, in the daylight, he can't really mean it. There has to be some other explanation for what happened to me last night. For the sleepwalking.

For the mud and the grass in my bed. The woman in the fog.

And in the bathroom mirror.

For all of it.

"Just listen." Cole reaches for my hands. "Please." His hair falls across his eyes, and I have this wild impulse to reach up and brush it back. "People here remember what happened to your mom. And they remember that little graveyard in the woods, too. The one where the women and children are buried. It scares the shit out of them. What the sea is capable of. It scares me." I feel the shiver that travels up his spine. It passes through his fingers into my flesh. "It should scare you, too."

There's no denying how afraid he is.

How afraid he is for me.

But something tells me it's more than that. He's afraid for himself, too. And I don't understand why. That fear is contagious, though. Like some kind of virus. The terror of finding myself standing in the waves hits me all over again. Hard. Suddenly I can't seem to get enough air.

I look at those words painted in red. My mother's name.

I almost tell Cole that there's more that he doesn't know. That it's not just the sleepwalking. But I can't find the words to explain about those moments when the lines have blurred.

Cole pulls his eyes away from mine, and they settle on that last line of cursive.

*What the sea wants, the sea will have.*

"Did you know," he says, "that on some whaling ships, if a sailor went overboard, nobody was allowed to throw him a rope? They believed, if the sea wanted to take you, there was nothing they could do to stop it."

"And you think the sea wants me." My voice sounds funny to my own ears. Like it belongs to somebody else. Somebody who believes in ghosts.

Or at least somebody who isn't so sure anymore.

Cole nods. "It wants me, too. It's wanted me my entire life. I've always felt those cold fingers, pulling at me." I shiver in my T-shirt. "But there's no way in hell I'm going to let it take you, Avril. I promise."

"What about you?" I ask him. Because I'm starting to suspect that Cole Culver's compass rose tattoo won't do him any good against whatever dark tide is pulling him out to sea. But he doesn't answer. And the look in his eyes scares me even more than what happened last night. There's so much sadness. A hopelessness that makes me afraid for him. For both of us. "Why did you show me this?" I need to know why he was waiting on my porch first thing this morning. Why he dragged me here when I should have been at breakfast with Lex and Val and Jude.

Cole takes a step closer. The darkness in his eyes lifts a little. But they're still deep gray, like the ocean in a storm.

"Because I need you to believe me. I need you to know you aren't safe here." He's searching my eyes, and I remember the two of us in the amphitheater. Watching that paper burn. I feel the heat of that in my cheeks. The flame of it low in my stomach. Being with Cole always leaves me reeling.

Uncertain.

I'm starting to feel dizzy. Overwhelmed by those red letters. The pressure of Cole's fingers. His eyes. And the brightness of the sun.

"I need to get to class," I tell him, and I take a step backward. I'm suddenly cold again. "I'll see you at rehearsal tonight."

I pick my way through the junk and head back toward the farmhouse. I slip into the library just as the morning workshop is starting, and I'm grateful to Lex for saving me a seat.

"Where were you at breakfast?" he whispers, but just then, Cole crosses the lawn. I stare at him through the tall library window, and it leaves me with almost the same feeling as seeing my mother dressed in moonlight, dancing in that empty field.

Lex follows my gaze. “I knew it!” he hisses, and he gives me a scolding look. “You’ve been keeping secrets.” His eyes are a hopeful shade of blue, and I can tell he wants this for me. Wants me to have something. Someone. Like he has now. With Jude. The two of them suddenly have inside jokes. And their bodies seem drawn together by some kind of invisible magnet. Knee touching knee in the cafeteria. Shoulder brushing shoulder on the sea porch steps. It hadn’t surprised me a bit when I caught them holding hands for the first time last night, outside the barn during a rehearsal break.

“Potential,” Lex tells me. “Remember, Av? You just have to be open to the possibilities.”

I reach into my pocket and feel the smooth bits of sea glass. But I have no idea how I feel about Cole Culver right now, except I’m starting to have this feeling that we wouldn’t be good for each other.

At lunchtime, Willa appears in the cafeteria doorway. She motions for me to come with her, so I grab a grilled cheese sandwich and a cup of tomato soup and follow her to the sea porch.

“How’d you feel about the first rehearsal?” she asks me as I ease my tray onto the picnic table directly across from her. She’s looking at me with those intense eyes of hers, so I pretend to be focused on not spilling my soup. I’m afraid if she sees my face, she’ll know somehow. About what happened last night. After the theatre.

On the beach.

In the sound.

“It was great,” I say. “It felt really good.” And that part’s not a lie.

It was later when everything went wrong.

Willa looks relieved. “You were a dream to work with,” she tells me. “Just like your mother. It’s almost like having Nicole onstage again." She looks at me for a few seconds. "You don't know what a gift that is for me, Avril."

"Is that why you gave me the lead?" It's something that's been nagging at me since she called my name and Jude handed me my script. I've seen the way some of the other girls stare. The way they whisper, and how their heads swivel in my direction when I walk into the room. Almost like I pulled off some kind of trick. That's why I'd planned to keep my secret until after auditions were over. Until after the cast was announced. I didn't want there to be any doubts about whether or not I earned my part, fair and square.

Willa laughs. She dismisses the idea with a wave of her hand. "Avril, I gave you the lead role because you blew all those other girls out of the water. There was never any question about who would play Eden." She narrows her eyes at me, and I guess she knows what I've been thinking, because she adds, "And if any of the other girls are giving you a hard time, it's just because they're jealous." She shrugs. "It comes with the territory when you're the leading lady."

"Everyone was really good at auditions," I say. "There are lots of girls you could've picked to play Eden."

"There are lots of girls who could've played Eden. That's true. But there was only one who proved she could truly *become* Eden. And that's the difference between good acting and great acting. Between pretending and art." Willa grins at me. Her eyes sparkle. "Ignore the haters. You can be the moon and still be jealous of the stars." She gives me a sly little smile. "Besides, you and Cole certainly have great chemistry together."

I blush. Take a nibble of grilled cheese. Try to figure out what to say to that.

Willa is studying me now. She hasn't taken a bite of her lunch. "You know," she says, "Cole could use a friend. He gets lonely sometimes." She pauses. Picks up her fork and holds it over her salad. "You could be good for him, I think."

"What do you mean?" I ask, because I genuinely don't understand how I could be good for anybody, but especially Cole Culver. If anything, being around me seems to bring out some kind of darkness in him. The circles around his eyes are blacker these past few days. His cheeks a little more hollow.

Willa smiles. "Cole needs someone to keep him grounded. Someone to get him out of his own head." She finally spears a forkful of salad, and she gives me a little wink. "Someone extraordinary."

I've never thought of myself as anything special before, but when Willa tells me I am, I almost believe her.

We spend the rest of lunch just talking. It's so much fun chatting with Willa about her life and about my mother that I almost forget about what happened last night. And about what Cole showed me this morning. My mother's name painted on the back wall of the scene shop. Red capital letters dripping like blood. I file those things away in some kind of separate drawer, just like Glory showed me with the invoices yesterday. I tuck them away in a folder. Label them TO DEAL WITH LATER. Then I slam the metal drawer in my head closed and try to forget it exists.

Willa makes that easy. She laughs. Tells funny stories. I feel like I could talk to her forever. I even like answering her questions about me, because Willa has this way of looking at you that makes you feel like, in that moment, there's nobody else in the world as important to her as you are. It isn't anything she does, it's just the way she listens. I've seen her do it in rehearsal, too. Not just to me. To Lex. To Val. To Jude. Even to the kids who only have one or two lines in the whole show.

When Willa is listening to you, you feel like somebody. It's like a little bit of her spark leaks out and bleeds onto you. And it's the best. Like some kind of drug.

As soon as lunch ends, though, the euphoria of having Willa's undivided attention starts to fade, and the fear of what happened to me last night starts creeping back in. It's like I keep opening that file drawer to peek inside. Even though I'm telling myself not to.

When I show up to work with Glory, she's watering the plants on the bookcase behind her desk. I say hello and pick up a stack of papers from the TO FILE tray. Glory is turned away from me, so I can't see her face when she says, "I knew your mother. She was a friend of mine."

I drop the papers I'm holding, and they flutter to the ground. They're all out of order now. "Shit," I say. "I'm sorry." And I bend down to scoop them up. My hands are shaking, so it isn't easy. I wasn't prepared for that.

Glory turns around to look at me. Her face is completely white and she blinks a few times, like she's just as stunned as I am. "I had no idea I was going to tell you that until I heard it come out of my mouth," she confesses. "I almost told you so many times yesterday, but I stopped myself. I wasn't planning to say it yet. Not until we got to know each other a little better."

"Willa told you," I say, but Glory shakes her head.

"It was George who got to me first, actually. As soon as I showed up for work yesterday morning." She laughs a little. "And that's not surprising. God. He was so obsessed with Nicole back then. He made a fool out of himself that summer. Pestering her. Following her all over the place. But Nicki never gave him a second look." I think about the way George stares at me, and my skin crawls. Because I know now, that he's been comparing me to her. "But then Willa told me, too, of course. It's all anybody around here has been talking about the last few days." Glory sets the little watering can on the floor behind her desk. She sinks into her office chair and reaches for a staple remover. "But I think deep down, I already knew it."

She looks at me and smiles.

"You seemed familiar to me, too," I tell her. "Like maybe I remembered you."

"I was nineteen that summer," Glory says. She's playing with the staple remover while she talks. Squeezing it open and closed, like a set of jaws. "I'd just broken up with my high school boyfriend. Dropped out of college. My life was a mess. God." She shakes her head. "I was just a disaster. And it was my first week working at Whisper Cove. Nicki was an old friend of Willa's, of course, and I met her the very first day she arrived here."

Nicki.

I've never heard anyone else call my mother that. Dad always calls her Nicole. Even Willa does.

"Were you close?" I ask.

Glory puts down the staple remover and takes half of my stack of papers. More invoices for the upcoming professional shows, she tells me. We sort them into her filing cabinet as she talks. But I have trouble remembering how to alphabetize.

"Nicki was thirty years old that summer. So eleven years older than I was. And it was less than eight weeks from that first day we met until . . ." She stops and picks a bit of fluff off her dress. "But you know how there are certain people you just click with right off? Like you know instantly this is someone you connect with? On a deeper level? It was like that with Nicki. For me." Glory's finished filing her half of the stack, and she reaches for mine.

There are so many things I want to ask, but I don't know where to start. It's a little paralyzing, having all this knowledge about my mother after years of begging Dad for scraps. It feels like waking up starving in the jungle, and then being led to an all-you-can eat buffet on the other side of the island.

"And I remember you, too, of course," Glory adds, smiling at me. "Your mother used to leave you with me while she was in rehearsal. You'd just sit on the floor and color for hours. You were never a bit of trouble. Everybody adored you. That snow-white hair and that curious expression on your face." She stops filing and looks at me for a few long seconds. "I knew even back then that you'd grow up to look like her." She pauses. Blinks. "Nicki was so beautiful, you know. Just luminous. But there was this sadness about her that summer, too." She goes back to the filing. "I guess that was partly because of the trouble with your dad."

I stop with a paper halfway in the file drawer. "Trouble with my dad?" I'm thinking about that almost-imperceptible frown of Willa's. The one I saw yesterday. Her fleeting disapproval.

"I figured you knew." Glory's face turns bright red. "I shouldn't have mentioned it, I guess. It's not my place. But I think there was some kind of trouble there. Or at least, that was my impression." She reaches for her water bottle. Takes a long drink. "That's what

Nicki was doing up here that summer, I think. She was trying to put some space between the two of them."

Dad's never mentioned anything about that, but then he barely mentions my mother at all. He told me she came up here because Willa practically begged her to take a role in one of Brody's shows that summer. They were on the brink of going bankrupt, he told me, and they needed her because she'd work for almost nothing. A favor for an old college friend.

Glory looks down at her polka dot skirt. She smooths it with her hands and fiddles with the hem. "What do you remember?" she asks. "About that summer."

I shake my head. "I don't remember anything."

She's staring at me now. "Nothing?" I shake my head again. "Well," she says, "you were so young. I just thought—"

"I don't remember anything before that, either."

She's really staring at me now. "So you don't have any memories of your mom?" I shake my head and Glory gasps. There are suddenly tears in her eyes.

And I come so close to spilling it all right then. How that lack of memory haunts me. How I've spent my whole life tiptoeing around that deep hole and trying not to fall in. How I lie awake at night trying to remember just one real, concrete thing. The sound of her voice. Her touch. The way she smelled. Anything at all.

Because I feel like until I know her, I'll never really be able to know myself.

But I don't say any of that. Because if I open up that crack, who knows what might come spilling out.

And it turns out I don't have to say anything anyway, because Glory has plenty to say.

We work together all afternoon, and instead of offering me more peppermints, she feeds me little bites of information about my mother. Just tiny morsels. But they're things I never knew. And I gobble them up because I've been hungry for so long.

Did I know she loved cats? "There was a little stray hanging around that summer. An orange tabby. Nicki named it Nacho and fed it every day. Scraps from her own meals."

Don't I remember what an ear she had for music? The way she was always singing. How she used to compose original melodies in her head and walk around humming them to herself under her breath. "Never whole songs," Glory explains. "Just the most beautiful little snippets. It used to drive me kind of crazy, but God, I missed it so much. After . . ."

Did anyone ever tell me she was obsessed with mint chocolate chip ice cream? The bright green color. The taste of it. The cold on her tongue. "Every Sunday afternoon that summer, we took you to Mitchell's Dairy, out on the highway. It was our little ritual. Just the three of us. They had these cows in a pen right beside the shop. So you could pet the cows who made your ice cream." Glory laughs. "Nicki thought that was the coolest thing. She always made sure you told them thank you."

And just for a second, I have a flash of actual memory. My hand reaching through a wooden fence to rub the soft head of a white cow.

These are the kinds of stories Dad never shares, but Glory talks about my mother almost like she's still alive. Like she's just in the next room, maybe, and she's going to walk in any minute and catch us telling funny stories about her. And we'll be in so much trouble.

"That whole summer was just incredible," Glory says. "There's never been another one like it. But . . . sometimes . . ." She freezes for a moment. Then she shakes her head. Takes a deep breath. She's folding a stack of printed mailers with astonishing precision. The creases are impeccable.

"Sometimes what?" I ask.

Glory stops folding. She picks up a bent paper clip and fiddles with it for what seems like forever before she finally says, "I don't know." She puts down the paper clip and gathers up the folded mailers. "It was a long time ago."

And that's the first thing she's said that doesn't seem honest.

"Please," I say. "Tell me."

Glory sighs. "Memories are strange, you know? There are things about that summer that are so clear. But there are other things that I can't quite call into focus. It's like living in a house, and every time you come home, something's just slightly different. Nothing major. Just tiny things. So it seems the same, until you realize the coffee cups are on the wrong shelf in the pantry. Or the bathroom door opens the wrong way." She reaches out and touches my hair, just the way Willa did at auditions. She runs her fingers over a long strand. "It's a lot like . . ."

"It's a lot like what?" I ask.

"It's a lot like being haunted."

# ACT II: SCENE 3

Rehearsal that night is strange. I have trouble focusing, which isn't like me at all. Or at least it didn't used to be. But I keep thinking about last night. The cold lap of the waves in the dark. And this morning. My mother's name on the scene shop wall. I'm combing through every little bit of information I have about her now. Every tiny thing I've learned from Willa. And from Glory. I'm stringing all those bits together like making a popcorn chain for a Christmas tree.

And I'm working on really getting to know Eden, too. Attempting to work off-book, because I already know my lines. I knew most of them before I ever got here. After all, I've been carrying that script around in my backpack for years.

I'm also trying not to turn fire red when Cole touches me during a scene. Or when I feel him watching me from across the theatre. It's a lot, especially when his hand lingers on my arm. The brush of his fingers feels like the striking of a match.

He catches me outside the barn after rehearsal, and he offers to walk me back to my cabin. The fog is already rolling in. It swirls around my feet. Alive and wet. Like a licking tongue. Or waves lapping over the sand.

Cole keeps his hand on my back as we move through the dark together. I feel the heat of him through my shirt. And by the time we reach the cabin steps, I think his palm print must be burned into my skin.

He's leaning against the porch railing, looking at me, but neither one of us says anything for a few seconds. I already miss the warmth of his hand on my back. The press of his fingers. And without even realizing it, I pull Lex's lighter out of my pocket and flick it with my thumb.

"You cold tonight?" Cole asks me, and I shrug.

"Maybe a little."

He steps in closer, and his arms go around me. I gasp out loud as he pulls me against him. His heart is beating loud in my ear. It pounds against my chest. "Feel that?" he whispers, and I nod. "We're still alive." I close my eyes and relax against Cole. "We're both alive. Right here. Right now."

"Keep reminding me of that," I say. And Cole laughs low. Under his breath.

"I will. I promise."

Our hearts are still beating against each other. And for a few minutes, it feels like that's all that matters. At least for right now.

We say goodbye, and Cole gives me one more piece of advice before he disappears. "Listen to music," he tells me. "Wear headphones. It sounds silly, but it helps."

I still don't know if I believe him. But later—when the fog gets thick—I take his advice. And I don't hear the whispers that night. Or the night after that. So maybe Cole's trick works. Maybe all I need to get through this summer in one piece is a little elevator music in my ear when I go to sleep.

It's Friday afternoon, almost the end of week one, when Glory sends me upstairs again. More files for Brody to look over. Only he's in his office this time, sitting behind a big mahogany desk. He looks up when I clear my throat from the doorway.

"These are from Glory," I say, and I show him the bright orange folders. He smiles at me and holds out his hand for the files.

"Avril," he says as I hand them to him. "Nicole's girl. Right?" I nod, and Brody puts the folders on his desk. He leans back in his chair to study me. "You know, when I saw you in here on Monday, it shook me for a second. Just looking at you standing there, from the back at least, I thought you were her." He's still smiling, but that same sad look is seeping through. The one Willa and Glory get when they talk about my mother. "I thought, here's Nicole, standing right here in my office. At least until you turned around." I remember his face. White. Like he'd seen a ghost. "And then Willa told me who you were, and it all made sense."

Brody stands up and pushes his chair back. He crosses over to the wall of photos, and I follow him. We stand side by side and look at that picture. Third row. Second photograph from the left.

"Nicole was a beauty," he tells me. "And so talented. Jesus. Not to mention, just brilliant. Willa had known her for years, but that summer was the first time I met her, and I knew right off. She just had it. She could have been a star. Broadway. Movies. Whatever she wanted." He frowns. "I wondered what she was doing, wasting her time down there in Texas." He leans in for a closer look at the photo. "I tried to talk her into sticking around. I wanted her here." He shakes his head. "Willa and I wanted her here."

I'm staring at my mother's gold sandals again. Her hot pink toes. And that terrified feeling is rising up in me. I shove it back down and focus on Brody's words. He's staring at me now. And something in his eyes makes me uncomfortable. I've seen that look before.

"If you've got any of Nicole in you, you'll have the world on a string, Avril."

But that's the thing. I don't know if I have any of my mother in me, because I don't know who she was.

At least not yet.

Brody gives me a pat on the shoulder. And I try to ignore the way his fingers play over my skin. The feeling of his hand lingering on my bare arm. I'm too busy adding that bit of information—the part about how my mother could have been a star—to my list of things to remember. It's like I keep gathering these left-behind pieces of her, hoping to stitch them together into something that might resemble an actual living, breathing woman. Flesh and blood. A kind of hand-sewn quilt I can cover myself with when I get cold.

"Thanks for bringing the files up," Brody says, and I nod.

"Sure."

There's that casual smile of his again. Just a little too broad and a little too relaxed to be real. I head toward the door. Down the hall to the stairs. But when I turn back to look over my shoulder, Brody is still standing there. Staring at the photo of my mother. He isn't smiling now, though. His face has hardened. There's something off about it.

When I get back to her desk, Glory gives me a nervous look. "Everything okay?" she asks. I nod and she asks me if I want to take a walk. "Fridays are pretty easy days around here," she explains. "Half the New York people don't bother showing up to their offices, so there aren't many phone calls for Brody. And everything else can wait."

I say sure, so Glory grabs her bag and her sunglasses, and we head out the back door onto the sea porch. I linger for a moment, hoping that flash will come to me again. That bit of memory. Me under the picnic table. Angry voices. My mother's gold sandals and pink toes. But nothing comes, so I follow Glory down the steps and onto the sloping lawn.

"I thought we'd head down to the beach," she says over her shoulder. And I'm grateful she can't see my face. I haven't been back to the beach since late Tuesday night, when Cole found me there in the fog, but I can't tell Glory that. So I keep following her.

When we reach the boardwalk that stretches across the marsh, she stops to lean against the railing. "Nicki loved it down here," she says. "I taught her how to fish for crabs. A little bit of raw chicken on the end of a string. She always tossed them back, though. Couldn't bear to cook them." Glory's voice is soft and far away. Almost like she's talking to the dune grass, and not to me. But then she smiles in my direction. "This is still where I feel closest to her."

She leads me on down the boardwalk. Up and over the dunes and onto the beach. I'm trying not to look at the water, but it's almost impossible to ignore a whole ocean when it's spread out in front of you.

Glory pulls a little blanket out of her bag and lays it on the sand so we can both sit. It's quiet for a minute, except for the waves. I keep hearing Cole's words.

*They believed, if the sea wanted to take you, there was nothing they could do to stop it.*

I take deep breaths. Unball my fists. Tell myself I'm being silly. That the waves aren't as loud as I think they are. Because I'm not the kind of person who believes in legends. Or ghosts. But I can't stop staring at the way the water washes up just a little higher with each incoming swell. Like it's reaching for us.

Reaching for me.

I'm staring at the floating swim dock. It's bobbing up and down. Sunlight bouncing off the metal ladder attached to the side. But Glory is looking down the beach to where a rock jetty marks the end of the Whisper Cove property. I turn my head and follow her gaze.

"That's where George found you," she tells me. "Washed up down there by the jetty."

My breath catches, and I turn back to stare at her.

"George found me?"

She nods. "He used to walk down here every morning before work to check on his crab traps. He loved to watch the sun come up over the sound." She pulls her eyes away from the rocks at the end of the beach and stares out toward the lighthouse. "He doesn't do that anymore. Not since that morning."

I've never known any of this. Just that someone found me. It never occurred to me to wonder who.

"He said he caught sight of something white down there," Glory goes on. "By the jetty." She swallows hard. Her face has gone gray. "He thought it was a plastic bag, maybe. But it was the little nightgown you had on. He didn't have a phone with him. And he couldn't tell if you were—"

"Dead?"

"Breathing," she says. "He couldn't tell if you were breathing. But he couldn't leave you there. To go get help. So he scooped you up and ran up to the farmhouse with you." Glory closes her eyes, lost in remembering. "I froze. Couldn't move. Didn't know what to do. Willa's the one who called 911. I've never seen her that shaken. I still remember the look on her face when she saw George running up the lawn. Screaming for help. With you in his arms." Glory shudders. "She never really got over that. God, she loved Nicki. None of us ever got over it." She pauses. Searches the sea like she's looking for someone. "We loved her so much."

I can't believe I'm finding all of this out now, at seventeen, when I should have asked Dad ages ago. It's weird the holes I didn't even know I had. All the things I don't remember forgetting.

Glory runs a hand over her hair. It's frizzing up in the damp. She tugs her sweater around her shoulders. "Then the ambulance came and Willa rode with you to the hospital. We wanted someone to be there in case you woke up. So you wouldn't be alone. Your dad couldn't get here until that evening. And then a bunch of us—me, George, Brody, a lot of the other people who were here that summer—we came back down to the beach and stayed here, just standing around and looking out at the sound all day. We knew, if you were in the water, Nicki must be out there, too. Somewhere. We were hoping for a miracle, I guess. And then dark came and I couldn't leave. The others all went home eventually, but I spent that whole night sitting right here. Waiting. Because I couldn't give up. Not on Nicki." She chokes a little. "I thought, if you were alive, maybe there was a chance she—" She stops again. Takes a deep breath. "The tide didn't bring her body in until the next morning. She must've gotten hung up somewhere. On the rocks, maybe. Or a fishing line."

"I've never known any of this," I tell her.

Glory hesitates for a second before she pulls something out of her bag and hands it to me. A pink sweater. Soft and worn. It's wrapped around a spiral notebook. The cover is a faded green. "I found these at my place when I finally went home that next day. The two of you had been there just a few nights earlier. I'd made spaghetti for the three of us, and we'd watched old Disney movies. Then everything happened, and I walked in the front door, and there Nicki's things were on my couch. Like she'd just wandered into the kitchen for a glass of water." Glory is staring at the pink sweater. "Nicki was always leaving things lying around." She almost laughs. But then she stops. Takes a deep breath. "And I just scooped them into a box and put them in the closet. I couldn't throw them out, but I never touched them again." She hesitates. "I thought you might want them."

The sweater is soft. I hold it close and try to breathe in my mother. I want it to smell like her, but I have no idea what she smelled like. I get the faintest whiff of lavender, though—like the ghost of a scent—or the scent of a ghost—and it makes the hair on my neck stand up.

I hesitate, but then I pull the sweater over my head. The morning air still carries a chill, but I feel instantly warmer. I pick up the notebook and thumb through it. A photo falls out and flutters into my lap. Me. At five years old. In the farmhouse library. I recognize the wood paneling and the leather sofas immediately, and I remember telling Lex and Val that I thought I used to play in there. Evidently, I'd been right.

I'm looking at the camera and laughing. My image is blurry. Like maybe I'm moving too fast to be captured on film. And behind me, just peeking out from behind the long drapes, I see a shock of dark hair. A flash of gray eye.

"That's you and Cole," Glory tells me, but I already knew it. "You two were inseparable that summer." She smiles. "And I guess that made sense, being so close in age. But it was funny how the two of you just took to each other. Like you were made for one another."

I study that one gray eye peeking out from behind the library drapes.

The lost playmate I never knew I had.

"Of course, that was before all the trouble started with him," Glory says. She's staring at the photograph in my hand. "The two of you were so innocent that summer." I hear her sigh, long and deep. "We all were."

"What do you mean?" I ask her, and I give in to the urge to run my fingers over the two little ghosts in the photo. A boy and a girl who don't exist anymore. "About the trouble with Cole?"

"You wouldn't know it to look at him," Glory tells me, and she drops her voice to a whisper. "But he's had a tough time." She glances over her shoulder, like she's worried he might be standing right behind us. "Willa sent him away last year. For a couple of months. She was worried about him. Brody was, too. We all were." She stops all of a sudden. Realizes she's said too much. "He's so much better now, though."

I wonder if that's true. I'm thinking about that bone-deep weariness on his face. The dark circles around his eyes. Those stories about the sea. The way he believes them.

"Thank you," I tell her. "For all of this." And I mean the information just as much as the sweater and the notebook. "I've never really had anything of my mom's."

"I know you must have questions," Glory says slowly. She's polishing her glasses with the hem of her blouse. "About what happened to your mom that night."

"What do you mean?"

My mother wasn't used to ocean swimming, that's what Dad said. A Texas girl who didn't know the dangers of being so far from home. That's all there was to it.

Glory sighs, long and deep. When she speaks again, her voice shakes.

"From the beginning, people were talking. Saying that the sea had lured her to her death. The whispering. You've probably heard the stories. And they said she'd tried to take you with her. Now, that's a bunch of nonsense, obviously. Because Nicki never would have hurt you." There's something fierce in her voice. "I want you to know that. Not ever." I'm relieved to hear her say it. Cole's been getting to me, I guess. "But—"

"But now you have questions."

Glory shakes her head. "It's not about me. Not anymore." She reaches out. Touches my cheek with one trembling hand. "I just thought you might need answers." The expression on her face looks an awful lot like regret. "I don't know what's in there." She nods toward the green notebook in my hand. "Probably nothing. I was never able to look. It felt like such an invasion of privacy. You should look, though. Whenever you feel ready."

Glory says she needs to get back to her desk, so we stand up and shake the sand out of her blanket. We move toward the boardwalk. But I stumble over something. There are wide, flat stones buried in the sand. My foot catches the edge of one.

"Careful," Glory warns me. "There are pieces of the past buried all over Whisper Cove. It's easy to get tripped up." We head back up to the mansion. It's a long walk, along the boardwalk, over the dunes, across the marsh, and up the great lawn. And I think about what Glory said. How George ran that distance screaming for help. With me in his arms.

"I'm glad I'm getting to know you," Glory says, and she reaches over to take my hand. "It's good to know you're okay." She hesitates. Almost like she's holding her breath. "You have been happy, haven't you? I've wondered that so often over the years. I've hoped for it."

"Yeah," I tell her, and she looks so relieved that I almost cry. "I've been happy. I've got a good life."

I don't tell her that sometimes I feel like I'm mostly made of holes.

"I'm so glad," she says, and it hits me hard that she's been thinking about me all these years, and I've never even known she existed. Never would have known if I hadn't come here this summer. So maybe I've already accomplished something.

"Thanks again for the sweater," I tell her. "And the notebook."

She nods. "If you find anything in there, you let me know. Okay?"

There's something about the way she says it that makes me uneasy. "What do you think's in there?" I ask her.

Glory shrugs. "Who knows? Maybe nothing." I watch her fiddle with the buttons on her dress. She pulls on the middle one so hard that I'm afraid she'll pop it off.

"But everyone has secrets."

# ACT II: SCENE 4

All the rest of that day, I wear my mom's pink sweater. I keep her notebook in my bag next to my script for *Midnight Music.* I haven't worked up the nerve to peek inside it yet, but when I go into rehearsal that night, it's like I'm carrying a little bit of my mother with me. A physical part of her. And that feels good.

We've spent the last three days working on the first couple of scenes, but now we're ready to move on to something new. "Remember," Willa tells us after warm-ups, "this is scene three. Orion comes back to the courtyard the day after they meet, and he finds Eden there again."

"Right," I say. I know the whole play by heart.

Cole leans down to whisper in my ear before we begin. I feel the brush of his dark waves against my cheek. It reminds me of that other tickle—seaweed against the backs of my knees—and I shiver.

"You sleep okay last night?" It's code between us now, and I know what it means. He's asking if my feet stayed dry. If I heard any whispering.

"Yeah," I tell him, and I wait for a relieved grin. He just nods, though. There's something different about Cole's eyes tonight. That tightness in his jaw is more noticeable. "What about you?"

He gives me a little bit of a smile. "I don't sleep," he says. "Remember?"

His fingers brush against mine. It's just the briefest of touches, but it shakes me. I want to ask him if he's okay, but Jude calls, "Lights up," and we have to jump into the scene.

I'm sitting on the bench, and Cole is walking toward me. He's humming that song, Eden's melody, when he slides into his spot.

**ORION**: Here you are again.
**EDEN**: Yes, here I am.
**ORION**: And here I am again.
**EDEN**: What a funny coincidence.
**ORION**: I brought you a flower.
**EDEN**: It's beautiful.
**ORION**: You're beautiful.

I blush then, even though I know it's ridiculous. He's just reading the script. But when I look up, Cole isn't looking at the page, he's looking at me. I look back down because I can't bear the intensity in his eyes.

**EDEN**: I'm not really. But flowers make me happy. Thank you.
**ORION**: What else makes you happy?
**EDEN**: Why do you want to know?

**ORION**: So I'll know what to bring you tomorrow.
**EDEN**: Let's see. Stars. Orange slices. Fresh snow on the ground.
**ORION**: I'll do my best. But the snow might be tricky.
**EDEN**: Are you flirting with me?

Shit.

I've read this scene a million times, but saying that line out loud to Cole hits different. He looks up and catches me staring at him, but he doesn't look back down at the script for the next line. He just says it from memory, with the beginnings of a smile.

**ORION**: If I say yes, will you flirt back?

I know the next line from memory, too, so I let myself fall into those gray eyes.

**EDEN**: What if I already am?

We sit there in silence for a few seconds, just watching each other, before Cole speaks again.

**ORION**: Come on. I want to show you something.
**EDEN**: Where are we going?
**ORION**: Just over there. Closer to the river.

Cole gets up and moves across the stage. And I follow him. We stand side by side and stare out into the rows of chairs.

**ORION**: Look at that, Eden. It goes on forever.

**EDEN**: It seems as wide as the sea, doesn't it?

**ORION**: It looks so much different up close. So much stranger and deeper.

**EDEN**: Wilder. Darker.

Cole locks eyes with me. I hear Eden's melody floating across the theatre, even though he hasn't picked up the guitar. And he isn't humming. I blink, and suddenly I'm standing in an ankle-deep ocean. It goes on for eternity, as far as I can see in any direction. I feel the water lapping around my bare feet—cold and wet. My heart is racing.

I make myself take a deep breath. Because I know I'm getting swept up in the moment. That's all it is. To be standing here. In this barn. In my mother's sweater. With Cole right there. So gorgeous. And so close. It's too much.

**ORION**: It's more beautiful.

**EDEN**: But also more dangerous.

**ORION**: More . . .

**EDEN**: Real.

**ORION**: It scares me sometimes when I stand this close. I wonder what would happen if I fell in.

There's this ache in Cole's voice. And it feels so familiar. Like an echo of my own heart. Without even thinking about it, I reach out and take his hand. It's instinctive. An actor's reflex.

**EDEN**: If you ever fall, I'll save you.

Cole wraps his fingers around mine.

**ORION**: Maybe we can save each other.

It takes me a second to realize that the scene is over, but neither of us has let go.

"That's perfect," Willa whispers. "Avril, I love that you reach out for him there. You make the choice to see where this is going to go. You light the fire."

I see one corner of Cole's mouth twitch up at that, and my face flushes.

We run that scene five or six more times to set it before we move on, and each time I find myself looking forward to that moment. That physical connection. Skin to skin. Cole's hand and mine.

After rehearsal, we gather up on the steps outside the barn. Me, Lex, Jude, Val, and Cole. I look around the group. It seems so weird to think that we've known each other less than a week. We're all joking around. Teasing each other. Talking over the little moments of our shared day. It feels like we've been friends forever.

I'm falling so in love with every single one of them. And that scares me a little. It sets off alarm bells inside my head, because I'm not the kind of girl who just falls in love with people.

Or at least I wasn't before Whisper Cove.

Val and I are pressed close together on one of the hard stone benches. She lays her head on my shoulder and sighs. "Tonight's the night," she tells me. "I'm gonna go call Chester. I have to break things off with him. For good."

"You sure that's what you want?" I ask her.

"Yeah," she says. "I just need something more. You know?"

"Like what?" I ask, and she shrugs.

"I can't even say. I guess I just want to become."

And I know exactly what she means.

"Wish me luck," she says, and I give her hand a squeeze before she heads up to the cabin.

Lex and Jude are leaning against a railing, talking low and private. Lex brushes his golden-red hair out of his eyes, and Jude leans in close to kiss him. Just a quick press of lips, but the casualness of it tells me it isn't a first kiss. Not by a long shot. They giggle when they catch me watching.

Lex comes over to whisper in my ear. "Potential, Av." Then he gives me a wink and a hug before he and Jude head off into the dark, hand in hand.

When they're gone, Cole and I are left alone. He slips into the spot where Val was sitting. "I heard you had lunch with my mom again today," he says.

"Yeah," I tell him. "It was nice."

I'm pretending not to notice the pressure of his thigh against mine.

"She's worried about you," he tells me. "She says it has to be hard. Being here. She asked me if I thought you were holding up all right."

"What'd you tell her?"

Cole rubs his palms on his jeans and laughs, but it isn't that beautiful laugh that I love. This one is twisted up. A little bit painful.

"That if she was really worried about you, she shouldn't have cast you as Eden in the first place."

"Is that all you said?"

He looks at me. "I didn't tell her I caught you lighting fires in the amphitheater. Or about your midnight swim, if that's what you're worried about." I nod, relieved, and Cole stares at me for a few seconds. The heat of his thigh against mine is getting harder to ignore.

"Thanks," I tell him. "For not telling your mom." He shrugs.

"There's plenty of stuff my mother doesn't need to know."

"Does she know about you?" I ask him. "About what you told me. That you hear the whispering."

"I've never told her in those words exactly." He runs his other hand over his face. Rubs at his eyes. I can see how exhausted he is. "I've never said it to anybody else. Besides you. But I think she knows."

I want to ask him about what Glory said. About how he got sent away last year, but I can't find the right words.

"Is that why she's afraid of the water?" I ask. "Because she's afraid for you?"

"Partly. Maybe." Cole sighs. "It wasn't always like that with her. We had a sailboat when I was little. My mom and dad actually won competitions."

"You mean races?"

He laughs, and it sounds more like him. "Say regattas. It sounds fancier." The smile slides off his face. "But all that changed, after . . ." He stops, and I've seen that pause enough times to know what it means.

"After my mom died?"

He nods. "She was different after that. Scared to let me out of her sight. Just totally terrified of the ocean. It was like she saw firsthand how cruel the sea could be, and she wasn't taking any chances with her family. Our house is built on a little cliff, and you used to be able to sit on our back porch and see the ocean. But my mother had a fence put up. There's a gate with a padlock and everything." He shakes his head. "Spent all that money to buy a house overlooking the water, and then put up a huge privacy fence to block the view."

"What did your dad think about that?" I ask, and Cole rolls his eyes.

"Dad isn't allowed to have opinions. My mom's the one who dropped the cash for the house. And the view. And the whole damn theatre, actually. It's all in her name. Officially, she owns Whisper Cove outright, at least on paper. My dad doesn't own shit." I'm not sure what he's getting at, but he lays it out for me. "My mom comes from money. A lot of money. When they met, my dad was a broke off-off-Broadway director with this crazy dream of running a big summer theatre on the shore, but no capital to make it happen. And my mom was a rich girl with big dreams of being famous for something besides being rich." He shrugs again. "So that's the bargain they struck."

"But they must have loved each other," I say. "Right?" And Cole looks at me like I'm being naive.

"I mean, maybe. I'm here, so there's proof they did at least spend time in the same room at one point. But growing up in that house, I can promise you, there's not much love left there, if there ever was any to start with." He looks at me. "What about your mom? What do you remember about her?"

"Nothing," I say, and I feel the hurt of that. I pull my hand away from Cole's and dig the old green notebook out of my bag. "But Glory gave me a couple of things today. Stuff that belonged to my mom. And that helps." I pluck the photograph of me and Cole from its hiding spot between the pages and hand it to him. He stares at it for a long time. I feel the warmth of his body next to mine on the bench.

He radiates heat. And I'm so sick to death of being cold.

"I was lying," he finally admits. "When I said didn't remember you." He touches the little boy in the photograph. That younger, half-hidden version of himself. "I don't remember much, but I remember that we played together."

"I remember you, too," I tell him. "At least kind of. I didn't realize it was you until I saw this photograph. But I remember playing hide-and-seek in the library."

He's studying my face. And he's right there. I can feel his breath against my cheek. I let myself reach out and run my fingers over his tattoo. That compass rose on the soft inside of his wrist. The mark of safety in rough waters. I see him shiver at my touch. And I shiver, too. He's looking at me so intently.

"I'm not making up stories," he tells me. "About the whispering. And the sea." His jaw is clenched so tight he has to work to get the words out. "And I'm not crazy." He looks down at the photo, then back up to me.

"I know," I tell him. But part of me still wonders.

Cole reaches for the strand of hair that's slipped from behind my ear. He takes it between his fingers, and I lean into his touch.

It's instinct.

"Have you ever heard that quote about how life can only be

understood backward," he asks me, "even though it has to be lived forward?" Cole tucks the strand of hair back into place behind my ear, and I shake my head, because I'm feeling a little bit lost. Or distracted, maybe. By his fingers in my hair. "What if you knew how our story ended?"

"There's no way to know that," I say. "We can't know."

"What if we could?" he presses. "Would it matter to you?"

"Is it a sad ending?" I ask him.

"Maybe." He pulls his hand back. Lets it drop to his lap. "Probably."

"I'd still rather enjoy the journey," I tell him. "No matter what." He looks at me for a long time. "What is it?" I finally ask, and he smiles. Hands me back the photograph.

"All this time we were missing each other, and we didn't realize it."

And there's one more hole I hadn't even known I had.

Cole walks me back to my cabin. He says I need to get in. Before the fog comes. We stand together on the front steps. "Thank you for finding me," I tell him. "The other night." I'd been too scared and confused to say it then. Too exhausted. So I say it now.

Cole's eyes burn in the dark. He leans in close. The brush of his lips against my ear feels more like a kiss than a whisper, and goose bumps break out all up and down my arms. "We found each other, Avril."

"Again," I remind him. "We found each other again."

He stares at me for a minute, and I think he really is going to kiss me. That wild intensity in his eyes makes me wonder what his lips would feel like.

He doesn't kiss me, though. He just reaches out and touches

my cheek. Trails his fingers down my neck. And something inside me sparks. "Let's make sure we don't lose each other this time," he says. And all I can do is nod.

When he's gone, I make my way to the bathroom, and by the time I come out, the fog is rolling in. I hurry toward the cabin, anxious to be inside, locked away.

Safe.

I hit the front steps just before it gets too thick to see, and I'm just in time to catch a glimpse of someone disappearing around the corner of the cabin. It's not so much that I see someone. It's more just a sense of movement. A disturbance of the fog.

I run to see who's there. To get a closer look. Because I refuse to be afraid. Not of ghosts and shadows. But it's too late. There's nothing but an ocean of white.

I turn and head back to the front porch, and an overpowering scent hangs heavy in the thick, wet air. It mingles with the salt. Seeps into the dark.

There on the railing, beneath the weak shine of the porch light, I find a little bundle of fresh purple flowers. Lavender. It's tied with simple brown string. And I know it wasn't there before.

I stare for a long few seconds, but I can't bring myself to touch it. Because I don't want to know if it's real.

I push open the door and creep into the cabin. The overhead lights are off, and the girls who are still awake turn to look in my direction, but then they go back to their phones. Or the scripts they're studying by flashlight. Their whispered conversations.

I glance toward Val's bunk, but she's already passed out, so I sit cross-legged on the green rug with my mother's old notebook. I'm afraid to open it up. I can't stop thinking about what Glory said. About how everyone has secrets.

What if I don't find any answers in her notebook?

Or what if I do?

I use my phone for light, thumbing through the pages, running my fingers over the handwritten notes. My mother's very own thoughts in curling, loopy script. It hurts me that I don't even recognize her handwriting. It's nothing like mine.

Each page is dated, starting at the front of the notebook with the very beginning of that last summer. Most of the pages seem to be full of rehearsal notes and character work. But there are also little scrawled reminders to herself. Phone numbers and email addresses. A recipe for lemon pie. A Chinese takeout order. Meeting times. Doodles of sunflowers and spirals.

Nothing really stands out to me until I come across a page in the middle of the notebook. It's mostly blank, just a few words scrawled in the center. They're written in purple ink, and my mother has circled them over and over, pressing hard with the tip of the pen. So many circles that she's almost torn right through the paper.

I close the notebook and slip it back into my backpack, then I crawl into my bunk and shiver beneath the thin, scratchy blanket.

I whisper the circled words into my pillow.

*We know who we are, but not who we may be.*

# ACT II: SCENE 5

The next day is Saturday. There are no classes or work assignments, but it's a full day of rehearsals, so we don't get to sleep in. I groan along with all the others when my alarm goes off, and I join the zombie-like procession of girls headed to the bathroom.

The bouquet of lavender is still lying on the porch railing this morning. It's damp and drooping. Wet with fog that's settled into dew.

But it's still there.

Which means it's real.

Which means someone left it there. For me.

I fake my way through breakfast. Laugh at Jude's jokes while my mind works. Promise Lex and Val that everything's fine. Eat half a muffin, just to make it more convincing. But the whole time, I'm wondering about those little purple flowers.

Ghosts don't leave gifts. Right?

In rehearsal, we spend the morning and the first part of the afternoon working scenes we've already done. Willa wants those sections polished before we move on. And things go so well that I start to feel a little better. When I'm onstage and things are really clicking, I can almost convince myself that all the strangeness of the past week never happened. That Whisper Cove is just what I told Lex it was on that very first night, summer camp without the god-awful canoeing.

"Beautiful work, lovelies," Willa finally tells us late in the day. "Time to move on to something new. This is the third meeting between Eden and Orion. It's nighttime. Dark outside. And Eden comes to meet Orion beside the river."

Jude picks up the blanket from the prop table and tosses it to Cole, who spreads it out on the stage floor.

"Okay, you two," Willa says. "This is the scene where things really start to heat up between Eden and Orion. So I need you to dig deep."

I nod and sneak a glance at Cole as he bends to pick up the guitar. His fingers glide over the strings, and suddenly all I can think about is his touch. Last night. Him reaching for my hand. Those fingers on my neck. The brush of his lips against my ear.

Shared secrets.

"From the top of the scene," Willa says. "Whenever you're ready." So I give Cole time to get settled on the blanket. He plays the opening notes of that melody. Eden's song. And my heartbeat slows to match the music. Some memory is tugging at me. It's right there. Just below the surface. But I can't get my mind around it. It's still too slippery. So I let a few bars go by before I take a deep breath and start with the first line.

**EDEN**: Hi.

Cole stops playing and turns to look at me.

**ORION**: I didn't know if you'd come tonight.
**EDEN**: You were playing my song, so I had to come.

Cole raises one eyebrow at me. He's almost smiling, but not quite.

**ORION**: Promise me you'll always come if I play that song for you.
**EDEN**: I will. I promise. It's the only song I know.

Cole smiles at me then. A real smile.

**ORION**: Come and sit beside me.

I walk toward the blanket, and Cole holds out one hand. I take it and lower myself to the floor, but Cole doesn't let go. My palms are sweaty, and I'm afraid to look at his face.

**EDEN**: Why did you want me to meet you here tonight?
**ORION**: So I could give you the stars. You said they made you happy, so I wanted you to have them. They're yours, Eden. All of them.

Cole makes a sweeping gesture with one arm, and I lift my eyes up toward the loft, but instead of stage lights, I see stars. A million twinkling stars are strung out across an inky night sky like sparkling jewels on a necklace. They're too beautiful to be real, and I know that. It makes me ache to look at them, so I close my eyes. And when I open them again, the stage lights are back. The stars are gone.

And I miss them.

**EDEN**: Thank you. I wish I'd brought something to give you.

**ORION**: You came tonight. That's enough.

**EDEN**: Do you believe in fate?

**ORION**: I don't know. Do you?

**EDEN**: I never have before. But I guess maybe I do now, because I think you and I were meant to find each other.

Cole touches me, and one by one I watch the stage lights turn to stars. "Again," he says. "We were meant to find each other again, Avril."

"It's beautiful here," I whisper. "The water. And the moonlight."

His fingers are on my cheek. I can't breathe. I feel dizzy and drunk. And Cole is leaning in. His mouth is so close when he whispers that I'm beautiful. I know he's finally going to kiss me.

But before his lips touch mine, the scent of lavender fills my nose.

I turn my head and my mother is standing there, silhouetted against the dark like a lighthouse. White-blonde hair. Flashing green eyes. She's a signal beacon. A warning to sailors.

She reaches for me. There's the *clickety-clack* of bony fingers. And the sound of wind chimes. It's a beautiful, musical tinkling. Light and breezy and carried on the wind.

But for some reason, it fills me with dread.

That pretty sound makes my blood run cold.

And then my mother is gone. She's vanished. Just disappeared.

One minute there. The next minute not.

My stars start to drop from the sky. They streak across the blackness and land in the water.

*Plop.*

*Plop. Plop.*

*Plop.*

Like the sound of an almost memory.

*Look at the stars.*

Blinding light. I cover my eyes. Close them tight.

Something goes around my wrist. Something cold. I want to scream, but I can't. I'm frozen. Someone is tugging on me. I grab for something. Anything. But my mother is gone and there's nothing in the whole world to hang on to.

And then I'm falling.

Falling.

Falling.

Falling.

I don't hit the ground this time. Because someone catches me. I open my eyes, and Cole's face swims into focus. His eyes are dark. More the color of heavy storm clouds than fog. "Hey," he breathes into my ear. "You almost passed out."

I untangle myself from Cole and take an unsteady step back so I can breathe. My chest heaves. I'm panicking. Everyone is watching me. Lex is on his feet in the second row.

"I'm fine," I say, but my voice sounds funny. Like it's coming from deep inside a well.

"Avril . . ." Cole takes a step toward me. I feel myself start to fall again, but this time I'm tumbling toward his eyes.

"Let's take ten," Willa says. "Avril looks like she could use a break." She glances around the theatre. "Everyone step outside. Get some fresh air." The way she says it, it's clearly more than a suggestion. The others all file out, but Lex and Val are looking over their shoulders at me even as Jude is leading them away.

"Come on," I hear Jude tell them. "She's good. Willa has her."

The barn door creaks closed, and Willa turns to Cole. "Give us a few minutes," she says, but he doesn't move.

"It's okay," I tell him. "I'm okay."

"You sure?" Cole asks me, and I nod. Because Willa has me. He doesn't look convinced, though.

When he's gone, Willa leads me over to a couple of chairs in the first row.

"How are you?" she asks, and I can see the concern in her eyes. "Tell me the truth." Her voice is firm, but gentle. Motherly. And suddenly I don't want to hide anymore. Not from Willa.

"Something weird is happening to me," I admit. I almost tell her about the woman in the fog and the lavender on the front porch, but I don't. Instead, I start with the pieces I might be able to make sense of. "It's like my brain is trying to remind me of something. But I don't know what it is."

Willa sighs. "What do you remember?" she asks. "About the night your mother drowned."

"Not much," I tell her. "Not anything, really. Just bits and pieces. But it's all out of order."

"Tell me anyway," Willa urges. "Maybe I can help you put some of those pieces together." She reaches up and runs a hand over my hair. "Maybe that would bring you some healing." Her hand slips down to touch my cheek. "God knows you deserve a little peace after all these years."

I hesitate, because I've never really talked to anyone about this before. But she's listening in that way she has. Nobody else has ever listened to be me like that. And it makes me want to be heard.

"It starts with this crazy bright light. Like blinding. Right in my eyes." I swallow hard. Will myself to stay present in the barn. I refuse to get lost again. "That's a new memory," I tell her. "I didn't remember it before I came here. And somebody—my mother, I guess—has a death grip on my wrist. That's new, too. And I remember the cold. Just this awful, freezing cold." I shiver. "The kind of cold that goes so deep it hurts. And I almost remember something about my mother's eyes, I think. And the dark. The sound of wind chimes, maybe."

I feel goose bumps break out along my arms. That brand-new memory. I've never heard that sound until tonight. A strange musical tinkling carried on the night air. Even just thinking about it leaves me feeling so afraid.

Willa looks confused. "Wind chimes?" I nod, even though I know none of this makes sense.

"Then there's a feeling of falling," I say. "Or flying, really. And—" I stop.

"And what?" Willa prompts. "There's something else."

I shake my head. "The rest of it is so weird."

"Go on, Avril."

"None of this makes any sense. I was dead. When they found

me, I didn't have a pulse. I wasn't breathing and—" My heart starts to race. Panic rises in my throat.

"I know." Willa's hand is on my knee, and her voice is so gentle. I remember what Glory said about that morning. When George found me on the beach.

"Glory said you went with me to the hospital. She said you didn't leave my side until my dad got here."

Willa nods. "You were so little. I didn't want you to be afraid."

"But that's where this weird memory comes from," I tell her. "At least that's what the doctors said. It's just my brain playing tricks."

"Tell me anyway," she says. "Maybe it'll help." Willa is like a bulldog. I wonder if she's ever given up on anything.

"Okay." I breathe in the smell of the theatre. No horses today. Just the familiar scent of wood and paint. "I remember falling stars."

"You mean like shooting stars?" Willa asks. But I shake my head.

"No. I mean falling stars. I have this bizarre memory of stars falling right out of the sky and landing in the sea. I remember the glow of them. And the sound they made when they hit the water. And I remember this voice saying, '*Look at the stars.*'"

"What kind of voice?" Willa asks, and I shrug.

"My mother's voice, I guess. I can't ever hear it when I'm awake." There's this gulf of hurt that opens up inside of me and I guess Willa can feel it, because she puts her arm around me and pulls me close. It's a little weird at first, but then I relax. And it feels good to be held like that. By her. "I told you it didn't make any sense. But I dream about it all the time. For as long as I can remember. Those falling stars. And that voice."

"Nicole had the most beautiful voice," Willa tells me, and I hear that same ache in her words. The one I feel in my heart. It's like the hurt is a magnet. It pulls us together. I let my head fall against her shoulder, and she sighs. "It's one of the first things I noticed when we met."

"I wish I could remember what she sounded like." I sigh, too. A soft sound that matches Willa's. "I wish I could remember anything about her."

"You don't remember her voice at all?" Willa seems so surprised, but I just shake my head. "You've never heard it on tape or anything?"

"We don't have any videos," I explain. "Dad says they were all in a computer file that got deleted somehow." Secretly, I've always wondered if maybe he erased them from our lives on purpose, like he erased everything else about her.

"What about your grandmother?" she asks. "Nicole's mother. Surely she—"

I cut her off. "She died not long after my mother did. I'd only been out of the hospital a few weeks when it happened."

"Wow," Willa says, and the softness of the word gets absorbed by the old wood of the barn. "I can understand. To lose a child like that. Her heart must have been literally broken."

"Dad says we need to move on," I tell her. "That I need to move on. Forget about it, but . . ." I hesitate, because I'm never sure how to explain the way I feel about all of this. "How do you forget something you can't even remember in the first place?"

"I have some videos of Nicole," Willa tells me. "Really old ones from college, but some from that last summer, too. I'll dig them up and we can watch them together."

My heart is in my throat. I have to talk around it. "I'd like that."

Willa gets this faraway look in her eyes. "It was just so perfect, having her here that summer. I mean, things were hard. Whisper Cove was losing money fast, and we were having trouble getting performers to sign on. But then Nicole agreed to come, and to me, that was the same as winning the lottery. That's why it was so awful—so out of the blue—when she—" She stops. I feel her breathing. "When she did what she did."

I'm confused. "What do you mean?"

Willa stares down at me. "Avril. Honey." Her voice is so gentle. "Your mother killed herself. Didn't you know that?"

I sit up and pull away. Because that's not true. It can't be true. "It w-was an accident," I stammer. "I—"

Willa shakes her head. Squeezes my hand. "It wasn't an accident. It couldn't have been. That's the thing that haunts me." She reaches up to tuck her hair behind her ear. "That's the thing that haunts all of us."

"How do you know?"

"It was so early in the morning when George found you down there. On the beach. It was cold that morning. Huge waves. It had been raining, and there was a storm rolling in. And you were still in your nightgown." Glory told me all that, but I hadn't thought about what those details might mean. "Who takes a little girl swimming late at night? Or at the crack of dawn? In rough surf. In her nightgown."

My head is spinning.

"I don't—"

"And there were other signs. The way we found her sweater folded on the beach. Her shoes lined up there, so neat. It's something people do sometimes, evidently, when they—" She stops. Pulls me hard against her. "I'm so sorry, Avril. It's all in the official report. I didn't realize you didn't know." I feel her tense up. "Your father should have told you."

"Why?" I say. "I don't— Why would she do that?"

Willa shrugs. "It's impossible, isn't it? To really know what's going on inside someone else's head." She looks up toward the loft of the barn. "I know what some people think. What the stories say. But I don't expect I'll ever know the truth."

"You mean the stories about her being called into the sea."

Willa nods. "And I think they're at least partly true."

I can't believe she'd say that. Cole is one thing, with his sea-glass tokens and his campfire stories. His sailor's tattoo.

But Willa?

"What do you mean?" I ask her. "How can that be true?"

"I think Nicole was being pursued. I think she always had been." Willa turns to look at me, and I guess I look as surprised as I feel. "Not by ghosts," she clarifies. "Or by the sea. By something harder to identify. Something inside her own head."

I remember what Cole said the first night I was here, when he gave me that blue sea glass.

*There are lots of ways to be haunted.*

"Maybe I shouldn't have told you that," Willa says. "But you came here because you wanted to know your mother, and I figured you deserve to know all of her." She gives me a long look. "I think you're strong enough to handle the truth."

Jude pokes his head in the door and apologizes for interrupting. "Almost time for dinner. Should I let everyone go?"

“Might as well,” Willa says. “It’s been a long week. Let’s just leave it here for today.”

Jude closes the barn door, and I hear him yell that everyone can leave. Willa gives my shoulders a squeeze, then gets up and starts gathering her things. But I can’t move yet. I’m struggling under the weight of her revelation.

Willa is refolding the blanket that Cole tossed onto the prop table. I hear the jangle of bracelets. She shakes her head. “That kid never could clean up after himself.” She puts the blanket where it belongs and turns to look at me.

“Was she unhappy with my dad?” I ask. “Was there something wrong between them?” I’m grasping for a reason that makes sense. I need to know if Glory was right about her having a secret. Something she was keeping to herself. Anything that might explain what she did.

“That’s a question for your father, Avril. I can tell you what I think, but he’s the only one who can answer that for sure.” Willa comes back to where I’m still sitting. She squeezes my shoulder. “It’s a lot to process,” she says. “I’m sorry.”

“No,” I say. “Thank you for telling me.” I get up to gather my things, and Willa watches me.

“You deserve to know the truth.” She moves the ghost light center stage. Reaches down to plug it in. It starts to glow. Soft and warm. “These kinds of things are worse if you leave them in the dark.” She gives me a little smile. “Get some sleep tonight. Okay?” She looks so beautiful there, one half of her face in shadow. “I can tell how tired you are.”

"Yeah," I say. "I'll try."

Val is waiting for me outside. Lex, too. He's stretched out on a bench with his head in Jude's lap, but he sits up as soon as he sees me.

"You okay?" he asks.

"Yeah," I tell him. "I just wanna go change before dinner." The day started off sunny, but the sky has turned gray and it's threatening rain. The temperature is dropping and I'm suddenly cold.

So, so, so cold.

"I'm gonna come with you," Val announces, and she links her arm through mine.

"No," I tell her. "I'm fine. I promise. I really just need to be alone for a few minutes."

Val and Lex exchange looks.

"You know you can talk to us, right?" Jude is staring at me with those big brown eyes. He pushes his curls back off his forehead and looks around the group. "We're all here, if you need us."

"Thanks," I tell him. "But I don't even know what I need right now." I smile. Try my best to look okay. "You guys just go on to dinner. I'll catch up."

"We'll save you a spot," Val says. "Okay?"

"Yeah," I say. "Thanks."

"Av—" Lex starts. He's reluctant to leave me, but Jude pulls him along. "Come on," I hear him say as he slips an arm around Lex's waist. "Give 'er a little space." And the three of them start off toward the cafeteria.

I wander toward the cabin, but I change course at the last minute and head across the lawn to one of the hugest trees I've ever seen. It's gnarled and twisted, with branches moving in all directions. Low ones. Like thick arms snaking across the grass. Reaching for something.

Reaching for me, maybe. Welcoming me home.

There's a tiny stage tucked into the base of the tree, almost totally surrounded by leaves. The Hidden Theatre, they call it. It's one of the private rehearsal spaces. There are three or four of them nestled in quiet spots around the Whisper Cove grounds.

I step onto the stage, and it's like I've been swallowed by the tree. I'm protected. Safe. And that feels good.

I wonder what kind of tree this is. Dad would know. That's one of his areas of specialty. Trees. A long time ago, he taught me the names for all the ones we have in Texas. Back when we were still trying with each other.

There are a few little benches, but I choose to sit on one of the giant, gnarled limbs. It's low enough that my feet just barely brush the ground. I dig Lex's lighter out of my bag and flick it with my thumb a few times. The last time, I hold the wheel down and the flame glows hot. I hold my palm just above it. I leave it too long, and the pain is intense. I'll have a blister there. I know it. But I do it again. Just to make sure.

And it hurts like fuck. It hurts so bad. It burns. Turns red. Blisters. Like I knew it would.

And finally I can cry. Because I know I'm still alive.

"Hey." The word is whispered. Soft. Like the brush of leaves against limbs. But it still makes me jump. When I turn to look over my shoulder, Cole is leaning against the trunk of the tree. Watching me. He's almost hidden in the shadows.

"What are you doing here?" I ask. It sounds a little like an accusation, but Cole smiles.

"This is my hiding place," he tells me. "You found me this time."

Maybe I should feel ashamed. Embarrassed that he caught me. Crying like this. But I'm not. All I feel is relieved that something drew me here. To Cole's hidden sanctuary.

Something drew me to him.

Just like it drew him to me that night on the beach. In the fog.

When he comes to sit beside me on the branch, it doesn't even move under our weight. That's how big it is. How solid. "What happened?" he asks me. "Tonight at rehearsal?"

"I don't know," I tell him. Because I'm too tired to pretend. "It was like I got lost. Inside my mind. Or my memory. Or whatever."

I wish I'd chosen other words, because I hear the echo of what Willa said earlier. About my mother being pursued by something inside her own head.

Cole nods, like he knows exactly what I mean. "Sometimes I remember things that didn't happen. Couldn't have happened. You know? Or I'll go to do something, and I'll know that I've done it before."

He takes my hand and turns it palm up. He looks at the mark the fire left there. It's red. Blistered. Just a little kiss from the flame.

He runs a hand over the blister, and I suck in air between my teeth. "Fuck," I say. And I flinch. But it feels good to be touched.

It even feels good to hurt.

"Feel that?" he asks, and I nod. Tears sting my eyes.

"Yeah. I feel it."

He slips his arms around me and pulls me against his chest.

"Whatever's happening to you, tell me. I'll understand. I promise." He tilts my chin up toward his face. "And I'll help if you'll let me."

"How?"

"When you feel that tug, that pull toward the sea, I can pull back. In the other direction. I can refuse to let you get close to the edge." He pauses. "And you can do the same for me." He drops his voice to a husky whisper. I feel the reverberation of it under his ribs. "And if we do that, maybe we can save each other."

I'm watching the shifting patterns on the ground in front of me. Moonlight filters through the leaves. A gust of wind shakes the branches, and the tree is suddenly alive. Everything is in motion. Blowing in the wind.

"What do you need saving from?" I ask him. I want him to tell me about the circles under his eyes. The darkness around the edges of him. The parts of him that are sore and broken. I want to hear about the things that haunt him. I need him to name his ghosts for me. Because I have this aching need to know Cole Culver. Really know him. Again. Like when we were little. "What is it you're so afraid of?"

He opens his mouth, and I think he's going to tell me. But then I feel his fingers in my hair. Something inside me twists, and before I stop to wonder if I should, I'm pressing my lips against his neck. I hear Cole gasp in surprise, and he drops one hand down my back to slide it under my shirt.

My breath comes in a rush. I'm pressing myself harder against him. I want more contact. More of my lips on his neck. More of his heart beating against my ribs. More of his fingers on my skin.

I find his ear. Tease it with my lips. And my teeth. I feel him shudder. He breathes my name into the dark. Slides his palm across my back.

It's the scratch of a match.

The sizzle of flames.

My whole body has been lit on fire. And I've never felt heat like this.

Not when I first crouched in the courtyard of our apartment back home, hunkered against the Texas wind, trying to get a pile of leaves to ignite.

Not when I was ten and set off the school sprinkler system lighting toilet paper in the bathroom sink.

Or when I burned my gym bag in the alley eighth-grade year, just to see how big the flames would get.

Definitely not when Denton Erikson rammed his tongue down my throat in the back seat of his car after the winter formal last February.

Not with anybody else. Ever.

But Cole makes me feel so much. And not all of it is good. Some of it is confusing. And a lot of it is scary. But all of it is real.

Because Cole makes me feel alive.

He pulls back a little and takes a shaky breath. "You okay?" he asks. And that strikes me as funny. It makes me giggle, because I feel so strange and giddy all of a sudden. Disoriented. Like I just got off some spinning ride at the fair.

It's dizzying, going from desperate and lost and hurting to this wanting feeling that's so strong I can't see straight. But Cole's face is serious. So I nod.

"Yeah," I tell him. "I'm okay." And I really feel like I am. At least for this moment.

He reaches out to touch my cheek. Something sparks inside me again. But it's a candle this time. Not a bonfire.

"This is a second chance," he tells me, and I nod. "For both of us."

I let Cole take my hand and lead me back toward my cabin. The fog is suddenly everywhere, when it was nowhere just moments ago. It has a solidness to it. A heaviness that makes it hard to move. It's like walking through deep water. That swirling mist reaches for me with damp fingers, but Cole's hand keeps me anchored.

We don't get lost.

He touches my face again before he says good night. And then he slips into the dark, and I climb the wooden steps. I'm suddenly disappointed, because I realize I still haven't felt his lips against mine.

"Avril."

I turn back toward Cole and smile. Because maybe this is when he kisses me.

Finally.

Except there's nobody there.

Nobody at all.

But then I hear my name again. "Avril."

"Lex?"

I put my hand on the wooden railing and feel my way down the stairs.

One step.

Two steps.

Three steps.

Then four, five, six.

There shouldn't be that many. Should there?

Then the crunch of gravel. More whispering. I'm still hanging on to the handrail.

"Who's there?" I ask.

I let go and take one step into the fog. Just one. And I'm immediately swallowed up. Lost. There's nothing. I can't even feel the ground under my feet anymore. It's like trying to touch bottom in a pool that's deeper than you think.

The smell of lavender fills my nose.

"Avril!" My name again. But different this time. It's shouted. Not whispered. "Av, where are you?"

"Lex?" I'm certain that's who it is this time. That Tennessee drawl gives him away.

I see the beam of a flashlight slicing through the thick fog.

"Av?"

"I'm here," I say, and I reach for the handrail. I was just holding it a second ago. But now it's not there, so I start to tumble.

Lex grabs me by the arm. "Holy shit," he says. "You're a block of ice." He's waiting for me to say something. But I can't. "Av? What are you doing back here?"

"I . . ." My voice isn't working any better than my brain.

"What's that in your hand?" Lex asks me. And I look down at the little bundle of lavender clutched in my fist. I drop it fast. Like the flowers are on fire. "Where am I?"

Lex turns the light away from me then. It bounces off a white wall just a few feet in front of us.

My mother's name. Bright red. On the back of the scene shop. The date she died.

*What the sea wants, the sea will have.*

My head spins and I sway on my feet. Lex's arm is suddenly tight around my waist.

"I was with Jude," he tells me. "In the garden. And I heard you talking to someone."

"I don't remember," I tell him. "I don't remember anything."

How I got here.

Where that lavender came from.

Lex studies the red words. His flashlight beam slips over every bloody letter. "That's your mother, isn't it?" he asks, and I nod. "Come on," he says. "Let's get out of here."

Lex leads me back to my cabin. "I'm staying with you tonight," he tells me as he half drags, half carries me up the steps.

One.

Two.

Three.

"You don't have to do that, Lex."

"It's a done deal," he says firmly. "I never should have left you alone tonight to begin with." And I can tell by the sound in his voice that there's no point in arguing with him, so I let Lex take me by the hand and quietly open the door.

We tiptoe toward my lower bunk, kick off our shoes, and slip in under the covers together, both of us still dressed.

"Talk to me, Av." Lex's voice is low in my ear. Tender and gentle. "Please." The sound of it cracks open some sealed-up place inside me.

"All this time, I believed it was an accident." I'm staring at the bunk above me. Whispering. But my words still feel too loud in the silent cabin. My throat is hoarse. "What happened to my mother. And to me." I turn to look at Lex, because I need to see his eyes in the dark. "But that was a lie."

A lie my father told me.

"People think she walked into the water because the sea was calling her. That's what Jude said." Lex doesn't say the next part, but I feel it hanging in the air between us.

"And she tried to take me with her."

He nods, close enough to me that I feel the kiss of his red hair against my forehead. "That's how the story goes."

When I first remembered that cold hand on my wrist, I thought—assumed, I guess—that it was my mother's hand, and that she'd been trying to save me. To save both of us. But what if she'd been trying to drag me down with her instead?

That fits with the images that have been running through my head. The weird bits of memory that have been bubbling up to the surface in all those strange moments.

I can't really believe that story. That my mother was the victim of some kind of curse. Or whatever.

But I also don't want to believe that my mother made the choice, all on her own, to hold my hand and walk into Long Island Sound one stormy summer night.

It's all too fucking much. I want to cry some more. Or scream. Kick and punch something. But I can't. Because I'm numb again. Cold.

Empty.

Shivering.

I feel Lex's arms go around me. He pulls me into the warmth

of his body. So solid and real and strong. And just knowing he's there—my best friend—sharing the darkness with me, gives me so much comfort.

It doesn't stop me from sneaking out of bed, though, later that night. It doesn't keep me from wandering to the window.

And it doesn't stop the shock that runs through me when I see the figure moving in the moonlight. Whispering through the fog.

It isn't my mother, this time, though.

It's Cole.

I watch him cross the muddy field from the farmhouse toward our cabin, and when I creep to the door and ease it open, he's sitting there on the front steps, back hunched against the chill. Dark hair clinging to his forehead.

"I couldn't sleep," he tells me, without turning his head to look behind him. "So I figured I might as well sit here as anywhere else."

I step out onto the porch. Touch his damp hair. Then I settle down on the step beside him. I slip my hand into his.

Cole doesn't look at me. His eyes are searching the fog. "You don't have to stay up," he says. "Go on to bed."

"No." I shake my head. "I'll sit with you tonight."

Because this is how we save each other.

# ACT II: SCENE 6

Cole and I sit together though the darkest, coldest part of the night. Side by side. Until the sun starts to come up. It's Sunday, our day off. So once the fog clears, Cole tells me to go to bed. I don't want to leave him, but I can barely keep my eyes open. So I go and crawl under the covers with Lex, and he pulls me into his arms without even opening his eyes. I fall asleep there, curled up in the crook of his shoulder.

When I wake up again, the sun is already bright outside the window. Some of the other girls are still asleep. But Lex is gone.

And I'm sure Cole is, too.

We're all supposed to go out for lunch together. Me, Jude, Lex, Val, and Cole. Jude got permission from Willa to use the van. There's some seafood place he wants us to try.

I roll over and grab my phone. It's almost ten o'clock, so I've got like two hours to kill. I decide to take a shower and then find a quiet place to go over my lines. We're working new scenes starting tomorrow, and I want to be prepared.

I get cleaned up and head back over to the Hidden Theatre. And maybe that's because I'm halfway hoping Cole will be there again. But it's also because there's something I love about the way this little space is almost a part of the tree. How it's separate from everything else at Whisper Cove.

I open my bag to get out my script, but I get distracted by the sight of my mother's notebook. I pull it out and flip through it, studying each entry. I'm looking for any possible clue. Something that might explain why she did what she did. But it's so hard. The pages are crowded with notes and doodles. And most of the scribbled phrases are impossible to decipher. There are random words scrawled in the margins.

*Need more.*

*Not enough feeling.*

*Too much.*

Acting notes? Maybe? Probably. But what if they mean something darker? I can't tell what makes sense and what's my imagination filling in the blanks.

I turn to the page I noticed the other night. Those words circled again and again, so many times that my mother has almost destroyed the paper.

*We know what we are, but not what we may be.*

I whisper the words out loud, and the leaves of the tree seem to whisper them back.

Nothing else leaps out at me, though. At least not until I turn to the very last page my mother ever wrote on. It's dated August 22.

It's the exclamation points that make me take notice. There are three of them. But it's also the way the letters seem tense. More angled and desperate than the others.

*B. C.—Figure out how to end it!!!*

I stare at the words, and at first I can't figure out what they could possibly mean. My brain is kicking out hundreds of possibilities, but none of them make sense.

Then, suddenly, I feel queasy. Dazed and sick. Because I realize there's only one B. C. around here. Everybody knows that.

Brody Culver.

I think about that picture on the wall in his office. The way my mother was looking at him. All smiles. Laughing. With her hand on his arm.

I remember how he told me himself that he'd wanted her to stay. The way he stood there staring at her photo, even after I left. That look on his face.

Oh fuck. Please don't let this mean what I think it means.

Before I can talk myself out of it, I reach into my backpack and pull out my phone. Dad picks up on the first ring, and it's strange to hear his voice. We've texted a few times, but I haven't talked to him since he dropped me off at the airport in Dallas. That was six days and a lifetime ago.

"Everything okay?" he asks after I say hello. His voice is tense. He's worried. I can tell. Afraid he was right. That this wasn't a good idea.

But there's no way I'm going to give him that.

"Were you and Mom having problems that summer?" There are a few moments of stunned silence on the other end of the line. "Dad?"

"I'm here," he says. But his voice sounds like maybe he really isn't.

"Is that why we came up here, me and Mom?" I hesitate, but I can't resist twisting the knife just a little bit. "Was she trying to get away from you?"

He mutters something under his breath. Something in French that I don't quite catch. Then he says, "She was mostly trying to get away from herself, I think." There's another long moment of silence on the other end of the phone. "But we were having problems, yes."

"Why didn't you ever tell me that?" I ask.

"Why would I have?" He sounds genuinely confused. And that pretty much sums up our relationship. Two perpetual hiders, trying to live with each other. "Did *she* tell you that?" he asks. And I don't have to ask who the *she* in question is. There's a sound in his voice that reminds me of the look on Willa's face when I mentioned my father. It's the vocal equivalent of a frown.

"Yeah," I say. "She's told me a lot of stuff I never knew about Mom."

"Did she tell you your mother wasn't planning on coming home?" There's a bitterness in his voice I haven't heard before, and it throws me a little bit, because it makes it seem like he might have really cared.

"What do you mean?" I ask.

"She called me not long before—" He stops. Seems to backtrack a little. "Just before she died. And she said she wasn't coming back. That she was going to stay up there."

She.

But he means *we*. Right?

Again, I'm an afterthought. He's never seemed to understand that I'm a part of this equation. That I'm a real, actual person, and even if I can't remember it, whatever happened up here that summer affected my life in a huge way.

"Did she say why?" I ask him.

"I think she must've met someone, Avril. That's all I could figure out. We never got the chance to talk about it."

And there it is. I didn't even have to ask him.

My mother had met someone. Someone she was planning to start over with. Somebody worth leaving for.

I guess, in the end, she couldn't figure out how to end it with B. C. So she was ending it with my dad instead.

Maybe she'd decided she was finally ready to *become*.

"I gotta go," I say, and I hear my father start to say something, but my finger is already ending the call.

My legs feel funny, and I slump against the giant tree. It's hot today. And I'm sweating.

My mother was having an affair with Brody Culver.

Her best friend's husband.

I jump when I hear the van horn honk. It can't be noon already, but I check my phone, and it is. I cram my script and my mother's notebook back into my bag and hurry across the lawn to where Jude has the van parked in front of the big yellow farmhouse.

Lex is already in the passenger seat next to Jude, and he gives me a worried look when I climb in. I flash my biggest smile, though, to prove that I'm okay. Because he deserves to enjoy his day off. Without worrying about me.

Val is in the middle seat. She has her backpack and sweater spread out, so the only real spot for me is in the back. Next to Cole. Val gives me a not-at-all-subtle wink, and I know things have been arranged that way on purpose.

I think about last night. Cole's breath on my skin. The way his fingers tangled in my hair.

"Hey," he says as I slide in beside him. Then he drops his voice to a whisper. "You get any sleep?" I'm looking out the window, but I feel his hand on my thigh. The press of skin on skin.

My stomach knots up. This is who we are now. We're two people who touch each other. Like this. And that seems so strange. But also so absolutely right.

It feels like it was inevitable.

"Yeah," I say.

I should tell him about what happened before he came to sit vigil on the front steps. But I don't, because I'm still not sure what that was.

How did I end up behind the scene shop, when I had just stepped off the cabin porch?

And I should tell him about what I just read in my mother's notebook. About B. C.

But I can't. How do I say that I've just discovered my mother was having an affair with his dad?

I push all that away. Because I just need a break from everything this afternoon. A little bit of seafood and sunshine.

Something normal.

We're making our way down the long, winding driveway now, heading toward the main road. It's hard to believe it was just one week ago today that I first laid eyes on Whisper Cove, that evening Jude picked me up at the train station. It feels like I've been here forever.

George is putting up a sign at the main entrance. MIDNIGHT MUSIC, it says. JULY 18, 7:00 P.M. TICKETS ON SALE NOW!

Our show. Starring me as Eden. Just three weeks away.

"He kind of gives me the creeps," Val admits. "The way he's always watching us."

"George isn't so bad," Jude says. "Did you guys know he's friends with Jimmy Buffett? Like they used to hang out and shit."

"Who?" Lex asks.

"Seriously, Lex?" Val shakes her head.

It only takes us a few minutes to reach the restaurant, a little shack just up the road from the theatre. ANSON'S LOBSTER, the sign says. It's right on the water, and a six-foot-tall, bright red crustacean greets us in the parking lot. He's cut out of plywood, his arm frozen in a permanent wave, and he looks awfully cheery, considering he stands around presiding over the murder of his kin all day.

"You ever had lobster before?" Cole asks me as we pile out of the van.

"Yeah." I roll my eyes at him, because I'm from Dallas. Not Mars. "We have a Red Lobster like two minutes from our apartment."

He laughs out loud, and it hits me again how much I love the sound of it. It's deep and real and open. "Trust me," he says. "That doesn't count."

We wait in line to place our order. I settle on a hot lobster roll and clam chowder, and we all gather up at a picnic table on the water.

Val leans against me. Her head is lazy on my shoulder. And it feels so good. "Jesus," she says. "Could this place be any more perfect? This whole summer is like a fucking postcard."

Jude has his arm slung around Lex, and Lex looks so happy and relaxed. They're taking selfies. The two of them with wide smiles and sunglasses. Big, colorful sailboats in the background. I have this pang of sadness when I wonder what happens for them in three weeks. But I push that thought out of my head. I don't want to think about it.

I don't want to think about what happens to any of us when this ends.

Not yet. Today is for living in the moment.

Jude leaves to use the bathroom, and a crackly voice comes over the loudspeaker. "Number twenty-seven."

"That's us," Cole says, and he gets up to grab our order. Val offers to help him. When they see how long the line at the pickup window is, Cole looks back at me and shrugs.

Lex slides into the seat next to me, filling Cole's empty space.

"How you doing today?" he asks me. His voice is low, and his blue eyes are worried.

"That depends," I tease. "Are you gonna share some of your clam strips?" But he doesn't let me get away with that.

"What were you doing back there, Av? Last night?"

"I don't know," I tell him. "I just ended up there somehow." The way he's looking at me, with so much obvious concern, it makes me want to tell him everything.

"Were you sleepwalking?"

I shrug. "Not really. I don't think I was asleep." He's staring at me. "I just got lost, I guess."

"Av—"

"How are things with you and Jude?" I nudge him with my shoulder, and he turns as red as the big plywood lobster out front.

"Good," he says. His smile spreads all the way across his face, and I know he's thinking about Jude's loose, dark curls and easy grin. "Really good. I've never had anything like this before. Shit. I've never had anything at all." He hesitates. "Not since Sam."

And boom. There it is. The name drop I've been waiting for all week. I knew there was someone.

"Who's Sam?" I ask him. "An old boyfriend?"

"No," Lex says. "Not really. Just a guy I knew." But the look in his eyes tells me different. "He's off at college now. Somewhere in Mississippi." Lex lets out a long breath. "He was a senior when I was a sophomore, and we used to sit out in his truck and listen to music for hours after football games and stuff."

"And?" I prompt.

"And that's it," Lex admits. "Nothing ever happened. I mean, we flirted a lot. But it never went any further than that. Not one single kiss. We never even held hands." He sighs. "But, God. The way we talked. I've never talked to anybody like that."

"Were you in love with him?" I ask.

"I think so." Lex shrugs. "But how the hell are you supposed to know, when you've never felt like that before?" He steals one of my oyster crackers. Crunches it between his teeth. "That summer, after Sam graduated and went away, I hooked up with some random guy from out of town in the back room at a friend's party. It was awful, but it was my first time." He sighs. "Fuck. I don't even remember his name. Dylan, maybe. Or something like that."

"So, you're writing a new story this summer," I say, and Lex nods.

"And maybe that turns out to be a love story," he tells me. "And maybe it just turns out to be a fun story. Either way. I'm sure as shit gonna find out." He looks at me. "What about you?"

I turn around to check on Cole. He and Val are still waiting in line.

"I've never had a love story," I say. "Not even a sad one."

Lex raises a red eyebrow in my direction. "It's time you had a real love story, then, Avril. You deserve one."

That makes me smile, but it makes me uncomfortable, too. Because I'm not ready to fall that hard. Lex is still looking at me, and I remember how he found me in the fog last night and took me home. How he curled up next to me and held me tight. "You can be my love story," I tease, and Lex grins from ear to ear. But it's totally true. I'm already so in love with him.

I know that's not what he means, though.

I look back at Cole again, and he smiles in my direction. Runs his fingers through those dark waves. My stomach drops. I can't stop thinking about his fingers in my hair.

Lex giggles. "Have you kissed him yet?" he whispers, and I shake my head.

"Not really." But I feel the striking of a match. My face flushes. I'm thinking about last night. In the Hidden Theatre. My lips on Cole's neck.

"Well, Jesus," Lex says, and he rolls his eyes. "Just fucking kiss him already." His eyes turn dark again. But this time I know it's the shadow of Sam that I'm seeing. "You don't wanna wonder later." He shakes his head. "Trust me. It's the what-ifs that'll kill you."

Cole and Val come back to our table with two huge trays full of food. The lobster roll is amazing. Cole was right. Nothing like Red Lobster back home. He teaches us how to eat steamed clams and mussels. Jude waves his arms and swears at the seagulls. And we all laugh in the sunshine while butter drips down our chins.

We spend the whole afternoon together. Just the five of us. Lobster. A sprawling old bookstore. Fudge from the candy shop downtown. And it's so easy to convince myself that everything is fine.

That this is all there is. Just these people. Just this good feeling. Used books and melted chocolate.

But later, when we get back to the theatre, Cole pulls a huge duffel bag out of the back of the van. He hoists it over his shoulder and heads toward the cabin with Lex and Jude.

"Hey!" I say. "Where are you going?" He turns to look at me.

"I figured if I'm gonna do the show, I should live with the rest of the actors. Right?"

I blink at him. He's grinning, but I know the truth. He's scared.

He's scared for me. And he wants to be close by.

"Yeah," I say. "Sure. That makes sense."

I wait on the front steps while he picks out an empty bunk and gets settled. I'm excited about having him right next door. But I don't like that he's worried about me.

Everyone seems to be worried about me these days.

"Well," Cole announces when he's finished unpacking, "the cabins are even shittier than I remembered." I laugh, because they really are terrible, and he smiles at me. "The neighbors are great, though."

"I'm sure your house is a lot nicer."

He shrugs. "It's okay. Nothing fancy." I'm suddenly trying to imagine what Willa's house might look like—at the exact same time, I'm trying not to imagine what Cole's bedroom might look like.

I feel my face flush.

"Do you wanna see it?" he asks. And I just stare at him. "My house. Do you wanna see where I live?"

"Yeah," I say. "Sure." And I feel my pulse start to race.

Cole grins at me. "Come on. We've got some time before dinner."

He leads me across the field and around behind the farmhouse. Then he starts down the lawn. I think maybe we're headed toward the beach, but then Cole veers to the right, toward the tree line of the thick woods that run along the edge of the property.

"Through here," he says over his shoulder. "It's not far, but it's a little bit of a climb."

I duck into the woods, and it's instantly dark and shady. A worn footpath leads away from the farmhouse and deeper into the trees. And then it starts to rise. It's steep and rocky, and I'm wearing flip-flops. Once or twice Cole reaches back, without a word, to give me a hand.

A few minutes later, just as I'm starting to think I'm an idiot and he's lured me into the forest to murder me, we come to a clearing behind a big old two-story house. It's square with wooden siding and a welcoming back porch. Overflowing tubs of pink and purple flowers sit along the railing, and a couple of cats lounge on weathered wicker furniture.

"Is this it?" I ask him, and he nods.

"Home sweet home. When my mom and dad started the theatre at Whisper Cove, back before I was born, they bought this place so they could be right next door. They were both putting in long days and nights back then." He stops to lean down and scratch a gray cat that's circling his feet. "Not that much has changed. My dad still spends more time in his office than he does here."

Suddenly I'm thinking about those initials in my mother's notebook again.

B. C.

And I'm worried about coming face-to-face with Brody Culver.

Cole doesn't head toward the house, though. Instead, we head down toward a tall privacy fence at the bottom of the yard. He pops open a rusty padlock and it makes a loud *click*. "My mom has no idea this lock is broken. So that's going to have to be a secret," he warns me. "Just between us." I glance back toward the house. The last thing I want to do is piss off Willa. "Don't worry," he says. "They're both in the city with important friends today."

When the gate swings open, I stop short and suck in my breath. Cole ushers me through and closes the gate behind us. My knees go weak. I take a few steps back, pressing myself against the wood of the fence. Because we're standing at the top of a steep cliff. It's a sheer drop down to the water below. And I've never been afraid of heights before.

But that churning water.

"Whoa." Cole shoots out a hand to steady me. "It's okay. I got you." I let him steer me over to a rusting garden bench where we can sit together.

"Your mom put up the wall," I say as soon as I get my voice back, "and the gate? After my mom . . ."

Cole nods. "I was still little. And I think it scared her, you know? That long drop to the sea."

"Why'd you bring me here?"

"Two reasons." He hasn't taken his eyes off me. "First, I just wanted you to see it." I sneak a peek toward the edge of the cliff. The abrupt drop to the waves below. "It's amazing, right?" He's watching my face so intently. "But also because I remembered something last night." He picks up a toy boat that's sitting in the grass next to the bench. It's simple. Clearly homemade. Just a little piece of wood cut into a wedge shape. It's painted blue and white, and there's a tiny sail attached to a drinking-straw mast. "Do you remember being up here? With me? That summer?"

I shake my head.

"Here." He hands me the little wooden toy. "Tide's on its way out. We have to do it now."

"Do what now?" I'm so confused.

"I made this one, but when I was little, my dad used to make them for me. Out of little bits of wood stolen from the scene shop. I loved tossing them off the cliff, here, and then picking them up later on the beach at Whisper Cove." He looks embarrassed all of a sudden. "I thought it might help you remember."

"What are you talking about?"

He laughs and it's magic, the way it makes me feel. "Just toss it," Cole says, so I pull back my arm and let the little boat fly. It sails through the air and lands in the water at the bottom of the cliff. I watch it get sucked out to sea. And then it's gone.

"Come on." He grabs my hand.

"Where are we going?"

He laughs again. "To get your boat back."

He pulls me through the gate and closes it behind us.

We move toward the woods, but we take another path this time. This one is less worn. Closer to the edge of the cliff. The waves are louder than before.

I'm trying to keep up with him, but Cole moves over the ground like some kind of wild creature. He's at home here.

I stumble over a big loose rock. When I stand up to yell for Cole to wait, I look around, and there are rocks everywhere.

No.

Not rocks. Stones.

All the same size and shape. Worn down by the wind and the weather.

They're arranged in neat rows. It's all overgrown, so it's hard to tell. But you can still see the pattern if you look closely. They remind me of a mouth full of broken teeth.

"Cole."

He's too far ahead of me to hear.

I pick my way around the toppled stones. Hurry to catch up. Don't let myself look back.

We emerge from the dark of the woods onto the Whisper Cove beach together. It's twilight. The sky is pink. The sea is pink. Everything is pink and perfect. We should be heading up to dinner. But instead we kick off our shoes and stand toe to toe in the sand. The wind pulls at our hair, and the salt burns our lips.

Cole pulls his shirt over his head and drops it on the sand. He walks toward the water and turns back to hold out one hand. I slip out of my T-shirt and shorts, and he stares at me for a minute. I'm standing there in my bra and underwear, but I feel so naked. I go to him and take his hand. Because I need that contact.

Cole anchors me. Grounds me.

Cole won't let me get lost.

We step into the sea together. The surf is cold, and it makes me gasp. He laughs and puts his arm around me, and he's so close now that I almost can't stand it. I feel the waves against my thighs.

Icy water.

Hot breath.

I feel dizzy and drunk, and it makes me bold.

"Do you trust me?" I tease.

He nods and I lean in, putting my hands on each side of his face and pulling him toward me.

But then he laughs and slips away.

Cole dives below the surface, and I follow him. It's dark and cold and beautiful under the sound. We pop up at the same time. Both laughing. Wiping seawater tears from our cheeks.

And then he starts to swim.

And I follow him again.

We swim toward the horizon line. Muscles burning. Lungs aching. Cold sitting inside our bones like it's made a home there.

We swim out farther than I went that first night. Past the swim dock. And the safety buoys. Past the lighthouse even. Until the shoreline curve of Whisper Cove seems more like a memory than a place.

And then we float. On our backs. Fingers linked. We don't fight it.

And the current takes right us back to shore.

All the way back to Whisper Cove. Like that's where it wants us to be.

We sit together for a long time in the sand, still warm from the sun. We write our names with a stick. I have this urge to draw a heart around them. But I don't. Because it seems silly.

Cole finds the boat for me. The one I tossed from the cliff. It's already washed up on the beach near the jetty. The mast and sail are missing. Stolen by the sea. But the rest of it is intact. Whole. He hands it to me and leans down low. I wait for the press of his lips. But it's the soft touch of his fingers that I feel. He wipes the sea from my eyes. The salt from my skin.

"Let me save you this time," he murmurs.

His mouth is so close. I feel our mingled breath.

The words are a kind of kiss. Pressed against my skin. But I'm so hungry for the real thing.

I pull him closer. My hands on his damp cheeks. His thumbs against my hip bones. "Do you trust me?" I ask him again.

It's getting dark now. We've missed dinner. But we still don't leave. We linger. Hands sliding over wet skin. The grit of sand.

And then the fog comes.

It rolls in so fast—so low and thick—that I can't tell if it's coming from the sea or rising from the ground beneath our feet.

"We need to go," Cole says, and we pull on our clothes. He grabs my hand, and we hurry toward the boardwalk. But I stumble over something buried in the sand. Those stone blocks. They keep tripping me up. I lean down to brush one off.

Cole is watching me. "Foundations," he says. "Of the old village. The bones of their houses are still here."

I can't stop staring.

I've been tripping over the past since I got to Whisper Cove.

Cole pulls me toward the boardwalk. Past the dunes. Across the marsh. Up the sloping lawn. He's moving fast. Flowing over the ground like water. And I move with him. Because I know he's racing that fog.

When we reach the little blue cabins, he pulls a piece of sea glass from his pocket. Pink like seashell. He tosses it into the air and catches it in his hand. Then he presses it into my palm.

"Sleep tight," he tells me. "I'll be right next door." He touches my face. Moves his thumb across my lips. So gentle. And I want to kiss him so bad. It feels like bones cracking, that desperate want. But I'm suddenly afraid.

What if I feel too much?

Cole watches me until I go inside. But I don't go to bed. Instead, I take the flashlight from under Val's bed, and I creep back out into the dark. Alone. I'm not sleepwalking this time. It's my choice to leave my bed. To relinquish the safety of the little blue cabin. Because I have this thought. This wild idea. And I need to know. For sure.

I move toward the thick of the tree line at the edge of the property.

The crush of the woods.

It takes me a little while. I wander for a bit. Lose my way. But eventually I find those stones again. The ones I tripped over between Cole's house and the beach. Only something is different. They stand at attention in the fog now. Not slumped. Not crooked. They aren't worn down. Not overturned and overgrown.

The neat rows are easy to see. The mounds of earth.

I breathe in the scent of fresh dirt. New flowers to mark the spot. And I marvel at the impossibility of it all.

The little graveyard made new again in the moonlight.

I'm not sure I can find my way back through the woods, so I take the path I took earlier with Cole. Running along the top of the cliff, then downhill toward the Whisper Cove beach. And I stand on the sand as the fog swirls around me.

But I don't move toward the water. Because someone is already there.

My mother stands with her back to me. At the edge of the ocean. She's beautiful. And still. But I call out one word.

"Mom."

She turns to look at me. Confusion on her face.

My face.

We are perfect mirrors of each other.

Because this isn't my mother.

It's me.

# ACT II: SCENE 7

"How far would you go to be with someone you love?"

That's the question Val asks us the next morning at breakfast. It's Monday. The beginning of our second week at Whisper Cove. And I'm staring, bleary-eyed, at a bowl of oatmeal I can't bring myself to eat.

Across the table, Jude has his arm slung around the back of Lex's chair. The two of them have been picking through Jude's fruit cup, but Lex turns his attention to Val now.

"As far as it takes," he says without hesitation, and I admire him for that certainty.

"So you'd do what Orion does?" Val asks him. "You'd give up everything? Just to be with him?"

"Yeah," Lex answers, like he's confused about why it's even a question. "Of course." He grins at me, and then at Jude. I can literally see the love coming off him like waves of heat rising off a Texas highway in the summer. And it's beautiful. Because he obviously means it. That's just how Lex is. He turns toward Val again. "Wouldn't you?"

Val shrugs. Swallows a spoonful of Cheerios. "I don't know," she says. "I wanna say no. I mean, I don't think I would." She frowns. "But maybe I've never really been in love."

I know she's thinking about Chester. They've been on and off more times in the past week than I can count. Right now I think they're together again, but I never know for sure. And it changes by the hour.

"What if you lost yourself along the way?" I hadn't meant to ask the question out loud. But the words hover over our breakfast table.

Jude grins. "Everybody gets a little lost sometimes." He gives Lex a squeeze. "You just gotta let someone find you."

I look around the cafeteria. I'd been expecting Cole to show up at breakfast, now that he's living in the cabins, but he isn't here. And after last night, I feel so weird and disconnected without him.

Unsafe.

My legs are covered in scratches from my midnight walk to the cemetery. Torn by thorns and brambles. I woke up with blood on my sheets.

All of it felt hazy.

But I can still see those tombstones, perfect and upright again in the fog.

I remember meeting myself at the edge of the ocean.

I managed to get out of bed, though. I showered.

Said good morning to Val. And Lex. Jude.

Walked to the farmhouse.

Filled my tray.

Now I'm pretending to eat my breakfast.

But everything feels different this morning. Not quite right.

Like I'm climbing a familiar staircase. Counting the steps. And I know how many there should be. But there's one extra today. Or one too few. So everything feels off. I raise my foot to take that next step and fall into nothingness.

Again and again.

Because I get it now. Cole was telling the truth. Whisper Cove is not like anywhere else I've ever been. Something happens here. In the fog.

Something I don't understand.

I fake my way through the morning class on improv techniques. And there's still no sign of Cole at lunch.

When I report to work with Glory, she sends me out to the scene shop to see if I can find a hammer. There's a nail sticking out of the baseboard, and she wants to fix it before someone gets a shoe caught.

I have no idea where to look for the hammer, though. I hear voices, so I brace myself for the bright red name on the back of the building, and I head around that way. George and a younger guy are taking a cigarette break in the shade of a tree. And I stop dead in my tracks. Because those bloody letters on the white wall are gone. There's only a clean, blank space where they used to be. And I wonder if Willa had them painted over. Out of kindness to me.

"You need something?" George asks.

"A hammer," I manage to say. "For Glory."

The other guy smiles then. "Anything for Glory," he says, and he disappears around the front of the shop.

"I remember your mama." George's voice is gruff, like maybe he's not used to using it much. "A real shame." He takes a bandanna out of his pocket and wipes at his forehead, and I wonder what's taking the other guy so long to find a hammer. Surely he knows where they keep them. "Real nice lady." I nod, but I can't say anything. I'm trying not to look at George. Trying not to look at that blank wall. "A beauty, that's for sure. Hard to forget a woman like that." George's eyes glide over my skin, and I shiver. "You're a dead ringer for her." He takes a step closer to me. "Anybody ever tell ya that?"

The other guy finally comes back with a hammer, and I practically snatch it out of his hands and take off running toward the farmhouse. I can't stand that blank wall anymore. Or George's sad voice. Those wandering eyes.

When I report back to Glory, she pounds the nail in. Then she stands there, the hammer dangling from her hand, and looks at me. Her hair is especially frizzy this morning, and she's wearing a soft yellow sweater. It makes her look younger than she is. She could be one of the students.

"Avril?" she says. "You okay?"

I nod, but Glory is still watching me. "Did you get a chance to look through the notebook?" I nod again, and Glory turns away. She busies herself with pulling dead leaves off one of her plants. "Find anything?"

"No," I tell her. "Not really."

The lie bothers me, but I'm not ready to tell anyone about B. C. yet.

Glory sighs, and I can't tell if she's relieved or disappointed. The two of us work the rest of the afternoon in a silence that's broken only by the ringing phone and the hum of the copy machine.

All day, I've been desperate to see Cole. But when rehearsal time comes, I'm nervous. Especially since we're going to be working the scene at the dance where Eden tells Orion she's in love with him. The monologue I did for my audition.

I get down to the barn early, and Cole is waiting for me outside the theatre. He slips his arms around me. "You been okay today?" he asks, and I nod. I want to tell him about the cemetery last night. I need him to explain to me about the tombstones. How they stood tall and upright in the fog. Fresh flowers on new-dug graves.

But I don't know how to make the words come out without it sounding like a dream.

And then Val shows up. And Lex. Jude is opening the door. And it's too late.

It turns out working the dance scene is so much fun, that I forget to be nervous. I forget everything. At least for a little while. It's so freeing to cast away Avril and all her questions and become Eden.

Because at least Eden knows one real thing. She's falling hard for Orion.

We reach the end of the scene, and I lift my face to Cole's to deliver my line. "This must be what it is to fall in love! I didn't recognize it at first, because it doesn't feel like falling at all."

I'm so unprepared for the way Cole is looking at me. The depth of feeling in his eyes.

The smoldering heat of it.

We're inside the barn, but overhead the stars blink on. Just like someone plugged them in. They shine against a black velvet sky.

I throw my arms around Cole's neck.

"It feels like I'm flying!"

He grabs my waist, just above my hips, and I remember the

feeling of his thumbs pressed there last night. He lifts me straight up off the ground with what seems like no effort at all. It really does feel like flying.

Graceful.

Free.

I'm soaring.

Safe. Because Cole is holding me. He has me. And I'm not afraid of falling.

Not anymore. Cole spins me around in a circle as I stretch my arms out as wide as I can and lift my face up to the stars.

"I'm flying in love!"

He brings me back down to earth, and when I feel my feet touch solid ground again, I have real tears on my cheeks.

"And blackout," Jude calls. Cole and I breathe in time with each other, neither of us willing to sever that connection we just made. The electricity of it still snaps and crackles between us.

"Wow," Willa whispers. "Wow. Beautiful way to end a scene. Avril, was that okay for you?"

I nod and then, suddenly, I burst into tears. I'm just feeling so much.

So much Eden.

So much me.

So much of my mother.

"Okay," Willa says, "company, take ten." People start to drift away.

Willa leaves Cole standing there, staring. She takes my hand and leads me over to a dark corner of the barn.

"Breathe," she whispers, and she pulls me into a hug. "You're okay." I nod against her shoulder. She's smoothing my hair, and it feels so good to have her petting me and making soothing noises in my ear. "Shhh. It's okay, my lovely."

For one short second, I have a flash of my mother. She's tucking me into bed. Smoothing my hair. Kissing me good night. She's humming something beautiful while she pats my back.

It's like a bolt of lightning straight to the heart, the shock of that memory. It makes me tremble with loneliness. And I ache for her. That woman I'm almost starting to remember. I have to bite my lip to keep from wailing.

"There's no shame in feeling, Avril. You can't make your audience feel if you can't feel." Willa's hand is making slow, soothing circles on my back. "Your mother was the same way. She kept a lot of things to herself. And I admired her for that strength." She shakes her head. "God knows I wanted it for myself." I pull back to stare at her, because Willa is such a force. I can't imagine her ever feeling weak. She reaches up, tucks a strand of hair behind my ear. "But that summer, here, Nicole was learning to let herself feel." I hear the jangle of bracelets as her hand drops back to her lap. "Whisper Cove has a way of teaching you what you need to learn."

I nod again, and Willa offers me a tissue. Then she sends me off to the bathroom to wash my face. But I'm afraid to turn on the sink, so I dab at my eyes with a dry paper towel. And when I'm finished, Willa tells Jude to call the others in.

Back to work.

"The show must go on," she says with a reassuring smile in my direction. "We're creating something extraordinary."

The rest of rehearsal is good. We work the scene over and over, but I keep it together. I let myself feel enough. But not too much. I'm finding that line. Walking an emotional tightrope.

"You okay?" Cole asks when Willa lets us all go. "That was intense. What happened earlier."

"Yeah. I just . . ."

"Felt too much," he finishes for me. Like he understands. I nod, and he takes my hand and walks me out of the barn.

It's a gorgeous night. Clear and warm and bright. Lex and Jude are making out under a lamppost. Red-gold hair and charcoal curls. They move together and it's beautiful, the way their bodies cast one shadow on the cement.

I turn to Cole. "What happens here?" I whisper. "At night. In the fog."

Cole looks startled. He opens his mouth to answer me, but Val grabs my hand. She grins as she pulls me away from Cole and slips an arm around my waist. "We're going night swimming," she says. "The three of us." She jerks her head toward Lex and Jude. "You guys wanna come?"

I'm afraid. Not of the water. But of the dark. Maybe. And of meeting myself on the sand.

Of the fog.

And of how much I want Cole.

But I remember what he told me my second morning at Whisper Cove. That conversation on the sea porch steps. It seems like a million years ago.

*I swim because the ocean scares me.*

And I think about what Willa said earlier tonight. About letting myself feel.

I want to become that person.

So I say yes. "Sounds like fun."

Cole gives me a look. He wants to know if I'm sure. So I take his hand. Squeeze it hard.

I need him to know I'm sure. This is what I want.

The five of us start down the lawn toward the sound. The waves get louder. But the night stays clear. Our feet move over the boardwalk. Across the marsh. And the dunes. Until we're standing in warm sand, staring out at the sea.

Val is leading the way. She looks back to smile at us. It's an invitation and a challenge. I watch her shimmy out of her shorts. She pulls her tank top over her head and tosses it to me. Then she slips out of her underwear. Her bra. She's sprinting for the water. Throwing herself headlong into the breaking waves. She squeals. Then she starts to laugh, and it echoes up and down the beach.

Lex looks at me. He raises one eyebrow. *Are we doing this?* The question is so clear on his face, but Jude is already shirtless, and now he's unbuttoning his shorts.

So I guess we are.

I pull my shirt off over my head and drop it in the sand. Lex and Jude have both stripped down to their boxer shorts. Lex hesitates, and for a second I think he's going to chicken out, but then he's wiggling out of his underwear. And so is Jude. I watch them racing each other toward the waves. Laughing. And free.

And I want to feel that for myself. The way Eden feels it when Orion lifts her toward the sky. After she admits that she's in love with him.

I turn back toward Cole, and he's standing there naked under a blanket of stars. My breath hitches in my chest. He's all tousled dark hair and smoky eyes and beautiful skin. Angles and edges.

He gives me a little sideways smile, and my heart is in my throat.

But I'm sliding off my shorts.

My underwear.

My bra.

I've never been completely exposed liked this. Not in front of someone else. Not in the moonlight. Toes in the sand. Just on the edge of the ocean.

Just on the edge of everything.

And it feels so unimaginably good.

I take Cole's hand and lead him toward the water. If the first shock of cold stops my heart, it's the electricity in his touch that starts it beating again.

Jude and Lex and Val are bobbing up and down like corks. Cole and I make our way out to them. And then we're all slicing through the sound. Pulling ourselves toward the swim dock. Arm over arm. Feet kicking. Salt water glistening on our eyelashes.

Jude disappears below the surface and my heart seizes. There's a moment of pure terror. Lex yells his name, and I can hear the fear in his voice. "Fuck!" Val says. Her eyes are frantic. Searching the blackness. But then Jude pops up ahead of us, shaking the water from his curls.

We reach the swim dock and pull ourselves up the slippery ladder one by one to collapse on top. We forget that we're naked, dressed in salt and moonlight. We're laughing. Teasing. Lex pushes Jude off into the water. "That's for scaring us, asshole," he says. But Jude manages to grab Lex by the ankle, and over the edge he goes, too.

They shriek and splash. And then they share a kiss, both of them clinging to the ladder, before they climb back up to rejoin the rest of us. We all stretch out on our backs. I'm lying in the crook of Cole's arm. My head is on his shoulder. My right hand and his left meet over his stomach. Our fingers intertwine and we move with the rhythm of the rocking swim dock.

"Cole," Val says, "do you really believe this place is haunted?" She's lying on her side, facing away from us, trailing her fingers through the dark water. I can't see her face, but I trace the curve of her hip with my eyes. The bend of her spine.

"Yeah," he says. "I know it is." My ear is to his chest, and I like hearing the vibration of his words before they leave his mouth. "These little seaside towns are full of ghosts. Every stretch of beach, from here up to Maine and all the way down to Florida, they've all got these wooden benches. And each one of them has a plaque in remembrance of somebody. A grandmother or an uncle or a town founder. Someone who donated books the library." He's stroking my arm. Trailing his fingers up and down my skin, like Val is trailing hers through the water. I shiver and nestle in closer to his body. "Every time you wanna sit down, you're rubbing shoulders with ghosts."

"You're sitting with the dead," I tell him. "Somebody's memory. That's not the same thing."

"No," he says, and I feel him pull me closer. "But a memory can haunt you, if you let it."

I feel the truth of that in the hollow pit of my stomach.

"Think about how much you'd have to love someone," Jude says, "to stick around and haunt 'em."

It's quiet for a minute. Just the slap of water against the wood of the dock.

"I'm not in love with Chester," Val finally tells us. "I wish I was." She lifts her hand out of the water, and I watch the little droplets fall from her fingers. "I tried to be."

"It's not your fault," Lex assures her. His head is resting on Jude's stomach, and Jude's hand is moving through his fiery hair. "You can't know what love feels like until you feel it."

We stay on the platform until we start to get cold. Then we follow each other back into the water.

We bob and float, content to let the current carry us home. Val and Lex and Jude are laughing. I watch Cole moving through the water just ahead of me. The shape of his shoulders in the moonlight. His arms. It's beautiful.

He's beautiful.

We reach the beach together—five strange creatures crawling out of the sea—all arms and legs and dripping hair—and we treasure hunt for our clothes.

A T-shirt here. "Found it!"

A pair of underwear there. "Oh my God! Finally!"

Some shorts that got tossed into the dune grass. "What the hell?"

Lex gives up looking for his second flip-flop. Jude thinks maybe he left it too close to the water and the sea took it as a prize.

The fog is curling around our ankles.

I look back out toward the swim dock, and just for a second, I catch a glimpse of us there. Silent-movie versions of ourselves. Bodies bathed in moonlight. And the soft glow of the lighthouse. I watch Lex push Jude into the water. Val throws her head back and laughs. Face to the sky.

We're achingly gorgeous. All of us.

"Av?" Lex touches my arm, and it startles me. "You okay?"

"Yeah," I tell him. "I'm good."

But when I look toward the dock again, we've vanished.

Cole points toward something winking in the sand. A tiny bit of polished glass. Milky white. He picks it up and offers it to me. And I slide it into my pocket.

Another lucky charm.

The others start toward the cabins. Val walks between Jude and Lex, the three of them holding hands. Jude lets go for a minute to spin on the boardwalk. And he's so graceful. Lean and muscled. I think about what a waste it is for him to become an accountant.

Lex looks back over his shoulder to smile at me, but Cole is pulling me in a different direction. "Come on," he whispers, and when I hesitate, he gives me a huge grin. "I know someplace we can be alone."

My stomach flip-flops, but I let Cole lead me away from the others, toward the rock jetty at the end of the beach. Along the cliff-side path into the tree line. Up the rocky hill toward his house.

I stop when we reach the tiny graveyard. Stones upright again tonight. Fresh flowers. My feet don't want to move. "Cole?"

He tugs on my arm. "We shouldn't stay here."

He leads me to the tall fence at the bottom of his yard again. To the gate with the broken latch. I follow him through, and he closes it. We stand and look at the sea laid out below us. It churns and tumbles and foams at the bottom of the cliff.

I tremble as the fog swirls around our knees. I feel the kiss of it against my skin. But it's Cole's kiss I'm desperate for.

He's so close, and suddenly I have to touch him again. To bridge those final inches between us.

*You make the choice to see where this is going.*

*You light the fire.*

I put my hands on his face and pull him to me. His hands go to my waist, and it's like his palms are electric. I feel the little sparks they give off. We're both still wet.

Water. And electricity. It's dangerous. But I don't care.

Our lips meet.

Then our tongues.

It's gentle at first. Tentative.

Until it isn't.

I slip both my hands into his hair, letting my fingers get lost in those dark waves. I felt him tense up, but then he relaxes and pulls me closer. I'm dizzy and lightheaded, but I don't want to break away for air.

Cole presses me backward until I feel the rough wood of the fence behind me. I let myself melt against the boards as he deepens the kiss.

He slips his hands under my shirt to rest against the bare skin of my stomach.

Rough.

Hot.

Strong.

*Real.*

I gasp against his mouth, and I feel him smile.

I pull my lips away from his, tilt my head back, and suck in a long, slow breath. I need a second just to focus on the feeling of his hands on my body and my fingers in his hair.

Cole is breathing hard. Then his lips are on my neck, and it feels so unbearably good that I'm afraid I might pass out. I open my eyes and look up at the big night sky.

*My stars.*

I'm kissing Cole Culver at the top of a cliff. With all of the ocean spread out below us. And I've never felt this much everything. It's almost unsurvivable.

I can hear the waves, but they don't frighten me. Not with Cole touching me like this. He whispers my name against my collarbone. And I shiver hard.

From somewhere far away, there's the scent of lavender.

My neck is so sensitive that Cole's lips are almost too much. I guide his face back up, directing his mouth back to mine. We're all lips and teeth and tongues. Searching fingers and pounding hearts.

Dripping. And sandy.

We've become sea creatures.

No brain. No bones. Just bodies.

I think I might die if he ever stops kissing me like this.

He does stop eventually, though, pulling back to look at me. And we stand there just taking each other in, trying to remember how to breathe normally. I feel so much more naked than I ever felt on the beach.

The fog is waist-deep now. It's like we're standing in calm water.

"That's all I've been able to think about. Since that first night I laid eyes on you." Cole leans in to me. Forehead to forehead.

"Again," I remind him. "Since you laid eyes on me again."

"Yeah," he breathes. And there is something so sad in his eyes. "Again."

I feel the tickle of his hair against my cheek. And, God, I want another kiss so bad I could die.

"I've been so scared," he admits.

"To kiss me?" He nods. "Why?"

"Because there's no going back now."

"I don't want to go back," I tell him.

"Nothing at Whisper Cove is real," he says. His hands are on my face. "It's all illusion. Smoke and mirrors. I need you to understand that." I can't help myself. He's so close. I kiss him again. But I still need more of him. I pull his body against mine and kiss him so deep that it's like being turned inside out. The fog blurs the edges of us until I'm not sure where my body ends and Cole's begins. "It's all theatre," he murmurs against my lips. His fingers on my neck make me shiver. "All of it. Except this. Except you and me. This is fucking real." His voice breaks. "Every single time."

"Is this why you brought me here?" I tease, and he smiles. Shakes his head.

"I brought you here to show you a magic trick."

Cole pulls me to the edge of the cliff and takes a flashlight out of his pocket. He aims it into the nothingness, over the edge of the drop-off. Then he reaches into his other pocket and pulls out a handful of sea glass. All different colors. Frosted and beautiful and smooth. He shows them to me in his palm as the fog wraps us up like a blanket.

"Watch," he whispers. And I'm mesmerized. By his words. His

breath hanging in the thick air. By the sea sounds and the wind. The taste of salty kisses on my lips.

And the rest of it happens in slow motion. It's the most beautiful thing I've ever seen. Cole pulls back his arm and flings the sea glass into the dark. And I think it's gone. Disappeared. Swallowed by the night. But then he hits it with that flashlight beam as it drops into the sea, and every single piece twinkles and shines, suspended for a moment before it streaks toward the water.

Like rain on fire.

Heavy and wet.

"Look, Avril." I think the next words in my head even before Cole says them out loud. "Look at the stars."

# ACT II: SCENE 8

*Plop.*

*Plop plop.*

*Plop.*

The stars are falling out of the sky again.

They hit the water, and I'm five years old.

I'm looking for my mother. But she isn't anywhere.

Then I see her. Just a glimpse. And she disappears.

Vanishes into thin air.

And I'm falling out of the sky.

Just like the stars.

"Avril?" I'm blinded. Cole clicks off the flashlight. Lays a hand on my arm. He's warm and alive. But I'm frozen.

A ghost.

A girl made of fog.

"Hey," he says. His voice is coming from somewhere far away, because I'm stuck twelve years in the past.

*Look at the stars.*

That single, strange phrase and the memory of those glowing streaks tearing a burning path toward the water. That's what's haunted me all these years. And I could never make sense of it.

Until now.

I back away from Cole, but I can't get as far away as I need to, because my back ends up against the fence. Again.

He reaches for me, one hand on my back. The other in my hair. And I let him pull me toward him.

I'm shaking.

"Hey," he whispers, low in my ear. "You're okay. I've got you. I promise."

I feel his lips against mine. Soft and salty. His fingertips against my skin. And I want him so bad that I ache all the way to the middle of my bones.

And that's how I know once and for all that I'm not dead. Surely that kind of longing is a punishment reserved only for the living.

"Avril," he says again. "What is it?"

But I can't answer him, because he was there.

Cole was there.

The night my mother died.

The night I drowned.

It wasn't just me and my mother, alone on that beach.

My mother was having an affair with Brody Culer. And Cole was there that night.

I don't know what those two things mean when you add them together.

I don't know what anything means anymore.

I untangle myself. Pull away. Step back.

Through the open gate.

"I have to go home," I tell him, and even as the words come out of my mouth, I don't know what they mean. Home to my bunk in the blue cabin? Home to Dallas? And my father? Or somewhere else entirely?

"Avril!" Cole shouts after me. "Wait!" I need to get to the tree line. I feel too exposed on the perfect grass of his perfect backyard. But I don't make it, because Cole catches me easily. He grabs my hand. Tries to pull me to his chest. But I jerk away.

"Don't," I beg him. "Please."

My feet are moving again. But this time, Cole doesn't follow. He lets me go.

I slip and slide my way back through the woods until I see the moon shining on the great green lawn. I step out of the tree line and into the open, like an actress stepping out of the wings and onto the stage.

But I can't find my light tonight. Even in the glow of the moon, it feels dark.

The fog is really starting to roll in now, and I race it to the cabin. I can't stand the feeling of it against my skin. Wet and heavy and cold. Like the touch of something dead.

I push open the door and slip inside. It's quiet. Glowing phone screens shine from a half dozen or so bunks. I tiptoe toward my bed and sink onto the thin mattress. I lie on my back and close my eyes. I try to think—to make sense of an impossible memory that's never made sense before—but my nose is suddenly filled with the scent of lavender.

Goose bumps pop up along my arms.

I open my eyes to see a little bundle of purple flowers tied with fraying twine. It's lying on top of the crooked dresser, beside my hairbrush and Val's paperback romance novel.

I recoil. Push myself up and away.

"Val." My voice is coarse. The scratch of sandpaper on metal. "Hey. Val." She rolls over to face me and opens one eye. "Do you know where these came from? The flowers?"

"No clue," she whispers. Her eye is already closed again. "They were there when I came back from dinner."

I take the little bundle of lavender and shove it under my bed. I don't want to think about it.

I don't want to think about anything. I only want to sleep.

But I know, as soon as I do, that old nightmare will find me.

And it does.

I'm standing in the dark. Looking up as those streaks of glowing light fall out of the sky and into the sea.

And there's that voice, only this time I know who it belongs to. I recognize it. Because I've heard it close and low in my ear. Felt it against my skin.

*Look at the stars.*

Cole's voice. The piece of the puzzle that's always been missing.

Then, suddenly, I'm blind. Blinking. The light is too much. I can't see.

There's the whisper of wind chimes. My skin starts to crawl. I'm afraid.

Then I'm not watching the stars anymore.

I've become one.

And I'm falling.

• • •

I sit upright in bed. Breathing hard. The smell of lavender is overpowering, and I need some fresh air. I creep to the door and open it up. Just a crack. So the fog can't come inside. But there's Cole. Slumped and asleep. Leaning against the railing.

I guess he followed me after all.

I step out onto the porch. Cole's arms are wrapped tight around his chest, and I know he must be cold. I reach out to touch his hair. It's damp. Glistening in the porch light. It makes my chest hurt to look at him.

I hear the foghorn. Feel the vibration of it in my bones. And under that lonesome sound, there's something else.

The whispering starts off so quiet that I almost can't hear it. It sounds like nothing. The dance of dune grass in the wind, maybe.

Then it gets louder, and it calls me off the porch into the night. I'm awake. Not sleepwalking. But I still have to go. I feel that pull so hard. It's like being hooked under the ribs. If I don't go, my skeleton will be ripped apart.

I make my way through the fog toward the light of the farmhouse porch, just across the little field. The distance seems as wide as the ocean. I count my steps out loud—one thousand—two thousand—until there are so many I lose track of the number somehow. I'm still trying to get to the farmhouse. I see the porch light burning in the fog. But something's stopped me. I can't go any farther.

I feel the rough wood of a rail fence under my palms. I run

my hands along it and hiss in pain as a splinter slices its way into my skin.

"Shit," I mutter. My mind is trying to make sense of what I'm feeling, but it sputters and stalls. Shuts down. Because nothing about this makes sense.

And there's something else. An odor that's almost unbearably strong in the night air. That manure smell again, but different from the barn. Thicker. More pungent.

I hear the grunting then. Not far away. From somewhere just on the other side of the fence.

Pigs.

I remember what Jude told us the night of auditions. How this used to a be a real working farm, back in the day.

But how long has that been?

Twenty years?

Thirty?

At least.

The whispers rise up in the night air again. I can hear them so loud now, even over the squeal of frightened pigs. They urge me on. Call me into the night.

So I feel my way down the fence until I come to where it turns a corner. Then I stumble across the field until I finally reach the farmhouse. The lights are all off, and a pair of boots sits beside the door, the mud and manure still fresh from the day's work. I wonder—if I climbed the front steps and crept inside—would I find Glory's reception desk—or something else? A straw hat on a peg? A basket for gathering eggs, maybe?

That thought scares me bad enough to get me moving again. I

work my way around the side of the house until I'm standing at the bottom of the sea porch steps. And there's a break in the fog just then. It gets blown away by the wind off the sound, and I see the sparkle of moonlight on the waves. The shimmer of water in motion.

Something is missing, though. There's no lighthouse standing sentry just offshore. It's gone tonight. I start to shake. And I wish for the lighthouse back. Because I'm badly in need of a beacon.

But like Cole said earlier, there's no going back now.

I take advantage of the moon and cross the lawn toward the tree line. I plunge into the dark of the forest and drag myself up the hill toward the Culver house. Toward the fence at the bottom of the yard. I pull on the padlock, like Cole did before, and it pops open. I wonder if it makes a clicking noise. I can't hear it because the whispering has grown so loud.

The gate swings and I step through. My heart is beating so fast in my chest, but I walk right to the edge of the cliff. Where Cole walks sometimes. With his eyes closed. Just so he can feel alive. Fifteen steps—blind—if things are bad enough, he told me.

There's nothing in front of me but nothing. Just air. A sheer drop to the water.

And there's nothing behind me but nothing. All the memories I can't remember.

But I know I'm right on the edge. Here on this cliff. And in my own mind. There's something just out of my grasp. Something I'm missing.

So I focus on the two things I know now.

One is that my mother was cheating on my father. She was having an affair with her best friend's husband.

The second is that Cole was there that night.

The stars fell into the sea because Cole Culver pulled them out of his pockets. They were his stars all along. Not mine.

*Look at the stars.*

His voice.

But what were we doing that night, the two of us?

And what was my mother doing?

"Avril." The voice is calm, gentle. Careful. But I'm not sure at first who it's directed toward. "Avril."

I don't move. I'm so confused. Stuck between the past and the present.

"April."

I turn my head to look over my shoulder, back toward the open gate behind me, and Willa is standing in the dark. Her long hair is loose and flowing. It floats around her face like fog. She has on a robe, and she holds out one hand to me. "Come on," she says. "Let me help you. Please."

There's something about the calm certainty in her voice. Something about the absolute authority. Even though her words are soft, they somehow drown out the whispers. So I reach out to take her hand, and I wince from the pain of the splinter buried under my flesh.

Willa pulls me to her and wraps her arms tight around me. "Shhhhh," she soothes. "You're safe now. I've got you."

I'm shaking so hard, but I let her lead me through the gate and up the stepping-stone path to the house.

The cats don't even look up as we climb the back steps. The

porch is crowded with all the things that make a place feel homey. Plants and bags of fertilizer. A little garden trowel. Overstuffed pillows. A book left open on a bright blue table. A forgotten coffee cup. A packet of seeds. And it's weird how all that stuff makes me ache for the kind of home I've never had. It's nothing like the sterile little apartment I share with my dad. And suddenly all I want in life is a porch like this.

A home like this.

A mother like this.

A leaf blower leans in one corner with a can of gasoline. Forgotten. And I wonder if they've been there since fall.

I imagine this house surrounded by colorful leaves. It must look like something out of a book.

Willa pushes open the door to a cozy kitchen, then parks me in a chair and crosses to the stove where a teapot is already steaming. She pours two cups of something that smells like mint, and then crosses back to the table to sit beside me.

I'm staring at a little painting that hangs on the wall over the breakfast nook. Beautiful girls with flapper-style haircuts and dresses. They're all in white, and they're dancing along the edge of a shining lake.

"The Greek muses," Willa tells me. "I found that painting at a thrift store when I was writing *Midnight Music*. We were so broke back then, and I was trying to fix up this ramshackle old house." She pauses. Blows on her tea. "Eden is Orion's muse, you know." She takes a tentative sip. "Every artist has one."

They're all so beautiful, but my eyes are drawn to one golden girl in particular. She stands shimmering in ephemeral light, waist-deep in the water. Her white gown floats around her, silver ribbons trailing in the rippling blue. There's something about her that makes me sad.

And then my eyes focus, and I see her more clearly. Water is streaming into the lake from a dozen invisible cracks in her arms, her chest, her face. She is a fountain, and water flows out of her from all those holes nobody can see.

I feel the water begin to pour from my broken places, too.

I'm crying.

Sobbing at Willa's kitchen table.

"What were you doing out there, Avril?" Willa's voice is gentle. Easy. But there's a firmness in it that tells me it won't do any good to ignore her. So I choke out the truth.

"Looking for my mother."

"Come on," Willa says. She picks up both of our mugs and leads me into the next room.

She points me toward a comfy-looking couch, but I can't seem to make my feet move. I'm staring at the photo of my mother that sits on the piano in the corner. It's just a snapshot. She's standing on the edge of a stage. Holding a bouquet of flowers. Bright lights shine above her head, and she's smiling. It looks so much like me that for a minute I can't figure out where I was when that picture was taken.

This must be the picture Cole told me about. The one he grew up seeing.

Willa steers me to the couch and settles me in one corner. "Here," she says, and she covers me with a thick, soft blanket. Then she reaches down and smooths my hair away from my face.

"If you're looking for your mother, you look in here with me. Not out there in the dark alone." She moves to the big television against the other wall and bends down to rummage around in the cabinet, then pops a DVD into the player. "We had all these old movies converted to disks a few years ago, but I kind of miss the tapes."

Willa picks up the remote and crosses back to the couch. She sits on the other end and tucks her legs up underneath her. Then she presses a button. And my mother is suddenly alive.

She's lounging on a blanket under a tree, reading. She's young. Not much older than me. And she's wearing a University of Texas T-shirt. Her ice-blonde hair is pulled back in a ponytail. "Whatcha reading?" a voice asks, and I recognize it as Willa's. My mother holds up a book. *Interview with the Vampire*. Then she rolls over on her back. And the camera shuts off.

She comes to life again. This time she's perched on a brick wall with a red plastic cup in her hand. She's laughing. I've never heard my mother laugh before. I freeze. Unable to breathe or move. That laughter in my ears. This is the most alive my mother has ever been for me. Then she looks at the camera. Blows a kiss in our direction. "Love you," she says. And I know she's talking to whoever is holding the camera. Willa, I guess. But to hear her say those words is still everything, and this deep and terrible yearning bubbles up from somewhere inside me.

I feel so robbed.

Cheated.

I set my mug on the coffee table in front of the couch and lean forward to stare at this woman who looks and moves so much like I do, but who has a different fire in her green eyes.

"She's beautiful," I say, and I turn to look at Willa. There are tears on her cheeks. She opens up her arms and I crawl to her end of the couch. I put my head in her lap, and she strokes my hair as I stare at my mother, back from the dead.

There are more little snippets of video. My mother driving and singing along to the radio. An Alanis Morissette song. My mother rehearsing a monologue from *Our Town*. Wearing cowboy boots and two-stepping at some country bar. Making faces in the mirror as she puts on red lipstick. Coming down the stairs dressed for some kind of formal event. She has on a dark green dress. Her hair done up. "Homecoming," Willa tells me. "Our junior year at UT." Then there's a trip to the zoo. And college graduation. Christmas. Somebody's birthday. A ski trip to Colorado.

And I love them all. Watching my mother move and breathe is mesmerizing. But it's hearing her voice that just undoes me. It unravels so much longing deep in my soul. I don't know if I actually quite believed she was real until right this moment. And now that I know she was, I want her more than ever.

Then there are the videos from Whisper Cove. That last summer. Splashing in the waves. Rehearsing a dance number in the barn theatre. Sitting shoulder to shoulder on the sea porch with Glory.

In that last one, I streak across the great lawn with Cole following behind me. Our laughter rings out in Willa's living room. I run to the sea porch steps where my mother is sitting and throw my arms around her neck. She scoops me up and pulls me onto her lap, and I feel my heart explode inside my chest. All I want—all I've ever wanted in the world—is to remember the feeling of her arms around me. She grabs Cole, too. She tickles us both. Turns her head to smile at Glory. Then she lets us go, and we take off around the corner of the farmhouse. Glory looks back over her shoulder. She waves at the camera.

"Cole was your shadow, right from the start." Willa's fingers are moving through my hair, but for a moment I imagine they belong to my mother. That we're sharing this memory together. Our couch. Our house. And she's made me tea. "From the very first day you met," Willa says, "you were two peas in a pod." She sighs. "It was a dream come true for me and Nicole, the two of us finding out we were pregnant at the very same time." She pauses. Takes another sip from her mug. "But we were so far apart during those early years, so when the opportunity came for her to come up and spend that summer at Whisper Cove, I knew I wanted her to bring you along."

Another video has started to play. Cole and I are chasing seagulls on the beach. We run toward a huge flock of them, waving our arms and laughing, and the birds all take to the sky at once. The screen is filled with white. I sit up to stare at the two of us. We both look so happy.

"You were quite a pair," Willa says. "Of course, you were both with Glory most of that summer. I was busy trying to get the theatre in the black. Making fundraising phone calls all day, every day. Filling out grant applications. Traveling back and forth to the city for meetings with donors. And Nicole was in rehearsal day and night." She smiles again, but it's a different kind of smile this time. The kind that comes with a raised eyebrow. "It doesn't surprise me a bit that you and Cole still share that special connection. I'm glad you found your way back to each other." She looks toward the picture on the piano. "There are people we're meant to walk through life with, Avril. If we're lucky, we find them. If we're really lucky, we manage to hang on to them."

And now I'm thinking that maybe I have things wrong. What if I'm getting one memory confused with another? If Cole and I spent those weeks mostly together, then there must have been so many summer nights. How do I know that memory of falling stars isn't from some other evening? Maybe my memories are bleeding together, the way sidewalk chalk runs and mixes in the rain.

But somehow, even as I think it, I know that's not true.

Cole Culver was there the night my mother died. I know it now.

I've always known it.

Willa takes my mug from the coffee table, even though I've barely had a sip. She goes into the kitchen to get us more tea.

I'm looking out the window. It's getting light outside. I should go, I think. Let Willa get ready to start her day.

And that's when Cole breaks out of the trees. He's moving fast. Jogging across the lawn. I know the exact moment he sees the open gate, because he breaks into a run. "Avril!" A beat. "Avril!" He's a blur moving across the grass.

I hear the back door open. "She's in here," Willa shouts. "Cole! She's fine! She's in here!"

A second later, Cole pushes his way into the living room, right past his mother. "Val came out and woke me up. She was headed to the bathroom. She said you weren't in your bed." Willa is leaning in the doorway, watching him. Watching us. "Avril," he says. "What happened last night? Why'd you take off like that?"

I'm not ready to tell him anything yet.

My memories are so strange and so jumbled. I need a little time to make sense of it all.

Cole moves to the couch. He kneels in front of me. His hands are on my face. He pulls me toward him. Kisses me. And his kiss is everything it wasn't last night. It's hesitant. Tentative. A kiss that asks a question.

A question I don't have an answer for right now.

"What time is it?" I ask him.

"Almost seven."

"I need to get ready for class," I say, and I start to stand up. But Willa steps in from the kitchen.

"Stay," she says. "You need rest. Both of you."

Willa has disappeared into the kitchen again, so Cole and I settle down on the couch together. I let him wrap his arms around me. Because what else can I do?

Another video is playing now. Cole and I are tossing toy boats from the top of the cliff. A white-haired girl and a dark-haired boy that I wish I could remember. Then I hear Glory's voice from behind the camera. "Careful. Not too close. It's dangerous."

Willa comes in and turns off the television. She covers us with the blanket and when she leans down to turn off the lamp on the end table, she touches my hair so softly. It's like a mother's kiss good night.

I'm almost asleep when I hear footsteps on the stairs but I manage to open my eyes enough to see Brody standing on the landing, looking at Cole and me curled up together on the couch. Fear tickles at me like a flame. But I can't swim through the exhaustion. It's too much. And before I know it, I'm sinking again.

"Shhhh," Willa says. "It's been a hard night. Let them rest."

My eyes have drifted shut.

"What's she doing here?" Brody asks.

Willa's answer is the last thing I hear before I slip away.

"She came home."

# ACT II: SCENE 9

It's almost noon when Cole wakes me up. "Hey," he says. "You okay?" My body is stiff and sore from sleeping so long in one position. And my mind is already spinning again.

I want to tell him the truth about what happened last night. How bad it scared me, realizing that he was the voice from my old nightmares.

*Look at the stars.*

But I don't, because the circles around his eyes are so dark this morning. And I'm not sure what it means yet.

Cole offers to make me lunch, but I need to take a shower and get cleaned up before I have to head to work with Glory, so he settles for sending me off with some peanut butter crackers and our first kiss in the bright light of day.

We're standing on his back porch, surrounded by tubs of brightly colored flowers and being watched by an old black-and-white cat. The forgotten leaf blower and the gasoline can. The garden trowel. All the pillows It's a beautiful day. Perfect. Crisp and clear and clean. The kind of summer day you never get in Dallas, where the afternoon heat and humidity are enough to melt the skin off your bones. And I want so much to pretend that this is all there is.

This beautiful weather.

This beautiful back porch.

This beautiful, beautiful boy.

But I can't pretend anymore. Because there's also waking up knee-deep in the water. Staring into my own eyes on the beach. The thick smell of pigs in the night.

Cole's pocket full of stars.

He takes my hands. The little blister from the lighter isn't bad, but I wince when he squeezes the one with the splinter lodged in the palm. He runs his finger over the raised, angry spot where the bit of wood is buried. "It's nothing," I tell him.

We should talk about the split-rail fence.

The boots on the farmhouse porch.

But in the daylight, my mind can't make those things seem real.

Even though my hand is throbbing.

I head back through the woods to Whisper Cove, and I make sure to go around the far side of the farmhouse, because it's lunchtime, and there are big windows in the cafeteria.

I sneak into the cabin the way I sneak into our apartment in Dallas sometimes when I've been out later than I'm supposed to be. Doing things I shouldn't. But there's no need for silence. The cabin is empty.

I find a pair of tweezers in Val's makeup bag, and I dig the splinter out of my palm. I stare at the tiny piece of wood. It's impossible for it to be there. But it is there. How do I make sense of that?

How far can you ask your mind to bend before it breaks?

I grab my things and head to the shower. The hot water feels good on my aching muscles. It clears my head a little, and when I show up at Glory's desk, she doesn't seem to notice that anything's off at all.

I'm getting awfully good at covering things up. Even better than I've always been.

I'm reaching for today's stack of file folders when Glory pulls something out of her purse. She starts to give it to me, then hesitates, like she can't quite bear to let it leave her fingers. "I found this," she says. "I knew I had it somewhere, but it had been so long since I looked for it."

She hands me a photo and hovers over my shoulder while I stare at it. My mother is sitting at one of the heavy wooden tables in the library. She's pecking away at a laptop keyboard, and she has a couple of notebooks spread out beside her. They're open, so I can't see the covers, but I wonder if one of them is the green one. The one I have now. She's looking down at the laptop screen, and a few strands of blonde hair hang loose in front of her face. You can see her eyes clearly, though. And they are so bright.

"That's my favorite photo of Nicki," Glory says. "God. I love that sparkle in her eyes."

"She looks happy," I say, and Glory nods.

"Nicki was happy. Most of the time. But I think she was torn between the life she had and the life she knew she could have, if she wanted it." Glory looks at me. "She was *becoming*. You know? She was getting ready to step out and be who she really wanted to be, I think. And becoming is never painless."

I hold the photo out to Glory. "Thanks for showing me this," I tell her. But she doesn't take it from my hand.

"No," she says, and she smiles. "Keep it. I have my memories of Nicki. You should have the picture."

All the rest of the afternoon, I keep thinking about what Glory said. It plays on a loop in my head while I'm filing invoices and answering Brody's phone calls. Because what if that's what I'm doing, too? What if I'm *becoming*? Only I can't become who I'm supposed to be until I know who I am. Where I came from.

Until I know my mother.

And what happened that night.

And like Glory said, there's pain in that.

When Lex and Val come crashing through the screen door for dinner, Lex looks so relieved to see me.

"Av!" he says, like we've been separated for seven years. "I haven't seen you all day!" He gives me a little grin. "How'd that private rehearsal session go, you lucky duck?"

"Huh?" I ask him.

"Willa told us that's why you weren't in the workshop this morning. She said she pulled you for a little one-on-one rehearsal time with her."

"Oh," I say. "Yeah. It was good." I don't like lying to Lex, and it worries me how easily the dishonesty rolls off my tongue. "Really good."

Val is staring at me, but she doesn't say anything. And I remember how Cole said she found him asleep on the cabin porch this morning. How she woke him up and told him I wasn't in my bed. How he probably took off like a wild man.

I follow Lex and Val to the cafeteria and fill my tray with spaghetti and salad. But I can't really eat any of it. I feel so disconnected from everyone and everything. Like I'm floating through the day.

Val pulls me aside after dinner. "What the fuck's going on?" she asks me. We're standing in the hallway outside the cafeteria, next to the big whiteboard with ITALIAN NIGHT written in blue block letters. Her long, dark hair is pulled back in a ponytail, and I watch it swing behind her as she stares at me.

"I'm trying to figure that out," I say. "I really am. But right now, I don't have a clue."

Val nods, like she can accept that. But then she says, "You don't have to figure everything out by yourself, you know." Her hand is on my arm. "If it's shit with Cole, you can talk to me. I know a thing or two about complicated relationships."

And I wish so hard that's all it was. Trouble with some boy. But this goes so much deeper, and I can't find the words, or the will, to explain it all. So I just nod and promise Val that I'm good.

But I know that's a lie. And judging from the way she looks at me with those cat eyes, Val probably does, too.

Cole greets me outside the barn before rehearsal, and when he slips his arms around me, I tense up. I keep hearing those words from my dreams.

*Look at the stars.*

Cole's words. How could I not have known that?

He takes my hand and turns it palm up. He touches the place where I pulled the splinter from my flesh. "Everything okay?"

It almost strikes me as funny. Cole Culver's ability to ask the most loaded questions is pretty much unparalleled.

"I don't know," I tell him. And it's the most true thing I've ever told anyone.

Cole's forehead is pressed to mine. I feel his breath against my eyelashes. The firmness of his lips against my cheekbone. "We have to be honest with each other, okay? No censoring. Or hiding."

"Yeah," I promise. "No hiding."

But I'm hiding so much right now.

I'm trying to convince myself that it doesn't mean anything, that memory of Cole tossing sea glass into the dark.

Like Glory told me, memory is weird. Stuff gets moved around. Distorted. Changed just enough to make it into something it wasn't.

You forget the wallpaper had cherries on it.

Or that someone's eyes were brown.

Somehow, something innocent becomes a nightmare.

But there's no explaining away the other part of it. B. C. scribbled in my mother's notebook, like lovers' initials carved into a tree.

Cole takes my hand to lead me into the theatre. "Come on," he tells me with a little smirk. "We can't keep our famous director waiting."

"Okay," Willa says when rehearsal begins, "this is the next Orion and Eden scene, after the dance. So far, we've been watching these two fall in love, and it's been a beautiful beginning."

Jude tosses the blanket to Cole. "We're at the edge of the river again," he says. "The scene starts with Orion already onstage, then Eden enters."

We take our places, and Willa gives us the nod to begin.

**EDEN**: It's so beautiful here.

Cole turns and watches me for a second before holding out his hand for me to join him.

**ORION**: I've seen it like this a thousand times, but it's never been more beautiful than it is tonight.

I cross to the blanket and sit down. Cole puts his arm around me, and I snuggle close. It feels good.

Right.

**ORION**: I wasn't sure if you'd come tonight.

**EDEN**: Look at the way my stars are shining. Did you polish them for me?

**ORION**: I did. It took all day.

He studies me for a minute, his expression slowly becoming more serious. Then he goes on with his line.

**ORION**: Where did you go last night? After the dance? Why'd you run away?

**EDEN**: I was afraid.

**ORION**: Of me?

I shrug, and Cole puts his hands on both sides of my face. He makes me look at him.

**ORION**: I would never hurt you.

**EDEN**: I know that. I'm afraid I might hurt you. What if I'm not good at this?

**ORION**: Good at what?

**EDEN**: At loving someone.

Cole almost smiles. His eyes are so beautiful.

**ORION**: Do you really love me, Eden?

His voice is teasing. But there's a serious question there. Something real behind the scripted line.

**EDEN**: I don't know. How would I know if I've never been in love before?

Cole is looking at me. I feel the heat from his eyes.

**ORION**: I love you.

**EDEN**: I don't remember anyone ever saying that to me before.

**ORION**: I'll say it to you every day for the rest of my life. I wish there was a better word, though. The word love doesn't seem big enough.

**EDEN**: We'll have to invent a new language, then. With a word that's just ours.

I know what comes next because it's written into the script, but it still takes my breath away when Cole reaches for me and pulls me into a kiss.

My head starts to swim and I hear the musical tinkle of wind chimes. Goose bumps pop up all along my arms. I'm afraid, and I start to tremble.

I know that if I open my eyes, I'll be lost in remembering. And I'll see stars.

Not my stars, though.

Cole's stars.

The grass. That night.

I'll be lost in that other world. Make believe.

Or memory.

So I squeeze my eyes tight and try to focus on what I know is real. The hard stage floor underneath me. The quiet buzz of the stage lights.

Cole's lips.

I let him be my anchor. He keeps me close to shore.

When the feeling fades, I open my eyes and we go on with the scene. And I don't get lost again. I stay grounded. Present.

Rehearsal runs later than usual. It's almost eleven o'clock when Willa calls it a night. She asks Jude and Cole to stay and help her get set up for tomorrow. We'll be working new scenes, and she needs help bringing some set pieces up from the shop.

Cole says he'll find me later, and I nod, because I know we need to talk. Even if I'm dreading it. Then Lex grabs my hand. "Come on," he whispers. "I've got a surprise for you." We step outside, and I glance up toward the sky. It's been threatening rain all evening, but it hasn't started yet. "Come on," Lex pleads. "Please?" So I let him pull me toward the farmhouse, around back to the great lawn where we can see the ocean spread out below Whisper Cove.

We settle onto the thick, soft grass. The hugeness of the lawn makes me feel tiny. The strangeness of everything and the gorgeous sparkle of waves in the moonlight. The dancing glow of the lighthouse beacon. The memory of last night. How that lighthouse wasn't there.

It all makes me dizzy.

Lex gives me a mischievous grin as he pulls a bottle of wine out of his backpack.

"Where'd you get that?" I demand.

"One of the other guys had it stashed under his bunk."

"You stole it." I'm pretending to be shocked, but Lex just laughs and unscrews the cap.

"Yeah, but who's he gonna complain to?" He puts the bottle to his lips and takes a long swig. Then he makes a face. "Ugh. This tastes like shit."

He hands the bottle to me, and he's right. It's overly sweet. Disgusting. But I take a long drink anyway. There's a peach on the label, but it tastes more like cough syrup than anything. I hand the bottle back to Lex and wipe at my sticky mouth with the back of my hand.

And that's when the sky opens up.

Lex grabs my arm and pulls me to my feet. "Come on!" he shouts.

We run, laughing together, toward the cover of the sea porch. But we're already soaked by the time we make it. We climb up on top of the picnic table to sit and watch the rain cascade off the roof like a waterfall. Lex hands me the wine bottle, and I take a long drink. The sound of the rain fills up the quiet. I pass the bottle back to Lex. I'm thinking about that weird flash of memory. Me hiding under the picnic table here. Hands over my ears. Angry voices. Gold strappy sandals and pink toenails.

"Av?" Lex is looking at me. We're both dripping. "What's going on with you?"

I watch a drop of water work its way down his nose. It moves between the freckles. Water is streaming down my face. Slipping down my neck like Cole's fingertips. Dripping down my back.

"Everything feels strange tonight," I tell him.

He nods. "It's so weird that this is all gonna be over in a couple of weeks." Lex takes another drink. He makes a face and shakes his head. "I don't know how to go home after this."

And I know what he means, because I keep thinking the same thing.

"It's like Willa said that first day," I tell him. "We're becoming different people."

"And that's a good thing, right?" His question is so honest and real, it's painful.

"I think so," I say. "I sure as fuck hope so."

We sit and talk for a long time, passing the wine back and forth while we listen to the rain.

Share a story.

Take a drink.

Lex tells me his dad is an asshole. "He moved away when I was little," he says. "And I only saw him a couple of times after that. Then the fucker moved back to town a couple of years ago and didn't even bother to tell me." He puts the bottle to his lips again. "I ran into him outside the liquor store."

"Seriously?" I say. "That's messed up."

"What about your dad?" he asks.

I shrug. "My dad isn't an asshole." I take the bottle from Lex and swallow another long swig. The sticky sweet warmth coats my throat. "He isn't anything at all."

It's quiet for another minute. Just rain and wine. And the comfortable warmth of sitting next to a good friend in the dark.

"I think I'm fucked, Av," Lex admits after he takes a particularly long drink. He sighs into the damp air. "I'm falling really hard."

"Jude's adorable," I say. "It'd be hard not to."

"I'm trying to just enjoy it, you know? Like, I don't want to worry about what happens later. But it's like, every second we're together, I'm counting down." He passes the wine in my direction. "Eighteen days to go." I watch him lean down to pick bits of wet grass off his ankles, and it reminds me of my first morning here. Waking up with that mud and grass in my sheets. I shiver, and Lex looks at me. "Seriously. You okay?" I nod. Scoot a little closer to him on the picnic table. He slips an arm around me, and I let my head fall against his shoulder. "How are things with Cole?"

"I think maybe I could fall in love with him, Lex. For real." I stare down at the weathered boards of the porch and wonder why I just said that out loud. Because I didn't even know I'd been thinking it until the words came out of my mouth. I look back up at Lex. "I've never been in love before." I see him taking that all in. "I mean, I'm not saying I'm in love with him after a week and two days. I'm not stupid. I'm not that girl. Jesus. I don't wanna be that girl. I just think maybe I could be. In love with Cole. Eventually. The potential is there." Lex is still looking at me. "Oh shit." I giggle. "I think I'm drunk."

Lex laughs, then fishes around in his bag and digs out a pack of cigarettes. "Just one left," he says. "We'll have to share." He pulls out a little box of matches to light it up, and I remember I still have his lighter. He takes a drag before passing it over to me.

I pull the smoke into my lungs. Breathe it out. Cough. "I think I'm starting to remember things," I tell him.

Lex takes the cigarette from my fingers. I watch him suck in and hold it. "About your mom?" He lets the smoke out in a slow exhale.

"Yeah. Nothing big. Just little bits, you know? Stuff from that summer here, mostly. Before she died." I'm thinking about the stars falling into the sea. Cole's voice in the dark. "But some of it doesn't make sense. It's confusing. Like it's all out of order or something."

Lex sighs. "Everything's fucking confusing."

It's some kind of Biblical magic how long that one cigarette lasts. A miracle. Like Jesus did with the loaves and fishes. We just keep passing it back and forth. Every time I put it to my lips, I taste Lex's minty ChapStick.

When the cigarette finally burns down, Lex gets up and crosses to the edge of the porch. He leans down to put it out on the wet steps. Then he flicks the butt into the bushes. He stretches one hand out into the rain and turns it palm up.

I watch the water slip between his fingers. He turns back to smile at me, and it knocks the wind out of me how beautiful he is. Red-gold hair and bright eyes against the dark blue of the night. That curtain of rain behind him. He takes my breath away.

Lex comes back to the picnic table and sits beside me again.

"Has anything happened to you?" I ask him. "Since you've been here? Anything weird?"

He raises one red eyebrow and grins at me.

"I mean—I went skinny-dipping."

"Yeah," I say. "Other than that."

He's quiet for a minute. Then he takes a long drink from the wine bottle. "A couple of nights ago, Jude and I were gonna sneak down to the barn. We were looking for someplace we could be alone. You know? And it was late. Maybe one o'clock in the morning. But Jude has a key, so we thought—" He stops. Swallows another swig of wine. "But we didn't make it."

"What do you mean, you didn't make it?"

Lex shrugs. "We never could find it. The barn. We kept walking. And I know we were walking the right direction. But we never came to it."

"I get so turned around here," I tell him, and I hope he can't hear the fear in my voice. "It's easy to get lost."

Lex turns toward me, and I think he's going to say something, but instead he leans in close and presses his lips against mine. I gasp in surprise, and when my mouth opens, I feel his tongue against the ridges of my teeth. Just for a second. His kiss is tender. Sweet. Then he pulls back and giggles. My mouth is tingling. That damn minty ChapStick.

"Oh shit," he says, and his hand flies to his mouth. He throws his head back. Laughs. Takes another swallow of wine. "I guess I'm drunk, too."

We're both laughing now. Leaning against each other and laughing so hard that tears are running down our cheeks.

I scoot down so I'm lying on the picnic table with my head in Lex's lap, looking out at my stars.

Cole's stars.

Lex is raking his fingers through my hair. "Promise me you'll be my best friend forever," he says.

I smile up at him. "I will if you'll let me."

Somehow I fall asleep like that. On the hard picnic table with Lex's fingers in my hair. The lullaby of the rain. And when I wake up, Lex is asleep, too. We're curled up together like kittens.

It's the foghorn that pulls me out of my dreams. Like always. It reverberates against my ribs. I look at my watch. Two o'clock. The rain has stopped. The night has turned cold, and the fog has crept up the lawn from the sea. I pick up the wine bottle. It's almost empty, but I take it with me as I cross to the steps to stare out into the dark. I tilt up the bottle to drain the last of the liquid. And it warms me. At least for the moment.

I turn back toward the picnic table to look at Lex. But he's gone. And just for a second, my mother is standing there. Gold sandals and pink toes. I see a little girl in a purple dress hiding under the table. Hands over her ears.

Then I hear my mother's voice so clearly. I know it now, from those videos Willa showed me. "*No more hiding!*" Her words come in a low, angry hiss. "*I want everything out in the open!*"

A flash of lightning turns midnight to noon, and I look out toward the great lawn. When I look back, the woman and the little girl are gone. Lex is sleeping on top of the picnic table again.

And I don't know if what I just saw was magic—or memory. The rain. Or the wine. But I know that Glory was right. My mother had a secret. One she was sick to death of keeping.

I think about those initials again. *B. C.* And the words my mother scribbled after them. *Figure out how to end it!!!* Those three desperate exclamation points.

More lightning splits the world in two. It's so beautiful that I wish Lex was awake to see it. It makes me lonely to think that everyone in the whole world is asleep, except me.

Then I see the little blonde girl in the white nightgown.

She's dancing on the dark lawn, oblivious to the swirling fog. She lifts one hand to wave at me. I don't wave back, so she just keeps dancing—twirling and spinning. Her mouth is open, and I can hear her laughing.

And then she isn't alone anymore. A little dark-haired boy has joined her. I watch them chase each other across the slippery grass. He grabs her hands and pulls her toward the trees. Toward the path to the Culver house.

The bottle slips from my hand and shatters on the stone steps.

Another flash of lightning draws my eyes up toward the heavens.

And then it's raining again. Water is pouring from the sky the way it pours from a bathroom sink.

When I look back down, the boy and girl are gone, and water is surging up the sloping lawn like waves washing up on the beach. A little higher each time. The rising flood sweeps away the picnic tables scattered across the grassy slope. It swallows the tallest trees. Foaming and swirling and rising and churning until the great lawn looks like the ocean in a hurricane.

I watch the water coming closer. It covers the lampposts that stand along the edge of the path, but they don't go out. I see them shining and blinking under the dark water, like strange luminescent jellyfish.

I'm still standing on the steps, and it's swirling around my ankles now.

I step up onto the porch and back away as seawater starts to creep over the boards. It's swirling around my calves. Getting higher and higher.

Knees.

Waist.

Chest.

The world is filled with water, and I wonder how long it will take to drown. And if I'll get it right this time.

I read a magazine article once about how drowning doesn't look like we think it does. How there's no screaming or choking or arm-waving. No yelling "help." Drowning is silent, the article said. Deadly silent. And most of the time, nobody else even notices.

The water is up to my neck now.

I'm worried about the broken wine bottle, the pieces of razor-sharp glass that I know are in the water. And I wonder about the girl in the white nightgown. And the little boy with dark hair. Have they been swept away? Or are they lurking somewhere under the black water, like the shards of the shattered bottle?

Then I have another thought. One that scares me more than any of the others.

Lex.

Lex is still sleeping on top of the picnic table.

And I know the water will cover him up.

Drown him.

Or wash him away.

That the pieces of glass will cut him to shreds.

Or maybe the girl in the white nightgown will drag him under the dark surface, where I can't get to him.

But when I turn to yell his name, he is standing right behind me.

It startles me, and I take a step back.

His hands are on my shoulders.

"Avril?" I want to warn him about the churning water, and about the broken glass and the girl in white—but I can't. I'm so cold and wet. Frozen solid. And the rain is still falling. "Avril." Lex says my name again, and this time he shakes me a little. "Hey! We need to make a run for the cabins. Before the rain starts again."

I reach out and touch his hair.

Dry.

The porch is dry.

He takes the wine bottle from my hand.

I feel myself trembling. I put my arms around Lex's neck, and he hugs me tight.

"Hey," he says. His voice is so gentle in my ear. "It's okay. I didn't mean to scare you."

I pull away and look around. The sky has the look of early morning. I hear the low rumble of distant thunder. "What time is it?" I ask.

"Five o'clock," he says. But it was only two when I woke up. And I'm wondering why Cole didn't find me. Cole always finds me. Lex's eyes look worried. He's smoothing the damp hair away from my face. "You'd tell me, wouldn't you, Av, if you were in trouble?"

"Yeah," I promise. "Of course I would." But I wonder how I'd know if I were really in trouble.

Would I even be able to tell?

"Come on," he says, and we gather up our things to dash across the field. The rain starts again just as we hit the front steps of the cabin. I hear the first cold, wet drops rattle on the roof. Lex tells me to get a few hours of sleep before breakfast, and I promise him that I will. But when I turn to head inside, I freeze. A bundle of lavender dangles from the doorknob. It's tied with twine, and the smell of it burrows its way inside my brain. I take it with shaking fingers and fling it into the rain. Then I creep inside.

I can't sleep, though. No matter what I promised Lex. I keep hearing those voices from the past.

My mother's. *I want everything out in the open.*

And Cole's. *Look at the stars!*

I pull out my mother's notebook again. I settle on the floor in front of my bunk and study it by cell phone light. There has to be something else in here about Brody Culver. I need another clue. Some proof. Something that will help me understand who my mother really was. And who she was becoming that summer at Whisper Cove.

But I don't find anything new. At least, not until I turn the notebook over. The back corner is water-stained and splotchy. But I can just barely make out something written in the top right corner. *#2,* it says. And at first I can't figure out what that could mean. Then I remember that photo Glory gave me. The one of my mother working at the table in the library.

I dig the picture out of my backpack to stare at it. And I was right. There are two notebooks lying open beside her laptop. I squint at the image, but it's too small and too fuzzy. I can't read any of the writing.

I tuck the photo inside the green notebook and slip them both back into my backpack. There are so many questions still unanswered, but the world suddenly seems a little more solid. Because for weeks I've been stumbling from random memory to memory, without anything concrete to connect them. And now I at least know what I'm looking for.

Notebook #1.

# ACT II: SCENE 10

The next morning we're sitting at our usual table in the middle of the cafeteria when I catch sight of Brody Culver. I've only seen him a few times since I've been at Whisper Cove, and I wasn't prepared to see him this morning.

He gives us all a big wave and a too-friendly smile, and I start to panic. But he doesn't come over to chat. He just grabs some coffee and a muffin and heads back to his office. And I'm relieved. I'm not ready to be face-to-face with him again. Not until I figure some things out.

As relieved as I feel, though, Val looks even more relieved. And I wonder what's up with that, but she doesn't say anything about it, so I turn my thoughts back to notebook #1.

We're dumping our trays when Val leans in close to whisper in my ear. "He touched me the other day. It creeped me out."

"Who?" I'm confused.

"Brody Culver," she says. And she makes a face. "I was working in the garden, and he came up behind me. Put his hands on my shoulders." I remember the way his fingers lingered on my bare arm. When he touched me in his office. "He told me he thought I had star potential."

"Seriously?"

She leans in even closer. Drops her voice a little lower. "One of the ladies who works in the kitchen told me he has a reputation for shit like that. With the actresses he works with." Val looks over her shoulder, then narrows those cat eyes of hers. "She said he has a temper, too. That he can go from nice to nasty so fast it'll make your head spin. So you watch yourself with him. Okay?"

"Yeah." I nod. "Okay." I knew that easygoing grin of his was fake.

"Girls gotta stick together," Val says, and she nudges me with her shoulder. "Too many fucking bastards out there."

"Yeah," I say again.

I'm wondering now if that's how things started between Brody and my mother. If he rubbed her shoulders and told her she had star potential. If he promised to help her start over. A new chance at a new life.

Somehow I make it through the morning workshop, wedged in between Val and Lex in the crowded library while someone from Actor's Equity drones on and on about how the union works. But all I'm thinking about is that missing notebook. It isn't in the box of things my father has in Dallas.

Did he throw it away?

Or did it get lost?

Does Glory have it?

She had notebook #2. She kept it all these years. So that seems like the most likely answer. At least it's someplace to start.

When I show up at her desk that afternoon, I hit her square in the jaw with my question.

"My mother had another notebook," I say. "That summer. Do you have it?"

Glory looks up from the email she's writing, and I see the panic on her face.

"Another notebook?"

I nod. "The one you gave me was marked number two. I need to know if you have number one."

She shakes her head. "I don't know anything about another notebook."

I feel the frustration bubbling up inside me. Because nothing is ever easy. But I'm in the mood for answers this afternoon, and I intend to get one. So I fire off another round.

"My mother was cheating on my dad. Wasn't she?"

Glory looks up from her computer and stares at me for a second. "No," she starts. And she shakes her head. "That's not . . . I don't . . ." I can see her wheels spinning. "It doesn't really matter, does it? It was a long time ago."

She stands up and moves to the copier. I watch her open the lid and put a piece of paper on the glass. She closes the lid and presses the buttons. The air hums with the sound of the machine. The hiss of copies spitting into the sorting tray.

"Are you sure?" I press. Because I already know she's lying to me.

Glory's still facing the copy machine. "I don't—" she starts again. Then she stops and takes a deep, shaky breath. "Nicki was my friend," she tells me. "The closest one I've ever had. And, honestly, that's all I know for sure anymore." She turns around to face me, and there's so much pain on her face. She sits down in her office chair.

She's staring at her desk. "Everything else about that summer is . . . hazy."

I don't know what to say. I hadn't meant to upset her. Glory's been so good to me. I just wanted to see if she might know anything else. Something she hadn't said yet.

Because I'm getting desperate.

When I walk into the cafeteria for dinner, Lex, Jude, and Val are already gathered at our usual table. I grab a pork chop and some rice and slide into one of the plastic chairs.

"You ready to die?" Jude asks me. He's dumping ketchup on top of everything on his plate. And the question throws me, until I realize he's talking about rehearsal.

We're working Eden's death scene tonight.

The scene where she drowns.

Lex looks worried. He's studying me with those bright blue eyes. "You sure you're up for this? It's gotta be weird."

"It's an intense scene," Val agrees. She stabs at a cucumber slice with her fork. "Even without the—" She stops. "The personal connection."

"It's fine," I tell them. "I'm actually looking forward to it."

Any actress would be, because Eden is the role of a lifetime. And her death is the kind of stage moment we all dream about.

Any actress but me, anyway.

Because the truth is, I've been dreading it since that first time Lex and I discussed it in the amphitheater, and every day at Whisper Cove that dread has gotten deeper.

There's no way I'm going to tell them that, though. So I do my best to push my worry aside. I laugh at Jude's jokes. Roll my eyes with Val. I let Lex fuss over me. But by the time we're ready to head down to the theatre, I'm so nervous that I feel like I might throw up. The two bites of dinner I managed to eat sit heavy in my stomach.

Cole is waiting for me outside the barn. He grabs my hand to pull me around the corner for a kiss. I kiss him back, but it's not as deep as I need. Or want. I'm afraid, if I kiss Cole too deep, he'll be able to guess all the secrets I'm keeping. Maybe he'll see the shape of them in my eyes or feel them hidden like rocks under my tongue.

"You ready for this?" he asks me. He's searching my face. There's so much tension in his jaw tonight. He's afraid for me, just like the others. But I nod.

"I'm ready." Then I hear the sound of the waves from down at the beach, and I shudder.

"If you fall in," Cole promises, "I'll save you."

He leans in to kiss me one more time before we head into the theatre and take our seats between Lex and Val. I feel everyone's eyes on me. Lex takes my hand and whispers in my ear, "I'm here, Av. I've got you." Val gives me a reassuring nod, and Jude hits me with his best grin. And that all helps. It helps a lot. But how do you prepare to drown? Again? Suddenly I don't feel ready at all.

"Okay," Willa says before we begin, "Avril, this is all you. There's no dialogue in this entire scene. Not one single spoken word. It's all very intense and physical." She looks at me, and I see a hint of worry in her eyes. "If you're uncomfortable in any way, or if anything doesn't feel right, I want you to call 'hold' immediately. Okay?"

"I can handle it," I say. "No worries."

Willa nods. "I know you can." The smile she gives me makes me feel so much braver. "You're not one to back down." She stares at me for a second. "Your mother would be so proud of you."

Willa looks at her papers, and Jude takes his cue. "Okay, people," he announces, "let's do this. It's nighttime again. Eden and Orion have agreed to meet by the river, but it's been raining all day. Eden gets there first."

One of the techs stands up to explain how we'll create the rain effect with lighting and sound. Same with the flood.

Willa walks me through what she wants. The mechanics of it are easy.

Enter from upstage left.

Cross to the edge of the stage.

Stand there and look out at the rising water. If I see it, she tells me, the audience will see it.

Then I look up at the stars and wait for the sound cue. Eden's music. When I hear that melody, I'm supposed to move. Just like I did at auditions. Then slowly the music will fade out, and the sound of rushing river will fade up. More lighting effects. Louder sound.

Until the dam breaks, and Eden is swept away in the blackout.

"Does that all make sense?" Willa asks, and I feel my heart racing in my chest. But I nod. Try to look braver than I feel. "How is Eden feeling when she dances here?" she asks me. "By the river. In the dark. And the pouring rain?"

The answer to that question is so obvious to me. "Mostly she feels free."

Willa smiles. "Why?"

"Because for the first time ever, she feels loved. Seen."

Willa nods. "That's it." She looks around the theatre at all of us. "You know, lovelies, we hear so much talk about 'finding ourselves,' but really I think it's not as much about finding ourselves as it is finding other people who know who we are, and who can reflect that back to us when we've forgotten it. Everyone needs someone who will sing your song back to you." She looks at me for a few long seconds, and I wonder if she's thinking about my mother. "God. What a rare gift that is." Then she smiles again. "So, Eden comes. She waits for Orion, and she dances to that music in her head, just for a few minutes, in this really private moment of letting go. Being free."

I'm starting to feel panicked. That music is so powerful for me, and I'm a little afraid of it. I guess Willa sees that on my face, because she says, "Just let us see what you showed me at auditions, and you'll be beautiful." She puts her hand on my arm. "That's what made me see you as Eden in the first place. You were so honest in those moments. And that's what good acting is all about. It's not about pretending. It's about becoming. Just for a little while."

"All right," I say. "I'm ready. Let's do it."

I move to the edge of the stage to make my entrance, and I close my eyes, just for a few seconds, to center myself before I step into Eden's world. I let her thoughts fill my mind and her feelings swell my heart.

She's remembering the first time Orion kissed her.

Then I correct myself.

I.

Not she.

Reliving. Not remembering.

I feel Cole's lips on mine. His fingers in my hair.

Reliving.

And then the music starts.

My music.

First it fills me up. Then it lifts me up.

I stop fighting. I give in and let it move me.

Stretching.

Reaching.

Twirling.

Spinning.

Lithe and limber.

I am a breeze blowing through the dune grass.

Movement. Memory. Motion.

And my feet aren't even touching the ground.

Because I am finally free. No more hiding. Someone finally sees me.

Someone knows me.

Someone loves me.

The rain is coming down. And the river is so close. It's rising. Getting higher. I can't even hear my melody anymore. Not over the sound of the water. But it doesn't scare me. The water is just a different kind of music. And I can dance to that, too.

Because Cole loves me.

Water swirls and bubbles.

It falls into my mouth.

Fills up my ears.

I spin in a slow circle, arms outstretched, and the music of the water is replaced by the soft tinkle of wind chimes. It's an ominous sound. Like the creaking of a door when you're alone in the house.

Footsteps on the stairs at night.

The quiet breathing of the monster under your bed.

I blink, and I can see my mother. She's standing at the edge of the cliff. She screams. And I know it's her voice. I recognize it now. She yells my name. Calls me April.

But I'm crouching in the damp night air. Hiding. The grass is thick and wet. I feel it sticking to my bare feet. Clinging to my legs.

My mother is there. And then she's not.

She's vanished. Over the edge.

I stand up and scream for her.

And then I'm blind. Staring dead-eyed into a light so bright it hurts.

Suddenly the sky is on fire. Bits of colored glass streak toward the water like fragile rain.

*Look at the stars!*

I hear the echo of that voice in my head. And I know now it's Cole's. It has to be. Because that's his magic trick. The stars all belong to him.

But someone else is there. Someone who isn't Cole. This person is bigger. Taller.

A grown-up. Not my mother, though. Someone who scares me.

A cold hand tight around my wrist. I'm being jerked. And dragged. I grab for something to hold on to. But it's too late.

I'm flying.

Flying. Flying. Flying.

Then falling like the stars. Rain on fire.

I'm a toy boat flung into the sea.

I hit the water hard. It hurts. I feel the crack of bones. Like hitting cement. I hold my breath as the water washes over the top of my head. My mind is calm, but my body fights involuntarily. My legs kick and my arms claw.

I'm sinking.

I look up toward the surface. Toward what's left of the stars. They're melting together and blurring with the movement of the water. They haven't all fallen. Some of them still hang in the sky.

Then, one by one, I watch them blink out and go dark.

Like the light cue at the end of a scene.

Then there's nothing.

Just dark. Just cold.

Until I feel hands on me. I'm being lifted up and carried. And I'm so frozen. Everything hurts.

I try to scream. To call out for my mother. But I can't make any noise.

I can't see.

But I do hear sounds.

Someone shouts.

And someone else is sobbing.

So many voices.

Sirens. Far away.

More shouting.

Snatches of conversation.

What happened . . .

. . . already gone.

. . . so little.

Where's Nicole? Somebody find Nicole!

. . . pulse . . .

Shit.

. . . losing her.

Fuck.

Hang on.

. . . too late.

Then the high-pitched whine of a siren. So close that it feels like it's inside my head somehow. It hurts my ears, and that's the moment I know for sure that I'm alive.

Someone is touching my hand. Calling my name.

"Avril."

Warm, gentle hands on my face.

"Avril, it's Cole. Open your eyes."

Suddenly I'm sucking huge breaths of air deep into my lungs. Gasping and gulping and choking.

"Easy," he says. "Just breathe." He wraps me up tight, but I pull myself free from Cole's arms. Untangle myself. Because he was there that night.

Cole Culver was there the night my mother died. The night I drowned. He told me to look at the stars.

He was there.

He was there.

He was there.

But someone else was there, too. Someone who took me by the wrist and tossed me in the water to die.

My mother didn't kill herself.

She didn't try to kill me.

Someone else was there that night.

Someone who murdered us both.

And there's only one person that could be.

Brody Culver.

I remember what Val told me. How Brody has a reputation for being too friendly with his actresses. How he can go from nice to nasty in an instant. And it all falls into place.

Everyone is staring at me.

Willa lays a hand on my arm. "Avril, that was incredible. I've never seen anything like that. It was heartbreaking. Terrifying to watch. Just perfect."

Cole stares at his mother. "Are you fucking kidding me?"

Willa looks from me to Cole. "Why don't you two take the rest of the night off?" she soothes. "I'll work with some of the others."

"Fuck you." Cole spits the words at his mother. Willa looks stunned. But she covers well. Doesn't even flinch.

Cole takes my hand and leads me off the stage. Toward the big double doors of the barn. Lex and Val are on their feet in the second row. Lex calls out to me.

"Avril!"

It reminds me of how my mother called my other name. Just before she vanished into thin air.

Over the edge of the cliff.

But I can't answer Lex. Just like I couldn't answer my mother. My mouth has stopped working.

"Let her be," I hear Willa say. "It's a hard thing, what she just did."

"Fuck," Val says, and I want to tell her I'm okay, but Cole is already pulling me out into the dark.

Somehow we end up around the corner. In the amphitheater. We're at the top. All that empty space below us. So high. And it reminds me of his house. The cliff in the back.

How we threw that tiny boat in the water. And the water took it home.

The amphitheater is spinning.

My mother and I didn't walk into the water at Whisper Cove. We were thrown into the sea from the cliff behind Brody Culver's house. And then the current took me back to the beach.

Just like that little boat.

My whole body is shaking. My heart is racing. I can't seem to get control of my breathing. It feels like being caught in a riptide. Pulled out to sea.

I'm getting farther and farther from shore. Nothing but black emptiness on the horizon.

"Avril." Cole's hand is on my cheek. His voice is in my ear. "What happened in there?"

And I can't tell him. I can't say that his father and my mother were having an affair. And that I think his father is a murderer. But that's what my mind is screaming at me over and over.

And I need it to stop. Just for a second. I need to think. I need to breathe. I need something to hang on to. Something to stop me falling. I need—

I put my hands on Cole's chest and move him back toward the wall of the barn. I need the feeling of his whole body pressed against mine—solid and real—as our lips find each other.

I have never in my life kissed anyone like this, so deep that it's like we're the air in each other's lungs. Like I'm trying to find a way under his skin.

We're making a home inside each other. Burrowing our way in.

If I can just get deep enough, nobody will be able to find me.

Cole will keep me safe.

I slip my hands under his sweater and rake my fingernails across his stomach. I tease him. Just the lightest touch. One finger dipping below the waistband of his jeans. His mouth is open.

Tongues. Lips. Teeth.

Cole moans, low in his throat. I catch the sound in my mouth and swallow it. It makes me feel powerful and sexy.

Like I'm in control of at least one goddamn thing. At least in this moment. Right now I know who I am and what I'm doing. Who I'm with. Where I am.

What is real.

And what I want.

Cole is still kissing me. His tongue is insistent against the soft inside of my cheek. Then tickling against the roof of my mouth. He slides his hands under my shirt, up my back to unhook my bra. I hear him say my name, deep and throaty. It sounds like waves against the sand.

I shiver hard, and I know Cole feels it. Because he stops.

He's breathing so heavy, but he puts his hands on my shoulders and pushes me back. The space between us feels cold. He's watching me with gray eyes.

"Avril," he says. "What happened to you in there?" I just stand there with my mouth half open. I don't know what to tell him.

"Whatever that was," he warns me, "you can't ever do that to yourself ever again. I don't give a shit about the play. Or what my mother wants you to do. Wherever you went there, it wasn't a safe place for you."

"Since when did you give a fuck about being safe?" I'm teasing. Reaching for him again. But Cole hears the truth in my voice.

"I'm serious," he says. "It's dangerous. Looking into the darkness like that." His eyes are full of fog. "Believe me. I know."

I untangle myself from Cole. I can stand on my own.

"Why didn't you come and find me last night?" I ask him. "After rehearsal."

He runs a hand through those dark waves. "I got lost last night," he tells me, and I'm staring at that compass rose tattoo. "I couldn't even find myself."

I picture him. Eyes closed. One foot in front of the other. Along the top of the windy cliff. And I ache for him. For both of us.

"I remembered things tonight," I say. "During that scene." Because I owe him at least a little truth.

"What kind of things?" Cole's voice is full of sharp edges.

"I won't get that close again. I promise." He doesn't look like he believes me. "I just need to keep a little distance."

And I need to figure out what I'm going to do next.

Cole walks me back to my little blue cabin. Lex is sitting on the porch step waiting for me.

I let Cole pull me close for another kiss before we say good night. "I'm right next door," he whispers. His hand is on my cheek, and his eyes are locked on mine. "I'm sorry about last night. Next time you get lost, I'll find you. I swear."

I nod, and I want so much to make him the same promise. I want to tell him that I'll pull him back from the jagged edge. But I don't know if that's even possible. And I don't want to lie.

When Cole heads off toward the other cabin, I go and sit next to Lex on the steps. He doesn't say anything. He just hands me his half-smoked cigarette and digs another one out for himself.

"I thought you were out," I tell him.

He shrugs. "I bought a few off George. I figure he can't bust me for smoking shit he sold me in the first place."

"Good point," I say, and then the two of us just sit there smoking in silence, watching the fog creep up the lawn in our direction.

"You okay?" he finally asks me.

"I don't even know how to answer that," I tell him.

Lex nods and ashes his cigarette with a quick flick of his wrist. A few more silent minutes slip by. He takes a long drag and blows smoke up toward the stars.

"We should go to bed," I say. "Fog's coming in."

But Lex doesn't move.

"What's been going on with you, Av?" he asks me. "And don't fucking tell me it's nothing."

"I don't know," I admit. "I'm remembering things, I think. But it's hard to make sense of it all. I'm not sure what's real anymore."

"Tell me what you need." The words are so simple, but they make me want to cry. Because I don't think anyone's ever said them to me before.

"I need you," I tell him. "I need a friend."

*I need someone to keep from slipping away.*

*Or being dragged out by the tide.*

Because if Brody Culver killed my mother—if he tried to kill me—then I'm going to lose Cole. And Willa. There's no way around that.

Lex puts his arm around me, and I rest my head against the solidness of his shoulder.

I look up and see the moon gazing down at us from a vast dark sea, but there aren't any stars tonight. Not a single one is shining. The sky is an infinite coal-colored plain.

It's like someone stole them.

Or scared them away.

So I look up at the empty sky and make a wish on the blackness.

# ACT III: SCENE 1

I spend the next few days going through the motions.

Breakfast. Class. Lunch.

Work. Dinner. *Midnight Music.*

I'm avoiding Cole as much as I can. Getting down to the barn just barely in time for rehearsal. Always with Val or Lex. Never alone.

But then he touches me during a scene. Or leans in close to whisper a line. I feel his breath on my cheek. And I'm lost again.

During every free moment, I'm studying my mother's notebook. Pouring over her scribbles and doodles. Looking for another clue. Something that will tell me what went wrong. How we ended up at the top of that cliff that dark night, with Cole and Brody Culver.

How the two of us ended up in the water.

But I know I only have half that story. Because that first notebook is still out there somewhere.

I make it through Thursday and Friday somehow, even when Glory sends me upstairs with a delivery for Brody. My legs feel weak on the stairs, and I sigh in relief when he isn't in his office. I leave the package on his desk and give myself a moment to look at that picture. My mother on the sea porch steps. Her hand on Brody Culver's arm. Laughing. Those gold sandals and pink toes. I close my eyes and try to put myself back there. Under the sea porch picnic table. I hear my mother's voice again.

*I want everything out in the open!*

I'm listening for more bits of conversation, but all I hear are angry voices. It's too muffled. So I head back downstairs to Glory, who spends the afternoon sneaking worried glances in my direction.

Then it's Saturday. All day in rehearsal with Cole watching me. Something dark has settled behind those fog-gray eyes of his.

He knows I'm hiding from him.

On Sunday, our day off, I'm sitting in the cafeteria with Val and Lex and Jude when Willa sticks her head in the door. She motions for me, so I leave my tray on the table and go to see what she wants. We step out into the hall.

"How would you feel about coming over to my house tonight?" she asks. "After dinner?" I'm panicking, trying to think of a way to say no. Because it makes me queasy, thinking about spending the evening with Cole and Willa. With Brody. But she goes on. "The boys will be gone, so it'll just be the two of us." She smiles. "A girls' night." And her eyes are so warm. "I thought I'd show you some more videos."

"I'd like that," I say.

When I knock on her kitchen door that evening, Willa is wearing shorts and a T-shirt. She's barefoot and her hair is loose. She has a glass of wine in her hand, and she looks so relaxed and comfortable. It makes me feel incredibly special that she's invited me here. To her house. To be with her like this.

And then it makes me feel impossibly guilty. Because I know what my mother was doing.

What Brody did.

What they did together. Behind her back.

Willa is at the counter. She's arranging some cheese and crackers on a tray for us, and my eyes are drawn to that little painting of the muses again. Those beautiful girls dancing by the edge of the lake. There's something about it that speaks to me. That girl who is a fountain, water streaming from her invisible holes. It's beautiful and strange. Like everything at Whisper Cove.

Without even thinking about it, I reach for the frame. I just want to lift it off the wall. To hold it in my hands and get a closer look. I need to see if that girl with all the holes looks as much like me as I think she does.

But Willa is pressing a wineglass into my hand. It's less than half full. "Don't tell the others," she warns me. She's trying to look stern, but her eyes are sparkling. And I laugh.

I forget about the girl with the holes.

Willa leads me into the living room. This time I notice a bookshelf tucked into one corner. I hadn't even seen it before, but now I'm staring in awe at her Tony. It sits next to a half dozen other major awards. Drama Desk. Drama League. Critics' Circle. Others I don't recognize. All for *Midnight Music.* I can't stop staring.

Willa is leaning in the doorway watching me. "Do you want to hold it?" she asks, and I nod. I sit my wineglass on the shelf, and I'm barely breathing as she lifts the Tony and puts it in my shaking hands. It's heavier than I expect it to be.

I'm looking at my reflection in the shiny silver plaque on the front of the award. BEST PLAY, the lettering says. MIDNIGHT MUSIC. WILLA CULVER.

"Did you know *Midnight Music* wasn't the original name?" she asks me. "It was called something else at first." Willa gives me a little wink. "That's a bit of trivia for you."

"What was it called originally?" I ask. It's so weird to think of *Midnight Music* being called anything else. The name is so iconic. It's like finding out *Death of a Salesman* once had another title.

Willa smiles and waves away my question with a flick of her wrist. "It doesn't matter," she tells me. "*Midnight Music* is what it says on the Tony." She takes a sip of wine. "Original names don't matter much. Do they? What matters is who we become."

I'm still staring at her name in bold letters. All caps.

**WILLA CULVER.**

"So many people spend all their time trying to find out who they are," Willa says. "But that's such a passive act. What you really have to do is create yourself." I look up at her, and she cocks her head to one side. "Who do you want to be, Avril?"

"I don't know," I tell her, and she sighs.

"You can't dream yourself a life. You have to hammer and forge yourself one. It takes a lot of courage." She stops. Takes another sip of wine. "Your mother was brilliant. She could have been anything. She could have had such a life. My God. She could have been a star." I watch her swirl the wine around in her glass before she swallows the last of it. "I think about that a lot. What Nicole could have been. Would have been. If things had been different."

I hand her the Tony award, and she puts it back on the shelf among the other trophies. "She could have been extraordinary," Willa tells me. "And really, that's the whole point of being alive, isn't it?" She pauses. Polishes the Tony with the hem of her T-shirt. Wipes away my fingerprints. “To do something amazing with our one brief, beautiful moment on earth.”

I turn back to look at all those awards again. There are pictures, too. Photos of Willa with famous people. A couple of movie stars. Some Broadway people who look familiar. President Obama.

“Wednesday night,” Willa says, “in rehearsal. The drowning scene.” My face turns red. I feel the heat in my cheeks, and I’m glad I’m looking at the shelf. Not at Willa. Because we haven’t talked about this yet. How Cole cursed at her and pulled me out of the theatre. What happened to me before that. “You got too close, didn’t you?”

I nod. My eyes settle on a picture of Brody Culver, and I think about what I remembered that night. My mother’s scream before she disappeared over the cliff. Cole’s voice. The undeniable presence of someone behind me. That tight hand on my wrist. Flying and falling.

I reach for my glass of wine.

“Cole still isn’t speaking to me.” She smiles a little. “He thinks I pushed you too far. That I asked too much of you. That’s why he reacted the way he did.” Willa pauses. “He was scared for you. So he lashed out at me.” I can’t move. I don’t know what to say. “Avril. Look at me.”

I make myself turn to face Willa. My hands are shaking. The wine is sloshing in my glass. But Willa’s eyes are so calm. So clear. Looking at her instantly makes me feel better.

“I think Cole’s wrong. I think you can handle it,” she says. “Because I think there is greatness in you. Great talent. Great strength.

And a great capacity for facing what scares you." She looks at me. Takes a sip of wine. "You remember that."

We settle onto the couch and Willa picks up the remote and pushes play.

My mother is alive again.

There's some kind of party happening on the great lawn behind the farmhouse. A big white tent has been set up. There's music and dancing.

"We had a big fundraiser," Willa says, and she nods toward the television. Her voice sounds far away, not in distance so much as time. "That last night. Before Nicole died."

I tighten my grip on the wineglass. Finally take a drink. It's not sweet like the wine Lex and I drank on the sea porch. This tastes expensive. I take another sip. Then I lean forward and study the video. I'm watching my mother weave in and out of the crowd. She's smiling and laughing. Pausing to hang on Brody Culver's arm and beam up at him. I watch her bat her eyelashes, and I'm wondering how Willa didn't see it. How she doesn't know.

It hits me that I'm watching the last scene of my mother's life. Right before she made her exit.

But then I remind myself that's not right. There was another scene. A curtain call. High on a cliff overlooking the water. In the dark. Behind a house with a big porch full of flowers.

This house.

My mother's final bow.

Whatever happened to her—to us—it happened not long after this video was recorded. And not far from where I'm sitting now.

"Tell me again what you remember," Willa says. And I freeze. "About that night."

"I don't know," I tell her. "It's just a jumbled mess."

Willa gets up and moves into the kitchen. She comes back seconds later with the wine bottle. The little tray of cheese and crackers. I watch her fill up my glass. She sets the bottle on the coffee table in front of us.

"Sometimes our brains play tricks," she says. And I nod as I swallow more wine. Because I know she's right. But I feel so sure about what happened that night. Every minute it feels more like the truth. "It's so easy to get lost inside our own minds." She frowns. Refills her own glass. "Did Cole tell you he went away for a while last year?"

"No," I say. I don't tell her that Glory mentioned it.

"He got lost. Inside himself. He was confused. All turned around." Willa takes a deep breath. "Cole will tell you he's a musician, not an actor." She shrugs. "But it doesn't matter. He feels deeply." She smiles at me. "Creative people like us always do."

The wine is making my head feel fuzzy. Sleepy. Willa takes my wineglass. She sets it on the coffee table and puts a pillow in her lap. "Come on," she says, and I slip off my flip-flops to stretch out. She pulls the blanket off the back of the couch to cover me. Willa's hand is in my hair. She strokes my head as I watch my mother spin across her television screen. "Whatever you remember, Avril, let it come. I'll help you face it. You don't have to do this alone. We can make sense of it together." She pauses. And when she speaks again, there is something about her voice that breaks my heart. "I owe Nicole that much."

And being with Willa makes me feel so safe. So taken care of.

But if I do what she's asking me to do—if I let those memories come—I'll lose her. And Cole, too.

I can't think about that anymore, so I watch my mother spin and smile. I let myself sink into the softness of Willa's couch. Her hand in my hair.

The comfort of a mother's touch.

It's everything I've always wanted.

"I love you," I murmur as I float away. But I don't know if I'm talking to my mother, or to Willa.

And I'm not sure which one of them whispers it back.

# ACT III: SCENE 2

Eden's melody wakes me up. It drifts into my ears like fog. Each familiar note vibrates against a thought that's buried so deep inside me. Some memory that's just out of reach.

I open my eyes, and someone is at the piano. Bent over the keyboard. Dark hair falling across his face. I listen to him play. And I ache.

That song.

Those fingers moving across the keys.

It's more than I can stand.

"Cole?" He stops. Turns around to look at me. "What time is it?"

"Almost midnight."

I'm so confused. Groggy. My head hurts.

"I fell asleep," I mumble, and I try to sit up. But it's so hard. "Where's your dad?"

"He went up to bed."

I manage to push myself up.

"I have to go."

"Stay," Cole says. He's kneeling in front of the couch now. He presses his lips to mine, and I crave more of him. He tastes salty. Like the sea. But I pull back.

"I can't stay here." Cole is tucking the blanket around me. But I can't be in the house with Brody. I know that. It isn't safe.

I shove the blanket onto the floor. Stand up. Slide my feet into my flip-flops. I'm heading toward the back door.

"Wait," Cole says. "I'll walk with you back to the cabins." I let him follow me out into the dark.

The fog.

I'm instantly confused. Turned around. But Cole leads me back toward the path to Whisper Cove, and when it gets steep, he reaches for my hand. Holds on tight.

We come out of the woods onto the great lawn. But I still can't see a thing. The fog is thicker than I've ever seen it. It's like looking at a gray wall.

Cole is still holding my hand. We feel our way across the grass. And neither of us speaks. If we did, I don't know if we'd even be able to hear each other. The fog would probably absorb the sound. Swallow the words and leave us with silence.

It seems like we've been walking forever.

Finally I see the flicker of lights in the farmhouse windows. Upstairs in one of the rooms—Brody's office, maybe—someone has left a lamp on. And tonight, it's our lighthouse.

We make our way to the sea porch so we can sit together on the steps. I'm grateful for the familiar feeling of the rough stone under me. My legs are shaking. I'm cold. Wet and exhausted.

I tilt my head back to look up at the green-and-white-striped awning. Maybe it will jog my memory. If I can remember something else about that fight, the one I overheard here when I was five, maybe somehow all of this will make sense.

But tonight there is no awning to block out my view of the stars. I see them shining, dim and far away, through the fog. It reminds me of looking up at them from underwater while I was drowning.

"Cole," I whisper. But he's staring over his shoulder. I look back to see what he's looking at, and there are no picnic tables, either.

A broom leans by the door. There's a braided rug. A bucket.

A child's wooden toy.

"Cole." My voice is threaded with fear. He holds a finger to his lips.

"Shhh," he whispers. "We'll wake them up."

"What is this? What's happening?"

"Folie à deux," he tells me. His mouth is so close to my ear. I feel the words more than hear them. "Madness shared by two." Cole takes my hand and pulls me up off the steps. "We need to go."

We step into the fog, and Cole slips an arm around me, but I pull away. I'm so confused.

"Tell me what's going on," he says. "If I did something to piss you off, or if—"

"Your father was having an affair with my mom." The words hang like water droplets in the heavy air. We're standing toe to toe. No space between us. It's the only way we can see each other.

"No," Cole says. He shakes his head. "No way."

"She wrote it in her notebook," I tell him. "And then my dad confirmed it."

Cole shakes his head again. "I don't believe that."

"I get why you don't want to believe it," I tell him, "but—"

"No," he says again. "You don't understand." He glances up at the light in the farmhouse window. Pulls me farther away from the sea porch. "It's not like that. It's just, my dad would never. Not because he loves my mom or he's such a good man, or whatever. He just—" Cole stops. He shakes his head. "My dad's a fucking coward. He likes the girls. Sure. But he'd be too chickenshit to take it that far. There'd be too much to lose."

"What do you mean?"

"I told you all of this belongs to my mom on paper. The house. The whole fucking theatre. Everything they built together." Cole shakes his head again. "He'd never risk her finding out. She wouldn't put up with it. My mom, I know she seems so warm, and she is. Or she can be. But she's ruthless, too. Willa looks out for Willa. She'd snatch it all away. Leave his ass with nothing. And he wouldn't survive that. This fucking theatre is all that's ever mattered to him. It's his whole goddamn life."

I hear the echo of my mother's angry whisper. Those words she said on the sea porch while I was hiding under the picnic table.

*I want everything out in the open!*

Cole thinks he's clearing his father's name, but all he's done is assign him a motive for murder. If my mother wanted everything out in the open—if she wanted to stay and build a life with Brody—if he'd made her a promise and she'd already told my father she wasn't coming home—but then Brody decided he couldn't risk letting Willa find out—what would he have done to keep that quiet?

How far would he have gone to hold on to everything?

"You were there that night," I tell him. "I remembered that." I don't tell him about the stars. My old nightmare. I'm afraid to talk about that. It still has so much power over me. "I know you were there."

"What night?" he asks me.

"The night my mother died." I swallow the sick feeling that's rising up in my throat. "You and your dad were both there."

Cole looks like I hit him in the face. He stares at me for a few seconds. Then he shakes his head.

"No," Cole says. "I wasn't there. I'd remember that."

"On the cliff," I tell him. "Behind your house."

"I wasn't there, Avril." Cole looks so confused.

"You were," I tell him. "We both were. And your father threw my mother into the sea."

"No."

"They were having an affair, and I think she must have threatened to tell everyone. To tell your mom. And he must've panicked."

Cole is shaking his head. Blinking hard.

"No way," he says. "That's crazy. He wouldn't—"

"Cole!" My voice is rising. I hear the hysterical edge underneath it. "He tried to kill me, too."

But the water took me home. Back to the beach at Whisper Cove.

"You're confused," Cole says. "Things are all mixed up. You said that yourself."

He reaches for me, but I pull away.

"Don't tell me I'm confused." I spit the words at him. "I know what I remember."

It's taken me twelve years. But I know now.

"You don't remember that, because it never happened." Cole sounds so certain. But I know he's wrong. And I can't be here anymore. Talking to him like this. I let go of his hand and walk into the fog.

"Avril!" Cole shouts. He's forgotten all about waking up whoever is sleeping in that nightmare version of the farmhouse. "Don't." He grabs for me, but I've already slipped away. "Fuck!" I hear the frustration in his voice. "Avril, come on. Jesus Christ." And then I hear the frustration turn to fear. "Where the fuck are you?"

And the thing is, I'm still standing right there. So close I could reach out and touch him. But he can't see me. I might as well be a ghost. So I just turn and walk. I can't even tell what direction I'm walking. One step after another in the blinding fog. No idea where I'm going. At one point I get tangled up in something. It grabs at me. Wraps around my face. And I gasp. Struggle free.

Damp cloth.

I feel the long ties of a cotton apron. Overall buttons.

Laundry hanging on the line.

My legs have turned to Jell-O, but I keep walking until I can't go any farther. Then I sink down in the wet grass and wrap my arms around my chest.

I'm lost.

And I'm so cold. So, so, so cold.

I find Lex's lighter in my pocket, but the tiny flame doesn't do a thing against the dark that's swallowed me up. I wonder if Cole can see the orange glow of it. I wonder if he's still looking for me.

He promised me he'd find me.

Thinking about Cole opens up a painful crack somewhere inside my chest. It feels like being split in two.

And then I hear the whispering.

I flick the lighter again. And again. I close my eyes. Hum a tune. Count to ten.

But there's no way to block out the sound.

So I take just one step toward those voices. Just one.

I'm pulling wet air into my lungs. It's like breathing water.

Then I register the slap of ice-cold waves against my knees.

I'm standing in the sound again.

My mind can't make sense of it. It doesn't know how to bend that far. But I feel the truth of it.

Ice-cold water.

The kiss of seaweed and the squish of thick sand.

I walk backward and backward. One foot. Then the other. One tiny, shuffling step at a time. Until I can't feel the water slipping over my toes anymore.

Lex's lighter is still clutched in my hand. I flick it. But nothing happens. It must have gotten wet. I stand at the edge of the ocean, trying to remember how I got here.

And then I hear a sound behind me. A single soft word in the fog.

"Mom?"

And I turn to look into my own eyes.

# ACT III: SCENE 3

I back away from myself, and the fog fills up the space between me and her. That other girl with the white-blonde hair. And my face. I can't see her anymore, and I feel better with that distance between us.

Until I back into someone else.

I spin around to face George, the Whisper Cove caretaker. He's standing right there. I can smell alcohol on his breath. That's how close he is to me.

"You're not supposed to be down here. Late like this." My voice won't work. I've forgotten how to form words. "Come on," George says, and he clicks on a huge flashlight before he turns to go. But I can't make myself follow him. Not George.

Where's Cole? He's supposed to be the one who finds me.

When I hesitate, George grabs me by the arm and pulls me along behind him. "Come on," he grumbles. "I can't leave you down here." So this will be the second time in my life that he's found me on the beach and dragged me up the hill.

His fingers are tight on my arm as I struggle through the damp sand. It shifts and moves under my weight. It's deep tonight. Drifting.

But I don't look back. And I'm relieved when we come to the boardwalk and George finally lets me go.

I don't know what I'm more scared of, George with his alcohol breath and his roaming eyes—or the dark of the not-quite-empty beach. So I give up and follow his flashlight between the dunes. Over the marsh. Up the hill. He never checks to see if I'm still behind him. And he never says another word. Not until we reach the farmhouse.

The awning is there again. The picnic tables. And I wonder about the child who owned that wooden toy. The one that was lying on the braided rug by the back door.

Where is that little boy or girl now?

I'm rubbing at the bruised places on my arm. Trying to massage away the feeling of George's fingers on my body. "You shouldn't be out there," he tells me. His voice sounds irritated. Like it's a big pain in the ass—the worst part of his job, maybe—hauling meddling kids off the beach while they're staring at phantom versions of themselves. "You got no business runnin' around in the dark like that." He clicks off the flashlight and sits on the steps. Where Cole and I sat not long ago. He pulls out a pack of cigarettes and shakes one out. I watch him light it up and breathe out smoke.

"What are they?" I ask him. "They're not ghosts."

The girl on the beach.

The woman in the fog outside my cabin window.

George sighs. It's a long, deep sound. It reminds me of the foghorn. "No," he says. "But that's what most people would call 'em."

A stiff sea wind blows across the lawn. It carries away the fog for a few seconds, and I see the sound laid out below us.

George is looking at the water. Same as me. The cigarette is dangling from his lips, so he talks out of one corner of his mouth. "They built that lighthouse in 1906," he tells me. But it isn't standing there tonight. There's no glow on the horizon to mark the opening to Whisper Cove.

And the smell of pigs is in the air.

"They're echoes." I breathe the words out like they're made of mist. "Memories."

"Not your memories," George says. But I already knew that. Because I've never had any memories.

These are Whisper Cove's memories.

My mother feels so alive to me at Whisper Cove because some part of her is still here. She still crosses the field. Stands on the sea porch. Dances on the grass. Like those home movies of Willa's. Only more real.

I remember the little girl I watched. That night when Lex and I shared the wine. Before the rain came back.

Somehow, five-year-old me is still running across the lawn with Cole tagging behind.

"Things get trapped here," George says, and he ashes his cigarette on the sea porch steps. "It's the fog, maybe."

I watch that thick gray curtain settling onto the lawn again.

It's filling up the space between the farmhouse and the beach.

The space between me and George.

All the space in my lungs.

I can't breathe.

"You've seen your mama," George says. "Haven't you?" But I don't answer, because I don't owe him anything. "I like to see 'em sometimes," he says as he blows out smoke. "The ones like your mother. God, she was beautiful." He's looking at me, and the expression on his face makes me uncomfortable again. I hate the way his eyes travel up and down my body. Slip over my bare shoulders. My thighs. "It's nice. Once you know what they are." George stands up, and I take a little step back. "They can't hurt you." He clicks on the flashlight. It's so bright. I have to shield my eyes. "You just make sure you don't hurt yourself."

He reaches out to touch my hair—runs a damp strand between his dirty fingers—and I hold my breath. Stare at the cigarette between his teeth. His mouth twists into an almost smile. "You look like her," he says, and he leans closer.

"Don't," I warn him. And I'm surprised how loud my voice sounds. How strong. "Don't you fucking touch me."

He smirks at me then. "Act like 'er, too." He takes a step back. "I saved your life. Did you know that? You'd have died, probably, if I hadn't found you down there washed up like a drowned rat. After your own mama tried to get rid of you." And maybe that's true. But it doesn't give him the right to look at me the way he is. "Get on to your cabin." He drops the still-burning cigarette and grinds it into the damp grass with the heel of his boot. "And goddamn stay there," he adds before he disappears into the dark. "Shoulda let the sea fuckin' have you." I watch the bounce of his flashlight until it's gone. And all I want is to go to bed. Like George said. But my legs are shaking. I don't know if I can cross that distance tonight.

That muddy field as wide as an ocean.

The split-rail fence where the pigs are.

I drop down to sit on the sea porch steps. I pull my knees to my chest and hug them tight. I'm reluctant to leave the little glow of the back porch light.

I've only been sitting there a few minutes when the fog blows away again. The clearing only lasts a couple of seconds, but it's long enough to watch a solitary dark-haired figure emerge from the tree line. My heart leaps into my throat, because I'm not ready to see Cole again yet.

Then I realize this isn't Cole. It's Willa.

I watch her walk up the lawn toward the sea porch. The fog is settling in behind her as she moves. Like it's following her. It's the long, dragging train on a gown made of night. And there's something strange about the way Willa is moving. Something about her that looks like a ghost.

Or a memory.

She reaches the stone steps of the sea porch, and I can see that she's real. Flesh and blood. So I say her name out loud. "Willa?"

Her eyes are open, but she walks right by me. Like I'm not even there.

I follow her in the back door of the farmhouse. Down the twisting hallways. Past Glory's reception desk, where the only light comes from the glowing computer screen. We move through the empty cafeteria. But she stops in the library doorway. The room is dark.

"Willa." She doesn't respond. Doesn't turn around to ask me what I'm doing out so late.

*Nobody outside the cabins after eleven o'clock.*

It's hard to see. The lights are off, and fog presses against the windows from the outside. It blocks out the moon. But I can make out the shape of her as she moves to the shelf and begins to pull the books and scripts from their places. She's digging through them. Knocking them to the ground. Like she's looking for something she can't find.

The lights suddenly flick on. It's so bright. For a split second, I'm five again. Blinking. Blind. Then Cole is standing beside me. His hand is on the switch.

"She's sleepwalking," he tells me. But I already figured that out. "Mom." His voice echoes loud in the empty library, but then it soaks into the long curtains. Gets absorbed into the pages littering the floor. "Mom!" he says again. Louder.

Willa turns around to stare at both of us. She blinks. Looks around the library. Takes in the pile of books at her feet. Then she sinks to her knees. She's staring at the mess she made.

Cole and I move toward the bookshelf. We're picking up the books. Putting them back on the shelves. Reorganizing and reordering.

But Willa is still slumped on the floor. She's staring at her hands now. I see them shaking.

When we're finished, Cole takes her by the arm and lifts her to her feet.

"I'm sorry," she says, "if I scared you." I don't know which one of us she's talking to. Both of us, I guess. Her eyes look so different tonight.

"We all get lost sometimes," I say. But all Willa can do is stare at her shaking hands.

"I'll take her home," Cole tells me. He jerks his chin toward the leather sofa in the corner. "Sleep here tonight, okay?" He glances toward the window. "Don't go back out there."

"Yeah," I tell him. "Okay." I'm trying to come up with something else to say, but I can't.

"I'm coming back," he promises, and I can only nod. He starts toward the doorway with Willa, and suddenly more words come to me. "Cole." He turns back to look at me, and there's something unreadable in his gray-fog eyes. "Be careful."

When they're gone, I look around the library. I'm thinking of that picture Glory gave me of my mother. Her bent over the laptop. Notebooks spread out beside her. Two notebooks. Eyes on fire. I can almost see myself playing hide-and-seek while she works. My little dark-haired playmate concealed behind the long drapes.

I curl up on the comfortable leather sofa. It's soft. Well-worn. And I wonder if my mother ever sat here. I lean my head against the arm and try to feel her, but I don't close my eyes. I'm staring out the window into the thick fog. And I know there's probably nothing there. But I keep seeing shapes. And faces.

Hands pressed against the glass.

I get up and go to untie the golden cords holding the curtains back. I pull them closed before I head back to the sofa.

It's been such a long, strange night. First the wine with Willa. Then waking up to Cole playing the piano. The fight about his dad. Being alone in the fog. Then not alone on the beach. That conversation with George.

And now Willa. Sleepwalking.

I'm exhausted, but I don't close my eyes.

Not until later, when Cole slips back into the library. He puts his arms around me. Pulls me against his chest. I feel his beating heart. So I know he's alive.

Real.

"Has she always done that?" I ask him. "Your mom?"

"The sleepwalking?" I nod. "No. I don't think so. I think it started . . ." He hesitates.

"After my mom died?"

"Yeah," Cole says. "That's what my dad says."

It's weird to think that I'm not the only one who was forever changed by my mother's death. There are so many other people who live with that hole. Just like I always have.

It makes me sad to know that, but somehow it also makes me feel less lonely.

Cole kisses me then. Soft and gentle, and with so much tenderness. And I feel it all the way down in the deepest, most hidden parts of my heart. So I know that I'm alive, too.

And finally I let myself sleep.

With the lights on.

The last thing I hear before I slip away is Cole humming that melody in my ear.

Eden's lullaby.

A song for a drowned girl.

# ACT III: SCENE 4

It's early morning when Cole wakes me up. I'm confused. I don't understand why we're in the library. But then I remember everything about last night. And it's like being knocked down by a big wave at the beach.

We walk back to the blue cabins together, and Cole kisses me again. Says he'll see me later. He doesn't mention anything about his mom. Her sleepwalking last night. And he doesn't tell me I'm crazy. That his father isn't a killer. He just brushes the clinging hair back from my face and promises me that everything will be okay. But it's a promise I don't really believe.

I don't see Willa all morning or all afternoon. She doesn't pop in to the cafeteria to wave at me. She doesn't stick her head in the door and ask me to bring my lunch to the sea porch.

But when I get to the theatre for rehearsal that evening, she's standing in the middle of the stage, staring up into the rafters of the barn. I'm lingering in the doorway with Lex and Val and Jude, and Jude finally coughs to let her know we're there. Willa turns and beams at us—at me—like nothing happened last night. I wonder if maybe she doesn't remember pulling those books off the shelves in the darkened library.

She waves us in. "Come on, my lovelies, we've got a lot of ground to cover this week." She's gorgeous tonight. Glowing. Long, dark hair and the jangle of silver bracelets. All lit up by the stage lights. There's no hint of the woman who sat slumped on the floor, surrounded by jumbled scripts and papers.

Cole slips in just as we're beginning. He finds a spot a few chairs away from me, but I can still feel him.

It's Monday night. The beginning of week three. We're just over halfway to the finish line, and I don't know how to feel about that. There's still so much I need to figure out. And it all seems so impossibly tangled and confusing. I'm worried that there isn't enough time left. And I have no idea what happens after this.

I can't imagine going back to Texas and picking up where I left off. I'm not that girl anymore.

But I'm also starting to wonder if I'll survive another two weeks at Whisper Cove.

"Okay," Willa tells us, and she claps her hands to get our attention. "We're working the scene at Eden's funeral tonight." Val is sitting beside me, and I can feel her excitement, because this is her first really big moment. "Eden's older sister, Anya, finds Orion after the funeral. Everyone else is gone, but he's still sitting there. And she tries to talk some sense into him." Willa winks at Val, then turns her eyes toward Cole. "You two ready?"

I'm glad I'm not in this scene. It gives me a chance to watch.

And think.

Cole takes his place in a folding chair onstage, and Val enters from the right. She crosses down to stand beside him. I notice the stubble along Cole's jawline. He's wearing the same wrinkled clothes from last night. And his eyes are so dark. Rimmed with black circles. I wonder how long it's been since he slept.

Days?

Weeks?

Years, maybe.

Probably.

Val puts her hand on his shoulder.

**ANYA**: You can go home now, Orion. She's gone.

**ORION**: What if there was a way to bring her back?

Cole turns his head to look up at Val. The two of them are striking, onstage together. All that beautiful dark hair and intensity.

**ANYA**: You can't—

**ORION**: Maybe I can.

**ANYA**: That's not how it works. No matter how much you loved her—

**ORION**: I more than loved her.

**ANYA**: Everyone more than loves the people they love.

**ORION**: Nobody has ever loved anyone the way I love Eden.

**ANYA**: Even if you could, she wouldn't be the same.

**ORION**: That doesn't scare me.

**ANYA**: It should.

**ORION**: I promised her I'd save her.

**ANYA**: No one can really save anyone else.

**ORION**: But I promised.

I'm sitting in the first row. Cole isn't looking at his script now. He's staring at me, and I get so lost in the bottomless gray of his eyes. And I know he's lost, too. We can't breathe. Can't look away from each other. It's like we're holding each other prisoner. Trapped in this moment together.

**ANYA**: You shouldn't have promised that. It wasn't fair.
**ORION**: But I meant it.

Cole's voice is so broken. There's real pain there, and I hurt for him. He drops his head to his hands. And I think, for a second, he's crying. But his shoulders aren't moving. He isn't making any noise. It's like he's turned to stone.

And I'm not sure that he's acting anymore.

I'm not sure he ever was.

Everyone in the theatre waits. We're holding our breath. The seconds seem to stretch on forever. But he doesn't go on to the next line. Val looks from Cole to Willa. Then to me. She doesn't know what to do.

But I know.

I get to my feet and move to where Cole is sitting. He's so still. But I kneel down in front of him, and I put my hands on his knees. I press my lips to the top of his head. Those beautiful dark waves.

He raises his head to look at me, and he whispers that he's sorry. It's so soft I can barely hear the words. They drift across my skin like fog. And I pull his face toward mine. I want to tell him without words that it's okay. That he doesn't have to save me. That I'm fine. That whatever is happening, I can handle it. All I want is for him to find a way to save himself. That's the only thing I need. But I don't know how to say all that, so I kiss him.

Cole's lips are so soft, and the kiss is deep. It's long and warm and lingering. And when it's over, everyone is staring at us. Of course.

I'm not sure what to do, but Willa steps in and saves both of us. "That's what good theatre does, my lovelies. It makes us feel," she says. "And that is never a bad thing."

And I love her so much in that moment.

Everyone applauds, and my face turns bright red. I find my way back to my seat, and Lex slips his arm around me. "You good?" he whispers, and I nod. But I'm not really sure that's true. Cole gives me a little smile, and I do my best to smile back. Because we each need the other one to be okay. Even if it's just for a little while.

Cole and Val go on with the scene, and they run it a few more times before we move on to something else. I'm not onstage in any of the scenes we work, and that's okay with me. I've already been the center of attention for way too many nights.

I open up my script to go over some lines. I flip to the back. The very last scene. And a few tiny flowers fall into my lap like purple snow. They've been pressed flat between the pages. I pick them up and hold them between my fingers.

I look around the theatre, but no one seems to have noticed the overwhelming smell of lavender. Or the fact that I've stopped breathing.

When rehearsal ends I look for Cole outside the theatre, but I don't see him. It's a perfect night. Beautiful and clear. No fog. No damp. No chill. Everyone seems to have found someone to enjoy the gorgeous weather with.

Lex is leaning against the wall of the barn. Jude goes in for a kiss. They whisper together, forehead to forehead, and Lex giggles as he slips his hands into Jude's back pockets. They're completely wrapped up in each other. Oblivious to everything else in the world.

Val is flirting with one of the guys. A blond named Nixon who's wearing a *Star Trek* shirt. She tosses her long, dark curls over her shoulder and laughs. He tells her she was really good in the scene tonight, and I see her touch his arm. Bat her long eyelashes. I wonder if this means she's broken things off with Chester for good. I also wonder if she's taken Nixon skinny-dipping yet.

Finally I spot Cole. He's sitting on the edge of the steps. Alone. Just staring off into the dark. I walk over and touch his hair, but he doesn't look up.

"Come on," I say, "we need to talk." I reach down and take his hand. Then I pull him to his feet and around the corner toward the amphitheater. But there are people there, too. Some of the techies are hanging lights. Gearing up for the big performance. *Midnight Music* by Willa Culver, starring all of us.

"Shit," I mutter. Because I don't know where to go.

"It's okay," Cole says. "I know a place." He leads me toward a little gravel path that runs around behind the barn.

There's a bench against the back wall of the building. Two big coffee cans filled with sand sit at either end. "This is where the crew comes for smoke breaks," Cole tells me in a voice that sounds like he's apologizing. But it feels like the perfect spot to me, because we have it all to ourselves. We just sit there for a few seconds. Grateful to be alone.

We're facing a clearing that extends from behind the barn to a line of trees not far away. A little trailer sits off to one side. There's a tiny garden. And couple of beat-up lawn chairs.

"George's place," Cole tells me. I see lights inside the trailer. The flicker of a television screen, maybe. I think about George finding me on the beach last night. In the fog.

"Remember that first night? At the bonfire?" I say. "On the beach." Cole nods. "You told me Whisper Cove was different from other places."

"I remember."

"What is it that happens here? At night. In the fog."

"It's hard to explain," Cole says. "I don't even know for sure myself, really. And I've lived here my whole life." He raises one eyebrow and gives me a crooked little grin. "Besides, you don't believe in ghosts. Right?"

"They aren't ghosts," I say, and Cole's grin disappears.

"No," he says, "they aren't. But I also told you that first night that there are lots of ways to be haunted."

"George told me they're memories. The things I've seen."

Cole lets out a long breath and leans back against the outside wall of the barn. "I don't think they're memories, exactly. At least not all of them." He's studying the coffee can full of cigarette butts. "Or maybe they are memories, and things just get out of order sometimes."

"What do you mean, out of order?"

Cole looks off at the tree line. Then up at the moon. He's looking anywhere but at me, and my brain is firing off little warnings that there's something I'm not getting.

"Mostly they're things that have already happened," he says, "but every so often, I catch a glimpse of something new. Something that hasn't happened yet."

"Like something in the future?"

I remember how, days ago, I stood on the beach and called out to what I thought was my mother. Just one word whispered into the fog. *Mom.* Then she turned to look, and there was the shock of looking into my own eyes.

And how, last night, I stood at the edge of the water, and turned around when I heard myself call out.

Two moments out of order. Circular memories. Like a dog chasing its tail.

It makes my head hurt. I feel dizzy, and I have to reach for Cole's hand to stop me spinning.

"It doesn't happen often," Cole tells me. "It's only happened to me a couple of times over the years."

"What did you see?" I ask him. But he won't answer. He just runs his fingers over the tattoo on his wrist. That compass rose. Then he leans down to kiss me. It isn't a long kiss, but there's something desperate about it. And it leaves me breathless.

Broken and afraid.

Cole's hands are in my hair, and his lips are at the corner of my mouth. Sweeping across my cheekbone. My forehead. Then he's breathing against my ear. "It doesn't matter. None of it's real. Smoke and mirrors, remember?"

But the fear in his voice tells me Cole doesn't believe that. It's a lie to make me feel better.

To make himself feel safe.

"You saved me tonight," he says. I close my eyes and lean into the brush of his fingers across my cheek. "During that scene. In the theatre. I fell in. And you saved me."

"Anya says that nobody can save anybody else," I remind him.

He pulls me against him, and it feels good to be wrapped up in his arms. But there is so much sadness in his voice. His words are thick with it. "We can't, in the end. But maybe we can save each other in little moments, like you did for me tonight. And maybe that has to be good enough."

"I love you."

I don't mean to say it. It just slips out. And I'm not even sure exactly what I mean by it. Because I'm feeling so many different things right now. I just know that it feels true. And that seems so weird, because it's only been two weeks. But then I remind myself that I've known Cole Culver almost all my life.

I just didn't remember it.

"I love you, too," he tells me. "I'm pretty sure I always have."

"You mean since we were five," I tease him, but he shakes his head.

"I mean always." He looks at me for a few seconds. I can't resist reaching up to run my fingers over the stubble along his jaw. I want to feel all of him. So I can remember him this time. I don't ever want to forget again.

"My father didn't kill your mother, Avril. It doesn't make sense. He's fucking spineless. He would never have had the guts."

I'm almost sure he's wrong. My memories of that night are so clear now. There are gaps. Pieces missing. But everything points to Brody Culver.

"Cole—"

"We have two weeks left," he tells me. "There's still time to figure it all out."

I don't tell him that it's actually less than two weeks. The performance is eleven days away. And the day after that, everyone will leave Whisper Cove.

Everyone except for Cole. He never gets to leave.

Eleven days.

That's not much time to untangle twelve years' worth of secrets. Or to figure out who my mother really was.

To become whoever it is I'm meant to be.

But maybe Cole is right. Maybe there's something I'm missing.

I want there to be another answer. Because the thought of losing Cole and Willa is almost too much to bear. And I don't see how it can go any other way, if I'm right about what Brody Culver did that night.

The wind changes direction then, and goose bumps break out all along my arms. The hair on my neck stands up. The overwhelming scent of lavender is drifting on the night breeze.

"Cole?" I whisper. "Can you smell that?"

"It's lavender," he says.

"I think my mother loved lavender," I tell him. "It reminds me of her."

"It's good that things like that are coming back to you." Cole smiles. Squeezes my hand. "It's all those little things that keep people alive for us, I think."

But he doesn't understand.

"Cole, someone has been leaving me little bundles of lavender."

He looks confused. "On the porch of the cabin. And in my bed. Between the pages of my script, even."

"Why?"

"I don't know," I tell him. "To scare me, I guess. That's the only reason I can figure out."

So that I'll know I'm being haunted. Not by a ghost. But by a person.

"It blooms this time of year," Cole tells me. His dark eyebrows are drawn together. "It wouldn't be hard to find around here."

"Where does it bloom at Whisper Cove?" I ask him.

Cole looks toward the little trailer with the flickering windows. "It grows wild all along the edge of George's place."

# ACT III: SCENE 5

I follow Cole's gaze down toward George's trailer, and something flickers across his face. Something that looks like hope. "You said you remember someone else being there that night." His words come out in a rush. An exhale that sounds like relief. "Someone who scared you." I nod. "Maybe it was George. He can be mean as a snake, Avril. I've seen it. That side of him."

I can't help wondering if he's ever seen that side of his father. The one Val whispered about in the cafeteria. That quick-to-anger side. And it suddenly hits me that there's not any real difference between George and Brody Culver. The way they look at women. Men like that are all the same. They feel entitled to stare. Or to touch. The only thing that separates the two of them is that Brody Culver has money and George lives in a falling-down trailer behind the barn.

But one isn't any better or worse than the other. It could've easily been either one of them.

Maybe it was more than a coincidence, George finding me washed up on the beach that morning. Almost dead.

Maybe he knew exactly where to look for my body.

I'm confused now. Grasping for those memories again. But I'm having trouble pinning them down tonight.

Someone hits me in the face with that bright light.

Then the hand around my wrist.

And I'm flying—falling—into the dark.

I think about the look on George's face when he talked about how beautiful my mother was. How Glory said he made a fool of himself that summer, pining away after her. I remember the way his eyes slipped over my shoulders. My thighs. How he touched my hair and told me I looked like her. My mother. And I shiver.

*Act like her, too.* That's what he said when I told him no. *Shoulda let the sea fuckin' have you.*

"Maybe," I say even though something about it doesn't feel quite right. "But I know my mother was having an affair with your father," I remind him, and I dig my mother's notebook out of my backpack. I show him the page with the initials on it.

*B. C.—Figure out how to end it!!!*

"Fuck," Cole says when I shine my phone light onto the page. It's the first time he's actually seen it. "In a million years, I'd never have believed he'd cheat on my mom. It's too risky."

"My dad confirmed it," I say. "He said she wasn't coming home. That she'd met someone. And that had to be your dad."

The scent of lavender drifts into my nose again. I look down toward the trailer, and a shadow moves across the window. "But I think maybe George was in love with her, too," I say. "And he gives me the creeps. The way he—"

"Avril." Cole's eyes flash. Bright and angry. "Did George say something to you? Or do something?" I hesitate. "Because if he has, you need to tell my mom. There was some trouble with one of the girls a few years ago. If he—" Cole stops. Gives his head a shake. "My mom made it clear she wouldn't put up with that. He'll be out of here."

The irony of that is hard to miss. Willa probably has no idea what people say about her own husband. Nobody would have the nerve to tell her.

"It's nothing," I tell him. But I keep thinking of the way George touched my hair. The way he looks at me. I don't want him gone, though. If there's a chance he really had something to do with what happened all those years ago, the last thing I want is for him to disappear right now.

"I don't believe my dad's a murderer, Avril. I can't believe that." Cole's eyes are on fire. They burn with a promise. "But I'll help you figure this out. No matter what the answer ends up being."

He walks me back to the cabin and kisses me good night. But he doesn't head toward the cabin next door. He just settles onto the front steps and leans against the railing. And I know he'll be there until morning. Staring out into the fog.

Keeping watch.

Cole's vigil doesn't end when daylight comes, though. For the next couple of days, he's my shadow. He eats every meal with us in the cafeteria. He waits for me outside my morning classes. Checks in on me when I'm working with Glory in the afternoons. I find him leaning against the outside wall of the bathroom when I come out after my shower. Waiting for me at the door when rehearsal is finished. He tells me he wants me to stay away from George. Not to ever let myself be alone with him. That it's not safe.

And every night he ends the day by sitting guard on the steps. I sit up with him, as long as I can. He presses pieces of sea glass into my palm, and we pour over my mother's notebook by cell phone light. Looking for clues. I tell him about the missing notebook. The one that will have "#1" written in the upper right-hand corner. On the back.

We talk through every memory I have. Every piece of the puzzle. Until my head gets too heavy, and it falls against his shoulder. Or until he sees me shivering. Then he sends me in to bed. But he promises he'll stay. That he won't leave. That he doesn't mind. Because he doesn't sleep anyway.

He doesn't say it out loud, but over and over again he's promising that he'll save me.

And I'd give anything to be able to save him, too. But his cheeks are more sunken and hollow every day. His eyes are dimmer. There's this darkness swelling in him. A kind of hopelessness. I can see it when I look at him. And I feel it when he kisses me.

By Thursday, we're not really any closer to figuring out what happened the night my mother died, and I'm becoming more worried about Cole than I am about me.

"I didn't find it," he tells me that evening when we meet up before rehearsal.

"Find what?" I ask him.

"That first notebook," he says. "I tore the house apart. Top to bottom. Every drawer. Every closest. But it isn't there."

And I know how bad he must have been hoping he'd find it, and that there would be something in there that proved me wrong.

Some clue that would point toward someone other than his father.

It's written so plainly on his face.

We're in the final few days before we move out to the amphitheater to start working with sound and lights, and everyone is feeling the pressure. The lack of sleep. The ticking clock. The stress of wanting to do justice to this beautiful piece of theatre we're creating together.

"The curtain goes up one week from tomorrow," Willa tells us after warm-ups. We're working the scene where Orion calls Eden back to him. It's the first time they meet after she dies. And it's always been my favorite scene in the play. "So we're going to keep forging ahead. Courage, my lovelies. Putting on a play is a kind of birth. And there is always pain in creation."

As tired as everyone is, there's still this tingle of excitement that buzzes through the room whenever Willa speaks. She looks at me and smiles, and I instantly feel better. Because it's like the whole world has turned to liquid and I can't find a foothold anywhere. But Willa still feels solid. She's my touchstone. The shoreline. And I have this rush of gratitude at having found her again. If I can't have my mother back in the flesh, at least maybe I can have a mother figure in Willa.

And maybe that's enough.

Maybe it has to be.

But that thought is followed by this cold dread when I think about Brody. And what I still believe he did. I've been going back and forth for the last few days, trying to decide if I'm going to tell Willa what I remember. Like I told Cole. And I'm running out of time to make a decision. I still don't have any real proof.

And I'm terrified to lose her.

Cole is convinced that it must have been George who grabbed

me by the wrist and threw me from that cliff. That he was pining away over my mother. Like Glory said. That he killed her because he couldn't have her. And he tried to kill me, too. But then, when I didn't die on cue, he decided to play the hero to make himself look innocent. So he brought me up from the beach that morning. Half-drowned.

We've whispered over all the possible scenarios as we sat huddled on the steps together these last few nights. But I'm still not sure. Wandering eyes and those creepy gifts of lavender don't make George a murderer. Brody's the only one with real motive.

Those are his initials in the notebook.

It's his backyard where the land drops away to the sea.

He's the one who had everything to lose. Cole said that himself.

Val nudges me, and I look around.

"Avril," Willa says. She's waiting for me, and I realize I've been staring off into space. "Let's take it from the top of the scene."

I nod, and Cole and I move to our places. He's sitting on the bench, and he pulls out that guitar. His fingers slide across the strings, and Eden's melody fills the barn. I feel every single note so deep inside my chest, and before I even realize it, there are tears sliding down my cheeks. No piece of music has ever affected me like this.

Just for a second, I have the very beginnings of a memory. Something about my mother. But then it slips away before I can wrap my fingers around it. And it feels like having her ripped out of my arms. My chest is being squeezed so hard my heart and lungs have surely turned to powder. I'm a girl with chalk dust where her insides should be.

I walk toward the bench where Cole is sitting. "That's a beautiful song," I say. My cheeks are still wet, but I don't bother to wipe away the tears. I don't have anything to hide from Cole. "Is it okay if I sit here?"

He turns to look at me, and there are tears in his eyes, too.

"Eden?" When Cole breathes that name, it sounds like a kiss. "I knew you'd come back."

"I think I used to know a girl called that," I say. "It sounds familiar."

"Don't you know who I am?" he asks. "I wrote that song for you."

I walk around the bench and sit beside him. I shake my head.

"You must have me confused with someone else."

Cole puts out his hand to touch me, and I shrink back from him.

"Please don't," I say. "I don't know you."

I look out toward the river. And something about the way it looks in the moonlight scares me. It's still and perfect tonight. But somehow, I remember it swirling. Bubbling and rising. I remember it pulling me down. Below the surface.

I remember being swept away.

My breathing is fast and shallow. My pulse flutters. I need more air.

"I know you," Cole tells me, and those three words are my anchor. Cole knows me. He remembers who I am. "I'll always know you."

"This is such a lovely spot," I tell him. "But I don't know why I'm here. "

"I know why I'm here," he says. "I'm waiting for someone. A girl I knew once."

"I hope you find her."

He smiles. "Maybe she'll find me."

"Is she someone you love?"

Cole reaches out to touch my hair. And this time I don't pull away. "Someone I more than love."

I sigh. "I think I more than loved someone once. I can almost remember him."

"Here." Cole picks up the guitar again. "Maybe this will help."

He starts to play, and his song fills up all the holes in my heart. It flows into me the way water flows out of the cracked muse in the little painting that hangs over Willa's breakfast table.

I close my eyes.

"The water," I whisper. "I was flying. I remember . . ."

The sound of wind chimes makes me shiver.

"Do you remember me?" Cole asks.

"I remember a dark-haired boy who kissed me and gave me the stars."

He pulled them out of his pockets and flung them into the ocean. For me.

Cole leans in and kisses me, and when I feel his lips on mine, I'm as fragile as sea glass. This isn't a stage kiss. This kiss is everything. I have to fight back the urge to whisper Cole's name. I want him so bad. I need him. He pulls away, and I open my eyes to look at him.

"It was you," I say. And Cole nods. "It's always been you. Hasn't it?" Something breaks deep in my heart. "I'm so sorry."

"Why?" he asks, and I reach up to run my fingers over his face. The angles and edges of him.

"Because I think it's too late for you to save me."

"Blackout," Jude announces. "End of scene."

Cole and I are staring at each other. My hand is still on his cheek. I'm holding my breath. My heart has forgotten to beat. Everything in my body is still. Waiting.

What comes next? For us. Avril and Cole. Where do we go?

"Wow," Willa tells us. Her voice is hushed, like she's afraid to break the spell that Cole and I have been weaving together. "That's incredible. There's a lot of honesty there." She looks from me to Cole. Then she turns back toward all of the others, who are leaning forward in their folding chairs, hanging on her every word. "This is what brilliant theatre is, my lovelies. This is what we are capable of when we don't pretend. When we *become*." She crosses back to me and crouches down in front of the bench. "Do you feel it, Avril?" Her hand is on my knee. I nod, and Willa smiles. "You're becoming Eden. She's so alive now." She gives my knee a little squeeze. "Your mother would be so proud of you." She looks at me for a second. "I'm proud of you."

I have this wild urge to jump up and hug her. There are so many empty places inside my heart that Willa fills up.

She waves a hand in Jude's direction, and I'm half-hypnotized by the jangle of those silver bracelets. "Let's run this scene a few more times before we go on to something else."

Later, after rehearsal, while Jude is shutting down the lights, Cole pulls me into a dark corner of the barn. His mouth is on mine before I have a chance to take a breath, and I'm not prepared for the way he kisses me. There's so much hunger in it. There's no gentleness tonight. Nothing tender. Cole is all urgency. Nothing but need. He's more teeth than anything else.

"God, you were beautiful, in that scene," he whispers. His lips are pressed to my neck, and his words vibrate against the soft part of my throat. "I keep thinking about how scared Orion must be. How it must terrify him to think he might lose Eden, when he'd just barely found her."

"Again," I say, and Cole pulls back to look at me. Those gray eyes of his are deep with fog.

"Again," he whispers back. "When he'd just barely found her again."

Jude plugs in the ghost light then, and we follow him out into the night.

I don't sleep much. I toss and turn. And I wake up exhausted. Then I feel guilty for being tired. Because I know that Cole hasn't slept in so long.

I'm still thinking about that scene. The one we worked at rehearsal last night. Eden's returning. It lingers in my head all through our morning class on British dialects. And through lunch.

It's Friday. One week until the curtain goes up on *Midnight Music.*

That afternoon, Glory sends me back out to the scene shop. She wants me to find a knife so I can break down some boxes.

Brody gets a lot of packages.

But for some reason, I find myself following the little path that leads around behind the barn. I stand against the building and stare at George's trailer. In the daylight, it's easy to see the little purple flowers that grow among the rocks at the edge of his garden.

I want Cole to be right.

I want it to be George.

Not Brody.

I want it for me. For Cole. For Willa.

For all of us.

I take a look around, but George isn't anywhere to be seen. I move toward the flowers until I'm close enough to touch them. I breathe in lavender. It mixes with the salty scent of the sea. And the smell of decay from down at the marsh.

My fingers find one of the purple clusters. They're so delicate. Each one made up of a dozen tiny blooms.

"Did Glory send you down here?"

I whirl around, and George is staring at me.

"No," I say. But neither one of us moves. "I just wanted to see the flowers."

George narrows his eyes at me like he's trying to figure out what kind of game I'm playing. He takes a step in my direction, and I suck in a quick breath. We're so isolated here. Behind the barn. Nobody even knows where I am. Glory thinks I'm down at the scene shop.

George pulls out a pocketknife. He flips it open. And I'm frozen. For one split second, I know for sure that Cole was right. George is a killer who murdered my mother.

Who murdered me. Once. A long time ago.

But then he turns toward some tomato plants. He's cutting away dead leaves. Letting them flutter to the ground. "I figured maybe she needed some more," George says.

I stop. Confused. "What do you mean?"

"Glory. She's been cuttin' lavender all summer."

George doesn't look up from where he's working. I watch him tie the plants up to the trellis. Fraying brown twine.

My heart starts to beat even faster.

"Glory," he repeats. Like I must not have heard him the first time. "She's been down here after lavender a couple of times a week." He points to a place where the bush has been trimmed back. "And it's not like I care. It grows wild. She can have all of it, far as I care. But I don't have time to be bundling it up for her. She can do that part herself from now on." He looks back over his shoulder at me. "You tell her that. Okay?"

I nod and back away from George. I'm moving toward the path. And I'm still half expecting him to stop me. But he doesn't. He doesn't even look up from his tomato plants.

I stumble back up toward the farmhouse. I can't feel my legs. My whole body has gone numb. I'm trying to form a coherent thought. To figure out what I'm going to say when I get back to Glory's desk. But even as I'm climbing the front steps, I have no idea.

She looks up when the screen door slams behind me. I'm just standing there in the doorway, staring at her.

"Avril?" she says. "Did you find a box knife?"

I need somewhere to go. Somewhere Glory isn't. I need time to sort through what George just told me. To see if I can force it to make sense.

"Um. I—" Glory is staring at me. Her eyes are full of concern. They're kind eyes. And I almost tell her what I know.

But then I think about how scared I've been. The lavender on my pillow. Pressed between the pages of my script like a memory.

And I know I need to get away.

From here.

From her.

"I feel sick," I say. And it isn't a lie. "I need to go back to the cabin."

"Sure," Glory says. "Of course. Do you want—"

But I'm already out the front door. And before I really even know it, my feet are carrying me down the great lawn. Across the marsh.

Over the dunes.

To the beach.

I hadn't been looking for him, but it doesn't surprise me when I see that Cole is already there. Because we have a way of finding each other.

Over and over.

And over.

He's standing on the floating swim dock, facing away from me. Out toward the lighthouse. And he doesn't know I'm watching him. So I stop and stare. That wild dark hair is blowing in the wind. He's shirtless. Beautiful.

And he looks so alone, standing out there surrounded by all that water. Something swells up in my throat. It's the feeling I get sometimes when I wake up in the middle of the night wanting my mother, and she seems so close. But I know there's no way to get to her.

No way to touch her.

Or to save her.

Cole turns to face me, but I don't know if he sees me. I'm still standing on the boardwalk. Dwarfed by the dunes on either side. And as I'm watching, he falls backward. Into the sea.

My breath catches in my throat. Because one minute he's there. And the next he's gone.

Just like my mother on the edge of that cliff.

I kick off my flip-flops and step into the deep sand. I'm waiting for Cole to pop up again. Scanning the surface of the water for that shock of dark hair.

But he doesn't come up.

And he doesn't come up.

And he doesn't.

And he doesn't.

And he doesn't.

And then I'm running toward the edge of the water. My heart is beating so hard.

Because he's gone. And it's been too long. Way too long.

But then I catch sight of him. He's pulling himself out of the waves. Down by the rock jetty at the end of the beach. Collapsing on the hard-packed sand.

I yell his name, and he lifts his head. But I'm already running in his direction.

I drop down to kneel beside him in the wet sand. And he rolls over on his back to look up at me. His chest is heaving, and I lean down to press my lips to his. He's cold.

So cold.

But he kisses me back. My hands are on his arms. His chest.

"You scared me." I can still taste my heartbeat inside my own mouth. It's wild. Afraid.

"Don't worry." Cole gives me a little smile. "This isn't how I die."

I stare at him for a minute. Something about the way he reaches up to touch my hair makes me think he didn't mean that as a joke.

"Did you hear it?" he asks. I'm wiping the sand from his cheeks. "It was so loud this afternoon."

"Hear what?"

The relieved look on his face tells me what he's talking about, and I shiver.

"I love you," I say. And it's not like the first time I said it. The last time. Behind the barn. When it just slipped out on accident. This time I say it on purpose. Because I want him to know.

He needs to know.

"I more than love you," he tells me. And I know he's telling the truth. "I always have."

Cole sits up and puts an arm around me. He pulls me against his side, and we keep each other warm as the waves lick at our toes. I run my fingers over his compass rose tattoo, and I wish it had real magic.

But we both know it can't keep him safe.

And he can't keep me safe.

"It wasn't George," I say, and I tell him about the lavender. How Glory has been cutting it all summer. "It had to be her leaving the flowers for me."

"Why?" Cole asks. I see the confusion in his eyes. "Why would Glory want to scare you?"

"I don't know," I say. "I don't have any idea."

"Just because he didn't leave the lavender," Cole says, "that doesn't mean he isn't responsible for what happened to your mother. And you."

I see how badly he still wants to believe it was George. How bad he needs it not to have been his father. But there's some huge piece of the puzzle I'm not seeing. Something that's just out of reach.

Cole and I sit together on the beach until we've missed dinner and it's time to head up to rehearsal. Lex and Jude and Val are waiting for us out front, and they look us over when we show up hand in hand. Damp and sandy.

"You guys okay?" Val asks. Her eyes move between my face and Cole's.

And I have no idea how to answer her in any way that sounds convincing, so I just nod.

"Av," Lex says. "What's going on?"

Jude opens his mouth to say something, but Willa arrives just then. Jangling bracelets and keys. She's unlocking the door and waving us all inside. "It's the home stretch, lovelies," she tells us. "No time to waste."

We're working the next scene between Eden and Orion tonight. Their second meeting after Eden's death.

And when Cole takes his place on the bench and picks up that guitar, I brace myself. Tell myself to be prepared. But that haunting melody still seeps into my soul. It tears at something buried in my memory.

Or in my heart.

With every note, I feel it coming closer to the surface.

So when I cross to Cole and look at him through tears, it's not acting. It's not even becoming.

It's just me existing.

"I know that song," I tell him. "I hear it in my heart sometimes."

"Come and sit beside me," he says, so I do. And I feel the soft press of his thigh against mine. He's so warm and so alive.

I wonder for a second if he can feel the heat of me. But then I remember that he can't. Because I'm dead.

Cold. And gone.

"I knew you'd come," Cole says.

"Again," I say. "You knew I'd come again."

He smiles. "I knew you'd come again."

"I thought about being somewhere else," I admit. "But I didn't know where that was."

Cole takes my hand. He's moving his thumb back and forth across my wrist. Rubbing the spot where my compass rose should be.

"This is where you belong," he tells me.

"It's late," I say. "You should go home."

He looks at me, confused. Gray eyes. Dark circles.

"I already am home."

"This isn't your home," I tell him, and I reach out to touch his face.

"You're my home, Eden. I want—"

I put my fingers to his lips and stop him in mid-sentence.

"I'm not the same," I warn him. "Being dead changes you."

"Living changes you, too," Cole says, and he puts his hand under my chin and tilts my face toward his. "But I know that I will always love you."

He bends down and kisses me, slowly and gently. Then he puts one hand on each side of my face and looks into my eyes. I feel my world start to tilt—I hear the sound of wind chimes, the pounding of the waves—and I bite my lip to bring the real back into focus.

"I love you, too," I say. "I know now that I always have. It's always been you and me. Hasn't it."

"Over and over," he says, and I nod.

"Over and over."

"Maybe we'll get it right, next time." Cole's voice is so sad. "Maybe next time I really can save you."

I reach out and run my fingers through his dark waves. "You save me every time." I smile. "Maybe next time I'll save you."

Cole shakes his head. "Next time we'll save each other."

"Blackout!" Jude says, but nobody in the theatre moves. Cole and I are still staring at each other, and Willa is watching us.

Someone starts to clap. And pretty soon the whole barn is filled with applause. It should make me feel good. That sound. Because to an actress, there's nothing better. But I can't tear myself away from Cole's eyes.

"Avril. Cole." Willa is crouched down in front of the bench where we're sitting. "Let's take five," she says. "Get some air."

"Yeah," Cole says. "Okay." And he gets up and moves toward the door. I start to follow him, but Willa grabs my hand.

"Avril," she says. "Wait." Her voice is low and gentle. Barely a whisper. "I told you before that Cole gets lost sometimes. Trapped inside his own head." I nod. "He has dark thoughts. And he gets confused. Do you know what I mean?"

"Maybe," I say. "I don't—"

"Has he told you that the sea wants him?" I freeze, because to answer that feels like a betrayal to Cole. But I don't want to lie to Willa. "Has he told you the sea wants you?" She waits, but I don't answer, and Willa sighs. It's a long, sad sound. "All those stories—" She stops and thinks for a moment before she goes on. "The sea has always been Cole's own darkness, Avril. I've tried to save him. We've all tried to save him." She reaches out to touch my hair. "And I know you're trying, too. But if you can't save him, don't let him pull you under." Her hand is on my cheek. "Cole is my son, and I love him. But Nicole would want me to look out for you."

"There are things I'm remembering," I tell her. And the part about Brody is on the very tip of my tongue. But I can't make it come out.

"Memories are funny things," Willa says, and she frowns. "They seem so concrete. So real. But they can be slippery." She lets her hand fall back to her side. "It's almost impossible to know if you can trust them, isn't it?"

I nod. But it's almost impossible to know if you can trust anything at Whisper Cove. Nothing here is exactly what it seems to be.

I remember what Cole said the first time I kissed him. How nothing here is real. It's all theatre, he told me.

Smoke and mirrors.

After rehearsal, Cole and I gather up with Lex and Jude and Val under the lights outside the barn.

"One week left," Jude tells us. "A week from tonight, it's all over." He's leaning against the railing with Lex, and they are so tangled up in each other. I'm expecting Lex to say something about how sad that makes him, but he doesn't. He just smiles.

"Nothing we started here ends next week," Lex says, and he leans in to give Jude a long, deep kiss. "This summer is just the beginning for all of us."

Val slips her arm around my waist, and her long, dark hair spills over my shoulder. "You gonna go find what's-his-name?" I ask her. I've seen her flirting with that blond guy—Nixon—a couple of times lately, but she shakes her head.

"Nah," she says with a laugh. "He's not really my type. I can only talk so long about *Star Trek*." But then her face turns serious. "I broke it off with Chester for good last night." Lex rolls his eyes, and Val punches him in the arm. "No. Seriously. We were together a long time, you know? And I think maybe I just need to be by myself for a while."

"Damn, girl," Jude says, and he nods. "Good for you." Lex nudges him in the side.

"Tell them your good news," Lex prompts, and Jude grins.

"My mom called this afternoon. I got a letter from the University of North Carolina. Full ride scholarship. In fucking ballet." He shakes his head like he can't believe it.

"So no accounting?" Val asks.

"Hell no!" Jude says. "I'm a fucking dancer!"

We laugh. And it hits me. They've all managed to do it.

They've *become*.

Like Willa said on that very first morning we all huddled on the farmhouse porch.

Every one of them is someone different than they were when they got here.

And I guess I'm someone different, too. I came here wanting to know my own mother. To find out who she was. So I could have something of her to hang on to. And I still want that.

But now I want something else, too.

I want answers.

I want to know what happened that night. At the top of that cliff.

And I'm running out of time.

Cole walks me back to the cabin, and we sit together on the front steps. I ask him if he's going to sit out here all night. Again. And he nods. Then he looks at me for a long while before he finally says, "I found something. Something you need to know about."

"What is it?"

"I was looking for that notebook of your mom's again, like I told you before. But I didn't find it."

"Okay." I'm trying to figure out where this is going.

"I found something else, though." He pulls a folded piece of paper out of his pocket and hands it to me. "This was crammed into a box of my dad's personal papers. Way down at the bottom."

It's yellow. The bottom layer of some kind of carbon copy pad. The kind where you write on the top layer, and it goes through to the other layers. But when I open it up, I can't figure out what I'm looking at.

Cole points to the logo in the top corner. *Alton Towers,* it says, and there's a picture of a building. "Okay," I say again. But I still don't know what this is.

"It's in New York City," he tells me. "I looked it up." Then he points to something scrawled at the bottom. "That's my dad's signature."

And then I see a name in the middle of the paper. Printed in neat letters.

*Nicole Kendrick*

The rest of it is faint and hard to read.

"What is this?" I ask him.

"It's proof you were right."

"I don't understand."

"It's a lease agreement," Cole says. "My dad put down money for an apartment. For your mom. And for you, I guess."

It's dated just a few days before she died.

"Cole—"

"I think he was trying to buy her off. I think he wanted to set her up in the city, maybe. Away from Whisper Cove. To keep my mom from finding out." He stops and stares at that scribbled signature. "So the shit wouldn't hit the fan." He swallows and shakes his head. "So he wouldn't lose fucking everything."

"My mother wanted it all out in the open. I remember hearing her say that." Angry words on the sea porch. Me under the picnic table with my hands over my ears. "I think she was sick of keeping secrets."

"I wanted it to be George. It seemed to make sense, you know?" Cole looks so tired. "But if all that's true," he says, "then my dad must have been scared shitless." He's staring at me with those fog-gray eyes. "And that's more than enough motive for . . ." His voice trails off. And he can't make himself finish that thought.

But I can.

"It's more than enough motive for murder."

We look at each other for a few long seconds before we say good night. Because there's nothing else to say. At least not at the moment. We both need some time to digest what Cole just told me.

He kisses me before he goes next door, though. Swears to me that we'll figure it out. Together. And when he murmurs that promise against my lips, I wish I could swallow it like medicine.

I pull myself up off the steps and start to head inside. I can hear the other girls talking and laughing. And suddenly I'm longing for my paper-thin bunk bed mattress. My slightly damp sheets. The idea of being with Val and the others—inside the warm, brightly lit cabin—sounds so appealing. It's a thousand times better than being out here. In the fog. Alone.

Or worse. Not alone.

But then the scent of lavender drifts into my nose.

The quiet crunch of careful feet on gravel.

I freeze. But those other feet keep moving. A step closer. Now one more.

"Who's there?" I call out.

The crunching stops. But lavender still hangs like thick perfume in the suffocating fog.

Then, just at the edge of the porch, something moves back toward the shadows. Away from the light. It's more a sense of movement than it is a shape. But I don't intend to let it slip away.

I'm down the steps and around the corner of the cabin in an instant. Quicker than I can exhale into the night. Faster than I can consider whether or not it's a good idea to chase a ghost into the fog.

There's a quick gasp. Not mine. Someone else's. And I start to move in that direction. But the swirling wall of fog messes with me. The sound seems to come from every direction at once. It echoes off the moisture in the air. Reverberates inside my chest and blends with the furious beating of my own heart.

"Glory!" I shout. "I know it's you."

But there's no sound. No breathing. No feet moving in the dark.

Then a face emerges from the shroud of gray. No body, at first.

Just pale features. Damp and shining in the moonlight. Eyes so bright and wide behind those huge glasses.

I take a step back. The trapped look on her face scares me. She's like an animal that's been taken by surprise. There's nothing about her that feels familiar tonight.

Not out here. Like this. A bouquet of lavender still clutched in her hands.

I'm wondering if the girls inside the cabin would hear me if I yelled for them. Would Val come to my rescue? Because something about this feels all wrong.

But then Glory takes a step in my direction. She moves out of the fog and into the glow of the porch light. And I can see her more clearly. Wet curls and a soggy pink sweater. Muddy tennis shoes.

She's just Glory again.

"You're the one who's been leaving me flowers," I accuse. "Lavender." She glances down at the evidence in her hands, and her face goes all pale. "Why? Why would you want to scare me like that?"

Glory is staring at me. Her eyes are huge and blinking. Her mouth opens, then closes. Then opens again.

"I wasn't trying to scare you." She looks toward the cabin window and lowers her voice. "I was trying to help you remember."

"By sneaking around in the fog and leaving me creepy flowers?"

"I—" Glory looks so genuinely surprised. "I didn't mean them to be creepy." She stops and looks down at her hands again. "Your mother loved lavender. I just thought maybe . . ."

"Maybe what?" I'm so bewildered.

"Scent is one of our most powerful senses. I thought maybe if you could remember the way Nicole smelled. If you could breathe her in." Glory looks so lost. "I thought it might help you remember her." I don't know what to say to that. She wipes at a stray tear with the back of her hand. "You and Nicki loved each other so much."

My anger is gone now. And the fear, too. It's evaporated like the fog in the morning. But it's left me so exhausted. Suddenly I can hardly stand up. I lean against the cabin wall and close my eyes.

I'm so, so tired.

I keep going around and around and around. But nothing at Whisper Cove makes sense.

"It just seems so unfair that you can't remember her," Glory tells me. "I have so many good memories of Nicki. I just wanted you to have some for yourself." She pulls at the bottom of her sweater. "I've tried to tell you things. But secondhand memories aren't the same. And I know that."

I think about how good Glory's been to me these last few weeks. The photos she's given me. The stories she's told me.

"I know you only wanted to help," I say, and the relieved smile that comes over her face makes me sad for her. She seems so lonely. And I wonder if Glory has anybody in her life. If she's had anybody at all since my mom. "But—"

Glory cuts me off. "Why don't you come over to my place?" she asks me. "For dinner tomorrow. After rehearsal." She gives me a nervous smile. "I have some more pictures and things I can show you."

With less than a week left, I can't turn down an opportunity like the one Glory is offering me. She has me hooked, and something tells me that she knows it.

"Yeah," I say. "Okay."

"Great!" Glory's beaming now. "I'll pick you up at six. Meet me on the farmhouse porch. I live just down the road." She holds out the lavender to me. She's shy now. Like a little girl handing her teacher a flower. But when I take it, she smiles at me again.

Then she's gone. And I really am all alone in the fog.

I stand there staring at the drooping bouquet clutched between my fingers and wondering why something still feels so off.

# ACT III: SCENE 6

The next morning is Saturday. No classes. No work assignments. Just a full day of rehearsals. And right from the start I can tell Cole is struggling under the weight of what he told me last night. How he thinks I'm right. About his dad. I see the pain of it in his eyes whenever he looks at me. And I feel it in his fingers when we touch.

I catch him during a break and tell him what Glory said about the lavender. How she was leaving it for remembrance. Almost like lighting a candle for the dead. "She thought she was helping me."

He nods. But I can see how distracted he is. How fast he's sinking.

It's like I'm watching him get swallowed up by a sea monster. If Willa was right about what she said, about the sea being Cole's own darkness, then it scares me for him. Because he's on the brink of drowning.

When rehearsal finishes, I talk with Lex for just a couple of seconds, and then I look around for Cole. But he's already gone. That worries me, but it's almost six o'clock, and I can't pass up an opportunity to finally get some real answers. So I head up to the farmhouse porch.

Glory pulls up at six on the dot in a rusted blue Subaru. I smile at the faded THERE IS NO PLANET B sticker on the back window.

"I've had this car forever," she says as I climb in, and the statement sounds like it's part apology and part brag. "Your mom hated it." She looks at me out the corner of her eye. "It was a piece of shit even way back then."

It's weird to be in the car with Glory, but the ride doesn't take long. In less than ten minutes we're pulling up to a tiny little brick home with a lighthouse flag out front.

She leads me in the front door and closes it quick behind us. "The kitties like to escape," she says. "So I have to be careful."

"Something smells good," I tell her, and she seems so pleased.

"Homemade chicken noodle soup," she says. "My one and only specialty. It should be ready soon."

We settle on the couch together, and I'm glad when a big orange cat crawls into my lap. I'm stroking his head, and he's purring so contentedly.

"That's Nacho," she tells me. "The cat Nicki was feeding that summer. When I went back to the farmhouse the next day, he was just sitting there looking so sad. And he was just a scrawny little guy then." She shrugs. "I couldn't leave him there." She is staring at the cat in my lap, and I wonder if she's seeing my mother holding him instead of me. "He's so old now. My grumpy old man." She stops for a second, and I see her thinking about something. "But Nicole will always be just the way she was that summer. That same age. Always." She gives me a little smile, but there's so much heartbreak underneath it. "It's funny, when you think about it."

I scratch the cat behind his ears. “Hey, Nacho,” I tell him, and he rubs his head against my side. I wonder if he thinks I’m my mom, finally come back after all this time.

Glory points at a framed photo that sits on a little end table beside the couch, so I reach over to pick it up. I’m sitting under a tree with my mother, and we both have ice cream cones. Mine is chocolate, and it’s running down my chin. Dripping down my arm.

And the two of us are laughing.

I just stare at that photo for a few seconds. It feels like such a punch in the gut to know that, while I was down in Texas not knowing anything about my mother, or about myself, really—all those long, hungry years—there was someone up here in Connecticut with a framed picture of us on her living room end table.

Proof that we ate ice cream together.

And that we laughed.

That somebody loved us.

“I have more pictures,” Glory says. “If you want to see them.” I nod, and Glory gets up to pull a cardboard box out of the closet. She takes the lid off and rifles through it until she finds what she’s looking for. “Here,” she says, and she hands me a stack of photos. “These are mostly you and Cole. You both spent so much time with me that summer.”

I shuffle through the stack. A little blonde girl and a little dark-haired boy.

Swinging in the park.

Building sandcastles at the beach.

Sitting on the floor behind Glory’s desk. Surrounded by paper and crayons.

"Here are some more of Nicki," Glory tells me. "God." She sighs as she hands me the pictures. "Sometimes it still knocks the wind out of me, seeing her." She smiles at me. "Look how beautiful she was." She sighs. "But she was so much more than that, too. The way her brain worked. The ideas that just came into her head." Glory smiles a genuine smile. "I've never met anyone else with that kind of raw creative energy."

I'm thumbing through the images. My mother on the farmhouse porch. In the library again. With that laptop. And then standing waist-deep in the sound. She's wearing a neon-green bikini top.

But I stop when I come to a picture of my mother with Brody Culver. It's just the two of them. The photo was taken in the barn theatre. They're sitting in folding chairs under the stage lights. Heads close together. Like they're telling secrets.

The photo makes me feel sick. I stare at it for a few seconds before I decide that I have to know. And there's less than a week left, so I don't have time to tiptoe anymore.

"My mother was having an affair with Brody Culver, wasn't she?" My voice is low. Almost a whisper. But I know Glory hears me, because she turns completely white.

"What?" Glory is shaking her head.

"She was cheating on my dad with Brody Culver. And he was cheating on Willa with her."

"No." Glory looks so shaken. And so confused. "No," she says again. And she takes the picture out of my hands. Stares at it. Like she's trying to see what I saw. "Why would you say that? Why would you even think it?"

"I found something in her notebook," I say.

"No." Glory shakes her head. "That's ridiculous. Brody has a certain reputation," she admits. "People talk. He can be a little handsy with his actresses." It grates on me, the way she says *his* actresses. Like they belong to him, and not to themselves. "But he'd never cheat on Willa." She scoops all the photos up and puts them back in the box. "And Nicki would never have— Not in a million years. Not with Brody." She puts the box back in the closet and closes the door. "Your mother loved Willa so much."

But I'm not letting this go.

"My dad said he was pretty sure she'd met someone."

Glory shakes her head. "Nicki would never have done that. Not to Willa."

"He said she wasn't coming home." I get up and walk to where Glory is still standing. Near the closet. "My dad. He said it was over between them."

"I don't know anything about that." Glory is so clearly flustered. I know she's lying.

"Brody put down money on an apartment," I say. "In New York City. An apartment in my mom's name."

"How do you know about that?" Glory looks stunned. She chews on her lip. Searches her sweater for cat hair.

"It doesn't matter," I say. "But why would he do that if they weren't together?"

"The apartment w-was Willa's idea," Glory stammers. "She and Brody both wanted to help. That's all. Your mom wasn't happy in Texas. Willa and Brody both wanted her closer. They thought—"

"Why won't you just tell me the truth?" My voice is sharper

than I mean for it to be. "My mother was cheating on my dad with Brody Culver."

"No. She wasn't."

"It was all so long ago. Why lie about it? Just tell me the truth. If they—"

"No, Avril. You've got it all wrong."

"Jesus!" I'm so frustrated. Because the answers feel so close, but still so far away. "I can handle the truth. I promise!"

"It was me."

"What?"

Glory turns around to look at me. "It was me, Avril." She's staring at me, but I still don't get what she means. "Your mom and I were together that summer. I was the one she met. I was the one she fell in love with."

"I don't—" I shake my head. I thought I had things figured out. But now nothing makes sense.

"It was me."

"Oh." It's the only word I can think of.

"That summer was perfect," Glory tells me. "We were both figuring so many things out together. It was all brand-new. For both of us. But I knew right from the beginning what I wanted. I wanted Nicki to stay here. With me. I thought if she stayed on at the theatre, it would be so great for all of us, you know? For the two of us, sure, but for Willa and Brody, too."

"So she was staying with you," I say. "At Whisper Cove." But Glory shakes her head.

"I wanted her to. But she wouldn't."

"Why not?"

"She was— There was something she needed to do. Someone she wanted to be. So Willa and Brody were going to set her up in the city. Help her get started. Then she was gone, and I just—" Glory stops. "A lot of times, in movies and stuff, when someone dies, you see people fall apart. The ones who are left behind. They're on their knees weeping and banging their fists on the ground. But it's not always like that in real life. It wasn't like that for me. There should have been all this sadness and pain, you know. But there wasn't any. At least not at first. There was just this huge, empty hole. All this—*nothing*. I would get up and shower and eat and answer emails and go to work and do whatever. But inside, I'd totally stopped existing. It was . . ."

"Like you were dead?" I say, and Glory nods.

"And so, later, when that grief did finally come, it almost felt . . . good . . . somehow. The pain was so much better than that awful nothingness."

I'm not sure what she's getting at. So we just look at each other for a few seconds.

"I'm going to go make a salad," Glory tells me. "And then we can talk more. Okay? There's so much I want you to know about your mom."

"Yeah," I say, "I'd like that." But I feel so weird. Just when I thought I had things figured out, everything gets turned upside down. None of it fits. It doesn't make sense.

If my mother wasn't having an affair with Brody Culver, then what does that B. C. mean in her notebook?

And if there was no affair, there was no reason for him to kill her.

Or me.

But someone grabbed me by the wrist and threw me from the cliff that night.

Maybe Cole was right all along. About George.

It's like I'm feeling my way across that muddy field at Whisper Cove and finding that split-rail fence in my path. When I know it shouldn't be there.

Glory disappears into the kitchen, and I just stand there for a second. I'm still half-stunned. I listen to her opening and closing cabinets. Pulling things out of the refrigerator.

And I'm desperate for another clue. Something that will tie all this together.

So I open the closet door and pull out that cardboard box. I hold my breath as I dig through it, scared to death that Glory will pop back into the living room. But she doesn't. I still hear her working in the kitchen. Turning the water in the sink on. Then off. Chopping something.

I've almost given up on finding anything in the photos when I catch sight of something blue on the bottom of the box. I move the photos aside and lift the worn spiral notebook out so I can get a better look at it. I flip it over to check the back, and there it is in the upper right corner.

**#1**

I stuff the notebook in my backpack and slip the box back in the closet.

Glory calls to me from the kitchen. "How do you feel about avocado in your salad?"

"It's good," I tell her. "I love avocado." But my heart is beating so fast. I can barely breathe. I look around the room and see a set of sliding patio doors. "Is it okay if I step out and get some air?" I say.

Glory sticks her head around the corner. "Sure. Of course. I know it's a lot." Her face flushes deep red. "I wanted to tell you so many times before. But I just wasn't sure how." She glances toward that framed photo on the end table. Me and my mother. Chocolate ice cream. "I've never been good at putting it into words, what Nicki meant to me." She smiles. "What both of you meant to me."

"I'm glad you told me."

And I really am. It makes me glad to know my mother had that. That she'd found something special. With Glory.

Except now I'm back to square one. With less than a week left. So I'm praying maybe the answer is in that blue notebook hidden in my backpack.

Everything that's happened tonight has me feeling dizzy. I just need a few seconds to clear my head.

Glory disappears back into the kitchen, and I slide open the glass door to step out onto the porch. The night breeze is so cool and fresh. I take a deep breath, and I instantly feel a hundred times better. I hadn't realized how stuffy it felt in that tiny living room.

I sit down at an old picnic table on the porch. I run my hands over the rough boards.

And suddenly I'm shaking. Terrified and small. The fear slams into me like a tidal wave. It washes over me and sweeps me out to sea. And I hear my mother's voice.

*I want everything out in the open!*

I stare at her hot pink toes. Her gold strappy sandals. And I press my hands over my ears. But that doesn't keep me from hearing Glory's angry voice.

*Then stay here with me, Nicki! That's what I want, too!*

My mother again. *Will you just listen to me!* she shouts. She sounds so frustrated. I jump when she bangs her hand hard on the picnic table. It rattles my teeth.

*I'm trying to be honest about what I'm feeling! I can't stay with you any more than I can go back to him! I need something more than that! I'm becoming something more than that!*

I hear someone crying. And when my mother speaks again, her voice is gentler.

*I really think I love you,* she says. *But this is my chance to be something extraordinary. And I have to take it. For me and for April.*

*What about me?* Glory asks, and there's so much bitterness in her words. But my mother doesn't answer. She just bends down to pull me out from under the picnic table and scoop me up in her arms. My hands are still over my ears. *What about me?* Glory shouts again. *Nicki!* But my mother and I are already gone.

My hands are shaking. I spread them out on the rough wood of the picnic table. That fight happened here. It was never on the sea porch at all. It was Glory's picnic table I was hiding under the whole time. I had it all confused.

Glory was in love with my mother. And maybe my mother was in love with her, too. But it didn't matter. Because she was ending it.

She was ready to become.

The wind picks up, and the sound of wind chimes floats across the dark. I turn my head, and there they are. Hanging from the corner of the porch. Dangling silver wind chimes, strung with seashells. They tinkle and dance in the breeze. And all the hair on the back of my neck stands straight up.

Because I've heard that sound before. I recognize it. Just before I died.

I jump when Glory slides open the door behind me.

"Avril," she says. "Dinner's ready."

# ACT III: SCENE 7

Somehow I make it through dinner with Glory. Chicken soup and salad. I listen to her talk about my mother. How much they loved each other. How it started as friendship for them. But then it caught fire. Almost overnight.

I manage to smile. Say the right things. And never let on that I remember now. That I know how things ended between them. With angry words and my mother's hand slammed down on the picnic table.

With the sound of wind chimes that still makes my blood run cold.

When Glory drops me back off at Whisper Cove that night, I'm desperate to find Cole. But he isn't on the cabin steps. And I know he isn't in bed. So I can't figure out where he could be. Then I remember how bad he was at rehearsal. How dark. And I think I might know where to find him.

The fog is just starting to roll in, but it isn't thick yet, so I hurry toward the farmhouse. George is leaning against the front porch railing, smoking. But if he sees me, he doesn't act like it. And anyway, I refuse to be afraid of him. He's a pathetic creeper. But he's not a murderer.

At least I'm pretty sure he's not.

I head toward the path into the woods and climb the steep hill to the Culver house. The gate at the bottom of the yard is open, and Cole is standing with his back to the edge of the cliff. His heels are hanging over the edge. And there's nothing but churning water below him. His eyes are closed. Arms spread wide.

It's the same way he was standing on the swim dock. Before he fell backward into the water.

I stare at him for a minute, afraid to so much as whisper his name. I don't want to startle him. But somehow, he knows that I'm there. He opens his eyes to look at me.

"You were right," I tell him. "Your father didn't kill my mother. They weren't having an affair. I don't know what B. C. means, but it isn't Brody Culver. I had it all wrong. He didn't have any reason to kill her." Cole takes a breath. Closes his eyes again. I see him sway a little on his feet, and my heart stops. "Cole," I say. "Listen. I thought it had to be him, because I remembered you being there that night. But we were with Glory most of the summer, you and me. If you were there, it's because she was there."

Cole opens his eyes and blinks at me. "Glory?" I nod.

"They were in love. My mother and Glory. I can explain it all," I tell him. "Just give me your hand. Okay?"

I reach out toward Cole, but he hesitates.

"Please, Cole," I beg. "I need you."

He reaches for me then, but the edge of the cliff crumbles under his heels, and he pitches backward.

"Cole!" I grab his hand and jerk hard, and he topples toward me. We're both lying in the damp grass at the edge of the drop-off. My heart is pounding so hard I'm sure my ribs must be breaking.

We lie there—tangled together—trying to catch our breath. And when we both stop shaking, I explain about the fight I remembered. How it happened at Glory's little house. Not on the sea porch.

And about the sound of wind chimes. How something about them makes the hair on my neck stand up and my insides turn to ice.

How I think I heard them not long before I died.

"You really think it was Glory?" Cole asks. He's pale. And I see his mind working behind those gray eyes. He's trying to get it to make sense. Trying to decide if he really believes the nice lady with the peppermints and the cat-hair sweaters could be a murderer.

"I need to check out the notebook I stole from her place," I tell him. "But yeah."

"Notebook number one?"

"Yeah. She had it." I feel sick all of a sudden. Glory's been so good to me.

"Shit," Cole mutters.

"I know it's hard to believe," I tell him. "Glory's so—"

"That's the thing." He cuts me off. "It isn't hard to believe. It should be. Maybe. I wish it were." He sighs so long and deep. "But the things people are capable of. The secrets we all keep from each other." He tilts his head back to look up at the inky sky. "We don't know anybody. Not really."

I reach for Cole's hand, and I lace our fingers together. I squeeze tight. Because I will refuse to let his head slip under the water. Not tonight. I need him too much.

"I know you," I tell him. "And you know me."

Cole starts to say something, but I see him decide not to. And that's when I know for sure that Cole Culver still has secrets. Parts of himself that I haven't unlocked yet. Shuttered places deep inside. Rooms that there are no keys to. And suddenly all I want in the world is a chance to know him. Really know him. Even the dark, scary parts of him. I want it even more than I want to know what happened to my mother.

"What about that lease agreement with my father's name on it?" he asks me. "The apartment in the city?"

"Glory says that was your mom's idea," I tell him. "They just wanted to help." I feel the weight of everything that's happened in the last twenty-four hours settling on my chest. "She's going to get away with it, Cole. Glory. I don't have any proof. There isn't any way to prove it." We're sitting side by side in the grass, staring down at the foaming water.

"We'll figure something out. I promise. But even if we don't—" Cole stops and pulls me into a kiss.

His hands are on my face, and he's running his thumbs over my cheekbones. I feel him trembling. There's this sadness that seeps into me through his skin.

Something feels different. This kiss isn't like any of the others we've shared.

This is a goodbye kiss.

"What's wrong?" I ask him. But Cole won't say. He just walks me back to the little blue cabins. We skirt wide around the hog pen. But I can hear them grunting tonight.

The smell burrows its way into my nose.

Before I go in to bed, Cole presses a piece of green sea glass into my hand.

"For protection?" I ask him. But he shakes his head.

"To help you remember me," he says. "Next time."

"You're scaring me," I tell him. But he just pulls me into another kiss, and when it's over, he's smiling at me. "What?" I ask him.

Cole touches my arm, and I feel the heat from his fingertips radiating out through my body.

"Do you want to know how the book ends?" he asks me.

I can't answer him. The lump in my throat is too big.

I look down at our feet, but he tilts my chin up so he can see my face. And then he asks again. His voice is warm and soft, like a winter coat.

"Do you want to know how the book ends, Avril?"

My heart is in ten thousand pieces, but I still know my line.

"That would ruin the surprise."

"But what if it makes you sad?" he asks, reaching out to brush a strand of hair away from my face. His voice is barely a whisper.

Wind in the dune grass.

"I'd rather take my time to find out all the lovely things that happen along the way, without worrying about the ending." I press myself into his chest. "Wouldn't you?"

"Yes, I think I would, too," Cole says. He's pulling me tighter against him. "Now that you mention it."

He kisses me one more time.

And then he's gone.

The next day is Sunday. Our last day off at Whisper Cove. It's supposed to be the calm before our final wild week. I spend the day in the library pouring over my mother's notebook, but I don't find much. There are some things in there about her and Glory. Just little notes about the things they did together.

How it felt the first time they kissed.

And I guess that's why Glory didn't want me to have it.

There are more notes labeled with those initials, too. B. C. And I still don't know what they mean. Phrases like *love isn't enough* and *no promises*. And scribbled adjectives like *lonely* and *secretive* and *passionate*. But if my mother was in love with Glory, I can't figure out who B. C. could be.

I keep waiting for Cole to find me. I want to show him the passages I've highlighted. The parts I don't understand. But he never shows up.

At breakfast on Monday, it hits us all that this really is the beginning of the end. Our last week together. There are no classes or work assignments these last few days. With the curtain going up on Friday night, we're focusing on the show. And I'm grateful for the fact that I don't have to spend my afternoons filing invoices with someone who probably murdered my mother.

It's a busy day of costume fittings and working with the props crew to find the last few things we need. I don't get much time to talk to Cole, but whenever I have so much as a free minute, I'm looking through that blue notebook for some kind of proof that the cold hand around my wrist belonged to Glory. Because I know I can't go to the police with evidence like wind chimes and childhood memories. And there's no way I'm leaving here without writing the final scene.

I'm surprised when my dad calls that evening after dinner. I'm walking down to the barn, and I let Lex and Val and Jude go on ahead so I can have some privacy.

"Hello?" I say, and a few seconds of silence slip by. I almost hang up. I figure it was an accidental call. But then I hear my dad's voice.

"You okay?"

"Yeah," I say. "Busy." I'm trying to figure out why he called. Because he definitely isn't a chatter.

"Your play is this weekend," he says.

"Yeah. Friday night."

"And then you come home. When? The next day?"

"Yeah," I say again. "I fly home on Saturday morning."

It's quiet for a few more seconds.

"It'll be good to have you home," he says. And that catches me so off guard that I almost don't hear the next part. "It's too quiet here. Tu me manques."

I miss you.

I don't say anything.

"What part do you have?" he asks me. Not that he knows anything about the play. But it's nice that he's asking.

"Eden," I tell him. "It's the lead."

"Eden," he repeats. "That's nice." A few more moments of silence. "That was your mother's favorite name."

"Really?" That seems so weird.

"She wanted to call you that, but I didn't want to." He stops and sighs. "I don't remember why now."

I wonder if Willa knew that. If that's why she chose that name. To honor my mom. Or if it was just a coincidence.

"Break a leg," Dad tells me. "I'll see you on Saturday."

I start to tell him that I miss him, too, but he's already hung up.

I hurry down to the barn. It's our last night working inside before we move out to the amphitheater for three nights of tech rehearsals. And we're working the last scene in the play. The final meeting between Eden and Orion.

Willa already has everyone gathered up in the front row when I slip into the theatre. She turns to smile at me. "This is it," she tells us all. "One last scene. It's short and sweet. No long, drawn-out goodbye for our two lovers. But there's so much to think about."

Jude sets it up for us. "Okay," he says. "This the last moment of the play. Eden and Orion meet one last time at the bench by the river. And if I say anything else, I'm gonna cry."

Cole goes to take his place on the bench, and I see him pick up the guitar. That song is almost more than I can stand tonight.

I walk onstage and stand right behind him—close enough that I know he can feel me breathing—until his fingers stop moving and the theatre goes silent.

It hits me how hollowed out and sunken in he looks. And I'm trying to remember exactly when he became Orion. But I can't. I guess I was too focused on becoming Eden.

"I know you're there," he tells me. "I can feel you."

"I almost didn't come tonight," I say.

"Then why did you?"

"Because I wanted to say goodbye."

Cole turns to look back at me. Then he holds out one hand. "Come sit with me," he says. And it's such a simple request.

So I do.

"Don't you love me anymore?" he asks, and it's like a knife to my heart.

"I more than love you," I tell him. "But things change. People change."

"You've changed," he says, and I nod.

"You'll change, too," I promise him.

"What if I play your song again?" he asks.

"I'll always hear your music. It's the song inside my heart."

"But you won't come back again."

"No," I say. "I won't come back again."

"What if I write you a new song?" he pleads. "Something better." He almost smiles. "Or louder."

"Okay." Willa holds up a finger. "Let's pause there for a moment before we go on." You could hear a pin drop in the barn, it's so quiet. There's just the sound of our breathing. "Why does Eden say she can't come back? She clearly loves him. This is killing her. So why is this goodbye?"

I see everyone turning that question over in their minds. And I know the answer, but I can't figure out how to put it into words.

It's quiet for a long time.

"Nobody?" Willa asks, and she looks around the barn. She sighs, clearly disappointed. "Eden's changed too much," she tells us. "She's outgrown Orion. And that's sad. It's a tragedy, maybe, if she really loves him. But she's become someone different than she was before her death. Before the chaos of all that. And there's no going back."

But that's not right.

I know Eden inside and out now. She lives somewhere inside me. And that's not it at all.

Eden won't come back to see Orion because he deserves the chance to change, too. She wants that for him. She knows that he can't spend the rest of his life waiting for a ghost. He needs to hurt. And grow. Learn. He needs a chance to *become*. Because he's the one still living. And she won't take that chance away from him.

It seems so strange that Willa could misunderstand her own play like that.

I don't say anything, though. Because it doesn't matter whether Willa knows it or not. I know it. She may have created Eden, but I'm the one breathing life into her. It's my heart that pumps her blood.

So I turn to Cole and deliver the last line of the play.

"No more songs for me, Orion. Write a song for yourself. Something that you'll always be able to hear inside your own heart. And I'll be a part of that tune, I promise. Because that's what it means to more than love someone."

There's a moment of eerie silence before the barn erupts in applause, because we've finally done it. We've worked our way through all of *Midnight Music*.

"Good work, my lovelies!" Willa Culver is clapping the loudest of all. "Extraordinary work!" But I keep thinking about how strange it is that she could write a play and get the ending so wrong.

When Cole walks me back to my cabin that night after rehearsal, he looks at me for a long time. "You can't save me," he finally says. "And that's okay. That's the way it's supposed to go." I want to tell him there's no way he can know that for sure. But I can't. I'm too sad. Too scared. Too confused and exhausted. Cole pulls another piece of sea glass out of his pocket. But I shake my head and close his fist around the tiny chunk.

"Keep it," I tell him. "I don't need anything to remember you by. I'll hear your song inside my heart."

"Always?" he asks me.

"Always," I tell him.

# ACT III: SCENE 8

The next few days are kind of a blur. Tech rehearsals last for hours. There are light cues and sound cues. All the new props. And set pieces. But it feels good to be working in the amphitheater.

Even when the sound of the waves seems too loud.

Even when the fog creeps in late at night to lick at our ankles.

Even when Cole's eyes seem darker than they used to be.

It's like we assembled the play together in the barn, but it didn't truly become a living thing until we brought it outside and let the night air fill its lungs.

Now it's breathing.

This is a play that wants to be performed by starlight.

After rehearsal Wednesday night, I linger in the amphitheater. I'm hypnotized by the movements of the lighting crew. The way they navigate the tall ladders with heavy equipment tucked under one arm like it's nothing. They're making final adjustments. There's a kind of grace to it. It's like ballet. Up and down. Reaching. Stretching. Nimble and fast. They seem so sure of their footing. It makes me jealous. Lately I feel one wrong move from falling to my death, even when I'm standing on the ground.

When I turn to go, Glory is standing right behind me. Shit. I hadn't heard a thing. But she's right there. Looking at me. For a second, I stop breathing.

"I like to watch the crew work," she tells me, and I nod. "So I come sometimes. At night." She's waiting for me to say something, but my mouth has gone dry. It's the first time I've been face-to-face with her since her house. When I stood outside in her backyard and heard those wind chimes. It's quiet for a long minute. Finally, she sighs. "I made mistakes, Avril. With Nicki, that summer. I was so young. And I'd never been in love like that before. There are things I wish I'd handled differently. I wish I hadn't—" She stops. And for one crazy moment I think maybe she's going to confess to me. That maybe she'll just say it. Out loud.

But she doesn't.

Instead she says, "You can't know how you're going to react in a situation like that. Not until you're there." I nod, and she reaches for me. I let her pull me into a desperate hug. And I grit my teeth against the urge to pull away. To push her to the ground. "I'm sorry," she says. "I'm so sorry."

Her words feel loaded. The weight of them is like an anchor tied to her tongue. And I can't help wondering exactly what it is she's apologizing for. Falling for Nicole Kendrick all those years ago? Not being able to save the woman she loved?

Or maybe for throwing my mother to her death from the cliff behind Willa Culver's house. For trying her best to kill me, too.

I pull myself away from Glory's embrace and make my way into the fog. Away from my mother's lover.

My mother's killer.

The next afternoon, I ask Willa a question during a rehearsal break. "Did you know there was something going on between Glory and my mom?"

She glances up from the notes she's studying to give me a strange look. She's startled, clearly. But there's something else behind her eyes, too. "I suspected. I never knew for sure."

"They were in love," I say, and I cross to sit beside her. Willa wrinkles up her nose like I've said something distasteful at Christmas dinner.

"No," she tells me. "I don't think so. Glory was in love, I'm sure. I could see that. It would be hard not to be. But Nicole . . ." Willa shakes her head. "Glory is so completely ordinary." Willa says the word like it's the worst thing in the world a person could be. "She's nothing special. I mean, she's lovely, of course. Nice. But she's . . ."

"Ordinary," I say, and Willa turns that magic smile on for me.

"Glory is one of those people who seems happy with the life she has. And there's nothing wrong with that. But Nicole, she was like us." Willa slips an arm around my shoulder. "She was destined for real greatness. She never would have settled for an everyday life. It would have destroyed her."

There's a hardness in her voice. A cold steeliness. "She was after something special, and you have to want that. You have to fight for it." Something sad creeps in behind her eyes. "You have to be willing to take it. You have to—"

I'm quiet, waiting for her to finish that thought. But she seems stuck. It's the first time I've ever seen Willa get lost. Then that sadness passes almost as quickly as it came, and that hundred-watt smile comes back. Brighter than ever. She gives me a squeeze. "You have to be willing to take it. No matter what, Avril. You have to be willing to die for it. Or kill for it. Lie for it. Steal for it. And then you have to be prepared live with the consequences. Or all you'll ever be is exactly what everyone else is." She shrugs and takes her arm from around my shoulders. Turns back to her notes. "Like Glory."

It hits me then that it would have destroyed Willa, too. For sure. Being ordinary. That when she says the only point of life is to be something extraordinary, she means that. It's not just an inspirational line she's feeding us. She just burns brighter than everyone else. She needs more. And she fought tooth and nail to become. To turn herself into something bigger and better and more special. Something so brilliant, it's almost blinding.

And I guess my mother would have, too, if someone hadn't put her light out.

If Glory hadn't thrown her into the sea so she wouldn't have to let her go.

I wish I had more of their fire burning inside me. I've always given up too easily. But not anymore. I promise myself that I won't go home without unraveling this whole thing. No matter what the consequences of that unraveling are. I'll pull at the tangled knots of my memories—study the clues—until I find some kind of proof. Until I can say for sure what happened all those years ago. To my mother.

To me.

But everything is moving so fast now. I don't have much time. It's our very last rehearsal.

The curtain goes up tomorrow evening.

Before we call it a night, Willa asks everyone to circle up. We form a ring under the stage lights. Soak up each other's energy. Soak up Willa's humming energy. One last time.

"This is how we leave things," she tells us, and we exhale together. Grip each other's hands a little tighter.

A prayerless prayer circle.

I'm standing between Cole and Lex. Holding their hands. Lex is crying. And I marvel at the way he just lets the tears roll down his cheeks. I can do that onstage. Be that honest. That free. But offstage, it's still hard for me.

There are so many things running through my mind . . . the show tomorrow night and the pride over what we've created together . . . the fear I feel for Cole . . . what exactly happened at the top of that cliff twelve summers ago . . . how I'm failing my mother . . . how Glory is going to get away with it . . . the impossibility of going back to my life in Dallas less than forty-eight hours from now . . . how I can't bear the thought of leaving Lex or Val or Jude.

Or Willa.

Or Cole.

It feels unbearable, the grief of finding him again. Only to lose him.

Again.

I'm so lost in our stage circle, and in those circular thoughts running on a loop inside my head, that I don't hear the sirens at first.

But I see the others react to the sound. And that pulls me out of my thoughts and back to reality.

By that time, the ambulance is already screaming down the long Whisper Cove driveway. We can't see it from where we're all standing at the bottom of the amphitheater, but there's no way not to hear it now.

It's the loudest sound I can imagine.

It tears through my brain, and I'm frozen for a minute. Wondering if they've come for me.

Have I drowned without realizing it?

Am I finally dead?

Maybe I'm imagining this circle. The warmth of the stage lights. And Willa's voice. Cole. And Lex. Maybe I'm dreaming of their hands in mine as I sink to the bottom of the sound and fade away. For good this time.

But then everyone is scattering and I'm being swept along with them. And Willa is shouting, "Wait! Stay calm, my lovelies!" It's too late, though. We're all running toward the farmhouse. The ambulance sits in the driveway. Sirens silent now. Lights still flashing.

"Avril!" Cole is shouting my name, but I've lost sight of him in the commotion, so I just follow the crowd around to the back of the house. To the sea porch steps.

Lex reaches for my hand, pulls me to him. And we shove our way through the group until we're standing at the front. We stare at the scene laid out in the moonlight. Like something from a Greek tragedy.

"Oh my God." Jude crumples to his knees. Puts his hands over his face. He's trying to block it out. Because this is what real-life nightmares are made of.

George is standing at the bottom of the steps, cursing at us. "Jesus Christ! Get back," he growls. "Stay the fuck back! All of you."

"George!" The crowd is parting like the Red Sea for Willa now. She's wild-eyed and frantic. I've never seen her like this. "What's—"

She stops when she sees what we're seeing. I hear her gasp. Then choke.

Glory is laid out on the weathered wood of the sea porch. I can't stop staring at her wet curls. Soggy white sweater. Her staring eyes and the unnatural angle of her arms and legs. The paramedics are bent over her, working with an intensity and focus that tells me everything I need to know about how serious this is. One of them is doing chest compressions. I can't see what the others are doing. Their bodies block my view. And I'm glad for that.

Some of the other kids are crying now. Hands over their mouths. They're clinging to each other. A few are praying out loud. But I just stand there silent and staring. Cole on one side of me and Lex on the other. They're both holding my hands again. But this time I know I'm not dreaming.

"What happened?" Willa's voice cuts through the chaos. She's regained her control now. Her composure.

"I found her down by the jetty," George says. "I had a little—" He stops. Looks almost embarrassed. "I went down there for a smoke break is all. And that white sweater of hers. It caught the light. Got my attention. Just like—" He stops again. Nods in my direction. "So I pulled her out of the water. Brought her up here and called for help."

Behind him, the paramedics are still working on Glory. They're loading her up on a gurney to take her away. One of them looks back over her shoulder at Willa. "Ma'am, you wanna get those kids out of here? We need a clear path."

Willa claps her hands. Like she's signaling the start of a rehearsal. "Everyone to your cabins," she announces. Nobody moves so she claps again. The musical sound of those jangling bracelets floats into my ears. "Now, my lovelies. There's nothing you can do for Glory tonight." She looks back toward the motionless body on the gurney. "There's nothing any of us can do." The crowd starts to drift away. Everyone is moving slowly. They're reluctant to leave. Wiping at their eyes. Holding on to each other. Whispering. Looking back over their shoulders. "Breakfast is at seven tomorrow," Willa reminds us. "We'll talk about it all then. Together."

I guess the show must go on.

Most of the others head back to the blue cabins, like Willa ordered. But Cole pulls me toward the Hidden Theatre. Lex, Val, and Jude trail behind us. The five of us seek some kind of shelter in the branches of the huge tree as we peek between the leaves and watch Glory get loaded into the waiting ambulance. The siren roars to life again, and they take off down the driveway.

We listen until the blaring noise fades away, and then it is so quiet.

So deathly still.

"What do you think happened?" Lex finally asks. "Some kind of accident?"

"I don't know." Jude sounds so broken. I remember that warm hug he had for Glory on our first morning. "It doesn't make sense. What would she have been doing down at the beach? At night. Alone."

"It wasn't an accident," Cole says. "She drowned herself, I think." Everyone turns to stare at him. His eyes are so black, and his voice sounds strange.

"No," Val says. "Don't do this, Cole. Don't make this into one of your ghost stories. The fucking whispering. I can't—"

"No." Cole shakes his head. "It isn't that. I just think she wanted to die." He's looking at me now.

"Why?" Jude is shaking his head. "Why the fuck would Glory kill herself?"

"Try to kill herself," Lex pleads. "We don't know if—"

"But why?" Jude asks again. "I don't get it."

"Guilt," I tell them. And I can feel their confusion. I don't know for sure if I'm ready to say it out loud to the whole group. But I can't see any reason to keep that secret anymore. So I let the words come out. "Because she murdered my mother."

There are a few stunned moments of silence. I see Lex and Jude and Val all trying to make sense out of what I've just said. But they can't. How could they? So I fill them in on everything I know. How Glory was in love with my mother. The fight at her house. Me hiding under her picnic table. How my mother said she was leaving. That she couldn't stay. Not even for love. Then the ominous sound of Glory's wind chimes. How it's one of the very last things I remember. Before the world went black. "She couldn't let her walk away. So she killed her. Threw her off the cliff behind Willa's house. It's the only answer that makes sense."

"And she threw you after her," Lex says. He's blinking. Trying to catch up. "Holy shit. Av. Oh my God. Av." He pulls me into his arms and it's suddenly all too much. I start to sob. Lex rocks me back and forth. He strokes my hair. Makes soothing noise in my ear.

"I think she tried to tell me the other night," I choke. I'm remembering that last, strange conversation with Glory in the amphitheater. "But she couldn't."

"She wanted you to know." Cole's voice cuts through the fog. "That's why she gave you that green notebook. Why she let you find the second one at her place." He pauses. Reaches for me in the dark. I let him pull me away from Lex and hold me close. Because I know he needs that physical anchor to keep him from drifting. He needs me. "That's why she left you the lavender. She was trying to trigger those memories. Hoping you'd figure it out."

"Why?" Val wants to know. "Why would she want anyone to figure out what she did?"

Cole's answer is so simple. So honest. "Because she was tired."

"But Glory was—she is—was—Fuck." Jude rubs at his eyes in frustration. "She was so sweet. You know? How could she—" He stops. Shakes his head. "How could she do something like that?"

"She *became*," Val says. "Whatever happened that last night, between her and Avril's mom, she let it turn her into someone else. Someone we wouldn't be able to recognize. Someone she probably didn't even recognize herself."

I think of that quote from *Hamlet*. Willa's favorite. A line from a girl who's doomed to drown. Our theme for the summer.

*We know who we are, but not who we may be.*

How had it never occurred to me that sometimes people become something dark and twisted and secret. Something that's nothing but a shadow of who they once were.

"I still don't understand exactly what happened that night."

Jude's voice is hoarse. Threaded with tears and thick with grief and confusion. "After the argument you remembered."

"How did the three of you end up at Willa's place?" Lex asks.

"I don't know," I admit. "Lots of the details are missing."

I don't know exactly what happened in those last hours. Or moments. Between the deadly tinkling of wind chimes and George pulling me out of the sea.

I don't know who B. C. is.

I don't know anything, really. Except that my mother is dead. And now the only person with any real answers is probably dead, too.

It's late and the temperature has dropped. We're all shivering. Damp. Numb from the cold. And from what we just witnessed. Jude says we should go to bed. Try to get some sleep. We still have a show tomorrow, after all.

Cole holds my hand as we slip through the tree branches like a band of ghosts. Nobody makes a sound. But just before I step out into the open, the foghorn sings out low and sorrowful in the darkness. I glance back over my shoulder.

And there they are. So real.

A slender woman with ice-blonde hair that falls just across her face. And another woman. Shorter. Smaller. Her hair is a mass of unruly curls. They sit pressed so close together. There's not even room for the fog to slip between them. Glory says something, and my mother laughs as she reaches out to run her long fingers though those wild curls. They're both giggling now. Foreheads touching. Nose to nose. I hold my breath and wait for the kiss I know must be coming. And I see the way they melt into each other when their lips meet.

Just like me and Cole.

"Avril?" Cole is waiting for me. Holding back one of the little limbs so the wet leaves don't brush my face. "You okay?"

"Yeah." I turn to look at him, and when I glance back over my shoulder, the Hidden Theatre is empty.

The memory ghosts have vanished.

But I know they're still here. Even if I can't see them. Because I'm beginning to understand that nobody ever really leaves Whisper Cove.

It's hard enough for the dead to escape. But it's even harder for the living.

# ACT III: SCENE 9

Cole leads us all back toward the cabins. The stench of farm animals is in the air, and we skirt around the fence that shouldn't be there. Val reaches for my hand when she hears the grunting of the pigs.

"I'm scared," she whispers, and I squeeze her fingers. Hope that it makes her less afraid. Because the pigs are only shadows.

The real danger at Whisper Cove had always come from flesh-and-blood people and the secrets they keep.

The next morning, Willa gathers us all up on the farmhouse porch before breakfast. I'm trying to read her face, to figure out what she's going to tell us. About Glory. But her eyes don't offer any clue. She gives us all a long look before she speaks. "I've just gotten off the phone with the hospital," she tells us. And it's the weirdest feeling. Two dozen people all holding their breath together. "As of this morning, Glory is hanging on. The doctors are optimistic." There's a collective sigh of relief, and I suddenly have no idea how I feel. Cole reaches for my hand. "She's not out of the woods yet." Willa closes her eyes and centers herself before she continues. "But I think we can be hopeful. And so the show will go on tonight. In Glory's honor." Lex looks at me, but all I can do is stare at Willa. "You've all worked so hard, and I know that she would want you to have this night." She tries to smile. "This is your moment to *become*."

Breakfast is strangely silent. Everyone should have been so excited this morning. The cafeteria should be vibrating with pure pre-show adrenaline. But now there's this cloud hanging over everything.

Somehow, though, I feel strangely at peace. Because I know my mother in a way I never would have if I hadn't come to Whisper Cove. I feel her with me now, almost all the time. And that's something I think I'll take home with me. That feeling of connection to a part of myself I thought was lost at sea. So all I can do is let go of the things I still don't know and hope that, one way or the other, Glory will pay for what she did.

And there's a kind of freedom in that.

Somehow we all make it through the rest of that last day, and almost before I can blink, I'm standing in the dressing room at the back of the barn, slipping on a simple white dress. Val helps me tie it in the back, and then she stands and stares at me in the mirror. She covers her open mouth with her hands.

"What's wrong?" I ask her, but she shakes her head.

"Nothing's wrong. You're just—her." Then she throws her arms around my neck. "Break a leg tonight," she tells me. "I love you."

And I hug her back so hard. "I love you, too," I say.

I finish my makeup. Pull my hair back.

Then I stand backstage holding hands with Lex.

"You're beautiful," he tells me. "Just fucking stunning."

"So are you," I say. And I mean that so much. I've never met anyone like Lex before. He's absolutely on fire with love and truth and curiosity, and I've been so grateful for his friendship and his light this last month.

I catch sight of Cole then. He's hidden in the shadows. Waiting. So I go to him. We're standing side by side.

The preshow music fades down, and Willa steps out on the stage to thunderous applause. She bows. Raises her face to the night sky. She's the most gracious host, welcoming the audience and saying that tonight's show is dedicated to someone very special. A much-loved member of the Whisper Cove family who is very much on our minds tonight. I'm blown away by her grace. Her poise. The steely strength of her.

If I could become anything, that's what I would choose for myself.

"Someone painted the memorial back," Cole whispers. "The one on the back wall of the scene shop."

My mother's name. And those blood-red words. *What the sea wants, the sea will have.*

"Why?" I ask. "I don't—"

"They think it was the curse. What happened to Glory. The whispering. Another tragedy at Whisper Cove."

"It wasn't," I tell him. "Nobody called Glory into the sea. That isn't—"

"No." He reaches for my hand. Squeezes it tight. "I know. The only one who cursed Glory was Glory."

He leans down to kiss the top of my head, and I have this sudden flash of terror. Almost like a vision. Or a premonition.

Something terrible is going to happen tonight. To me.

Or to Cole.

But I don't have time to think about any of that, because the lights are going down and I'm moving into my spot.

I sit on the bench center stage and shed my Avril skin, the way you slip off a robe before you step into the shower. I let the Eden thoughts replace the Avril thoughts, and I embrace all the places where they overlap. I let the edges melt together.

I'm sitting on the bench. Waiting for Cole to find me.

Because he will. He always does.

That's the only thought I keep. I let the others drift away like ashes rising into the wind.

I'm waiting for Cole.

I'm always waiting for Cole Culver to find me.

Always.

Then the lights come up. And we're off.

The show is going so well. The audience is eating out of our hands. And it feels so good. Because every single minute, scene by scene, I'm falling so in love with Cole over and over again. That dark wavy hair. And those gray eyes. By the time we get to the dance scene, where Eden admits she's in love, I don't know which one of us is more head over heels. Me. Or her. But I know when Eden tells Orion, that's me telling Cole, too.

I feel so open. Like every part of me is exposed. And it's the most amazing feeling. To be standing in the spotlight like that. No secrets. No hiding in the shadows.

But doing the show is also strange. Because each time I hear that song—Eden's melody—it pulls a little harder on my mind. It's like my memories are threads, and instead of plucking guitar strings,

Cole is tugging on those threads each time he starts to play. He's undoing me, bit by bit. Through all of act one, the longing for my mother builds and builds with each chord of that song. I feel the truth floating up, closer and closer to the surface. I can almost lean down and grab it.

Almost.

But then it sinks just out of reach again.

I can't focus on remembering, though. Can't focus on me. Not now. I have to focus on Eden. All I can do is let my mind work in the background.

And maybe that's why it finally comes to me. Because I'm just living inside the notes of that song. Experiencing it. Not trying to remember. Not trying to force it.

It's in the middle of the drowning scene that it hits me. The music is so loud in that moment, because Cole isn't playing it on the guitar. It's being pumped through the speakers, straight into my head.

I'm dancing on the edge of the river when it slams into me. Like a rogue wave.

And I stop dead in my tracks. I'm frozen.

My mother is tucking me in at night. The bed is warm and cozy. She lies down beside me to rub my back. And she's humming that song. Eden's melody.

Eden.

My mother's favorite name.

Suddenly I remember a hundred nights. The memories slam into me like waves. One after the other. A hundred hugs and kisses. My mother's hand on my back. That song against my ear.

Over and over. A thousand variations of the same tune.

I'm moving again now. Spinning and dancing, twirling. And the sound of the rushing water is getting louder in my ears.

Memories flood my brain.

My mother lifting me overhead and spinning me around.

My mother sweeping the kitchen floor.

My mother washing my hair.

And humming. And humming. And humming.

Always that same tiny bit of the same haunting melody.

I remember something Glory said to me. About what an ear my mother had for music. The way she was always singing. How she used to compose original melodies in her head and walk around humming them to herself under her breath. "*Never whole songs,*" Glory told me. "*Just the most beautiful little snippets.*"

The memories keep coming.

And coming and coming and coming.

The water gets higher.

And the music gets louder.

Until the dam breaks and I'm swept away.

And the world goes dark.

I stumble offstage and into Cole's arms. He's waiting for me in the tiny backstage area, and he wraps me up tight. I'm gasping for air. Drowning. Choking. On water. And on memories. "Breathe," he tells me. "I won't let go. I promise. Just breathe."

But I untangle myself and pull away. Because I only have that one scene. The one at the funeral. Between Orion and Anya. Cole and Val. And then I have to be back onstage.

I push my way through the kids that are waiting to go on. The funeral crowd. One of the girls has a script in her hands. She's looking over her lines. But I pluck it out of her hands. "Hey!" she hisses, but I'm already moving toward the prop table. I hold the script up to the light and flip to the very first page, where the production information is.

And fuck. There it is. Right there.

I was carrying the key around in my fucking backpack with me the whole goddamn time. Almost my whole goddamn life.

*Midnight Music* was first produced at Whisper Cove Theatre under its original title, *Before the Chaos.*

B. C.

*Before the Chaos.*

My mother wasn't trying to figure out how to end an affair.

She was trying to figure out how to end a play.

"Av?" Lex is standing behind me, looking over my shoulder. "You okay?" he whispers. But I can't move. Or speak. "Av?" he says again.

"Willa Culver didn't write this play," I tell him. I'm thinking of that picture of my mother. Hunched over that laptop. Eyes on fire. And all the other B. C. notes in that blue notebook.

Love isn't enough.

No promises.

Lonely. Secretive. Passionate.

And all the others.

They're character notes. Plot notes.

Not love notes.

"What?" Lex whispers. "What are you talking about?" He clearly thinks I've lost my mind.

"My mother did."

I push past Lex. I'm heading for the side exit.

As soon as I step away from the brightness of the stage, I'm aware of the fog rolling in to suffocate me. But I don't care. I'm already moving through the dark toward the farmhouse. The fog is so thick now, but somehow I find the little path that leads into the woods, toward the Culver house. And when I look back at Whisper Cove, the lights of the amphitheater have vanished. All I see are empty houses. Dark and deserted. Dead. No smoke curls from the chimneys. No candles flicker in the windows.

Laundry flaps on the lines.

Vegetables rot in the gardens.

And then I'm climbing through the woods. Racing toward the kitchen door. Willa is at the amphitheater, I know. And Brody, too. Cole. All of them. But I only have a few minutes before they all discover that I'm missing and *Midnight Music* comes to a screeching halt.

The kitchen door isn't locked. I knew it wouldn't be. I push it open and hurry toward that little painting. The one of the muses. The girl with all the cracks.

The one who reminds me so much of myself.

I lift it from the wall and turn it over in my hands. And there's an inscription on the back.

*To Willa,*

*Thanks for encouraging me to write. You'll always be my best friend and my greatest inspiration. Love you forever and ever!*

*Nicole*

The painting clatters to the floor. And I'm already moving toward the living room. I scan the shelves for other clues. But something tells me to look upstairs. In Willa's bedroom. If she's hidden any other proof, I bet it will be there.

I climb the stairs and stand in the hallway. I don't know which rooms are which. I don't even know which one is Cole's. I look down at the wood floor, and there's a worn path in the middle. It runs from one end of the hallway to the other. Like someone has spent years and years pacing back and forth.

"She walks at night."

I spin around, and Cole is standing at the top of the landing. He looks down at the worn path on the floor. "I hear her out here all the time. Walking back and forth." He lifts his eyes to look at me. "I don't— We don't sleep."

I remember that strange night in the library. Willa sleepwalking. Pulling books off shelves. Looking for something. Searching.

I wonder if she'd been looking for my mother's notebooks, maybe. She had to have known they existed. That they were full of clues.

The idea of them being out there somewhere must have haunted her.

I look past Cole to the big picture window at the end of the hall. The perfect view over the tall fence and out to the cliff beyond.

"Did you know?" I ask him. "Did you know she stole *Midnight Music* from my mother?"

"No." Cole looks like I slapped him. "I swear. I had no idea. Not until Lex grabbed me and told me what you said tonight. Before you took off." I'm trying to decide if I believe him. I want to believe him. But everyone at Whisper Cove is so slippery. They all move through my fingers like the damn fog. I can't seem to pin anyone here down.

They shift and change before my eyes. "It all makes sense now, though. The way she wrote it so fast. And we didn't know—nobody knew—that she'd even been working on a play. The way she's never written another thing. Not one fucking thing. In all these years."

A thought suddenly knocks the air out of me. "Did she kill my mother? So she could steal her play?" I have to lean against the wall to stay on my feet.

Did Willa Culver drown me?

Is that what Glory wanted me to figure out? Is that why she gave me so many clues?

"I don't know," Cole admits. And it's not the answer I wanted. I wanted him to say that stealing a play doesn't make his mother a murder. Because I love Willa. I love her so much. But he just repeats those three words again. "I don't know. I wasn't there that night."

"You were there," I tell him. My voice is rising. I'm frantic now. Desperate for an answer. Something that will finally put an end to all this. "You did that magic trick for me. The one with the sea glass and the flashlight, and—"

"No. That's one thing I know for certain, Avril. I wasn't there when your mother died. When you—"

"Cole. You told me to look at the stars."

"No." He sounds so certain. "I wasn't there. And I've never seen that part of it. The shadow of it. Or the memory. So I don't know. I don't know what happened." He reaches for me, but I back away.

"Oh my God," I whisper. "Cole." Because now that I've said it, I know it must be true. What would Willa Culver have done for a chance to become extraordinary? What would she have taken? Who would she have thrown away to get it? Or to keep it?

Cole freezes. He puts a finger to his lips. "Do you smell that?" he whispers. And it feels like déjà vu. But this isn't the smell of horses. Or pigs.

It isn't the smell of the past that's filling up our noses.

This is the smell of gasoline. Here. In the present.

"We need to get out of here," I whisper. "Now."

Just then I hear voices below us. Laughing. A boy and a girl. Cole takes my hand in his, and we creep back down the stairs.

A video is playing on the TV. Little Cole and little April are giggling at the edge of the cliff. Dusk is falling. It's almost dark. "Careful." It's Glory's voice from behind the camera. She's always nervous. Always cautious. "Don't get too close," she warns. "It's dangerous." She grabs Cole by the hand when he strays too far from her side. Then she pans over to the right, and Willa stands at the edge of the cliff. Her long, dark hair is blowing wildly in the wind. She holds a flashlight in one hand, and I stand in her living room, transfixed, as she pulls a handful of sea glass from her pocket. She tosses it into the darkness and hits it with the flashlight beam.

"Look at the stars!" she tells us, and we squeal with joy.

Me. Cole. Glory. Because Willa is pure magic.

The smell of gas burns my nose.

"Your mother taught you that trick," I whisper. And Cole nods. "It was her that was there that night. Not you. Not your father. Not George. Not Glory."

It was Willa.

"Cole!"

We both whirl around, and Willa glares at us from the kitchen doorway.

Cole takes a step in her direction but I reach out to grab his arm and stop him. Because I see the matches in her hand.

And the room is drenched in gasoline.

"She won't hurt you," Cole says. But I don't know if he's talking to me. Or to his mother.

If he's talking to me, I know he's wrong. Because Willa Culver murdered me once before. And there's nothing to stop her from doing it again.

"Get out, Cole," Willa says. But Cole doesn't move.

"Mom."

"I said get out!" Willa hisses.

"I'm not leaving." Two sets of slate-gray eyes, each locked on the other.

"Everything about you is a lie." I spit the words out like poison. "There's nothing extraordinary about you. You stole it all from my mother." It surprises me how much it hurts to say those words. Because I wanted so much for Willa Culver to be exactly who she said she was. I was so willing to love her for who she pretend she was. And I was so hungry for her to love me back.

"You can't steal from a dead woman," Willa tells me. Her eyes are so cold. How could I ever have thought they looked like Cole's eyes? "That play wouldn't have done your mother any good."

"How could you kill your best friend?" My jaw is clenched so tight that I'm not sure how the words can find a way out. "She fucking loved you!" There are hot, angry tears on my cheeks. Because Willa Culver took so much from me. She took my whole world.

Willa looks genuinely surprised. "I didn't kill your mother,

April. All I did was accept a bargain." She smiles at me. "I can't let you accuse me of murder in front of my son."

"It was Glory, wasn't it. We had that part right." Cole's voice is so quiet. He sounds so distant. I grab his hand to make sure he's still there. That he hasn't slipped away from me.

"They had a fight that night," Willa says. "A big one." She's playing with the matches while she talks. Holding one delicately between her fingers. Rubbing the head just so lightly across the side of the box. Reminding us that she could strike a flame at any moment. If she chose to. Because she's Willa Culver. And she's extraordinary.

"Nicole told Glory that she was leaving," she goes on. "That it was over. All of it was over. Nicole came straight here when she left Glory's place. Brody and I were going to set her up with a little apartment in the city. Just something tiny. A fresh start."

The scratching sound of the match against the striking strip. A barely audible warning. A reminder to us that we're not in charge here. That Willa is telling this story because she chooses to. Because there's nothing Willa Culver loves more than an audience.

"But Glory followed her here. I heard them fighting down at the edge of the cliff, so I stepped out on the porch to see what was going on." Willa finally strikes the match and Cole and I both suck in our breaths. "And that's when I saw Glory push her over the edge. I don't think she meant to do it. She just did it." Willa shrugs. "But there are moments of no return. Some things you can't take back."

"Glory offered you a deal, didn't she?" Cole says. "She knew

Nicole was working on a play. She knew it was good. That it would be something big. And she traded it to you for your silence."

"She bought you," I whisper. The match in Willa's hand goes out. But she immediately has another one between her fingers.

"She offered me an opportunity. A chance to become someone completely different."

"But you became a monster," I say. "You could have become anything. And you chose to become a thief and a liar."

"How did Avril end up in the water?" There is so much ice in Cole's voice that for a moment he sounds exactly like Willa. "Was that Glory, too? Or was that you?"

"I didn't know she was there. Not until Glory left." Willa is looking at me now. And just for a moment there's something soft in her eyes. Something genuine and sad. "I didn't know Nicole had even brought you with her that night. That's the truth. But then you popped up out of the grass. And I knew you'd seen. That you knew. So I did what I had to do."

"Jesus. She was a little girl." Cole sounds sick. Like he's going to throw up. "Was the fucking Tony worth it?"

Willa tightens her jaw. "I did what I had to do. Just like I did what I had to do last night."

"You tried to kill Glory." The realization of it comes to me so suddenly. "She was going to tell me, wasn't she? She couldn't live with it anymore."

Willa shrugs. "I did what I had to do." She strikes another match.

"And what are you going to do now that it looks like Glory's going to live?" It's Cole and the pain in his voice is almost the worst thing about this whole unfathomable night. "Are you going to try again? How many times are you willing to kill someone?"

"I'll do what I have to do. Just like I'll do what I have to do tonight. Whatever that is. I won't let anyone take my whole life away from me."

"I was your son," Cole says. And one word rings in my ears. *Was.* "I should have been your life." There's so much heartbreak in his words. "Not that play."

Willa is looking at Cole. The match in her hand has gone out, and I'm sliding my hand under the white dress. Into the pocket of the shorts I'm wearing underneath. I'm running my fingers over Cole's smooth good-luck charms. Finding Lex's lighter.

Willa Culver tried to drown me, and she failed. Now she thinks she can take me out with fire. But she doesn't know me.

I've never been afraid of the flames. I've always craved the burn.

"I'll kill you both," Willa says. "If I have to." And I know she means it. But she won't get the chance.

I pull out the lighter and flick it open. Then I grab Cole by the arm. "Run!" I scream. And I'm pushing him past Willa. She looks so stunned when I toss the lighter on the floor behind us and the carpet goes up with a *whoosh.*

Cole and I burst out the kitchen door into the dark.

Into the fog as thick as mud.

And somehow I lose my grip on his hand.

I start to panic, because the air smells like drowning tonight.

Not the ocean.

Or the beach.

It smells like drowning. Water over your head. The sting of it in your nose. Dead things and sailors' curses. The muck on the bottom. The stink of it. Sea monsters and whale bones and fish eating away at your eyes.

"Cole!" I whisper. "Where are you?"

"Avril!" he says. "Over here."

And I move toward the sound of his voice.

But I get distracted. Because the fence is gone tonight. And my mother is standing at the edge of the cliff. Her back is to the water, and her eyes flash bright and angry. She's arguing with another woman. Someone with wild curls and even wilder eyes. The curly-haired woman is frantic. She's waving her arms and my mother is backing away from her. She backs one step too far. Too close to the edge. I see her reach out for help. But the woman with the wild hair shoves her hard.

I hear my mother shout my name. "April!"

And then she's gone. Vanished into thin air.

Someone grabs me from behind, and I scream. "Avril. It's me." Cole spins me around and pulls me against him. I feel the quick press of his lips. His warm breath against my skin. "I didn't know," he tells me. "I never made sense of it all. Not until tonight."

"I believe you," I tell him.

I glance back toward the edge of the cliff and another memory is playing out now. This one is dark. The shapes are dim. And hard to see. Almost like shadow puppets on a wall.

A woman with blowing black hair stands at the edge of the cliff. She's staring down into the foaming water below, searching the waves with a flashlight.

A little blonde girl pops up from the tall grass. Her face is tear-streaked. She's crying for her mother.

The dark-haired woman swivels. Her face is tear-streaked, too, but her eyes go wide when she hits the little girl dead in the face with the flashlight beam. The woman recovers fast, though. She reaches out to the child and I hear the jangle of delicate silver bracelets. It's a pretty sound. Light and delicate.

It sounds exactly like the music of wind chimes.

"Cole," I whisper, and I reach for his hand.

"I see them," he tells me.

Then the woman pulls a handful of something from her pocket, and she flings it into the air. "Look at the stars," she says. And when she turns the flashlight out into the darkness, the whole sky is lit on fire.

The girl stands and stares. Because she's never seen anything so pretty. The stars are falling like rain, and she forgets to be afraid for just a second. Until the dark-haired woman grabs her by the wrist. She jerks hard. Once. Twice.

Cole pulls me to his chest. "Don't look," he whispers against my ear. "You don't need that memory." So I close my eyes tight. But I still feel myself flying.

Falling.

"I love you," I tell him.

"I love you, too," he says. "So don't be sorry. This is what I want."

I don't know what he means.

"Cole—"

Behind us, the Culver house is engulfed in flames. I feel the intense heat of it. Everything is tinted orange now. The air is on fire.

Cole's hands are on my face. "I more than love you. So don't you dare be sorry when I die."

"You're okay," I tell him. "We're okay."

He shakes his head. "I've seen it, Avril. I've watched myself die a hundred different nights. Out here. In the fog. Over and over. But I never understood it. It never made sense. Not until you showed up. And then I recognized your face. The very first second I saw you. And I knew, if I fell in love with you, it was all over. That this is how it would end. For me." He reaches out to touch my hair. So gentle. "But I did it anyway." He trails his fingers down my neck. "And it was worth it."

"What are you talking about?"

"I've always known I was going to die. I've seen myself go over the edge. I've been watching it like a movie my whole life. I don't know how it happens. I've never known that. Because I never see that part. The part that happens just before. I only see myself falling. And I know that you're there. I see you. I feel you. And I know I'm falling to save you. To keep you safe." His forehead is pressed to mine. "Somehow I know that. I've always known that. So it's always been okay."

"No," I tell him, and I know I sound hysterical. "Cole. No."

"What the sea wants, the sea will have."

"That's bullshit," I tell him. "Your mother is the sea, Cole. Willa Culver is the sea. She's deep and she's dark. And she's so fucking cold. She's the thing that's haunting you. The thing that's pulling you under." Cole is looking at me, but there's something in his eyes that's already gone. "But listen to me." I'm pleading with him now. "You can fight her. The way you've always fought the whispering.

The way we've always fought it." I stop and swallow back my rising terror. "She doesn't have to win."

"It doesn't matter now," Cole tells me. "This is real. All the rest of it is smoke and mirrors. Over and over." He kisses me again. It's fast and desperate. And it leaves me gasping for air. "But you and me? This is real. Every fucking time. You remember that." He squeezes both my hands. "You fight like hell to remember that. Next time. Okay?"

I nod, and the fog blows away. Just for a second.

Cole and I are standing at the edge of the cliff. Right on the edge of all that nothing.

There's a noise behind me. I turn around, and Willa is running in my direction. Hands stretched out in front of her.

And that's when Cole shoves me hard. Sideways. I go sprawling across the ground, and Cole steps into my place just as Willa's hands make contact with his chest.

I watch in slow motion as they both go over the cliff.

Willa's eyes go wide. She clutches at the air.

But Cole is peaceful.

And his eyes manage to find mine one last time.

I watch them fall like stars and disappear below the black surface of the sea.

I stare for a minute. I'm hypnotized by all that churning water.

But then I turn and run.

So many people are filling the Culver yard now. They all stand there and watch the house burn, drawn by the glow of the flames. The smoke and the sirens. I see George pushing his way through the crowd. And Brody. He's standing there with this stunned look on his face while the embers of his perfect life fall around him like fiery snow.

I wonder if he knew. About the bargain his wife made. Or if he at least suspected.

I catch sight of Lex's red hair. He sees me, too. And he shouts my name. Elbows his way through the crowd. He's sobbing. Reaching for me. "I thought you were in there," he shouts. But I can't stop. Not even for Lex.

I'm sliding down the path toward the beach.

I don't even pause to look at the upright stones.

New dirt.

Fresh flowers.

I can't stop. Not until I get to the beach.

Willa is lying facedown at the edge of the water. Near the jetty. Her long, dark hair floats out around her.

And I think at first that she's moving, but then I realize it's just the rhythm of the waves. It looks like breathing.

Cole is on his back not far from his mother.

The water brought them home together, and for a second I'm jealous. Because it didn't do that for my mother and me.

I drop to my knees in the cold water. I'm cradling Cole's head in my lap. Sobbing.

I brush the beautiful dark hair out of his eyes.

"Av?" It's Lex. He's standing on the beach behind me. Bent over. Hands on his knees. He's breathing hard. Val and Jude are running down the beach toward us. They came for me. The three of them. To make sure I was okay. And the sound of Lex's voice—confused and scared and so full of love—is enough to finish me off. This is more than I can survive.

The loss is too deep.

I take one more look at Cole's face. I lean down and press my lips against his. I don't want him to be cold.

But then his eyelids flutter open. He coughs up seawater and I choke out his name. The fog lifts, and the two of us are breathing together. We're alive. The rush of relief when Cole reaches up to touch my hair with a trembling hand is all the proof I need.

Now. In this moment. We're alive. Both of us.

The sea can't have us. Not tonight.

Cole pulls me to his chest. I feel the pounding of his heart against my own.

"I never saw this part," he says. I wipe the water from his eyes, and he almost smiles. "You and me. At the end of it all."

"This is the only part that matters," I tell him. "This is real. You and me. Always. The rest of it is smoke and mirrors."

And—

# EPILOGUE

I was five years old the night stars fell from the sky. They tore loose somehow and came down like rain. I remember the heavy, dull sound of them hitting the water.

*Plop.*

*Plop. Plop.*

*Plop.*

I'm watching—waiting for them to do that act again—but tonight they stay pinned to the vast blackness above us. Where they're supposed to be. Which is more than I can say for us, because we're supposed to be in our cabins. Curfew was like an hour ago.

But here we are on the beach.

# ACKNOWLEDGMENTS

First, I want to give a shout out to my mom, Anna Myers, and my sister, Anna-Maria Lane, who have been the most constant and solid forces in my life. There's no way I could ever thank you enough.

To my son, Paul, who shares my love of all things spooky and creepy. Thank you for being the best kid I could ever have asked for. When this book is released, you will have just graduated from high school and you'll be starting a new journey. I'm proud of your thoughtfulness, your creativity, your humor, and your tender heart. It is such a privilege to call you mine.

To the rest of my family who are always so supportive—my brother, Ben Myers, and his wife, Mandy; my brother-in-law, Bill Lane; my cousin, Becky Kephart; and Lela Fox, whom I claim as an honorary part of my family. Also to all my nieces and nephews and my aunts, uncles, and cousins on both sides of my family tree. I'm forever grateful to come from a long, long line of storytellers and story-lovers.

To my agent, Pete Knapp, who is the absolute best in the business. Thank you for being the most perfect blend of kind and tough as nails. I'm so grateful to have you in my corner.

Thanks also to the rest of the team at Park & Fine Literary and Media, particularly the awesome Stuti Telidevara, who is always so on top of everything, and Abigail Koons and Kathryn Toolan in the Foreign Rights Department.

To my editor, Ruta Rimas at Razorbill, who is a dream come true! The opportunity to work with someone who is not only a fantastic editor, but who also just inherently gets me and my stories has been such a gift.

And to everyone else at Razorbill and Penguin Young Readers, including Casey McIntyre, Simone Roberts-Payne, Jayne Ziemba, Felicity Vallence, Kaitlin Kneafsey, Gretchen Durning, James Akinaka, Abigail Powers, and Kristie Radwilowicz, who designed another cover to die for.

Thanks so much to Berni Barta at CAA, my film and television agent, and to the wonderful team at Electric Monkey/Farshore Books in the UK, particularly Sarah Levison, Lindsey Heaven, Lucy Courtenay, Laura Bird, Olivia Adams, Ellie Bavester, and Pippa Poole.

I also want to send love to Tiffany Thomason (and Carter), Catren Lamb, Brenda Maier, and Valerie Lawson. You all have literally kept me alive the past two years with a hilarious and wide-ranging group chat and innumerable brunches and afternoons at Panera. Also to Kim Ventrella, Scarlett St. Clair, and Alysha Welliver. You all know the answer to every question before I even ask it. You are funny and smart and powerful and I adore you beyond measure! And, of course, a huge thank you to all of my Margarita Night people and to Gaye Sanders and everyone at SCBWI Oklahoma!

This book is a love letter to the theatre. Although I love writing, it's the theatre that has had my heart since I was a very little girl, and I want to say a heartfelt thank-you to everyone who has ever shared a stage or a corner of a darkened theatre with me. There is a piece of every single one of you in this book. I particularly want to send love and gratitude to the following . . .

Lincoln County On Stage, the small-town community theatre that grew me up.

The University of the Ozarks theatre department, where I truly learned the craft and art of acting.

The Eugene O'Neill Theatre Center, where I was lucky enough to spend six wonderful summers as an intern soaking up seaside sunshine and rubbing elbows with legends. The beautiful, fog-soaked grounds of Whisper Cove were inspired by the truly breathtaking setting of the Eugene O'Neill Theatre Center in Waterford, Connecticut.

Also, thanks and all the love in the world to all of the Stages Theatre kids who shared so much of their lives with me in so many beautiful moments, on stage and off, over the years. To Caitie, Robert, Hannah, Lauren, Faith, Blakely, Cason, Dustin, Talley Beth, Weston, Jessica, Kelsey, Kimmie, Colton, Lexie, Suede, and all the others who I would love to be able to name here . . . but I'd need pages and pages. What we did together was magic, and you guys have no idea how proud I am of you and how much of my heart you take up, even after all this time.

And to my friend Bruce Brown, who shares my passion for the theatre. I will never forget our three-hour lunches and long conversations. I'm grateful for all the adventures we got to share, both in the theatre and out in the world.

Last, to my own bold, beautiful, brilliant, red-headed best friend, Weston Allen Kemp, to whom this book is dedicated. Thank you for being the kind of friend I never knew I needed until you took me so wonderfully by surprise. The shock of recognition between us was instant and inevitable. It's what you once called "the magic of you and me," and you were so right. You will always be my favorite partner in everything, on stage and off. You're my one big YES, and it gives me so much joy to be able to share this story with you. I'm so incredibly grateful for all the second . . . and third . . . and fourth . . . chances we've given each other over the years. It hasn't always been easy, but we have always been worth it. I more than love you, Wes. Please keep your candle burning, because you are anything but ordinary, and the world needs your light almost as much as I do.